Praise for *New York Times* bestselling author Kat Martin

"[Kat] Martin is a terrific storyteller."
—*Booklist* on *Season of Strangers*

"[Martin] dishes up romantic suspense, sizzling sex and international intrigue in healthy doses, and fans are going to be the winners."
—*RT Book Reviews* on *Against the Sun* (Top Pick)

"Kat Martin is a fast gun when it comes to storytelling, and I love her books."
—#1 *New York Times* bestselling author Linda Lael Miller

Praise for Nicole Helm

"An intimate, rewarding romance with a hot hero whose emotional growth is as sexy as his moves in the bedroom."
—*Kirkus Reviews* on *Want You More*

"Nicole Helm has done a great job of writing three-dimensional characters…a super beginning to this series. I look forward to the next book in the series, *Wyoming Cowboy Protection*."
—*Harlequin Junkie* on *Wyoming Cowboy Justice*

NEW YORK TIMES BESTSELLING AUTHOR

KAT MARTIN

AGAINST THE STORM

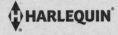

ISBN-13: 978-1-335-66255-2

Against the Storm
First published in 2011.
This edition published in 2023.
Copyright © 2011 by Kat Martin

Wyoming Cowboy Bodyguard
First published in 2019.
This edition published in 2023.
Copyright © 2019 by Nicole Helm

Recycling programs
for this product may
not exist in your area.

Harlequin Enterprises ULC
22 Adelaide St. West, 41st Floor
Toronto, Ontario M5H 4E3, Canada
www.Harlequin.com

Printed in U.S.A.

CONTENTS

Top ten *New York Times* bestselling author **Kat Martin** is a graduate of the University of California Santa Barbara. Residing with her Western-author husband, L.J. Martin, in Missoula, Montana, Kat has written seventy Historical and Contemporary Romantic Suspense novels. More than seventeen million of her books are in print and she has been published in twenty foreign countries. Kat is currently hard at work on her next novel.

Books by Kat Martin

Maximum Security

The Deception
The Conspiracy

Maximum Security novellas

Before Nightfall
Shadows at Dawn
Wait Until Dark

The Raines of Wind Canyon

Against the Mark
Against the Edge
Against the Odds
Against the Sun
Against the Night
Against the Storm
Against the Law
Against the Fire
Against the Wind

Visit the Author Profile page
at Harlequin.com for more titles.

AGAINST THE STORM

Kat Martin

To my personal assistant and friend, Rita Michell,
for her many years of hard work and support.
And for making all the hard work fun.

Chapter 1

Snow Dogs. Trace Rawlins sat at a table in back of the Texas Café thinking of his client and her white rapper husband, Bobby Jordane, the lead singer of the wildly successful rap music group, the Snow Dogs.

It seemed the perfect name for the mangy group, who sang about decadent society yet seemed to be the root of the problem. Only Bobby was married, his beautiful wife of the last three years was a creamy cocoa-skinned African American. Why she had ever married the guy, aside from his seven-figure bank account, Trace couldn't imagine.

Apparently, Shawna had come to the same conclusion, for she sat a few tables away next to her attorney, Evan Schofield, there for a meeting with Bobby.

Bobby Jordane was a wife beater par excellence, and

he was extremely unhappy that Shawna had filed for divorce. But Schofield had managed to set up a meeting at a neutral location kept secret from the media, in the hope something could actually be accomplished.

The restaurant was old and narrow, with wooden floors and a long, varnished-wood lunch counter, a place for locals where a guy like Bobby wouldn't even be recognized. This time of day, the lunch crowd was gone and it was too early for dinner patrons. Only two other tables were occupied, one by an older man and his wife drinking chocolate shakes, another by two young women eating hamburgers. One of them was a foxy redhead Trace tried not to notice, but his gaze wandered back to her again and again.

Unfortunately, he seemed to have a penchant for trouble where redheads were concerned.

He returned his thoughts to the meeting at hand, which was supposed to include only Bobby and his attorney, Shawna and Evan Schofield, Trace's longtime friend.

But Bobby was a hothead, and Evan was no fool. He didn't trust Bobby, and neither did Trace. Everyone in Houston had read about the couple's fiery clashes and Bobby's out-of-control behavior, which recently had landed him in jail. Shawna had threatened to file a restraining order, and Evan had hired Trace, a private detective and the owner of Atlas Security, to keep a protective eye on his client.

The bell above the café door rang, flipping the little ruffled curtain above the glass. True to form, Bobby sauntered in without his attorney, just the other two obnoxious members of the Snow Dogs.

Clyde "The Mountain" Thibodaux hailed from New Orleans. Big, bald and tattooed, he was bare-chested beneath his leather vest. A small black goatee clung to his chin.

Lenny Finks, known to his fans as Lenny the Sphinx, was the nerd of the group. Skinny and homely, with kinky auburn hair, he was the talent behind the act, the guy who wrote the music, though Trace refused to call it that. Lenny was harmless, except for the viperous tongue he used to lash at the group's critics. He was a necessary component and the reason for the group's unbelievable success.

Bobby himself was as tall as Trace, about six-two, and as lean and solidly built. Having taken years of martial arts, Bobby thought he was a tough guy. Trace flicked a glance at the bruises on Shawna Jordane's beautiful face, clamped down on a surge of anger and wished he could show him ex-Ranger tough.

Instead, he tipped back his white straw cowboy hat, shifted in his chair and sipped his coffee, his gaze fixed on Bobby, who swaggered over to Shawna's table, his friends close behind.

"Hey, babe."

"Hello, Bobby." Her voice held the faint edge of fear.

Bobby turned a hard look on the man beside her. "So… *Evan*…you wanted me to come down here so we could have a little chat. Is that right?"

The lawyer, a slender man with sandy brown hair and intelligent eyes, sat up a little straighter in his chair. "I was hoping we might be able to make some progress in the matter of your divorce," he said.

Bobby shifted, his legs splayed in a belligerent stance. "You get my wife to file for divorce and you want me to come here so we can *talk?*" Reaching out, he grabbed Evan by his red-striped power tie and hauled him to his feet. Shawna screamed and Trace went into action.

Tossing Lenny out of the way like the skinny little runt he was, he reached out and grabbed hold of the back of Bobby's black, silver dragon T-shirt. Trace spun him around, waited an instant for Bobby to throw the first punch, then ducked and nailed him solidly in the jaw. Bobby went down like a sack of wheat, his head hitting the wooden floor with a melonlike thump that had his eyes rolling back in his head.

"You son of a bitch!" Clyde's blunt, meaty hands balled into fists as he lumbered forward, swinging a roundhouse punch meant to send a man to his knees. Trace ducked, turned a little and threw a straight-from-the-shoulder blow that sank four inches into the big man's stomach. Clyde grunted, doubled over, and Trace took him out with an uppercut to the chin.

Blood gushed from his nose and Clyde flew backward, knocking over a table and sending the surprised older couple scrambling out of the way. It was exactly the kind of thing Evan Schofield had hoped to prevent when he had hired Trace.

"Sorry, buddy."

Evan held up a hand. "Not your fault. I should have known this wouldn't work." He grinned. "Besides, it was worth it to see Bobby get what he had coming."

Shaking off the ache in his hand, Trace reached down and picked up his cowboy hat, settled it once more on his head. Lenny stood next to Bobby with his mouth gaping and his eyes wide. "Y-you shouldn't have done that."

"You don't think so?"

"Bobby... Bobby's gonna be really mad."

Trace chuckled softly. "If you're smart, you'll get him out of here before somebody calls the police. He doesn't need any more trouble."

Evan pulled out Shawna's chair. "Let's go."

She rose shakily to her feet and turned to Trace. "Thank you, Mr. Rawlins. You have no idea how good that made me feel."

A corner of his mouth edged up. "Oh, I think I do."

Shawna turned and started walking, but before she had reached the door, a camera flashed, capturing her retreat. Then the photographer turned toward the man moaning softly on the floor. The camera flashed again and again, taking photos of Bobby Jordane that would be wildly embarrassing to a guy with an ego as massive as his.

Trace inwardly cursed. The redhead. Just as he'd figured, they were nothing but trouble.

Striding toward her, he reached out and jerked the camera from her hands, turned it around and deleted the last series of digital photos.

"Hey! What do you think you're doing? You can't do that!"

"Nice camera," Trace said. Walking over to the lunch counter, he handed it to Betty Sparks, the owner of the café.

The sexy redhead raced along behind him. "Listen, whoever you are—that's my camera! You can't just—"

"I just did. And you can have it back as soon as they're gone." Trace tipped his hat to the redhead and her friend, a tall, svelte brunette a year or two older. "Have a nice afternoon, ladies."

Turning, he strolled out of the café.

"Did you see that? Oh, my God!" The brunette's attention followed the man who strode down the sidewalk outside the window. "Who was that gorgeous hunk?"

Maggie O'Connell's gaze jerked toward the window

just as the tall, lanky cowboy in the white straw hat disappeared from view. "What are you talking about? That bastard just ruined my pictures. Bobby Jordane and his estranged wife? You know how much photos like that are worth?"

Maggie turned at the sound of a groan, saw the guy with the kinky hair—Lenny the Sphinx, his fans called him—help Bobby to his feet. Clyde the Mountain swayed upward until he was standing. Wordlessly, the small group staggered toward the door.

Maggie looked longingly at the lady who held her camera, but the older woman just shook her head.

Maggie sighed. She wouldn't be getting photos of Bobby Jordane sprawled on the old plank floor, beaten to a pulp. Not today.

"I hate to remind you, but you aren't the tabloid type," said her best friend, Roxanne De Mers. "You didn't come here to take pictures. You came for a late lunch with a friend. It just turned out to be a little more exciting than we planned."

Roxy swung back to the window, watching the rap stars as they made their way to the long white limo waiting out front. "I wonder who he was."

Maggie didn't have to ask who her friend was talking about. The cowboy was, at the very least, impressive. Tall and lean, with wide shoulders and slim hips, he had thick, dark hair neatly trimmed, golden-brown eyes and a set of biceps that were impossible to miss.

Still, she didn't appreciate his interference in her business. As the limo door closed, shutting the three men inside, she walked over to the counter to collect her camera, which the broad-hipped woman readily handed back to her.

"So who was he?" Maggie asked, nodding toward

the window. "The Lone Ranger out there…what was his name?"

"You a reporter?"

"I'm a photographer. Mostly I do outdoor shots. I just saw an opportunity and took it—or tried to."

"Sorry it didn't pan out."

"Me, too. I can always use a little extra money."

"Name's Betty Sparks," the woman said. "Me and my husband, Bill, own this place."

"Nice to meet you, Betty. I'm Maggie O'Connell. You make a great burger."

"Thanks."

The woman, who was in her late fifties, with a cap of short, curly gray hair, tipped her head toward the door. "His name's Trace Rawlins. Owns Atlas Security. He's a private investigator."

Walking up beside Maggie, Roxanne sighed dramatically, a hand over her heart. "I think I'm in love."

"The redhead's got a better chance," Betty said. "Trace has a weakness for 'em."

"No, thanks. I don't do cowboys."

Betty chuckled. "If I was twenty years younger, I'd dye my hair."

Maggie laughed. "How much do we owe you?" She walked over to the purse hanging on the back of her wooden chair and started digging for her wallet.

"On the house," Betty said. "It's the least I can do."

Maggie smiled. "Thanks."

"You new in the neighborhood?"

She nodded. "I just bought one of those town houses they built a few blocks away. Vaulted ceiling upstairs. Good north light, great place to work, you know?"

"Welcome, then. Maybe we'll see you again."

"If it's always this much fun in here," Roxanne said, "I'm sure you will."

Betty just laughed.

Maggie put her Nikon back in its case and slung the straps of the camera bag and her purse over her shoulder. Roxanne tossed a couple bills on the table for a tip, and the two walked out the door.

"You know that trouble you been having?" Roxy said.

Maggie paused. "What about it?"

"That cowboy...he's in the security business and he's an investigator. He might be able to help you."

Maggie started to argue, to say she didn't need any help. Then she thought of the way Trace Rawlins had handled those three men. "I hope it doesn't come to something like that."

But it might and both of them knew it. For more than a month, someone had been following her, phoning her and hanging up, leaving messages on the windshield of her car. So far it hadn't been more than that, but it was frightening just the same.

When she got home, she was going to look up the number for Atlas Security.

And write it down beside Trace Rawlins's name.

Trace returned to the Atlas Security office on Times Street. He lived in a house in the University District not far away, a place with a yard for Rowdy, his black-and-white border collie, with big shady trees and an old-fashioned, covered front porch. When his dad died, Trace had inherited the house along with the business, a company his father had started when he first got out of the army.

Seth Rawlins had been a Ranger, a tough son of a

bitch. Following in his footsteps, Trace had also enlisted and become a Ranger, figuring on a career in the military. Then six years ago, his dad had been killed in a car accident and Trace had come home to take over the business as he knew his father would have wished.

He slowed his dark green Jeep Grand Cherokee, pulled into the parking area in front of his office and turned off the engine. Recently, he had purchased the two-story brick structure—or rather, he and the bank owned it together until he paid off the mortgage. Which, since his profits were up and he was making double payments, he hoped wouldn't take too long.

In the years since he'd taken over his father's business, he had doubled the size of the company and opened a branch in Dallas. As a kid, with his dad gone much of the time, he had been raised on his grandfather's ranch, a place where hard work was expected of a man. Trace still owned the ranch, but it was leased out to a cattle company now. He only went out there once in a while, to check on the old house and the acreage he'd retained around it, but he always enjoyed the time he spent in the country.

He wiped his feet on the mat in front of the office door and stepped inside. The walls were painted dark green and the place was furnished simply, with oak desks for his staff and oak furniture in the waiting area. Framed photos of cattle grazing in the pastures on the ranch hung on the walls.

He looked over to the reception area. "Hey, Annie, what's up?"

Seated behind her desk, his office manager, Annie Mayberry, glanced up from typing on her computer.

"You got a couple of calls, nothing too exciting." Annie was in her sixties, with frizzy gray hair dyed blond, and a rounded figure from the doughnuts she loved to eat in the morning.

"Maybe you could give me a hint," Trace drawled.

She pulled off her reading glasses. "You got a call from Evan Schofield. He says Bobby Jordane is threatening to sue you for assault. Evan says not to worry about it. Bobby couldn't stand for anyone to find out he got his—I'm quoting here—'ass whipped' the way he did."

Trace chuckled, but Annie's penciled eyebrows went up. "So you got in a fight with Bobby Jordane?" Disapproval rang in her voice. "I thought you'd outgrown that kind of thing." Annie had worked for his father before Trace had taken over. She had mothered Seth Rawlins, who had lost his wife when Trace was born, then mothered Trace, since he didn't have one.

"It wasn't exactly a fight. More like a discussion with fists. Mostly mine." Absently, he rubbed his bruised knuckles.

"You know you're getting way too old for that rough stuff."

"I'll keep that in mind." She was a small woman, but feisty. She didn't take guff from anyone, including him, and that was exactly the way he wanted it. "What else have you got?"

"The Special Olympics called looking for a donation. I phoned the bookkeeper, told her to send them a check."

"Good. What else?"

"Marvin's Boat Repair called. Joe says he's finished working on your engine. *Ranger's Lady*'s running like a top."

Trace nodded. "I think I'll go down to Kemah for the weekend." As often as he could manage, Trace made the forty-mile trip to where he docked his thirty-eight-foot sailboat. He loved being out on the water. There were times he wondered if being a SEAL wouldn't have been a better fit than being a Ranger. But then he wouldn't have met Dev Raines and Johnnie Riggs, two of his closest friends, and guys like Jake Cantrell.

"Jake called," Annie said as if she read his thoughts, which she seemed to have a knack for doing. "He's taking a job down in Mexico for a while. He'll be gone at least a couple of weeks, maybe more."

Jake had come to Houston with Trace after they'd finished a rescue mission with Dev and Johnnie that took them into Mexico. Cantrell, a former marine, mostly freelanced, hiring himself out as a bodyguard for executives who worked for big corporations. He had worked in the Middle East but specialized in South America. Jake did pretty much anything that wasn't illegal and paid him plenty of money.

"That it?"

Annie handed over three more messages. "One's a potential client. You'll need to call him back. And Hewitt Sommerset called." He was CEO of Sommerset Industries. "He wants to talk to you about that report you just finished."

Hewitt believed one of his employees was embezzling funds. The surveillance equipment Atlas installed had proved he was right.

"I'll call him right now."

"The third message is from Carly. If I were you, I'd lose that one."

He scowled, stared down at his ex-wife's name scrolled on the paper. "Anything important?"

"The usual. Said she just wanted to hear the sound of your voice."

Trace crumpled the note and tossed it into the trash can beside Annie's desk. For some strange reason he was a magnet for needy women. It was no surprise he had married one. He'd been divorced from Carly nearly four years, something the petite redhead had a way of forgetting.

Trace walked past Annie's desk into the main office area. Sol Greenway was working away at one of his three computers. At twenty-two, Sol was Atlas's youngest employee and a near genius when it came to electronics. Sol handled background security checks, security problems, information retrieval, online forensic services, and just about anything else that had to do with computers.

In the middle of the office, Ben Slocum and Alex Justice, both freelance investigators, sat behind their desks. Ben had his cell phone pressed against his ear. Alex was cleaning his Glock 9 mm.

"How'd it go with Arnold Peters?" Trace asked Alex.

"I took him the photos. His wife was seeing some oversexed football player. Peters took one look, broke down and cried like a baby."

"Why the hell do they hire us? They say they want the truth, but what they really want is for us to tell them they're wrong and everything at home is just peachy."

Alex's grin cut a dimple into his cheek. "Far as I'm concerned, the best thing to do is stay single."

Trace thought of Carly and the trail of men she'd ushered in and out of his house while they were married. "You can say that again."

Continuing on, he went into his office and closed the door. He needed to return Hewitt's call. The investigation was over, but Trace liked the guy and knew Hewitt was taking the information hard. The embezzler was his son-in-law.

Trace had a few other calls to make, but he didn't

personally handle as many cases as he used to. These days, he could pick and choose, and since the weekend was coming up, he would probably give anything new to Ben or Alex.

Trace imagined himself stretching out on the deck of the *Ranger's Lady* in the warm Texas sun, hands behind his head and catching a few rays.

He smiled.

Sounded like the perfect plan.

Chapter 2

Maggie O'Connell walked out of her newly purchased town house and headed for her red Ford Escape hybrid parked in front. She loved the car, which got over thirty miles to the gallon, loved the room in the back for the cameras, tripods, meters, lights and miscellaneous equipment she used in her work.

At twenty-eight, Maggie had achieved an amazing amount of success as a photographer. What had started as a hobby while she went to college as an art major on a partial scholarship had ended up a career.

Part of it was luck, Maggie admitted. After graduation from the University of Houston, she had managed to snag a part-time job as an assistant to Roger Weller, a renowned Texas photographer—work that gave her an invaluable education in the field and also time to shoot the outdoor scenes that had become her trademark.

Weller helped her get her first gallery exhibition,

which was surprisingly well received. Several more shows followed and her clientele grew. Now her photos hung in some of the most prestigious galleries in Houston, Dallas and Austin.

Her mind on her upcoming show at the Twin Oaks Gallery and the photos she intended to shoot that afternoon, Maggie had almost reached her car when she jerked to a shuddering halt. Setting her camera bag at her feet, she reached a shaking hand toward the scrap of paper pinned beneath the windshield wiper. Very carefully pulling it free, she began to read the message.

My precious Maggie,
How long before our destinies are fulfilled? When
will you understand that your fate is entwined
with mine and I am the only one who can give
you the peace you need?

Maggie glanced frantically around. Only two other cars were parked in front of the six recently completed town house units where she lived, a Toyota Camry and a Chevy Camaro. Both vehicles were empty. The breeze ruffled the leaves on the freshly planted shrubs in the flower beds out front, and a couple of teenagers rolled by on their bicycles. No one who looked like he might have left the note.

She stared down at the torn slip of rough brown paper, which matched the two others she had already received. She had hoped, after moving into the condo two weeks ago, that whoever had been leaving the creepy messages would stop.

She hoisted her camera bag over her shoulder, holding the note with just two fingers in case the man had left prints. She scanned the lot once more for anyone who seemed out of place, but no one was there.

Maggie hurried back inside her town house, the paper fluttering in her hand, her stomach a little queasy. Easing her camera bag to the floor, she closed the front door and leaned against it. After couple of steadying breaths, she opened her purse and dug out her cell phone and pulled up her best friend's name.

She hit the send button, and with every unanswered ring, her anxiety grew.

Roxanne finally picked up.

"Roxy? Rox, it's Maggie. I—I got another note. It was under the wiper blade on my car."

Her friend softly cursed. "Where are you?"

"I'm back inside my house. I looked around the parking lot. No one was there."

"Listen to me, Maggie. You need to take that note to the police. What was the name of that police lieutenant you talked to before?"

"Bryson. But he isn't going to help me. He doesn't believe me. That isn't going to change."

"It might. You have this note and the two you got before."

"I didn't keep the first one. I thought it was just a prank."

But it wasn't really a matter of having the notes as proof. It wasn't a matter of the police believing her. The cops were punishing her for a crime she had committed years ago.

A crime she was indeed guilty of committing.

"I won't go back there," she said. "I won't be humiliated that way again."

A long pause ensued. Roxanne was one of the few

people who knew that as a teenager, Maggie had falsely accused the high school quarterback of rape.

At sixteen, she'd been stupid and irresponsible. The truth of it was she'd had sex that night with Josh Varner, though it certainly wasn't rape. She had encouraged the handsome football player, not fought him, but she'd been frightened of her dad's reaction when he found out.

"All right," Roxanne finally said, "if you won't go to the police, go see that private detective, the guy who runs Atlas Security."

"Who, Rawlins?"

"You have to do something to protect yourself, Maggie. You don't know how far this guy might be willing to go. Maybe Trace Rawlins can help."

Maggie didn't like it. The cowboy seemed cocky and far too self-assured. Worse yet, she didn't like the jolt of attraction she'd felt when he looked at her.

But she didn't like the snide remarks and sideways glances she had gotten at the police station, either.

Josh Varner was the son of a Houston police officer who was now a captain in the vice squad. Hoyt Varner had a score to settle for the unfair trouble she had caused his son years ago.

In a way Maggie didn't blame him.

"If you won't call him, I will," Roxanne said from the other end of the phone, jarring her back to the moment.

"All right, all right, I'll call."

"You want me to come over?"

"No, I'll be fine. I was just on my way to the grocery store, but I guess that can wait."

"Yeah, I guess it can."

Maggie ignored the sarcasm.

"Call me after you talk to him," Roxanne said.

"I will."

"Call him right now. Promise me."

"I said I would, didn't I?"

Roxanne signed off and Maggie hung up the phone. She glanced around the town house, which was still stacked with boxes she hadn't yet unpacked. Walking over to the breakfast bar separating the living room from the kitchen, she picked up the address book lying on the counter next to the phone and flipped it open.

On a yellow sticky note pressed inside the vinyl cover, she had printed the name Atlas Security. The address on Times Street was there, along with the company phone number and Trace Rawlins's name.

She stared at the yellow square of paper, then snatched it out of the address book. The office was in the University District, not that far away. Picking up the *People* magazine she had been reading while she drank her coffee that morning, she very carefully laid the note from her windshield inside the cover and closed it. With the yellow sticky note in hand, she grabbed her purse and headed back to her car.

As she crossed the lot, she scanned the area for anyone who might be watching, but whoever had left the note was gone. Maggie climbed into her little SUV and cranked the engine. As it began to purr, she shifted into gear and drove out of the lot, searching to the right and left, but seeing nothing out of the ordinary.

It didn't take long to find the brick building with the neatly printed Atlas Security sign on the front. Maggie parked the Escape, picked the magazine up off the passenger seat and got out of the car. She paused when she reached the front door.

Maybe Trace Rawlins wouldn't help her. Maybe just like everything else she had done in her life, she would have to find a way to handle this alone.

She drew in a shaky breath, thinking maybe this time money would solve the problem. Maybe—for a price—she could find someone willing to help.

Trace reached for his coffee mug and realized his coffee had grown cold. Seated in the chair behind his desk, he'd been going over some upgrades he wanted to install in the alarm system in the library at Rice University, one of the company's longtime clients. He looked up at the sound of Annie's voice.

"Someone here to see you," the older woman said. She tucked the yellow pencil in her hand above an ear. "Her name's Maggie O'Connell."

"O'Connell. Doesn't sound familiar. She say what she wanted?" He had been hoping to leave for home within the hour, pack up his gear and his dog and head for the shore.

"She didn't say, but you'd better watch out." Annie didn't bother to hide her grin. "She's a redhead."

He ignored a trickle of irritation. Annie knew his penchant for fiery-haired women and the trouble more than one of them had caused him over the years. And she didn't hesitate to goad him about it.

On the other hand... "Send her on in."

He stood up as the lady walked through the door. Five-four at most, slender yet curvy in all the right places. Once he got past the great body in snug jeans and a T-shirt with a Kodak ad on the front that read A Picture Is Worth a Thousand Words, he recognized her in a heartbeat.

The photographer he had clashed with three days ago in the Texas Café.

"Well, we meet again," he drawled. "I hope you

aren't here because Betty wouldn't give you back your camera."

"Betty gave it back. She seemed like a very nice woman."

He thought of the scene at the café, the sizzling temper the redhead had unleashed when he had deleted her photos, and amusement touched his lips. "What can I do for you, Ms.... O'Connell, was it?"

"That's right. After our little...disagreement, Betty mentioned you were a private investigator."

"That I am. You need something investigated?"

"Actually, I do."

He motioned for her to take a seat in one of the two dark brown leather chairs opposite his big oak desk, and sat back down himself. "Why don't you tell me how I can help you?"

She opened the *People* magazine he hadn't noticed she carried, being distracted by her nicely rounded breasts and shapely little behind. And there was all that glorious red hair.

With the magazine nestled in her lap, she opened the first page, then used the tips of her fingers to pick up a piece of brown paper that looked as if it had been torn from a grocery sack. Reaching over, she set it on his desk.

"Someone's been leaving notes like this on my car. This is the third one I've found. Whoever is doing it is beginning to scare me. I thought maybe I could hire you to find out who it is and make him stop."

Trace rose from his chair, leaned over and turned the paper around to face him, being as careful as she had been. If there were fingerprints on the note, he didn't want to smudge them.

My precious Maggie,
How long before our destinies are fulfilled? When
will you understand that your fate is entwined
with mine and I am the only one who can give
you the peace you need?

He didn't like the tone. He could understand why the lady might find the notes upsetting.

He sat back down in his chair. "You need to call the police, Ms. O'Connell. They'll make a report of the incidents and keep an eye out in your neighborhood for whoever may be leaving these."

"I've been to the police. It hasn't done any good. I want to know who this is and I want him to stop."

"And you think I can do that for you?"

"I saw the way you handled those three men. I imagine you could take care of this guy if you wanted to."

"I don't assault people for a living. That isn't my job. On the other hand, if my client is in danger, sometimes steps have to be taken."

She seemed to mull that over. "I guess what I'm saying is I'd like to hire you. Your receptionist told me what you charge, and that would be fine. If I'm your client and something happens, you would be obliged to protect me."

His gaze ran over her, the smooth skin and stubborn jaw, the big green, troubled eyes, the red hair curling softly around her shoulders.

He cleared his throat. "I'll need to see the other notes before I decide."

She bit her bottom lip. She wore peach-colored lipstick and her mouth was full and perfectly curved. He wasn't generally this taken with a woman, at least not at first glance. But there was something about her… He told himself it was just that damned red hair.

"Actually, I only have one."

"One?" he repeated, having lost track of the conversation.

"One of the other two notes. I threw the first one away. I thought it was a joke. I should have brought the second note with me. I wasn't thinking. I just wanted to get here, to talk to you, see if you could help."

She was worried, he could tell, maybe even a little frightened. She set her purse in her lap, then unconsciously twisted the strap one way and then another.

"As I said, I'd like to see the other note."

She rose from her chair. "I'll get it for you right now. My condo isn't that far away."

Trace stood as well. "I'd rather come with you. I can see where you live, take a look at the neighborhood, see where your car was parked when the notes were left."

"The first one was left on my car before I moved out of my apartment. It's about a mile or so away from where I live now. But I think that's a good idea."

She started for the door, but he caught her arm. "I'll drive. My car's right out front." He grabbed the white straw hat he had exchanged for his usual brown felt Stetson as the weather began to warm, and led her through the reception area. Opening the door, he waited while she walked outside.

"The Jeep Cherokee," he said, and one of her burnished eyebrows went up. "What? You were expecting a pickup?"

She shrugged, smiled. "You're a cowboy. I thought all you guys were pickup men."

He chuckled, thinking of the Joe Diffie song and wishing at the moment he owned one. "'Fraid I only drive one when I'm out at the ranch." He helped her into the vehicle and closed the door, rounded the hood and slid in behind the wheel.

She settled back and snapped her seat belt. "You have a ranch?"

"Technically, yes. The place belonged to my grandfather. My dad sold half when Granddad died and used the money to go into the security business. The land that's left is leased to a company that raises Black Angus beef. I kept the old ranch house and fifty acres around it. I pretty much grew up there as a kid. I stop by every once in a while just to keep an eye on things."

"The photos in your office...the rolling fields with the grazing cattle. Those were taken on the ranch?"

"Not by me, but yes. Gabe Raines, a friend of mine from Dallas, took them when we were out there together. I liked them so had them blown up and framed."

"They're very good."

"I'll tell him you said so." Gabriel Raines was Dev Raines's brother, one of his closest friends. They had worked together last year when Gabe was having trouble with an arsonist. Gabe was in construction. Taking pictures was just a hobby, but Gabe seemed to have a good eye.

They drove away from the office, leaving the small business district behind, moving along Kirby Street through a neighborhood of stately older homes and smaller, even older residences like the one in which he lived. Big sycamore trees overhung the streets, shading the asphalt. Manicured lawns climbed from the curb to the front of each house.

Heading south at Maggie's direction, they passed Holcomb Street, wound around a bit, eventually turned onto Broadmoor and into a six-unit town house development that looked very new. The units were nicely constructed, utilizing the land without destroying too many trees. The buildings, beige with redbrick trim, had a vaulted roofline, and each unit had its own brick chimney.

"That one's mine. The one on the end, unit A."

He pulled into a space Maggie indicated in front of a row of matching two-story dwellings. "This your usual parking spot?"

She nodded. "There's a guest space on the right. I keep my car in the garage at night."

They got out of the car and Maggie led him toward the door of her unit. He liked the way she moved, sexy and confident. He liked the way she looked, too, with that little spray of freckles across her forehead and the tip of her nose.

His groin tightened. His instincts were warning him to stay away from temptation, and Maggie O'Connell was certainly that. He would give the case to Alex or Ben, he told himself. As soon as he had a little more information.

She unlocked the door and Trace followed her in. "I'll get the note," Maggie said. "I'll be right back."

He watched her climb the stairs in the entry, admiring the firmness of the muscles in her hips and thighs. The lady stayed in shape, it was clear. He liked that in a woman, since he believed in staying fit himself.

As she disappeared, he glanced around the condo, which was almost empty. Just a beige, floral-print sofa and matching chair in the living room, a maple coffee table and a couple brass lamps, one of them sitting on the floor. Cardboard boxes were stacked everywhere. There was a dining table in an area off the living room.

She had a laptop set up there. Good to know she was computer literate.

Maggie returned with the note, carrying it gingerly but not as carefully. "I handled it when I first got it. Fingerprints never occurred to me until today." She walked to the breakfast counter and laid the note on the gold-flecked white granite top. Trace moved it a little so he could read the words.

> *Precious Maggie,*
> *Such a delight you are. Soon you will come to me. Soon you will understand we are meant to be together.*

There it was again, that odd, eerie tone. Trace couldn't put his finger on exactly what it meant, but he didn't like it. He placed the second note beside the first, compared the hand-printed letters. Bold. Well formed. No misspelled words.

Maggie looked up at him. "Will you help me?"

Give the case to Alex, a little voice said.

A muscle tightened in Trace's cheek. Alex Justice, with his good looks and dimples… Trace glanced down at Maggie and desire curled through him. Her eyes were on his, green and worried. A surge of protectiveness overrode his good sense.

So she was a redhead. So what? So what if he already felt a strong attraction to her? It didn't mean a thing. She could be in serious trouble and she needed his help.

"You have any idea who might have written these?" he asked.

Maggie shook her head. "I've tried to think. It doesn't sound like anyone I know."

"Educated. Forceful. Older, maybe. This is not some bum off the street."

"No, I don't think so, either."

"If I'm going to find this guy, you're going to have to help me. I'll need to know things about you. Things about your past, about your work. Some of it fairly personal. If you're willing to tell me what I need to know, I'll help you."

He watched the uncertainty move across her face. Unlike his ex-wife, talking about herself didn't seem to be high on Maggie's agenda.

"I'll tell you as much as I can," she said, which wasn't the answer he wanted. He guessed for now it would have to do.

"All right, Maggie O'Connell. If we're going to get this done, we might as well get to it."

Chapter 3

"Before we get started," Trace said, "I need to go out to my car. I'll be right back."

Maggie walked into the living room and sat down on the sofa in front of the empty brick hearth, waiting while he disappeared outside, then returned carrying a leather briefcase. He sat down in the floral-print chair at the end of the sofa, took off his cowboy hat and rested it on the padded arm. He was dressed in sharply creased jeans, a short-sleeved white Western shirt with pearl snaps, and a pair of freshly polished, plain brown cowboy boots.

His hair was a dark mink-brown, but in the sunlight streaming through the window, little streaks of gold wound through the ends. The man was broad-shouldered, lean and fit, but she had already discovered that during his run-in with Bobby Jordane in the Texas Café.

She had noticed the gold in Trace Rawlins's brown

eyes, his straight nose and white teeth. Now she noticed the sexy, sensual curve of his mouth, and found herself staring more than once. He was a good-looking man. But that and the fact he knew how to use his fists were all she really knew about him.

After the way he had bullied her in the café, she wasn't even sure she liked him.

The brass latch on his briefcase clicked open and Trace took out a state-of-the-art recorder, a Montblanc pen and a yellow legal pad.

"Let's start with the present and work backward," he said, turning on the recorder. "You're a photographer. Is that a hobby or what you do for a living?"

She smiled. "I'm lucky. I'm not rich, but I make a very good living doing the work I love."

Trace glanced at the barren white walls of the town house.

"My pictures are all still in boxes," Maggie explained in answer to his silent question. "I'm working on a photo project that's been keeping me really busy. I'm unpacking a little at a time."

"What kind of project?"

"A coffee-table book. It's called *The Sea*. It's set around the ocean and the different kinds of things people do that involve the sea—jobs, recreation, that kind of thing."

His gaze sharpened with interest. When he looked at her with that direct way of his, her skin felt warm. "Why did you pick that subject?"

"I love the ocean. I do mostly outdoor photography. I love shooting any kind of landscapes, but the sea has my heart."

His eyes gleamed and tiny lines appeared at the corners. She wondered if they were laugh lines or life lines, or just a reflection of the time he spent out-of-doors.

"I'd love to see some of your work," he said.

Maggie smiled. "I guess I'd better get busy and unpack those boxes."

They talked about her business a little more, about the people she dealt with in the galleries where her photos were displayed, and people she might have encountered during her shows.

"Do you keep a list of your clients?"

"As much as I can. I enter them into a file on my computer."

"Anyone in particular who's bought an extraordinary amount of your work?"

"Not that I can think of. I have clients who've purchased three or four pieces. That's not that uncommon." Maggie sighed. "As I said, the notes don't strike any sort of chord. I can't imagine I know this person."

"Maybe you don't. Starting tomorrow, I'm going to put a tail on you for a couple of days. It'll be me or a guy who works for me named Rex Westcott. I'll show you his picture, so if you happen to spot him, you'll know he's not the guy we're after. We'll keep tabs on you, watch for anyone who might be following you."

She felt a trickle of relief. "All right."

"Of course, that might not be the way he operates. Obviously, he knows where you live. He might know a whole lot more."

Maggie didn't like the sound of that. It was one of the reasons she stayed away from social networking sites like Facebook and Twitter.

Trace asked her more questions about roommates at school, old boyfriends, someone she might have jilted.

"To tell you the truth, I don't date that often. I had a

boyfriend when I went to college. We were pretty serious for a while, but it didn't work out."

"What was his name?"

"Michael Irving."

"Anyone else?"

She hated to mention David, since she had been the
one at fault for the breakup, and she didn't want to cause
him any more trouble.

"Maggie?"

She released a breath, determined to reveal as little
as possible. "I went out with an attorney named David
Lyons for a while. We lived together a couple of months."

"Bad breakup?"

His eyes were on hers. The man didn't miss a thing.
"Pretty bad. It was my fault. I didn't mean to hurt him,
but I did."

"When did it end?"

"First of April, two years ago."

"Where is he now?"

"I haven't seen him. I heard he was dating someone."

Trace stopped making notes and looked at her. There
was something in those golden-brown eyes that seemed
to see more than she wanted.

"What about now?" he asked. "Are you involved with
anyone at the moment?"

Maggie shook her head. "I've been way too busy."
She wondered if there might be something personal in
the question. She wasn't sure how she felt about that.
"And I really don't like the dating scene. I suppose eventually I'd like to meet someone, but not right now. I've
got my career to think about. I'm happy the way I am."

He studied her as if he wasn't sure he believed her.
She wondered if he was one of those men who thought
every woman was desperate to find a husband. Or

maybe exactly the opposite. That she was just another faithless female concerned with only herself.

"It'll take some time to check all this out," he said. "The thing is, you might know this person and not realize it. He—or she—could be using this odd style of writing so you won't figure out who it is."

She frowned. "You don't actually think this could be a woman?"

"Unless your sexual preferences go both ways, probably not."

She smiled. "I'm boringly heterosexual."

His eyes seemed to darken. Maggie felt a warm, unwelcome stirring in the pit of her stomach, and inwardly cursed her bad luck. An attraction to Trace Rawlins was the last thing she wanted.

"The handwriting looks masculine," Trace continued, "but there definitely are women stalkers. Jealousy over a past relationship with a man, or your success as a photographer. That kind of thing."

He kept asking questions, moving her backward in time. Thinking about the incident with Josh Varner, she began to grow more and more uneasy.

"Tell me about your family," Trace said, making notes now and again.

"My mom and dad divorced when I was four. Mom moved back to Florida where she was raised, remarried not long after and had another kid. I stayed here and lived with my dad."

"He still alive?"

"He passed away a couple of years ago."

"I lost mine a while back. I still miss him."

Maggie made no comment. Her dad had been demanding and a tough disciplinarian, but she had loved him and still missed him.

"How about high school? Anything stand out? Any old grudges that might blossom years later?"

She forced her gaze to remain on his face. No way was she telling him about Josh Varner. Josh didn't even live in Texas anymore. He had gone to UCLA on a scholarship and then taken a job in Seattle with Microsoft. She'd heard he made barrels of money.

And if he wrote her a message, it wouldn't sound anything like the words on the notes she had received.

"I, um, can't think of anything. Besides, if it was something from high school, why would the person wait all these years?"

Trace's pen stopped moving. "Usually something happens, an event of some kind. A stressor, it's called. A trigger that digs up old memories, sometimes twists them around in a weird direction."

She shook her head. "I really can't think of anything." At least nothing that had recently occurred. Still, she was glad he looked down just then to write another note. She had always been an unconvincing liar.

"It may well be that this guy has seen you somewhere but the two of you have never met. He could be fixated on you for no good reason other than the color of your hair, or that you look like someone he once knew."

A little chill ran through her. "I see."

Trace reached over and squeezed her hand. "Look, we're going to catch this guy. There are very tough laws against stalking."

She nodded. Just his light touch reassured her. Maybe this was a man she could count on, a man who could make things turn out all right.

They talked awhile longer, but he didn't bring up her past again. If something happened that involved her Great Shame, as she thought of it, she would tell him.

If she did, she knew the look she would see on his face. At the moment, she just couldn't handle it.

Trace rose effortlessly from his chair, to tower over her on his long legs. "On the way back to the office, you can show me where you lived when you got the first note." He packed up his stuff, closed the briefcase, clamped on his cowboy hat. "I'd like to take the notes," he said, "check them for prints."

"All right."

Trace bagged the notes and she led him to the entry.

"You keep your doors and windows locked?"

"I'm pretty good about it."

His glance was hard and direct. "You be better than pretty good. You be damned good."

She didn't like his attitude. On the other hand, he was probably right. Even in a good neighborhood, the crime rate in Houston was high.

"I'll keep the doors locked."

"Good girl. Let's go."

She felt his hand at the small of her back, big and warm as he guided her out of the house toward his Jeep, then opened the door and helped her climb in. They cruised by her old apartment. He stopped in front and made a thorough perusal of the area, then turned the Jeep around and headed back toward his office.

"Anyone in your old apartment building who might be interested in you in some way?"

"There're only four units. A retired lady school-teacher lives in one. There's a single mother and her four-year-old son, and an older man in a wheelchair. The one I left is still vacant."

"Looks like we can rule out the apartment residents."

They reached his office and Trace walked her over to her car.

"Remember what I said about keeping your doors locked."

"I will."

As Maggie drove back to her town house, she couldn't help thinking that in going to a private investigator she had done the right thing.

She didn't like the attraction she felt, but it was only physical, nothing to really worry about. Trace was a handsome, incredibly masculine man, and she hadn't been involved with anyone in years.

And she felt better knowing she had someone to help her.

Even if she had to pay for it.

Trace sat in front of his computer, staring at Maggie O'Connell's webpage. The black background showed off a dozen photos of the Texas Hill Country, including the imported African game that roamed the grasslands, and a variety of magnificent sunsets that lured the viewer deeper into each scene.

On another page, there were shots of small towns and beaches along the coastline bordering the Gulf, and wonderful action photos of various power-and sailboats skimming over the water in Galveston Bay.

The colors were brilliant, the angles of the photos showed the subject to the very best advantage, and there was always something a little different, something intriguing about each picture. At the bottom of the page, information on the three galleries in Texas that carried limited-edition prints of Maggie's work was listed, and a contact email address.

Trace searched through the dozens of other sites that popped up on Google when he referenced her name, and the more he searched, the more frustrated he became.

Damn, his client wasn't just a good photographer, she was practically a celebrity. She was a well-known, well-respected artist whose work had been viewed by thousands of people.

And any one of them could be the person who was stalking her.

Trace leaned forward in his leather chair and punched the button on the recorder, listening again to his conversation with Maggie. When he finished, he reviewed the notes he had taken.

He went to work on her list of names, verifying what little information he had. Nothing turned up. Michael Irving and David Lyons both had webpages. Irving was a certified public accountant in Dallas. Lyons was a corporate lawyer in Houston with Holder Holder & Meeks.

It was after seven by the time Trace finished. The office was closed. Annie had left for the night and Alex and Ben were out working cases. Trace had decided to postpone his trip to the shore until next weekend, and had called Rex Westcott to start the tail on Maggie tomorrow morning. He had sent Rex's photo to the email address she had given him: photolady@baytown.com.

Photolady. Looking at some of her work, he realized she was far more than that. He might have smiled, except that he didn't like complications, and Maggie O'Connell was nothing but. Her life was complicated. The possibilities of who her stalker might be were endless.

And the unwanted attraction Trace felt for her only made matters worse.

He sighed as he rose from his chair, plucked his hat off the credenza behind his desk and prepared to leave. A knock on the front door caught his attention. He glanced at the clock, saw that another hour had passed and wondered who knew he would be there this late.

He settled his hat on his head and started for the front door, turned the lock and pulled it open.

"Good heavens, Trace," said a familiar female voice, "where on earth have you been?" Carly Benson Rawlins stormed past him into the office, whirled and set her hands on her hips. "Why didn't you return my calls? I needed you, Trace. Why didn't you call me back?"

"Good evening, Carly. Why don't you come on in?" His sarcasm went unnoticed.

"How could you be so insensitive?" She was petite and voluptuous, with long, straight red hair that fell past her shoulders. She had the prettiest blue eyes he'd ever seen. He cursed as he watched them fill with tears. "H-how could you ignore me like that?"

"You aren't my wife anymore, Carly. I can ignore you whenever I want."

She sniffed, tilted her head back to look up at him. "What if something had happened? What if I'd been in a car wreck or something?"

"Were you in a car wreck?"

"No, but I could have been. Did you see that newspaper article in the *Chronicle* this morning? That woman who drove down to the shore and never came back? Her parents are frantic. She was my age, Trace—twenty-nine years old and she just disappeared."

"I saw it. The police think maybe she took off with her boyfriend or something."

"Or maybe she was *murdered*." Carly shuddered with feigned revulsion. "A woman needs a man to look out for her." She smiled, her tears long forgotten, looped her arms around his neck and went up on her toes to look into his face. "You know I still love you, Trace. Sometimes I just need to know you're still there for me."

He took hold of her wrists and eased her back down on her feet. "Look, Carly. You aren't in any sort of danger and you need to get on with your life. That's what people do when they get divorced."

"I never wanted a divorce and you know it."

"No, but you wanted other men in your bed. That didn't work for me."

Her chin angled up. "You weren't there, Trace. You were working all the time."

"I was trying to build the business, trying to make a life for us. I'm sorry I couldn't keep you properly entertained."

"It was all your fault and you know it."

Maybe some of it was, but mostly he had just picked the wrong woman, as his friends had tried to warn him. Carly was wild and self-centered. She hadn't been ready to settle down when he'd married her. She wasn't ready now.

Still, he felt sorry for her. She wasn't happy. He wasn't sure she ever would be.

He turned her around and urged her gently toward the door. "We've been through all this before." *A thousand times,* he added silently. "Things just didn't work out, that's all. Go home, Carly. Entertain yourself with someone else."

She jerked to a halt at the door. "You're cruel, Trace. Cruel and heartless."

If anything, he was too soft when it came to women. Years ago, he had learned to control his temper. He had come to value his self-control. He'd been raised to treat a woman like a lady. He did his best to do just that.

"Good night, Carly," he said gently, then waited as

she stormed out the door. Trace watched her drive her little silver BMW sports car down the alley out of sight, and wondered which of her many admirers had bought it for her.

He lifted his hat, raked back his hair, then settled the hat a little lower across his forehead. He had no idea why his ex-wife continued to plague him. They were never right for each other, never should have married. They might have been in lust at one time, but they were never in love.

That same kind of attraction to a good-looking red-head had hit him several other times in his life. None of those times had ended well.

Trace thought of Maggie O'Connell and warned himself not to go down that road again.

Chapter 4

It was pitch-black in her upstairs bedroom. Only the night sounds of crickets and cicadas intruded into the darkness of the high-ceilinged room. Maggie tossed and turned beneath the lightweight down comforter, unable to sleep with so much on her mind. She needed to get the photos completed for her coffee-table book. And she had a show coming up. She had most of the pictures ready, but could use a few more for the exhibit.

She sighed into the darkness. She had so much to do. Aside from her work, she needed to unpack, try to make the town house more of a home. There wasn't much furniture downstairs, and only a bed, two nightstands and a dresser in her bedroom, stuff she'd had for years.

She still had a few pieces to bring over from the apartment before the end of the month, when her lease was up, and some things she needed to buy, and of course her photos and some prized Ansel Adams pieces that needed to be hung on the walls. She wasn't much of a decorator but she could do better than the way it looked now.

She punched her pillow, turned onto her back and stared at the ceiling. Tomorrow was Saturday. She planned to drive down to Galveston, take some shots around the harbor. She needed to get up early. Which meant she had to get some sleep.

She closed her eyes, tried to clear her head.

That was when she heard it. The faint scraping of a chair against the ceramic tile floor in the kitchen. She listened, straining her ears. Was that the patio door sliding open? Was that a footstep she heard on the stairs? Her heart was pounding, thumping against her ribs. Her palms felt slick where she clenched the sheet. She thought of the notes she had received, wondered if the man who had written them was crazy enough to break into her home.

She listened again, trying to decide if she should call 911. The police would show up, she figured, even if they knew she was the caller. But as the seconds stretched into minutes, she realized the only sound she was hearing was the fear pumping through her veins.

When the noise didn't come again, she began to relax. She had imagined the intruder. There was no one in the house. As Trace had insisted, she had carefully locked the doors.

She glanced at the digital clock beside the bed: 2:15. She lay there in silence, her ears focused to catch any noise out of the ordinary, but she didn't hear anything more. The little button in the center of the bedroom doorknob was pushed. It wasn't much of a lock, but it gave her some sense of security. At least she would know if someone was trying to get in.

She watched the clock, the numbers slipping past. At

two thirty-five, she rolled out of bed. No other sounds had reached her. Maybe she had fallen asleep for an instant and dreamed the entire incident. Things like that had happened to her before.

Still, she had to know.

Reaching for the blue fleece robe tossed over the foot of the bed, she slipped her arms inside and tied the sash around her waist. After years of living in the Texas heat, she slept in the nude, but she always kept the robe handy in case there was some sort of emergency, like a fire, or just someone arriving unexpectedly at her door.

She listened again for a moment, heard nothing and quietly turned the knob. Easing the door open, she waited. Just the ticking of the antique clock that she planned to hang on the wall in the living room but hadn't done yet. Sticking her head out in the hallway, she glanced both ways, but no lights were burning; nothing seemed out of the ordinary.

After tiptoeing down the hall, she slipped into her photo studio and grabbed a makeshift weapon—a unipod, the one-legged stand she sometimes used to steady her camera. She quietly retraced her steps with it clutched in both hands, and descended the stairs.

No movement. No sound. Maggie flipped on the light switch, illuminating the glass lamp hanging in the foyer, casting a bright glow partway into the living room.

Nothing.

The tension eased from her shoulders. She turned on the light in the kitchen, turned on a lamp in the living room, took a look around. She had imagined the entire episode—thank God.

It was the note. The notes were making her edgy and restless, sending her into a tailspin. She hoped Trace Rawlins would find the man who had been harassing her.

She moved through the house, making a brief inspection of the locks, finding them all secured. She turned off the brass lamp in the living room, then padded back to the kitchen. Her hand paused midway to the light switch as her eyes caught something sitting on the breakfast bar.

A cold chill swept through her. The only things there when she had gone to bed were the telephone, the old-fashioned answering machine she still used and the address book she kept beside them.

Her mouth went dry. She forced her feet to carry her to the counter. Her hand shook as she reached toward the small porcelain statuette sitting on top. It was no more than five inches high, a man in a black tuxedo dancing with a woman with upswept red hair wearing a long, flowing, pale green evening gown.

Maggie swallowed. Her gaze shot around the kitchen, but she had checked the rooms and the closets and found no one there. Picking up her address book with a shaking hand, she flicked it open. Trace Rawlins's business card rested just inside.

Frantically, she dialed the cell number printed on the card, terrified that the man who had left the statue might be hiding in the house and she just hadn't found him. With the phone pressed against her ear, she listened to the ringing on the other end of the line and prayed Trace Rawlins would answer.

The boat was running with the wind, *Ranger's Lady* skimming over the surface of the frothy blue ocean. The early-spring air felt fresh and cool against his skin. Gulls screeched and turned over the top of the mast, circling the boat in search of food.

Trace was smiling, enjoying the perfect day, when

Faith Hill's sweet voice began to sing to him through his cell phone. In an instant, he was jolted awake, a habit from his days in the Rangers. His hand shot out and grabbed the phone off the bedside table, and he pressed it against his ear.

"Rawlins," he rasped in a sleepy voice.

"Trace, it's Maggie O'Connell."

"Maggie?" Worry slid through him. He rolled to the side of the bed, swung his long legs over the side. "Maggie, what is it?"

"Someone…someone was in my house tonight. He left…left something for me on the counter."

A chill ran down Trace's spine. "Have you called the police?"

"I—I called you instead."

His fingers tightened around the phone. "Are you sure he isn't still there?"

"I—I don't think so."

"Not good enough. Hang up and call 911. I'm on my way."

Trace hung up the phone, grabbed his jeans off the back of a chair and pulled them on without bothering with his briefs. After dragging a T-shirt over his head, he pulled on his boots and headed for the door. Sensing his urgency, Rowdy followed, but the dog was used to his master's odd hours and didn't make a fuss.

Trace's shoulder holster hung on the hat rack beside the back door. He used a Beretta 9 mm semiauto when he carried, which he hadn't needed to do lately. He slipped on the holster, snapped out the weapon and checked the load as he hurried outside toward his car.

It didn't take long to reach Maggie's town house. He was glad he had been there before. It was almost three in the morning, but the lights were on. As he strode up the walkway, he could see her through a small window over the sink in the kitchen, standing there in her bathrobe, her arms wrapped around herself as if she were cold.

No patrol car was in sight. Trace silently cursed the time it was taking them to get there. He knocked on the door. "Maggie? It's Trace."

She opened the door an instant later, her shoulders sagging with relief as he walked past her into the entry.

"Thank you for coming."

He glanced around. "I thought the cops would be here by now."

Her gaze strayed from his. "I, um, didn't call them."

Frustration tightened Trace's jaw. "Why the hell not?"

"You were on your way. I took another look around. I'm sure he's not here."

Trace shook his head. "Dammit, Maggie." Pulling the Beretta from its holster, he made a check of the rooms downstairs, the coat closet, the bedroom and bath. He made the same search upstairs, the master bedroom and bath, and the photo studio. Returning downstairs, he opened the door from the entry into the garage, flipped on the light and took the single step down.

Maggie's Ford Escape sat in the garage. The door leading outside was locked. There was no sign of whoever had come into the house.

"I checked the doors and windows," he told her as he returned to the kitchen. "They're all locked. No broken latches, nothing. Any idea how he got in?"

"I don't know."

"Show me what he left you."

She led him to the breakfast bar. "That." She pointed toward the item on the counter. "It's pretty innocuous, just a little porcelain statuette, but…"

"But it means something. At least to him."

Trace examined the dancing couple, carefully painted by hand. Using a paper towel, he lifted the piece to examine it more closely, noting that the bottom was uneven, as if it had been attached to something, and broken off.

He set the statuette back on the breakfast bar. "Does it mean anything to you?"

Maggie shook her head. "I've never seen anything like it. It looks a little like one of those things you put on top of a wedding cake."

"Yeah, but it isn't. Check the bottom." He showed her the uneven edges. "At one time, this was attached to something. Glued on, it looks like."

"I have no idea why anyone would leave that here," she said, her gaze still on the figurine. Her eyes were the same pale green as the woman's dress, her hair the same fiery red. The porcelain figure meant something, all right, and whatever it was, it wasn't good.

Trace glanced around the town house. "Your locks are a joke. Tomorrow I'll have my guys come over and install some decent ones, along with a security system."

"They're, uh, kind of expensive, aren't they?"

For the first time, he smiled. "You're a client. You get a special price. We'll just do the basics—the windows and doors, a couple motion detectors."

"I guess I don't have much choice."

He gently caught her shoulders, forcing her to look at him. "We need to call the police, Maggie. Someone broke into your home. This isn't the first problem you've had. You need to file a report, keep the cops in the loop."

She looked away, studied her slender feet, showing beneath the hem of the robe, the pale peach polish on her toenails. Trace's gaze followed hers and he found himself wondering how smooth her skin would feel, how responsive she would be if his hand moved up her thigh. He wondered what she was wearing beneath the robe, and felt himself harden inside his jeans.

Son of a bitch. He forced his attention back to her face, amazed that he had allowed his attraction to sidetrack his thoughts.

"What is it with you and the cops?" he asked. "You don't have a record, do you?"

Her eyes widened. "No, I... No, of course not."

But he thought that her face went a little pale. He pulled out his cell and dialed 911, and a few minutes later a white-and-blue patrol car rolled up. A Hispanic officer whose name tag read Gonzalez, and his slightly chubby, blond-haired partner, walked into the town house in response to the call.

The blond cop, Sandowski, searched the unit, while Gonzalez took Maggie's statement, which briefly recapped the events of the night.

"So that's it?" Gonzalez said, making a final note on his pad as she finished. "You heard a noise and found the statue on the counter?"

"That's what happened, yes."

"Was anything stolen?"

"I don't think so. I haven't noticed anything missing."

He looked at Trace. "What about you? You got anything to add?"

Trace explained that he had come over after receiving Maggie's call. "She was clearly upset. She's been getting threatening messages left on her car, hang-up calls, that kind of thing."

Sandowski returned from his search just then. "I checked the doors and windows. No sign of forced entry. Are you sure your cleaning lady or a friend didn't leave the statue there? Maybe you just didn't notice it before you went to bed."

Maggie's pretty lips thinned. "It wasn't there."

Gonzalez wrote something on his notepad. "We'll take a look around outside before we leave. I suggest you check with friends, see if maybe one of them was playing a joke or something."

"It wasn't a joke," Maggie said tightly.

The officers headed for the door. It was obvious they believed she had just overlooked the presence of the porcelain figurine.

Maggie had said the cops weren't able to help her. Clearly, they weren't convinced the threat against her was real. First thing in the morning, Trace would take the figurine down to his office, do a check for prints on it and the notes she'd received.

"Will you be able to sleep?" he asked once the police were gone.

"Probably not." She raked soft red curls back from her face. Sleep-tousled, they teased her cheeks and shoulders. His fingers itched to touch them.

"You need to get some rest," he said a little gruffly, thinking that under different circumstances he might have exactly the sleeping pill she needed. As it was, Maggie was his client, his responsibility. He had no intention of trying to seduce her.

He almost smiled. And he was pretty sure if he tried, his chances of success would be slim to none.

"I was planning to drive down to the shore tomorrow," she said, "take some shots for my book. Now... I don't know...."

"That might not be a bad idea," Trace said before he could stop himself. "Until you walked into my office,

I was thinking of heading to Kemah for the weekend. I've got a boat docked there."

One of her burnished eyebrows went up. "A cowboy who rides a boat instead of a horse?"

He smiled. "That's me."

"Kemah's a charming little town. I've gotten some great pictures on the boardwalk."

"Maybe we could drive down together. My men will be working here all day, installing the security system and changing the locks. You could get away from all that for a while and I could get in a little sailing."

And he could take Rex's place, keep an eye out, see if anyone followed them down.

Maggie looked at him with a combination of weariness and suspicion.

"I'll drive," he offered. "You can sleep on the way."

"And you'll bring me back tomorrow night?"

A cautious lady. In her situation that was good. "Unless you decide you'd rather stay and sleep aboard," he couldn't resist adding.

She sliced him a sideways glance. "I'll let you know in the morning."

Trace just smiled. "In case you haven't noticed, it is morning, Maggie."

Chapter 5

As soon as he got home, Trace stretched out on the overstuffed sofa in his living room still wearing his jeans and boots. Rowdy curled up on the beige carpet next to the sofa, and both of them fell asleep. Trace slept like a rock till six, then made himself some coffee, loaded his gear in the back of the Jeep and drove down to the office.

There was a fingerprint kit in the back room. He dusted the notes for prints, but as he had figured, the rough brown paper yielded nothing.

He held more hope for the little porcelain statuette, but after careful examination and dusting, it appeared the figurine had been wiped clean. Which in itself revealed something about Maggie's stalker.

Whoever it was was careful. Very careful. No sign of forced entry. No footprints that Trace had seen. He would bet he could dust the whole condo and no prints would turn up. Since the town house had recently been for sale, it wouldn't have been difficult for the intruder to get a key. Trace would talk to the Realtors who'd handled the listing and sale, see what might come up.

His Jeep was loaded and ready. The office wasn't officially open on weekends, but Ben, Alex and Sol were usually in and out. Annie came in whenever she needed to play catch-up. The alarm system installers worked for JDT Security Systems, the company that handled all the Atlas jobs. Trace phoned Ed Wilcox and got the guys going on what would be an overtime job at Maggie's.

By nine he was finished and heading back to the town house. He wanted to interview the residents in the other five units, see if anyone had heard or seen anything last night.

As he drove toward Broadmoor, he found himself smiling. He was working, sort of, providing a protection detail for his client—not that he planned to charge her for a trip to the shore. But the better part of the bargain was the day he would be spending at sea, sailing with the pretty little redhead on his boat in Galveston Bay.

Maggie was surprised she had agreed to the trip. But as Trace had said, the security people would be working in the town house all day, and she really needed to take some more pictures. She wanted to finish the coffee-table book and if she got lucky, she could get a few more shots for her show at the Twin Oaks Gallery in a couple weeks.

After Trace left in the wee hours of the morning, Maggie had returned upstairs and managed to get a couple hours of sleep. But it wasn't nearly enough. As she dressed in a pair of cropped navy blue pants, a red-striped top and sandals, she yawned, feeling groggy and out of sorts. Coffee helped but not that much. At least the weather was good. Still cool, but no longer cold, the air not too humid.

Trace returned at ten, his Cherokee loaded with gear. "You ready?" he asked when she opened the door.

"Just about." She looked down at the black-and-white dog standing next to him on her doorstep.

"That's Rowdy," he said. "Rowdy, this is Maggie."

Her eyes widened when the animal barked.

"Hi, Rowdy," she said, because he seemed to demand a greeting. "It's very nice to meet you."

He barked again.

She bit back a laugh. "I just need to load my camera gear." She turned to collect the Nikon D3S sitting in its case in the entry. It was equipped with a fantastic Tamron 28-300 lens she had purchased a few weeks back. The new equipment had set her back nearly seven thousand dollars, but in her line of work, it was an essential investment.

Trace walked past her, gently elbowing her aside when she reached for the bag, and hoisted the strap over one of his wide shoulders.

"I'm used to carrying my own equipment," she said.

"I'm sure you are." But he kept on walking, hauling the stuff out to his Jeep and loading it into the backseat.

"I hope you aren't charging me extra for that," she grumbled as she carried her yellow canvas swim bag out to the car.

He grinned, a flash of white in a suntanned face so handsome it made her breath catch. An amazing face, she thought, with those hard, sculpted features and intense, whiskey-brown eyes, so warm and direct they sent a little quiver into her stomach.

"No extra charge," he said, sliding her tripod onto the seat. "Not today."

She watched the flex of those incredible biceps she

had noticed at the Texas Café, and told herself there was nothing wrong with being physically attracted to a man. After all, she was a young, fully mature woman, though she rarely gave in to those sorts of urges.

"Oh, I almost forgot the sandwiches."

He smiled. "Sandwiches, huh? I like the way you think. I'm hungry already."

Maggie ran back inside and grabbed the small cooler she had filled with ham-and-cheese sandwiches on fresh rye bread, and a couple Diet Cokes. Mr. He-man probably drank the real thing, but today, diet would have to do.

Trace and Rowdy walked to the rear of the Jeep. "Load up," he said, and the dog hopped onto the tailgate, went inside and lay down on his bed. Trace left the rear window rolled partway down to let in fresh air, and the little dog seemed pleased.

"Rowdy looks very much at home back there," Maggie said as she climbed up in the passenger seat. "Do you always take him with you?"

"Most of the time. Rowdy loves to sail almost as much as I do."

"Smart dog."

"He's a border collie. They're bred to herd cattle and sheep, one of the smartest breeds."

"Where did you get him?"

"Gabe Raines—the guy who took the photos in my office? His brother owns a ranch in Wyoming. Rowdy was a pup from one of the litters up there."

Trace closed her door, then went around to the driver's side and slid behind the wheel. He wasn't wearing his cowboy hat today, just a white ball cap with an anchor on the front, plus jeans and a yellow knit shirt. No boots, either, just a pair of white canvas deck shoes that were clean but had seen plenty of wear.

The lack of sleep didn't seem to faze him. He looked every bit as good as he had the night before.

Not liking the train of her thoughts, Maggie sat up a little straighter. "I'd like to get a dog someday," she said, just to make conversation. "I had a cocker spaniel when I was a kid, but my mom took it with her when she went back to Florida. I keep thinking someday I'll get one, but right now I'm too busy."

Trace cast her a glance. "You said you were four when your mom and dad divorced. It must have been tough on you."

She felt the old familiar ache in her chest. "It was hard. My mother went on with her life and we barely stayed in touch. My dad did his best, but he had to make a living. He owned a small trucking company so he was gone from home a lot."

"Mine, too. My mom died when I was born. My dad was in the army, so my grandparents pretty much raised me."

"Out on the ranch," she said, remembering what he had told her.

"That's right."

When he didn't add more, she let the subject drop. Didn't sound as if either of them had had a fantastic childhood.

The Jeep rolled along the shady streets. From her town house, they drove through the University District onto the 59 Freeway, then took the 45 south toward the ocean. Kemah was one of a string of seaside communities that fronted Galveston Bay.

At the edge of the water, small weekend retreats that had been there for years sat next to sprawling, newly constructed mansions. Fine white sand surrounded them, lush vegetation and lots of palm and live oak trees.

Trace kept his boat—a sleek, white, low-hulled thirty-eight-footer—at the Kemah Marina, she discovered.

"What kind of boat is it?" Maggie asked. He climbed aboard, then reached down to take her hand and guide her up the steps and onto the deck. "Hunter Legend. Been a great boat to own."

It was immaculately clean inside, she saw as he gave her a quick tour, and nicely fitted out with blue canvas cushions and lots of teakwood kept highly polished. A dining area and a galley; two cabins and a head.

"So what do you think?"

"She's beautiful." *Ranger's Lady* was the name painted on the stern. "Name fits, too. Lone Ranger, right? That's the way I thought of you that day in the Texas Café."

Trace chuckled. "Not that kind of Ranger. U.S. Army. Kind of a tradition in our family."

"You were a Ranger?"

He nodded. "My dad, too. That was the reason he was gone so much."

"Where were you stationed?"

"South America, mostly. We were there but we weren't, if you know what I mean."

"I think I can figure it out." She cast him a glance. "I bet you've always been somewhat of a maverick."

Trace grinned. "Somewhat."

She looked away, not liking the flutter that grin caused in her stomach. "Mind if I take some shots?"

He glanced around. He had been doing that all day. Second nature, she imagined, for an investigator. And she was, after all, paying him to find a stalker.

"Go ahead," he said. "I'll get ready to cast off while you wander a little. Just don't go too far."

"No problem."

Trace went to work, and she watched his easy, economical movements. No wasted effort, just do the job and get it done. There was a certain grace there, too. She wondered what he'd look like on the back of a horse, and thought he would probably look as if he'd been born there.

Leaving him to his work, she climbed onto the dock and took some photos of the yachts in the marina. She wandered a bit, snapping a shot here and there: an old lady in a huge straw hat walking her little rust-colored Pekinese; two old men playing cards at a table next to the water; a little kid licking the biggest yellow-and-white rock candy sucker she had ever seen.

She returned to the *Ranger's Lady,* snapping photos along the way. When she reached the boat, she realized Trace must have been watching her the entire time she was gone. He was only doing his job, she reminded herself, nothing more. Which for reasons she couldn't explain, she found mildly annoying.

He helped her aboard, then went back to examining one of the lines that hoisted the sail.

He had stripped off his cotton knit shirt and jeans, leaving him bare chested in a pair of navy blue swim trunks. With his back to her, she couldn't help checking him out. His skin was a smooth golden-brown and rippling with muscle. His legs were long and corded. There wasn't an ounce of fat anywhere to be seen.

She couldn't resist a couple of shots of such a gorgeous man at work on his boat, but at the rhythmical click of the shutter, Trace turned. Broad, solidly muscled shoulders, a chest banded with sinew and lightly furred with dark hair, and a six-pack stomach...

She felt that funny lift again, only a little embarrassed to be caught staring. "I guess you really were a Ranger."

He just shrugged. "There were times being in condition meant the difference between life and death."

"You're not a Ranger now," she reminded him.

"Old habits die hard." He lowered a pair of wrap-around sunglasses over those whiskey-brown eyes. "You ready?"

She looked at him standing there with his legs splayed, his gaze on the horizon, and had the oddest feeling he was as much a Ranger now as he ever had been. The breeze gusted just then, rattling the ship's rigging. The Gulf stretched in front of them, blue and beckoning.

"You bet I'm ready."

Trace tossed off the lines and Maggie settled herself on one of the blue canvas cushions. Rowdy took a place beside her. His ears perked up as the boat began to move, anticipation clear on his little doggy face. Trace manned the wheel and the boat eased away from the dock.

"You'll have to earn your keep, you know." He flicked her a glance. "I'll need you to bring up the fenders and tend the dock lines, maybe take a turn at the wheel. You'll have to remember to duck when we come about, and of course you'll need to watch for pirates."

She laughed, gave him a smart salute. "Aye, aye, Cap'n."

Trace grinned. They settled themselves for the trip, the hull slipping smoothly over the water until they reached the open ocean, then the wind picked up and the boat heeled over. The stiff breeze tugged at Maggie's curls, blowing them across her face, so she dragged the heavy red mane into a ponytail held in place with a small hair elastic.

"I've been sailing only a couple of times," she said. "I went out with a friend when I was in college."

"Michael Irving?" It was a casual question, yet she thought Trace had just morphed back into a detective.

"A friend in my art history class. Her dad owned a forty-two-foot Catalina."

"Nice boat."

"Beautiful. So is yours. You really take good care of her."

Trace seemed pleased. "I do my best." He leaned back in the seat behind the wheel, his dark glasses hiding his thoughts.

The sun beat down so warmly she decided it was time to shed her own clothes. "I'm going to change. It's just too nice a day not to get some sun."

"Help yourself."

She disappeared below and came up a few minutes later in a red-and-white-striped bikini. The suit wasn't exactly modest, but it wasn't over-the-top risqué, either. She wore a loose-fitting white gauze shirt over it, but that didn't hide much. Though she couldn't see his eyes behind the glasses, she could feel his very thorough inspection, burning like a laser.

"I guess you like to stay in shape, too," he said a little gruffly.

She did. Very much so. And she was way too glad he noticed. "I ride my stationary bike in the mornings. I lift a few weights to build bone strength, and I play racquetball whenever I get the chance."

"Is that so? We'll have to have a match sometime."

"You like to play?"

His gaze moved over her again. "Oh, yeah, I like to play." But his drawl had deepened and she was no longer sure he was talking about raquetball.

They fell into a comfortable silence, enjoying the wind and the sea, and the gulls darting back and forth at the stern. When they approached a group of sportsmen fishing for tarpon, Maggie grabbed her camera and went to work. One of the men had hooked up to a real monster, and just as she focused, the fish jumped spectacularly into the air. She caught the shot, snapping a series of photos in milliseconds.

She laughed joyously as the tarpon plunged back into the sea. "My God, did you see that?"

Trace lifted his ball cap and settled it back on his head, a habit she had noticed when he was wearing his cowboy hat. "I sure did. Looks like you got a couple of great photos there."

She replayed the digital images. "Oh, this makes my day."

"Just being out here makes mine."

Maggie agreed. It felt so good to be out on the water, the boat sliding over the surface. They ate the ham-and-cheese sandwiches she had brought, but ignored the Diet Cokes. Instead, Trace cracked open a bottle of chilled chardonnay, poured it into two stemmed glasses, and they toasted the perfect day.

Relaxed, Maggie removed her cover-up, put on some sunscreen, stretched out on the cushions and let the warmth of the sun seep through her. With so little sleep last night, she must have dozed off. The sun had moved toward the horizon and Trace was turning the boat when she awakened.

"Time to go home," he said.

Maggie felt a twinge of disappointment. "I didn't mean to fall asleep."

"After last night, you needed the rest."

She inhaled a deep breath of the salty air. "It's been wonderful."

Trace seemed to share her mood. "Tomorrow's Sunday. We can spend the night if you want. Two staterooms down there. You wouldn't have to worry about your virtue."

She was surprised to discover she was tempted, but

then sighed. She hardly knew Trace Rawlins, and it was never smart to get involved with someone who worked for you. "Thanks for the offer, but I need to get back."

"Not a problem." Wheeling the sailboat expertly through the opening into Clear Lake, he turned toward the marina and his slip at dock A. Easing the vessel neatly into its berth, he tossed a line over the side and pulled the boat in close, then tied it in place.

They'd been out of cell phone range when they were at sea, but now Trace's iPhone started ringing down in the galley, where he had left it so it wouldn't fall into the water.

He hit the ladder, reached out and grabbed the phone, pressing it against his ear as he returned to the deck.

"Rawlins." The caller talked for a while and the lines of Trace's face went hard. "How'd it happen?"

More conversation, then a muscle tightened in his jaw. "Neither do I. I'm on my way." Trace hung up the phone and began to pull his jeans on over his swimsuit. "Looks like spending the night wouldn't have worked for me, either."

"What's going on?"

"One of my clients turned up dead. The police think he killed himself. I don't."

Maggie slid her pants over her bikini bottoms and adjusted the gauzy cover-up, tying it up around her waist. "You're saying it was murder?"

"Could be."

She slipped on her sandals. "I guess finding a murderer tops catching a stalker."

Trace shook his head. "One has nothing to do with the other. By the time we get home, your alarm system will be installed. As far as the creep goes who's been bothering you, you hired me to do a job and that's what I intend to do."

"What about the murder?"

He gave her a hard-edged smile. "Ever heard of multitasking?"

Maggie didn't doubt he could handle both cases. One glance at the dark look on his face and she felt sorry for the guy who had murdered his client.

"Besides," Trace continued, "if Hewitt was murdered, I already know who did it."

Chapter 6

They were headed back to Houston. The perfect day at sea had ended far too quickly.

As he dodged in and out of the heavy traffic on Highway 45, Trace mentally replayed the phone conversation he'd had on the boat.

"Trace, it's Annie. You need to get back to town. That Sommerset case you just finished? Hewitt Sommerset turned up dead half an hour ago in his study. The police are calling it a suicide."

Trace's stomach had knotted. "How'd he die?"

"Gunshot wound to the head. His son doesn't believe he pulled the trigger."

He clenched his jaw. "Neither do I." Hewitt was a good man. Trace needed answers and he was determined to get them.

The car in front of him slowed and he slowed as well, his mind drifting from Hewitt to the pretty redhead in the seat beside him. At least for a while, he had been able to keep Maggie's mind off her stalker. He wasn't sure how the man who had left the notes was keeping tabs on her, but there had been no sign of him on their way to the shore or at any time while they were there.

The figurine was another matter. Someone had broken into Maggie's house. There were no visible signs of entry, but the locks were paltry and there were ways to get in without leaving evidence. By now, the security alarm would be operational and the locks all replaced. Even so, the guy was a threat that had to be dealt with.

Trace had spoken to Rex Westcott and put him on notice to be ready for the stakeout tonight. Maggie was safe for the moment.

Trace thought of the day he had spent with her. He didn't have a problem mixing business with pleasure, not when it was a good way to do his job. He had let down his guard and relaxed more than he'd meant to, something he rarely did with a woman, but he liked Maggie O'Connell. She was smart and talented and vibrant. Along with that, she was sexy as hell.

He flicked a glance her way, caught a glimpse of soft lips and gorgeous red hair, and his groin tightened. He wanted to take her to bed, taste those pretty lips and lose himself in all those sweet curves.

It was a bad idea, he knew. Every time he got involved with a woman disaster struck.

This is different, he told himself. Nothing more than a physical attraction. He wouldn't let himself get in too deep.

Trace took a last glance at Maggie, told himself that time would settle the matter one way or the other and forced his thoughts back to the more immediate problem at hand.

The death of his former client, Hewitt Sommerset.

Trace's hands tightened around the steering wheel. The Saturday traffic along Route 45 had turned brutal. Maybe there was a wreck up ahead, roadwork, something. Whatever it was, his frustration was making him edgy and restless. He stepped on the brake for the hundredth time, bringing the Jeep to a halt behind the white Toyota pickup ahead of him.

He slammed a hand against the wheel. "Dammit! I need to talk to the police."

Maggie turned in her seat. "You're going to the crime scene?"

He nodded. "As soon as I drop you off, I'm heading for the Sommerset house."

Her gaze went to the dense trail of cars rolling slowly along the pavement ahead of them. "Where is it?"

"The Woodlands." Thirty miles north of Houston. "At this rate it'll be dark by the time I get there."

She studied the slow-moving traffic. "You're probably right. It'll be even later if you have to drop me off. Why don't you just take me with you? I've got a good book. I can wait in the car until you're finished. I can see this is important to you, and I really don't mind."

He started to say no, then paused. It wasn't as if there was a shoot-out in progress. The questions he wanted answered and the information he had to deliver wouldn't take that long. And with traffic the way it was, it would save him at least forty minutes.

"You sure?"

"Thanks to you I got some terrific material today. It's the least I can do."

Trace smiled, feeling a wave of relief. "Great." He wanted to be there for Jason and Emily. Hewitt's son and daughter were both good kids. It was his son-in-law, Parker Barrington, Emily's husband, who was the problem.

"So what's the story?" Maggie asked. "The police think it's suicide but you think it's murder. Why is that?"

He rarely talked about a case, but most of this would be in the news in a couple of days, anyway.

"A few weeks ago, the victim—Hewitt Sommerset—came to see me. He wanted to find out if his son-in-law was stealing money from the company."

"And you found out he was."

"Parker Barrington is chief financial officer of Sommerset Industries. At Hewitt's request, we installed a couple hidden cameras, put a live feed in his computer. We caught him doctoring the books, siphoning money off to an account in the Cayman Islands."

One of Maggie's wing-shaped eyebrows went up. "So his hands were definitely sticky."

"Definitely."

"You think Hewitt Sommerset confronted his son-in-law, who killed him to keep from being caught?"

"It's possible. Depending on what Hewitt told him, Parker may not have realized other people already knew."

The heavy traffic continued until they got a ways north of Houston, then the cars began to thin out. The Woodlands was a huge development of homes, shopping centers and offices, even a prestigious golf course. What made the area such a desirable place to live was that all those things were hidden among dense grooves of trees and beautifully cared-for landscaping.

Trace wound his way along the curving roadways lined with trees and shrubs, and turned onto a street with massive homes tucked away among the foliage on oversize lots. The Sommerset mansion sat at the end of a cul-de-sac. Two patrol cars were parked in front, along with Jason Sommerset's flashy silver Porsche. Emily drove a Mercedes, but it wasn't there. Trace wondered where her husband was.

He felt a jolt of hot, dark anger. Parker Barrington was in for a little surprise when he found out all the evidence condemning him was well documented. Hewitt was a decent, hardworking man who had built an empire though years of dedicated work. He didn't deserve to be killed by an ungrateful, thieving son-in-law.

"You look like you're going to explode."

Trace shoved the car into Park and turned off the engine. Under different circumstances he would have smiled at Maggie's words. Instead, he took a deep breath and reined in his temper.

"You're right. Hewitt was more than a client. He was a friend. Until I'm completely sure what happened, I don't want to jump to conclusions." He cracked open his door. "You all right here?"

"I'll be just fine."

"With any luck, I won't be gone long."

Maggie watched Trace stop to speak to one of the policemen, who let him into the house. It was quite a place, at least ten thousand square feet, and painted a pale, dusky rose. Done in the French style, it sported a mansard roof and arched doors and windows.

The mansion was grand and imposing, and she wondered if Hewitt Sommerset had been happy there. She knew a little about him, what she had seen on TV. He was a well-known figure in the Houston area, a self-made billionaire, a philanthropist who donated millions to charity. He'd been a dedicated husband and father, a man who had greatly mourned the death of his wife two years ago.

In the time since then, Hewitt had returned to work, immersing himself more deeply in the company than he had for a number of years. Maybe that was the reason he had uncovered his son-in-law's nefarious activities.

Maggie couldn't help feeling sorry for the daughter who had married such a dirtball. She smiled, thinking she would love to be a fly on the wall when Trace confronted him.

Hearing a soft whine from the back of the Jeep, Maggie got out of the car, went around to the rear and let Rowdy out for a quick pit stop. Several patrol cars were parked at the curb, and a number of officers wandered in and out of the house. Rowdy sniffed the base of a nearby tree, took care of business and returned to the Jeep.

"Load up," Maggie commanded, as Trace had done, and the dog jumped back up. Making himself comfortable in his bed, he rested his black-and-white muzzle against the cushion.

"Good boy." Maggie reached in to pet him, then shut the tailgate.

The light was fading but still good. The days were getting longer, the weather warmer. She glanced around, her photographer's eye kicking in. The sun was beginning to set, but at this time of day, the soft golden rays filtering down through branches of the gnarled old oaks brought out interesting details: the uneven texture of the bark, the faint curl of a newly budded leaf.

Maggie reached into the backseat and grabbed her camera. While she was waiting for Trace, maybe she could catch a few good shots.

Trace crossed the black-and-white marble-floored entry reminiscent of a French château, heading straight to Hewitt's study. He had been there in the late afternoon just a few days ago, bringing his employer the damning evidence that had been collected against Parker Barrington.

The study, a huge, walnut-paneled room with two-story ceilings and heavy brass chandeliers, swarmed with people now, the forensics squad hard at work poring over the scene. Hewitt's desk was in disarray and a large bloodstain remained where his body had been found slumped over the top.

"Trace!"

He recognized the youthful voice, turned to see Jason Sommerset walking toward him. He was twenty-four years old, golden-haired, handsome as sin and spoiled rotten. It was amazing he'd turned out to be such a nice kid.

"Jason. I'm so sorry. I liked your father very much."

His face was pale, his eyes red-rimmed. But he wasn't crying now, he was angry. "Dad didn't do it, Trace. He didn't kill himself."

"Take it easy—I don't think so, either. We talked just last week. He was looking forward to the trip the two of you were taking to the Bahamas."

"Someone killed him. They made it look like he pulled the trigger, but I know he didn't."

Trace settled a hand on the young man's shoulder. "That's why I'm here. To find out the truth one way or another."

Jason took a steadying breath. "I knew you'd come. Dad trusted you and so do I."

Trace just nodded. Clearly, Hewitt hadn't told his son what they had found out about Emily's husband. Jason was smart and he seemed to have inherited his father's gift for sizing people up. Trace wondered if the boy would be all that surprised to discover his brother-in-law was a thief.

Someone called Jason's name, and with a nod of his head that indicated they would talk again, he walked off down the hall, leaving Trace to the task he had come for. Returning his attention to the study, he scanned the room for anything out of place, and spotted the familiar features of Detective Mark Sayers, a classmate of his at community college and a longtime friend.

Trace walked toward him. "Got a minute?"

His head came up and surprise lit his face. "Hey, Trace." A little shorter, a little beefier, Mark had light brown hair and hazel eyes. Except for the cheap suits he wore and his overall rumpled appearance, he was a good-looking guy.

"Under different circumstances I'd say it's good to see you," Mark said. "But your timing's not great. I guess you must have heard—Hewitt Sommerset is dead. Looks like he killed himself."

"I don't think that's likely."

One of Sayers's light brown eyebrows went up. "That right? I didn't know the two of you were friends."

"Business acquaintances, mostly. Grew into a little more than that over the years. You and I need to talk."

The detective's interest sharpened. "Okay." Turning, he led Trace down a hall lined with expensive paintings in heavy gilded frames, and turned into one of the numerous parlors in the house, this one elegantly furnished with peach brocade sofas and dark green velvet drapes. There wasn't so much as a piece of fringe out of place on the Persian rugs that covered the polished oak floors.

"I guess you've talked to Hewitt's son, Jason," Trace said as Mark closed the door.

"We talked to him. His reaction isn't unexpected. No son wants to believe his father killed himself."

"When did it happen?"

"Last night. Hewitt was supposed to be out of town, but something must have come up. Apparently he keeps his study door closed when he's away. The body wasn't found until this afternoon."

"How was it done?"

"Thirty-eight caliber gunshot to the side of the head. The pistol is registered to Sommerset, who allegedly kept it in a drawer in his desk."

"But someone else could have pulled the trigger."

"There were no signs of a struggle."

"Maybe he was unconscious."

Sayers pondered that. "I suppose it's possible. There weren't any obvious wounds to suggest that."

"Maybe not. Doesn't mean it couldn't have been done some other way."

Sayers looked unconvinced. "Hewitt left a suicide note, Trace. We found it on his computer."

"Typed, then. Not handwritten."

"It's the twenty-first century, my friend. Nobody writes notes by hand anymore."

It was a good point, one Trace silently conceded. Not that he believed for a minute that Hewitt had actually written it.

"You need to find out where Parker Barrington was last night."

Sayers's gaze narrowed. "Why is that?"

"Parker was embezzling funds from the company. And not small change, either. Millions, Mark. Siphoning the money off to an account in the Cayman Islands."

"Jesus. You got any proof?"

"All you need. Hewitt came to me with his suspicions. We set up surveillance in Parker's office. I took him the cold, hard evidence two days ago."

The detective's eyes widened. "Two days ago? You're not thinking Parker Barrington killed Sommerset to cover up the theft?"

"Unless you can convince me otherwise, that's exactly what I'm thinking."

Sayers glanced away, as if he wished he could look back to the time of the murder. "I'll need to see what you've got."

"I'll have it in your office first thing in the morning."

"And I thought this one was going to be easy."

Trace's mouth edged up. "When are they ever easy?"

Mark friend laid a hand on his shoulder, walked him out of the parlor and back down the hall. Trace flicked a last glance into the study as they passed, and continued toward the foyer, lit by a huge chandelier.

"Have you talked to the daughter?" Trace asked.

"She and Parker were here earlier. She was really shaken up. We let him take her home."

Trace made a mental note to go see her. Once the dirt on Parker was uncovered, Emily was going to need all the support she could get.

Sayers stepped out on the wide front porch and Trace followed.

"Besides murder and mayhem," his friend said, "anything new and exciting going on in your life?"

Trace thought of Maggie, spotted her at the edge of the yard, snapping photos of beautiful flame-colored tulips growing around the base of a huge oak tree. They were almost the color of her hair. He watched the way she moved, with a confidence and ease that marked her as a professional. Why that turned him on, he couldn't say.

"Not much," he answered, but as he looked at Maggie, he was thinking maybe that would change.

Sayers's gaze followed his toward the tree and he started to frown. "That isn't... Jesus, Trace, tell me the redhead isn't with you."

Trace dragged his gaze away, finding it harder than it should have been. "She's a client. A photographer. Name's Maggie O'Connell. Matter of fact, I was planning to talk to you about her."

"I know who the hell she is."

Trace didn't like the sound of that. "Want to tell me why?"

Sayers drew him away from the hum of officers and people walking in and out of the mansion. "I shouldn't say this. I could get in a shitload of trouble, but..."

"What is it?"

"She came to us claiming she had a stalker. Said she'd been getting hang-up phone calls, that kind of thing."

"That's right. Go on."

"Captain Varner got wind of it. Turns out Maggie O'Connell brought rape charges against his son, Josh, when she was in high school. Josh was arrested. He claimed he was innocent, claimed Maggie was a willing partner. They were both underage or it would have been far worse. As it was, Josh got kicked off the football team and everyone in his school basically shunned him. They called him a rapist and a pervert, stuff like that. It went on for more than a week—until the O'Connell girl admitted she had lied about the rape."

"Maybe she was telling the truth and she just got scared."

"The boy was completely cleared. They'd been seeing each other for weeks."

"Son of a bitch."

"She's one of those women, Trace. She wanted attention and she got it. The charges were dropped and the records were sealed because of their ages, but it still caused Josh and his family all kinds of trouble. And believe me, Maggie O'Connell is still on Varner's hit list."

"Which is why the police aren't willing to do much more than show up if she calls them."

Mark shot Maggie a hard glare. "It's no secret in the department what happened. Captain Varner doesn't believe any of that bullshit about a stalker, and neither does anyone else."

Trace clenched his jaw so hard it hurt. Mark was the kind of guy who would check the facts, find out the truth. The story about the phony rape accusation was undoubtedly true.

"She's a good-looking woman, Trace, but I wouldn't trust her. Don't let her get under your skin."

Trace reined in his temper, which was beginning to build. "Thanks for the heads-up, buddy."

"Hey, man, we're friends. And you've already had more than your share of trouble with women."

Trace thought of Carly, remembered the sick feeling in his stomach when he'd found out she was sleeping with half the men in Houston. She was a liar and a cheat. He hated a liar, no matter how beautiful she was.

He just nodded as he walked away.

Chapter 7

Maggie was smiling as she stuffed her camera back in its case, nestled it in the backseat and closed the door, then climbed into the Jeep. "How did it go?"

"Remains to be seen."

"Did you tell them about the embezzling?"

"I told them." Trace didn't say more, and the way his jaw was clenched, Maggie didn't press him. He started the car, slammed it into gear and roared away, slinging her back against the seat. His hands gripped the wheel as if he wanted to tear it out of the vehicle. Whatever had happened, things hadn't gone well.

Maggie kept her mouth shut. Better to give him a little space. As they raced toward Houston, far faster than the speed limit, she considered trying again to start a conversation, but one look at Trace's hard profile and she changed her mind.

They rode back in silence, neither of them speaking

all the way to her town house. By the time they arrived and Trace turned off the engine, Maggie couldn't take another minute.

"All right, what is it?" she asked. "If it's the murder, I'll understand. If it's something else, something I've said or done wrong…"

He turned in the seat. "You're a liar, Maggie. In my book, that's as wrong as it gets."

Her stomach twisted at the look on his face. "What are you talking about?"

Trace climbed out of the car, rounded the hood and jerked open her door. "As of right now, I no longer work for you. Find some other sucker to buy into your bullshit."

Her eyes widened. Her own anger surfaced. "What the hell is going on? The least you can do is explain."

Instead of a reply, he caught hold of her arm and hauled her out of the Jeep. He pulled a key from a pocket of his jeans and held it out to her.

"Your new locks are in. The installers left a key with me this morning. You'll find another inside. I'll get your bag and your camera gear."

She planted herself directly in front of him, jammed her hands on her hips. "I'm not going anywhere until you tell me what happened back there that turned you into a maniac."

He ground his teeth, looking as if he wanted to throttle her. "I told you what happened. You lied to me. If you try real hard, I imagine you can figure out which particular lie I might have found a little disturbing."

An icy chill ran through her. He'd been talking to the police. They must have seen her, must have said something. They must have told him about her Great Shame.

Her hands dropped to her sides. She realized she was trembling. "Josh Varner, right?"

"That's right. Your old boyfriend. Now go unlock the door so I can carry your gear inside and be on my way."

Her heart was beating too fast, slamming against her ribs. She felt sick to her stomach. Not wanting to make a scene in front of the neighbors, she led him to the door of the town house, used the key he'd given her to open the door and stepped aside so he could carry her gear inside.

Wordlessly, he stalked past her into the hall, set her camera case and yellow swim bag on the floor. The muscles in his shoulders seemed to vibrate with tension. He was angry. Furious. And he had every right to be.

She took a deep breath. "Okay, I probably should have told you."

Trace whirled to face her, his dark eyes burning into her like twin laser beams. "Probably?"

"All right, I should have told you. I didn't because I was afraid you would act exactly the way you're acting now."

"I said I'd help you if you told me what I needed to know. You didn't think I needed to know you had an enemy in the police department? That you'd accused some poor kid of rape when he didn't do a goddamn thing but take what you offered?"

She hated the way Trace made it sound, though every word was true. In the past she would have cried, but those days were over.

Instead, she steeled herself, forced up her chin. "I was sixteen years old. My dad caught me coming in at two in the morning and I was scared to death. I was terrified of what he'd do if he knew the truth."

"Beat you?"

"No, but—"

"I'm done, Maggie. You lied to me before. There's no reason to believe you're telling me the truth right now."

She steadied herself, fought for control. "I was ashamed to tell you, all right? It's the worst thing I've ever done."

His hard look didn't soften. No more Mr. Nice Guy, she thought. The charming Southern gentleman was gone. In his place was the fierce Army Ranger he had been and clearly still was. Gold flecks glittered in his dark eyes, and the muscles tightened in his jaw.

"Goodbye, Maggie." He started to turn away, but she caught his arm.

"Trace, please. At least give me a chance to explain."

"You've already explained. We had a deal. You didn't keep your end of it. Now the deal is off."

"But...what about the stalker?"

His jaw tightened even more. "Call the police."

"They won't help and you know it."

"The locks are changed. Your alarm is in. I'll send over one of the guys from JDT to show you how to use it." His smile was harsh. "Though odds are you won't need it."

He no longer believed her. By his standards, she wasn't worthy of his trust.

"Thank you for that."

Trace made no reply. Without a backward glance, he turned and stormed out the door. Maggie forced herself not to run after him. She had her pride, didn't she? Sure, she should have told him about Josh, should have known he would find out sooner or later. But she had wrongly believed that if he did discover her secret, she could simply explain and Mr. Nice Guy Rawlins would understand.

Now she knew Trace Rawlins wasn't always the calm, controlled, soft-spoken guy she had believed. He was a man of fierce conviction and strong emotions.

As she watched his long strides carry him toward the Jeep, something stirred inside her. Some primal instinct that found such a hard, determined man even more attractive than the gentleman he had once seemed.

He jerked open the door and slid behind the wheel, and desire slipped through her. She watched him start the engine, put the car in reverse, then drive away. In moments, he was gone.

Maggie's insides felt heavy. It was ridiculous. She barely knew the man, and yet flickers of heat still tingled through her body, along with a need she had taught herself to ignore.

But she had always been a passionate woman. Passionate about life, about her work, about her family and friends. It shouldn't come as a surprise she would respond to a passionate man.

Maggie sighed, wishing things could have been different, grateful the relationship hadn't gone further than it had before it fell apart.

She turned to assess her surroundings. The town house had been left neat and tidy. Aside from a note and a business card belonging to JDT Security Systems lying on her breakfast bar, and a second set of keys, there was no evidence the installation crew had been there.

She walked over to the counter. The note read, "Installation complete. Trace can show you how to set the alarm."

Except that Trace was gone.

He would send a man over, he had said, and she knew that he would. He was reliable, steady. But he had a temper she hadn't expected. She would have liked to discover the man beneath his surface calm, test the fire he kept so carefully controlled and explore the attraction between them.

If things had worked out differently…

But things hadn't worked out, and that was the end of it.

Trace sat in his office Monday morning reading the newspaper. Except for his Saturday trip to the shore, he'd had a shitty weekend. Hewitt Sommerset was dead. Parker Barrington had very likely killed him. And Maggie O'Connell had turned out to be just another deceitful woman.

He folded the paper and set it on his desk. The headline stared up at him. Missing Woman Found. The article told of a teenage boy finding a woman's body washed up on a local beach. No positive identification had been made at the time the article was written, but the victim's clothing and hair led authorities to believe it was the young woman who had recently disappeared. An autopsy was scheduled to determine the cause of death.

Unconsciously, Trace glanced toward the door, expecting Carly to appear any minute demanding his protection. He wasn't in the mood for his ex-wife and her dramatics, or any other woman—at least not right now.

His thoughts returned to Maggie and the bitter disappointment he felt. She had lied about the false rape, about the police and probably about the stalker.

Worse yet, she had made Trace lose control.

It didn't happen often. Like honor and honesty, in his family, control was a valued commodity. His daddy had lost his temper only once, when Trace had lied to him about sneaking out to meet his friend Willie Johnson and drinking the pint of whiskey Willie had stolen from his mama's special medicinal supply. Trace had been ten years old and his father had used a hickory switch to show him the error of his ways.

Later, his dad had come to him and apologized, as if he were the one who had done something wrong.

"I lost my temper, son. A man can't afford to let that happen. Not ever."

And because Trace wanted to be the man his dad believed him to be, he made sure it never happened.

Well, almost never.

In the army, his nickname had been Ghost. It wasn't just because he had a talent for appearing and disappearing without being seen, a skill that often came in handy. It was also because of the way he remained in control, the way he always stayed calm no matter the situation. Calm and controlled, out of sight and out of mind, as quiet as a ghost.

But Maggie O'Connell had broken through his well-honed defenses. He had begun to trust her, begun to let down his guard.

She's one of those women, Mark Sayers had said. The kind who crave attention, the kind who'll do anything to get it. But she hadn't seemed that way. Which just proved what a piss-poor judge Trace was of women.

Worse yet, part of him worried that maybe Sayers was wrong. Maybe there *was* a stalker. Maybe—at least about that—Maggie had been telling the truth.

Trace leaned back in his chair, refusing to continue

dwelling on his brief relationship with another woman he couldn't trust. He glanced up at a knock at his office door, watched it swing open. Annie never waited for permission.

"Detective Sayers is here to see you. Wants to talk to you about the information you left for him."

Trace sat up in his chair. "Send him in."

Mark walked into the office and closed the door. As always, his light brown hair was neatly combed, while his J. C. Penney suit was slightly wrinkled.

"Parker's got an alibi," he said, cutting straight to the point. "His wife says he was home with her all evening."

"Bullshit." Trace came out of his chair. "She's covering for him. Emily's been a fool for Parker since the day she met him."

"We've still got the embezzlement charges. The D.A.'s on it. He's putting together a case. He doesn't want to move until he's got all his ducks in a row."

"I'll talk to Jason, tell him what's going on. I'll ask him to speak to his sister, see if he can get her to tell the truth."

"He doesn't know about the stolen money?"

"Not yet," Trace said. "But he's in line to take over the company. He's going to need to be told."

"Might not be a good idea," Mark said. "Word is the kid's pretty hotheaded. He might come to the same conclusion you did, and try to do something about it."

Trace thought of the son who had worshipped his powerful father. "You might be right."

"We're on this thing, Trace. If Parker killed Sommerset, he's going down for it."

He nodded. "The funeral is on Wednesday. Once it's over, things will settle down. I'll talk to Emily myself, pay my respects. I'll be sure not to mention that her no-good husband was stealing a fortune from her dad."

Mark chuckled. "Sounds good. Let me know how it goes."

Trace walked his friend through the office, out to the unmarked brown Chevy he was driving that perfectly matched his inexpensive brown suit.

"So what happened with the redhead?" Mark asked as he opened the car door.

"I wouldn't know. She's no longer my client."

"Wise move. I can tell you that as far as I know, she hasn't made any more 911 calls."

"That's good, I guess." But Maggie had always been reluctant to call the police. She didn't think they would help her, and pretty much, she was right.

Trace didn't like the way that made him feel.

"Like I said, keep me in the loop." Mark slid into the car and drove out of the lot, and Trace returned to his office. The kid, Sol Greenway, was working at his desk in the glass-windowed office next to Trace's, partly hidden behind a couple of forty-inch monitors. Trace was good at digging up information, but the kid was better. He could find out anything, legally or illegally. Trace was careful not to encourage him.

Most of the time.

The door was open, Trace walked in and Sol looked up at him. "Yeah, boss?"

"Think you can get into an old, sealed, juvenile arrest file?"

Sol grinned. He pushed his long, straight dark hair out of his eyes. "Sure. Just give me a name."

"Margaret O'Connell. I'll get you her address and phone number and whatever else I've got."

"Shouldn't take long." Sol cracked his knuckles, a habit Trace found mildly annoying, then replaced his fingers on the keyboard.

Silently cursing himself for giving in to his worry about Maggie, Trace turned and walked back out the door.

Chapter 8

The days slipped past. As promised, a man with JDT Security Systems arrived at her door within an hour after Trace had brought her home from their trip to the shore. Mr. Wilcox had carefully shown her how to set the alarm, and had checked to see that everything was working as it should.

"It's a wireless system," he explained. "Fairly basic, but it's all most people ever need. If the alarm goes off and you don't enter the proper codes to turn it off, the system automatically calls the security company. From there, the police are notified. You should be perfectly safe as long as you remember to turn it on."

"Thank you, Mr. Wilcox."

"No problem."

So far there hadn't been.

And she had to admit she felt safer with the alarm system in and dead bolts installed. Since nearly a week had passed and there hadn't been any more notes or hang-up calls, she was beginning to think she didn't need Mr. He-man Rawlins, after all.

The doorbell rang. It was Friday night. The weekend had finally arrived and Maggie had plans for the evening. She checked the peephole, smiled and opened the door.

Dressed in tight red leather pants and a red silk blouse that left her midriff bare, Roxanne sashayed through the door. "You ready, lamb chop?" With her black hair swept into a twist and soft tendrils curling beside her ears, Roxanne, at thirty, was a fox.

Maggie smiled. "I'm ready." Her own outfit was a little less flashy, a very short black skirt, gold silk halter top, gold jewelry and very high black-and-gold heels. "I'm overdue for a little fun."

They were going to Galaxy, an upscale nightclub that catered to the late-twenties through early-forties crowd. Maggie loved to dance. Anything from modern to ballroom, country to hip-hop. Anytime, anyplace, she was game. She was especially good at swing and ballroom dancing, since her dad had insisted she take cotillion. *Cotillion.* The old-fashioned word made her smile. Because she didn't have a mother "to teach her certain things," her dad had signed her up on her twelfth birthday, and insisted she attend classes once a week.

Now she was glad she had.

"Grab your purse, girl. Let's rock and roll." Roxanne was always up for going out. She liked drinking martinis and socializing more than actually dancing, but it worked out fine just the same. And since Roxy was leaving for a couple weeks to visit friends in New York, this was kind of a farewell evening.

"Car's out front," Rox said. "I've got Alonzo driving tonight so we don't have to worry if we get a little tipsy."

Roxanne had more money than she could spend, a legacy of her daddy's oil fortune. Though she was two years older than Maggie, they had gone to the U of Houston together, Roxanne starting as a freshman after she had spent a couple years jet-setting around Europe.

They had met in art history class, the one subject Roxanne knew backward and forward, since she had seen a number of antiquities up close and personal in her travels and developed an appreciation. Aside from their common interest in art, for reasons neither of them completely understood, they had become fast friends and still were.

Roxanne's white Mercedes S550 sat in front of the condo, with Alonzo, her good-looking part-time driver, seated behind the wheel. She and Maggie climbed into the backseat and headed for Galaxy, which was over by the Galleria.

It didn't take long to get there. Alonzo opened the door for them, and as they made their way toward the entrance, the doorman recognized them and waved them to the front of the line.

"Thanks, honey," Roxanne said to the big black bouncer with the thick Southern accent.

He just grinned. "You two gals be good tonight. Don't y'all go gettin' them boys stirred up and fightin' over ya."

Maggie laughed at the backhanded compliment. "We'll be sure to mind our manners."

They stepped inside, onto the stainless-steel floor in the entry, and were captured immediately by the heavy beat of the music. The place was slick and modern, with lots of brushed chrome and dark wood. Mauve and blue lighting gleamed beneath the bar and along the walls, and the ceiling glittered with tiny white lights that winked like stars. The stainless-steel dance floor was large and the DJ was really good at choosing songs, usually a combo of top forty and Latin, with a little disco and the occasional country song thrown in.

Since the crowd was her age or older and Maggie was a regular, she knew a number of people in the crowd. As she and Roxanne slid onto high, dark blue leather seats at the black granite bar, a face she hadn't seen in months was one of the first she recognized.

Roxy leaned toward her, raising her voice a little to be heard above the music and the crowd. "Isn't that your old flame, David, sitting over there?"

Since she had already spotted him, Maggie kept her gaze fixed straight ahead. "That's him."

"I thought he was dating someone."

"I thought so, too." But clearly, he was alone tonight. Their breakup two years ago hadn't been easy and Maggie felt a tightening in her stomach.

The bartender walked over just then, olive-skinned and handsome. "What can I get for you ladies?"

"Grey Goose martini, if you please, Enrique." Roxy had an amazing memory for the names of good-looking men. "Up, and very, very dry."

"I'll have a Cosmo," Maggie added, but one or two were her limit. She was basically a white-wine drinker, though occasionally the strong, fruity cocktail tasted good.

Roxanne leaned closer. "Don't look now, but I think he's coming over."

Maggie inwardly groaned. She told herself not to glance in David's direction, but her eyes went there just the same. He stopped in front of her, a tall man, very lean and perfectly groomed, with blond hair and pale blue eyes.

"It's good to see you, Maggie."

She smiled, tried to ignore the thread of guilt she felt for the way they had parted. "You're looking well, David."

"Thank you. You look beautiful. But then you always do." Very formal, always proper, that was David.

"You remember Roxanne?"

"Of course. Hello, Roxanne."

Roxy took a sip from her long-stemmed glass. "I'm surprised to see you here, David. You were never much for socializing."

David did corporate law for Holder Holder & Meeks. He was happiest behind his desk working on briefs, or researching case law. Just going out with another couple for dinner was a major undertaking for David. Which had been a problem for Maggie, since her job required she attend various gallery shows around the state, and meeting people was just good business. It was also something she enjoyed.

"Would you like to dance?" David asked her.

The DJ was playing a slow song. She didn't want to encourage him, but she didn't want to be rude, either. "All right." Slipping down from the bar stool, she let him guide her through the growing crowd onto the dance floor. When she stepped into his arms, they felt as comfortable as they had during the months they had lived together.

But Maggie had discovered that a comfortable relationship wasn't enough for her. She wanted more, wanted the heat and the passion, wanted the kind of enduring love that happened in romance novels.

Maybe she would never find it. But she was determined to try.

"I've missed you, Maggie."

She looked up at him, tried to smile. "I thought you were seeing someone, David."

"I was, but it didn't work out."

"I'm sorry to hear that."

"I thought… I asked around. You aren't seeing anyone, are you?"

Why Trace Rawlins's image popped into her head, she couldn't begin to say. The man didn't even like her. "Not at the moment."

"I was thinking…maybe we could go out sometime. We're both older, wiser. Maybe things would be different between us now."

Maggie bit back a sigh. "Nothing's different, David. I still care for you as a friend—but nothing beyond that. There's no point in going through all of that again." *All that* being the breakup David had taken so hard, the terrible guilt she felt for ever making him think they might have a future together, when deep down she'd known it would never work.

The song came to an end and he walked her back to her seat at the bar. "Thanks for the dance."

She managed to smile. "It was nice seeing you, David."

He leaned down and kissed her cheek. "Take care, Maggie." Then he turned and disappeared into the crowd.

Maggie released the breath she had been holding.

"How did that go?" Roxanne asked, arching one black eyebrow.

"Take a wild guess."

Roxy lifted her half-full martini glass. "So David and his girlfriend broke up and he's sniffing after you again."

"Yes, they broke up. And I hope he's not sniffing. I hope this was a one-time thing."

"I think the guy has masochistic tendencies. You've only told him a dozen times it's never going to work between you."

"I know, but even with his busy job, David is basically lonely. He's a really nice guy. He deserves to find a woman who truly loves him."

"You tried, kiddo. That's all anyone can do."

"I guess." But she should have followed her instincts, should have known from the start she was going to hurt him. He was a good man, but not the one she wanted.

Another guy walked up to them just then.

"This is a really great song. You wanna dance?" His name was Doug Winston, Maggie recalled. Early forties, attractive in a kind of too-slick way and carrying a few extra pounds around his middle. But he was a very good dancer. Which was all that mattered when she came to Galaxy.

"I'd love to."

Roxy lifted her glass in salute as Maggie headed once more for the dance floor. This time she was able to give herself up to the hot beat of the music, to relax and enjoy herself.

She deserved a night out.

She wouldn't think about anything else, she vowed, and flashed a bright smile as she and her partner moved around the floor.

It was a little after midnight when Trace drove into the two-car garage behind his house. He'd been out to a movie and dinner with Ben Slocum and Ben's current girlfriend, Rita DeStefani. Rita's cousin Haley was in town for a visit, a pretty little blonde Trace had met before. The trouble was that Haley was a talker, and most of what she said was about herself. He had gone as a favor to Ben—who now owed him big-time.

Rubbing the ache in the back of his neck, Trace climbed the back porch steps, pulled open the screen door and stepped inside the screened-in porch. He unlocked the door and walked into the kitchen, flipped on the light switch and punched in the alarm code, turning off the system. Rowdy raced up, tail wagging, and Trace reached down to scratch his ears.

"It's been a long night, buddy," he said, and he was damned glad to be home.

Rowdy whimpered as if he understood.

Then Trace's iPhone started to ring, and silently, he cursed. Nothing good ever happened at this time of night. He sighed as he pulled the phone out of the pocket of his tan slacks and pressed it against his ear. "Rawlins."

"Trace…? Trace, it's Maggie. Please…please don't hang up."

His fingers tightened around the shiny hunk of plastic. "I'm not going to hang up. Tell me what's happened."

"I went out tonight and when I—I came home…when I came back to the house, my phone message light was blinking. Nothing bad has happened, you know, not… not since the last time. So I didn't think anything about it, but this time it…it wasn't just a hang-up call. When I played the message…oh, God, Trace, this guy is really scaring me."

"Check your doors, make sure they're locked. I'll be there in ten minutes." Trace didn't consider not going. His instincts had been warning him from the start. And earlier in the week, Sol had dug into Maggie's sealed juvenile records. Reading the transcripts of what she had said when she had gone to the police to tell them the truth about the rape had moved him deeply.

I love my dad so much.... I didn't want to hurt him. (subject begins to cry) When he caught me sneaking into the house, he asked me what happened and I—I just couldn't...couldn't tell him the truth. Josh and I... we didn't mean for anything to happen, we just...somehow things just went too far. I started crying, and Dad asked me if Josh had forced me to have...have sex with him. I looked at him and I couldn't make myself say the truth, so I just nodded. I thought I could find a way to... to straighten things out in the morning. (subject continues to cry) Then I found out Dad had gone to the police and I—I was terrified for Josh. But I didn't know how to undo what...what I had already done.

Reading the transcript had left Trace with a sick feeling in his stomach. She was just a kid at the time, he realized. At sixteen, still innocent, a young girl trying to find her way. If it hadn't been for her dad going to the cops—which Maggie hadn't expected him to do—the boy would never have been arrested.

Maggie had been horrified and riddled with guilt. As bad as it was for Josh, it was also a terrible trauma for her.

Trace pulled the Jeep into a parking space in front of her condo and killed the engine. As he crossed the asphalt to the sidewalk, she opened the door and just stood waiting. Her face was pale, her chest rising and falling in rapid breaths. As he stepped onto the porch, Trace reached out and pulled her into his arms.

"You all right?" he asked softly against her ear.

Maggie clung to him. She was so upset she was shaking. No way was she faking it.

She nodded, held on an instant longer, then took a

deep breath and turned away. "I-I'm okay. Thank you for coming. I know the way you feel and I—"

"I was wrong. I should have listened to what you had to say."

She swallowed, looked as if she wished he would hold her again, but instead moved farther away. "Come on in and I'll play the message."

Trace walked inside and closed the door. He set his hat on the coat tree and turned. For the first time, he got a really good look at her. Black miniskirt, gold satin top that left her back and shoulders bare, sexy high heels. Her pretty red hair was clipped up on the sides, but soft russet curls hung down past her shoulders.

His groin throbbed. He'd been out with a gorgeous blonde all evening. He suspected she'd wanted him to take her to bed, but he hadn't felt the slightest urge. Now, just looking at Maggie, he was already hard and aching to have her.

He released a slow breath. "Let's hear the message."

He followed her into the kitchen, trying not to look at her ass.

He spotted her landline phone and the small black box next to it with the blinking red light.

"It's a little old-fashioned, but I can see the light and know right away when someone has called."

He waited while she punched the play button, and the message began. At first there was a scratchy sound he didn't recognize. Then a song began: "I…saw…you… I knew you would be my one true love. I…saw…you…a vision so pure and sweet, my only true love…."

It sounded like an old vinyl record, a little scratchy, a little wobbly, but he knew the song, had heard it a dozen times over the years. Still, he couldn't quite place it.

The voice that followed, electronically distorted, sent

a shiver down Trace's spine. "Mag-gie…my precious Mag-gie. Some-day soon you will awa-ken to me. You will come to me, my Mag-gie. Soon."

He hit the stop button, looked over at her face. The last of the color had drained away, making the freckles stand out on her nose.

"I know it's distorted, but is there any chance you recognize the voice?"

She only shook her head.

"How about the song? You know what it is?"

"I've heard it. It's been years. I can't remember where I know it from."

"I recognize it, too, but only vaguely. It won't be hard to find the name. The question is does it mean anything to you?"

She replied with a shaky breath, "Not a thing."

Trace reached out and hit the message button again, took note of the time of the call, 11:00 p.m. Then he replayed the message. He would have played it a third time if Maggie's face hadn't gone paler every time she heard it.

"You're all dressed up," he said, his gaze skimming over her sexy clothes. "Hot date?" He tried to keep his tone neutral. He had no hold on Maggie O'Connell, no say in what she did or didn't do. Still, he didn't like the idea of her seeing another man.

"Roxy and I went dancing. We went to Galaxy. I love to dance. We don't go that often, but when we do, that's where we usually go."

He knew the place, upscale and classy, catering to a mostly thirties crowd. "Anything unusual happen? Any of your partners say anything, do anything out of the ordinary?"

She hesitated an instant too long.

"Don't make the mistake you made before, Maggie. I need you to trust me. I need you to tell me the truth."

She took a shaky breath. "David Lyons was there. The guy I used to live with? We danced together, but only once, and he didn't say or do anything unusual. In fact, he was extremely polite."

"Why didn't you want to tell me?"

She glazed down at the toes of those very high heels, and Trace's gaze followed. Damn, she had the prettiest legs. Slender ankles and nice high arches. He forced his gaze back to her face.

"David didn't make that call," she said. "He just isn't the kind of guy to do something like that, and I don't want to cause him any trouble."

"You still in love with him?"

She shook her head. "I was never in love with David. That was the problem. I hurt him. I didn't mean to but I did. I don't want to do it again."

"You hurt Josh Varner—now you don't want to hurt David Lyons. Is that about it?"

She swallowed. "I guess maybe that's part of it. I just know David was really…upset when our relationship ended. He's a very nice man and he doesn't deserve more problems from me."

"I'll be sure to keep that in mind," Trace said drily. But now that he was back on the case, which apparently he was, he was going to see it through. David Lyons was on his list of suspects. For Maggie's sake, Trace would give the guy the benefit of the doubt, but he wouldn't overlook him completely. Not until her stalker was found.

"Anything else?"

Pondering the question, she worried her lower lip. It was plump, damp and shiny, and the muscles across his stomach contracted. He wanted to set his mouth there, find out how sweet those full lips tasted. He wanted to do a lot more than that.

Damn. This wasn't good.

"I can't think of anything," she said. "At least not at the moment."

"There are a couple of things we can do. You've already reported the calls, the notes and the break-in to the police. So far, they haven't been much help. That leaves the phone company. First thing Monday, arrange to get caller ID. You might get lucky and we'll be able to track another call backward if one comes in. Or if the caller number is blocked, which it probably would be, you can figure it's him, let it ring and not pick up."

"All right."

"Also, there's a thing they can do called a trap. Once it's set up, the phone company can figure out where any harassing calls are coming from. The bad news is you'll have to be here when the call comes in, and you'll have to log the time and date. Once the phone company finds the caller's number, they give it to the police, who track it from there."

"What if the police won't do it?"

"I've got a friend in the department. It shouldn't be a problem. The trouble is, if the guy was careful enough not to leave his fingerprints, he's probably smart enough to use a disposable phone. Even if we get a number, it might not lead us anywhere." There were a couple other alternatives, but the trap seemed to be the best option.

Maggie looked up at Trace. "I think we should try it, don't you?"

"Absolutely. I do a lot of work with the phone company. I'll talk to them, set things up."

He glanced at the clock. It was nearly 2:00 a.m. "Why

don't you get some sleep? We can talk again in the morning."

"I'll try." She gave him a wobbly smile. "I feel better now that I've talked to you."

So did he, he realized. He hadn't been able to stop worrying since he'd left her last weekend. She might still be in danger, but now he was around to make sure she stayed safe.

He stifled a groan. That he cared so much did not sit well with him.

"Lock the dead bolt and activate the alarm. Call me when you get up in the morning."

Maggie walked him to the door. She paused for an instant and looked up at him. "Thanks for coming."

He reached out and gently cupped her cheek. "I won't let him hurt you, Maggie."

She managed to smile as his hand fell away. He wanted to reach for her again, ease her back into his arms. He wanted to kiss her, strip off her clothes and make love to her.

She's the last thing you need, he told himself, as he turned and walked out the door.

Chapter 9

Maggie set the alarm, then climbed the stairs, trying not to think of Trace, and failing miserably. She was ridiculously attracted to him, more every time she was with him. And the heat in those golden-brown eyes said the feeling was mutual. The problem was, though apparently he was going to help her, Trace didn't really trust her.

Which was hardly the framework for any sort of relationship.

It's just about sex, she told herself. Just chemistry. Pheromones did strange things to people.

Maggie walked into her bedroom and flipped on the light switch. She changed out of her clothes, pulled on an oversize pink T-shirt she'd been given at a breast cancer fundraiser and climbed into bed. But sleep remained elusive.

Instead she stared at the ceiling, her mind going over

the notes the stalker had left, and the eerie message on her phone.

Who was he?

Someone she had met at one of her shows? Who had purchased one of her photos? Or maybe it was someone she had been introduced to by friends. His words hinted that he knew her in some way. She went over the last few months, the places she had been, the gallery shows where her work had been shown and sold.

Nothing stood out. There'd been a few men who had expressed an interest in her personally, even a couple of guys who had asked her out, but none had pursued the matter once she'd turned them down.

She was exhausted by the time the sun began to creep over the horizon, tired enough that she finally drifted into an uneasy sleep.

It was after nine when a knock at her door jolted her eyes wide open. Grabbing the robe at the foot of her bed, she pulled it on and hurried downstairs.

Wondering if Trace might have returned, ignoring a little curl of hope that he had, she gazed through the peephole. Not Trace. Instead, a young woman with a baby in her arms stood on her front porch.

Shock jolted through her. *Oh, my God.* Maggie reached for the doorknob, her mind trying to process the sight on her doorstep.

"Hello, Maggie. Long time no see." Blonde and slender, her half sister had grown taller than her by at least six inches. With high cheekbones, delicate features and big, thick-lashed blue eyes, Ashley had matured into an incredibly beautiful young woman.

Maggie finally found her voice. "Why don't you come inside?"

Ashley stepped into the entry. The last time Maggie

had seen her, she had been a gangly, rebellious teen. Maggie tried to calculate how long that had been.

"It's been six years, if you're counting."

They stood in the foyer, both of them uncomfortable, Maggie still trying to get her mind wrapped around the fact that the sister she barely knew was standing in her home. "That sounds about right. That would make you…"

"I just turned twenty-one."

Maggie forced a smile. "And you have a baby."

"That's right." Wrapped in a soft blue blanket, and no more than a few months old, the infant fussed. Ashley jiggled the child soothingly.

"Let's go into the living room so you can sit down." Maggie started in that direction, barely able to feel her legs moving beneath her. She was still in shock, still trying to grasp the notion of Ashley with a baby. And probably no husband. That was, after all, the modern thing to do.

The girl sat down on the overstuffed, beige floral sofa, cuddling the infant in her lap. Thank God, Maggie had mostly finished unpacking. At least the boxes were gone from the living room.

"Guess you're pretty surprised to see me," Ashley said.

She managed another smile. "You could say that." They had never been close. In fact, the few times Maggie had visited her mother in Florida, there had been a certain animosity between the two girls. At fifteen, Ashley had been wild and out of control, dabbling in drugs and drinking. Maggie, older and working to make a living, had not approved.

"So…what brings you to Houston?"

Ashley looked away, and for the first time Maggie realized she was nervous.

She smoothed the baby's fine dark hair and carefully kept her attention fixed on the child. "Six months ago, Mom kicked Dad out of the house. His business was going bankrupt and you know how much Mom hates problems."

Maggie knew, all right. A similar thing had happened to her own father. Tom O'Connell's small trucking company had been having financial problems. Money was tight and her mother couldn't handle it. So Celeste took off, leaving them high and dry, and returned home to Florida. As soon as the divorce was final, she'd married the first man who asked her, only to have it end in a quick divorce. A third marriage the following year had produced Ashley, and lasted, apparently, until a few months ago.

"I was six months pregnant when she gave him the boot. Dad was having his own problems. I didn't have anywhere else to go, so I stayed with Mom after he left. We fought all the time. After I had the baby, it got worse. Last week, I packed up my things and moved out. I thought... I was hoping you would help me."

Maggie just sat there. "Are you asking me for money?"

Ashley straightened and her chin angled up. "I was hoping you would help me get a job, you know? Find a place to live, figure things out." She stood up, the baby still tight in her arms. "It was stupid. We're not even really sisters." She started for the door, and the sight of her leaving, clutching the tiny baby so desperately in her arms, squeezed something tight in Maggie's chest.

"Wait!" She hurried after the girl, reached out and caught her arm. "We *are* sisters. We just don't know each other." She didn't let go. "Come back and sit down. We'll talk things out, see what we can do. It might take us a while, but we'll manage. You can start by telling me your baby's name."

Ashley gazed softly down at the infant she carried, and a tender smile curved her lips. "His name is Robert. After my dad. I call him Robbie."

They walked back into the living room and sat back down.

"Does Mom know you're here?"

"I told her I was leaving. At the time, I wasn't exactly sure where I was going."

"You'll need to call her or she'll be worried."

"I doubt it."

"Still…"

Ashley shrugged her slender shoulders. "If I stay, I'll call."

Maggie gazed at the infant. He looked like every other baby she'd ever seen, with chubby cheeks, big inquisitive eyes, a little pug nose. "What about… Robbie's father?"

Her sister sighed. "I was a fool. I thought I loved him and he loved me. But Zig didn't give a damn. All he cared about was sex."

"His name is Zig?"

"His name is Sigman Murdock. Kinda weird, huh? Zig hated his name so he called himself Ziggy—you know, from Zig-Zag, the rolling papers? Should have been a tip-off, huh? But Ziggy was charming and super good-looking. By the time I realized the kind of guy he really was, it was too late."

Ashley bent and kissed the top of the baby's head. "Mom and Dad wanted me to have an abortion, but I just… I couldn't do it, Maggie." She smoothed a finger over her child's cheek and his big blue eyes followed the movement. "Robbie's the best thing that's ever happened to me, and no matter what, I'll find a way to take care of him."

Maggie looked at her sister and felt a tug at her heart. "You don't have to go. We'll find a way through all of this."

They would manage somehow. She wasn't about to toss her out in the street.

Still, Maggie couldn't help thinking, *Dear God, how am I going to work with a baby in the house?*

She knew nothing about children. Almost nothing about the young woman who had come to her for help.

And there was the matter of the stalker. It was hardly fair to put Ashley and her baby in danger.

Maggie sighed. If she thought her life was complicated before, she hadn't imagined the problem that had just arrived on her doorstep.

At the first light of dawn, Trace headed for the office. He wanted to know the name of the song on Maggie's message machine. He wanted to read the rest of the lyrics. Maybe they would give him a clue to the stalker's identity.

It was early Saturday morning, not a scheduled workday, but security wasn't the kind of business that had set hours. He turned on the overhead lights, made a pot of coffee and carried a mug of the steaming brew into his glass-enclosed office.

It took a minute for the computer to boot up. As soon as it had, he typed the first line of the song on Google: "I...saw...you... I knew you would be my one true love."

To his amazement, the phrase popped right up. There were at least a dozen sites on the first page, along with the movie from which it had come.

"The Prince and the Maiden," Trace said aloud. "Jesus, that's eerie."

"What's eerie?"

He turned, to find Ben Slocum standing in the open doorway. "You owe me, brother," Trace said. "Last night was way above and beyond the call of duty."

Ben just laughed. "Does that mean you went home with Haley, or you didn't?" He was as tall as Trace, his features harder, his slightly crooked nose having once been broken. His eyes, an icy blue, drew women like a magnet. Rita DeStefani, the shapely model who was Ben's current flame, was just one among a long, ever-growing list.

"Are you kidding?" Trace grumbled. "I was damned glad to get rid of her. Next time, find somebody else to pawn her off on."

Ben smiled. "Shouldn't be too tough. She's a good-looking girl and she likes to party."

"You mean she's easy. I guess these days I'm looking for more than a quick piece of ass."

One of Ben's dark eyebrows went up. "That sounds interesting. Who is she?"

Trace frowned. "I didn't say there was anyone in particular."

"Maybe not, but I'm betting there is. I can see it in your face."

Trace refused to think of Maggie. He wasn't about to fall for another redhead. He had learned his lesson. He hoped.

"What're you working on?" Ben asked.

"The O'Connell stalker case."

"Thought you said you were dropping that one for personal reasons."

"She got a call from him last night. Played a song for her on her message machine. We both kind of remembered it, but we couldn't think of the name." He pointed at the computer screen. "It's from *The Prince and the Maiden*."

Ben leaned over and stared at the website, elyrics, showing on the monitor. "*The Prince and the Maiden?* That old animated kid's movie? That's weird."

"Guy electronically distorted his voice. Scared the hell out of her." Trace clicked the play button on the YouTube link and the music floated into the room. Both men listened, then Trace clicked it off. "I got a bad feeling about this one."

Ben straightened away from the desk. "They're all lunatics. Let me know if I can help."

"Thanks, Ben."

Ben headed for his office and Trace turned back to the computer screen, reading the words of the song again and again. The lyrics were relatively short: "I… saw…you… I knew you would be my one true love. I… saw…you…a vision so pure and sweet, my only true love…." The brief song played out, finally came to an end, a beautiful love song that could mean just about anything.

Could be the guy knew her or had met her somewhere, or as it said in the song, she was only a vision in his mind.

Trace clicked on a couple more links, discovered the film was first released in 1959. Which didn't mean much, either, since it had been released again and again over the years, and almost everyone had seen the movie at some point in their lives.

He pulled out his cell phone, brought up Maggie's number and punched the button. It took a while for her to answer and he wondered if she might still be sleeping. The image of her naked popped into his head, all that glorious red hair spread out on the pillow.

Maggie sounded a little breathless when she said hello.

"Maggie, it's Trace."

"Oh, hi. I meant to call but I...got sidetracked."

He thought of the ex-boyfriend she had danced with last night. "Mind if I stop by? I've found the song and I've got a few more questions."

"Well, ummm... Sure, come on over."

Ignoring the hesitation in her voice and trying not to think that a visit from the ex might be the cause, he printed the lyrics and shut down the computer. After he talked to her, he planned to hit the real estate office that had sold her the town house, speak to the agents involved in the transaction. First he wanted to know if the song or the movie rang any bells with her.

He waved to Ben, grabbed his hat off the rack beside the door and walked out. A few minutes later, he pulled up in front of the town house. As he neared the front door, he could hear conversation inside. It sounded female, but he couldn't make out what the women were saying.

He knocked and Maggie opened the door.

"Good morning. Come on in." She smiled at him and a rush of heat went straight through him. All morning, he'd been thinking about her, trying to forget the feel of her soft body pressed against him last night. Clearly, it hadn't worked, and he silently cursed.

He pulled off his hat, ran a hand through his hair. "You sleep okay?" he asked, then grimaced as the picture he'd imagined of her naked in bed popped into his mind.

"Not great." She stepped out of the way and he walked past her into the entry. "Before we get started," she said as she closed the door, "there's someone I'd like you to meet."

Trace pulled his thoughts back to business, and followed her into the living room. His gaze shot to the young woman on the sofa, a baby in her arms.

"Trace, this is my sister, Ashley Hastings. And her son, Robbie. Ashley, this is Trace Rawlins. He, um, he owns the company that installed my new alarm system."

Trace frowned. It wasn't a lie. After all, he was in the security business. It just wasn't entirely the truth.

"Nice to meet you," he said, but he was thinking that Maggie O'Connell kept more secrets than the CIA.

He focused his attention on the younger woman, a stunning blonde, tall and slender, with delicate features and a short cap of softly curling hair. She could have been a model for *Vogue* magazine.

"Mind if I steal your sister for a couple minutes?" Trace asked her. "There's a couple of minor items we need to discuss."

Ashley smiled. "Not at all. It's nice to meet you, Trace."

"You, too, Ashley."

"Why don't you go ahead and finish getting settled?" Maggie said to her. "I'm sure this won't take long. There's food in the fridge if you get hungry."

Trace set a hand at her back, guided her out to his Jeep, and they both climbed inside. He tossed his hat into the backseat but didn't start the engine. "Why is it I'm just finding out you've got a sister?"

Maggie's head snapped toward him. "I'm sure I mentioned her. I said my mom remarried down in Florida and had another child."

He grunted. "From the way you said it, I didn't expect her to be a grown woman."

"I haven't seen Ashley in years. This morning she showed up on my doorstep, babe in arms. I couldn't just send her away."

"No, I guess not. But it sure as hell complicates things."

"I know."

"I get the idea you haven't told her about your stalker."

"Not yet, but I will. I didn't want her to think I was just trying to get rid of her."

"Is that what you want?"

Maggie sighed. "Let's just say I've got enough trouble without adding more. I don't really know Ashley. I haven't seen her since she was fifteen."

"What else?" he pressed, sensing there was more.

"Fine. You're so high on the truth, here it is—I've always resented Ashley for being the daughter my mother loved. I wanted a mother so badly, but Mom barely knew I existed. I know it's silly, but that's the way I felt."

His mouth edged up. "You're both grown now."

Maggie released a slow breath. "I know. And she's got a newborn. She and my mother aren't speaking, which means I've got to help her. I can't just turn her away."

Trace made no reply. She was right, as far as he was concerned. The girl was family. That was enough. And she was Maggie's sister. Secretly, he had always wanted a brother. Maybe that was the reason he'd become so close to Dev and Johnnie, his buddies in the army. The men were more like brothers than just friends.

"Listen, Maggie, this morning I went on the internet and found that song you heard last night. It's from an old animated children's movie, *The Prince and the Maiden*."

Her green eyes widened. They were rimmed by lashes nearly as thick as her sister's. "You're kidding! I saw that film when I was a little girl."

"Anything you remember about it that might help us?"

She thought for several long moments. Then shook

her head. "I loved the movie. I guess I was a romantic even before I knew what it meant. Aside from that, I can't think of a thing."

He handed her the computer printout. "These are the rest of the lyrics. Anything stand out? Any flash of memory that could mean something?"

Maggie read the words, which were mostly a repeat of the first two lines. She sighed and dropped the sheet onto her lap. "I have no idea what this guy is thinking, Trace, I swear."

He picked up the paper, folded it, unsnapped his shirt pocket and tucked it inside. "It's not your fault. The guy is obviously a nutcase. You don't think the way he does. Probably better you don't."

"So where do we go from here?"

"I need to speak to your real estate agent."

She cast him a hopeful glance. "Can I go with you? The office is only a few blocks away. I need to get out of the house for a while, try to get my head together about all of this."

He should probably say no. The more time he spent with her, the more he thought about taking her to bed. "I don't see why not." At least with him, she'd be safe.

"Let me go tell Ashley."

On the other hand, as much as he wanted her, she'd probably be safer if she just stayed home.

Chapter 10

Maggie leaned back in the deep leather seat as Trace drove the Jeep away from the town house. The Garmin Real Estate office was a couple miles away, in a small shopping center on Bissonnet.

As they started toward the door, she felt Trace's hand at her back, guiding her up the walkway, and just that slight touch made her skin feel warm.

The office was mostly empty, she discovered as they walked inside, with just a few agents sitting at metal desks. Photos of homes for sale rested on pedestals in the front window, and sales licenses hung on the walls.

"Mike Jenkins was the listing agent for all six town house units," Maggie told Trace, pointing to a short, stocky man with thinning hair seated at the desk farthest away. "That's him over there."

Trace urged her in that direction. Mike stood up as they approached and greeted them with a smile. "Hello,

Maggie. It's nice to see you. I hope you're enjoying your new home."

"It's great, thanks. Mike, this is Trace Rawlins. He's an investigator. Recently, I had a break-in. Trace is hoping you can help me."

Mike turned to him. "I'm happy to do what I can."

"I need to know who had access to the key to Maggie's condo."

"No one lately. Not since the deal closed. Before that, we all did." He gestured to the entire office. "While the condo was for sale, the key was on the sales board. Agents just sign it out when they need it."

"Then you have a record of who might have used it."

"That's right. We put the property sign-out sheet in the file after the sale closes." He walked to the back of the office and pulled open a drawer from a row of metal files along the wall. Withdrawing a manila folder, he closed the drawer and returned.

Mike opened the file, took out a sheet of paper and handed it to Trace. "This is a list of anyone who checked out a key."

"Are these all salespeople?"

"Well, yes, and pest control, cleaning people, the guy who did the home inspection."

A muscle jerked in Trace's cheek. "So pretty much anyone on this list could have made a copy."

"Well, I guess so, yes. But we're all professionals here. We've never had a problem."

"At least that you know of. You might want to consider rekeying a home after you've sold it."

"Absolutely. We always advise our buyers to do exactly that."

Trace turned a hard look on Maggie and a guilty flush rose in her cheeks. "Mike said I should rekey. I just never got around to it."

The Realtor's chubby face broke into a smile. "We look after our clients in every way we can."

"Anyone show an interest in the place after you'd shown it to Maggie?"

"There couldn't have been many," she interjected. "I made an offer just a few days after I first saw it, and the offer was accepted."

"That's right. Once the property went into escrow, it was taken off the market." Mike took the sign-out sheet from Trace's hand, looked down at the names and dates. "I showed Maggie the condo on Friday, the first of March." He opened the transaction file, thumbed through a couple pages. "We made the offer on Monday, the fourth, and the property went into escrow later that same day."

Mike glanced back down at the list. "Jim Brewer signed out a key on March 3, the Sunday before we made the offer. That would have been after Maggie had been there. Jim held an open house."

"I'll need to talk to him," Trace said. "Any idea when he might be in?"

"He's sitting another open house, at 2255 Woodale. It's just off Braeswood. You can find him there."

"All right, that's it then." Trace offered a hand and the agent shook it. "Thanks, Mike."

"Let me know if there's anything else I can do."

Trace urged Maggie back toward the door and she let him guide her out to the Jeep.

"I guess we're going to an open house," she said.

She found Trace's eyes in the mirror. She thought he might say no, but instead he started the engine. "I guess we are," he said.

Maggie thought of the dozens of people who had been in the town house, people who could have made a key. It seemed impossible to find out if one of them had become her stalker.

"Why would this guy, my stalker, go to an open house? How would he even know I was interested in buying the place?"

"I'm not sure he did. But he got inside fairly easily, so either he had a key or he knew the layout, or both. Maybe he was following you the day Mike showed it to you. If he was, maybe he heard you say you planned to buy it, and he wanted to see where you would be living. Maybe he just went to the open house because you'd been in the condo and he wanted to be in a place you had been."

Maggie felt a chill. "I can't...can't believe he'd be that obsessed."

Trace flashed her a sideways glance. "You can't?"

She thought of the notes, of the eerie song left on her answering machine last night, and her insides tightened. How dangerous was this man? Just how frightened should she be?

And what about Ashley and little Robbie?

A sign appeared on the road: Open House, with an arrow pointing the direction.

"It's up ahead." Trace followed a trail of signs to an older, white, ranch-style home shaded by a cluster of big, leafy trees.

They walked inside and a thirty-something agent with short sandy hair and hazel eyes started over to greet them. He was wearing a suit and tie and a wide white smile.

"Mike Jenkins sent us," Trace said. "We aren't here to see the house, just to ask you a couple of questions."

The smile slipped away. "Oh?"

"I'm Maggie O'Connell. I bought one of the town

houses your company had listed on Broadmoor. You held an open house on my unit the Sunday before I made the offer."

"I remember the place. You got a good buy."

"I like to think so."

Trace tipped his head toward the guest book lying open on the table in the entry. "Did you keep a guest register that day?"

"I did. That's the way we pick up clients."

"Lots of people show up that day?"

"No, just a few."

"Did everyone sign?"

"I think so." He walked over to the book and flipped the pages back to an earlier date. "Here it is…2818 Broadmoor, unit A. Only two couples came in that day." He glanced up, frowned. "Wait, that's not right. There was a man…he said he wasn't really a buyer, at least not yet. He just wanted to take a look around, get an idea of values for when he was ready to purchase. Since the condo was empty, I let him wander a bit. He didn't stay very long."

"What'd he look like?" Trace asked.

"Big guy. Forties. Heavyset. A touch of silver in his hair. Nothing that really made him stand out. I only remember him because he didn't want to sign."

"Dark hair?"

"Yeah, but with silver running through it. He looked kind of distinguished. I figured he had some money. That's one of the reasons I let him wander."

Trace looked at Maggie. "Ring any bells?"

She shook her head. "A client, maybe. Someone who bought one of my pictures. No one specifically I can think of."

Trace turned back to the Realtor. "Thanks. We appreciate your help."

"Anytime."

They walked out of the house, heading for the car.

"You think the man Jim saw at the open house was him?" Maggie asked as they climbed into the Jeep.

"No way to tell, at least not yet. But it's something." Trace slid in behind the wheel. "If we get another lead that points to a guy who fits the same description, we'll know we have something."

"If it's him, it isn't David. He's younger than that, slim and blond, and he has blue eyes."

Trace grunted. "Sounds like a real pretty boy."

Maggie bit back a smile. "I guess you could say that." She looked at Trace from beneath her lashes. "You're kind of pretty yourself."

He laughed, white teeth flashing in a face so ruggedly handsome it made David look like a sissy. Trace turned to gaze at her and silence fell between them. He reached out and settled a hand on her cheek, and she could feel his working-man calluses, feel the strength. Leaning over, he very softly kissed her, just the lightest brush of lips before his mouth settled firmly over hers.

Maggie's pulse roared. Her breathing quickened and damp heat poured through her. Trace kept kissing her, soft moist kisses that made her toes curl inside her sneakers and need tighten like a fist in her belly. The kiss deepened, turned erotic. A soft moan escaped. He tasted like heaven. Like cinnamon and coffee and hot, sexy male.

God, she wanted this man. She wasn't sure what she wanted to happen after the sex, but she had never felt this kind of desire before, this strong an attraction, and she wanted to find out where it might lead.

By the time Trace ended the kiss, she had forgotten where they were, forgotten everything but the aching want clawing through her body.

When he settled his tall frame back against the seat, he was breathing as hard as she.

"I was afraid of that," he said, sounding almost angry.

"Afraid of what?" She couldn't concentrate. All she could think of was how much she wanted him to kiss her again.

"Afraid you'd taste as sweet as you do, and I'd want you even more than I already did."

Heat rushed into her cheeks. As much as she wanted him, she wasn't the kind of woman who jumped into bed with a man. She needed to know what she was getting into, needed to think this through before she did something stupid, the way she had with David.

A shuddering breath whispered out. She worked to slow her breathing, determined to force things back on a safer track. "So, um, how do we find another lead?"

He leaned down and cranked the key, and the engine roared to life. "We hope he calls after we set up the trap on your phone."

Maggie studied Trace's profile, tried not to think of that mind-blowing kiss. She was wildly attracted to him. But she didn't need any more trouble in her life, and it was clear this man was a handful. "You don't look optimistic."

He shrugged his broad shoulders. "There's a chance. But like I said, this guy doesn't seem the type to make that kind of mistake. He probably used a disposable phone."

"Like the ones you buy at the supermarket?"

"Right." Trace pulled the Jeep out into the street.

"I'm putting Rex Westcott on your place tonight. He's good. You won't see him. Neither will your stalker if he shows up."

Her senses went on alert. "You think he might?"

Trace didn't bother to answer. The man had been there before. "You need to tell your sister."

Maggie moistened her lips, which suddenly felt dry. "I'll tell her when I get home."

Trace drove Maggie back to her town house. He was still hard inside his jeans. One lousy kiss. Dammit, he'd known better. He had rotten luck with women, especially redheads. But his willpower was nil where Maggie was concerned.

"Where are you going from here?" she asked, which put his big head back in charge, thank God.

"I need to talk to Emily Barrington. I called her this morning, told her I wanted to stop by early this afternoon."

"Hewitt's daughter?"

"That's right."

"So you're still working on the murder."

"There's still no proof there was one. I need to find out if Parker Barrington really was home with his wife the night her father died."

"Is that what Emily says?"

"That's what she says."

"So the case is ongoing."

"The D.A.'s building an embezzlement case against Parker. In the meantime, I'm doing some digging on my own." Trace turned the Jeep onto Broadmoor. Maggie's condo was just down the block. "I want you to keep me advised of your movements. I don't want this guy getting you alone somewhere, okay?"

She stiffened. "I've got to work, Trace. I need to take some more photos, finish getting others framed and ready for the show. I've got a black-tie opening on Friday at the Twin Oaks Gallery. It's a very big deal for me."

"It that so? Unless we catch this guy, you'll be bringing a date to the party."

"A date? I'm not bringing a date, I'll be working."

"Maybe I should have said *bodyguard*."

Her russet eyebrows shot up. "You?"

"That's right."

She eyed him as if she were trying to decide if he'd come up to scratch. "You'd have to wear a tuxedo."

The corner of his mouth quirked. "I think I can handle it."

"Yeah?"

"Yeah."

Maggie didn't say more and he wondered if she was comparing him to Pretty-boy Lyons. She'd said she wasn't in love with the guy. Carly never loved any of the men she slept with but it didn't keep her out of their beds.

"I don't suppose you'd take me with you to see Emily?" Maggie asked. "I could wait outside in the car."

Trace grinned. "Which is it? The sister or the baby?"

"Both. I don't know Ashley, and I don't know anything at all about babies."

He chuckled. "Come on, Maggie. I never took you for a coward."

She laughed. "Just shows you how little you know about me."

His humor slowly faded. All too true. He knew very little about her, and he was a rotten judge of women. Maggie seemed different, but he could damn well be wrong.

He let her off in front of her town house. The look of dread on her face softened his mood. "You'll be fine," he assured her.

"Thanks for the ride," Maggie said darkly. Squaring her shoulders, she marched up the sidewalk as if she were facing a firing squad.

From Maggie's, Trace drove across town to an area off the Allen Parkway. It was an elegant, prestigious neighborhood, with some of the most expensive homes in Houston. Parker Barrington's house looked like a Southern plantation, sparkling white, with two massive Corinthian columns out front and a balcony that wrapped around the second floor.

When Trace rang the bell beside the big double doors, a short, thin, dark-haired man in a black suit and white shirt opened the door. *The butler.* The pretension was Parker all the way.

Trace wondered how the man was going to adjust to the eight-by-eight cell he'd be sharing with some big bruiser, and almost smiled.

"Trace Rawlins," he said. "I'm here to see Mrs. Barrington. I believe she's expecting me."

"Why, yes, Mr. Rawlins. Please come in." The butler reached for the hat in Trace's hand, which he surrendered. "Mrs. Barrington asked that you wait for her in the long gallery. I'll let her know you're here."

"Thank you."

The long gallery overlooked a huge, manicured yard studded with tall, leafy trees. Clusters of yellow crocus, pink petunias and purple and yellow pansies bloomed along the walkways.

He sat down on a rose velvet chair next to a matching sofa that looked out at the grounds through small paned windows. He had met Emily a number of times over the years, but had never been to her house before. She hadn't seemed the type to be quite so enamored of society, nor her tastes quite so lavish. But the house fit Parker like an expensive leather glove.

He looked up at the portraits hanging on the wall, gilt-framed paintings of various family members. Hewitt and Caroline Sommerset, Emily's parents, were prominently displayed. He assumed the perfectly groomed blond couple in the picture to the left belonged to Parker.

In beige slacks and an embroidered blue silk blouse, Emily walked into the gallery a few minutes later. She had short dark hair cut in a stylish bob, the same blue eyes as Jason and her brother's fair complexion. Trace rose as she entered, her hands extended in greeting.

"Good morning, Trace. Thank you for stopping by."

He took her hands, gave them a gentle squeeze, leaned down and kissed her cheek. "I came to express my condolences, Emily. I admired your father very much. And I liked him."

Her eyes misted. "He was…my father was a very great man. I still can't believe he's gone."

"Hewitt was larger than life. I figured he'd live to be a hundred."

Emily glanced out the window, her gaze fixed on a bird that landed in a small marble fountain. "I still don't understand why he killed himself."

It was the opening Trace needed. "Are you certain he did?"

She sank down on the velvet sofa and Trace returned to his chair across from her.

"I can't figure out why he would. He seemed happy.

He and Jason were planning a trip to the Bahamas. I thought he was really looking forward to it."

"I think he was."

She met Trace's gaze. "Jason believes he was murdered. That's why you're here, isn't it? You think so, too."

Trace steeled himself. "Yes, Emily, I do. I think someone shot him and made it look like he pulled the trigger."

"Is that…is that even possible?"

"It isn't easy but it can be done."

She clasped her hands in her lap. "Then that must be what happened. I don't think Dad would kill himself."

"There were circumstances, Emily. Before it happened, your father asked me to check into some…accounting problems that he had turned up. Do you know anything about that?"

She frowned. "No, why would I?"

"Because Parker was involved."

"Parker? You…you aren't implying…"

Trace made no comment.

"You're wrong, Trace. Parker wouldn't steal from my father. He…he wouldn't do something like that."

"I didn't mention stealing, Em. I think maybe your instincts have been telling you that something was wrong, and because you love Parker you don't want to face the truth."

She rose from the sofa, her spine stiff and her face pale. "I think…think you should leave now."

Trace stood up, too. "Was Parker home with you the night your father died, Emily? Or was he out well past midnight? Past the time that your father was killed?"

She swayed on her feet, seemed to shrink inside herself. "Oh, God. He wouldn't do it, Trace. He couldn't— could he?"

"You need to tell the police the truth, Em. You need to let them sort it out."

She swallowed, wiped at the tears rolling down her cheeks. "H-he wasn't home with me that night. H-he came in late. When I asked him where he'd been, he said he was downstairs in the library. We both...both knew he wasn't. I had looked for him there." She straightened, seemed to find some inner strength. "Find out what happened, Trace. Find out if my husband...if Parker murdered my father."

"I've got to tell the police, Emily. They need to know so they can continue their investigation."

She nodded, sank back down on the sofa. "Tell them. Find out the truth."

"You can't mention this to Parker. Not yet."

Tight lines formed around her mouth. "That won't be a problem. He's hardly ever home."

"Take care of yourself, Emily." Turning, Trace strode back to the entry, took the hat the butler held out to him and left the house.

The first call he made was to Mark Sayers.

Chapter 11

"So there you have it," Maggie said, finishing what she had finally gotten around to telling her sister. "I've got some creep stalking me, and staying here puts you and little Robbie in danger."

Ashley gently jiggled the baby in her lap, making him smile. "And Trace Rawlins is the man you hired to find this guy."

"That's about it. I should have told you when you first got here, but it just seemed like too much to handle all at once."

The infant wrapped his tiny fingers around Ashley's thumb and made a little cooing sound. A soft smile curved Ashley's lips, then she looked up. "Did you mean what you said about helping me and Robbie?"

"Of course I did. It was kind of a shock, seeing you out on my porch like that. But I meant it. We're sisters. I'll do everything I can to help you."

Ashley sat up a little straighter on the sofa. "Then we're staying. You've got this Rawlins guy working on the problem—he's a major hunk, by the way. If you're paying him, he's not going to let anything happen to you, right?"

"That's what he says." She ignored the "hunk" comment, though she certainly agreed. "The problem is we don't know what this guy might do next. Until we catch him, anything could happen."

Ashley shrugged. "I ran away from home when I was in high school. Mom probably never told you that."

Maggie shook her head. "No, she didn't. But we don't talk very often, and when we do, all she ever says is everything's fine."

"I lived on the street for a while. I wasn't a prostitute or anything, but I slept in the open and I bummed around with some pretty strange people. I made friends with a couple of girls who turned tricks, and they talked about guys who like to be spanked and stuff. There are some real weirdos out there. I learned real fast to stay away from certain kinds of men."

Maggie's heart squeezed to think of the young girl who had been out there alone, struggling to find her way. "I'm sorry you felt you had to do that. I'm glad you went back home."

"I figured out pretty fast that Mom and Dad weren't all that bad. I mean, they fought all the time and mostly ignored me, but at least I had a decent place to live. I went back to high school and graduated before I took off again."

Maggie watched the baby's eyes drift closed. At three months old, he slept most of the time. He was so tiny and sweet. "Where did you go after high school?"

"I got my own apartment and took a job in a cocktail lounge. Pay wasn't good but the tips made up for it. Unfortunately, that's where I met Ziggy."

"Robbie's dad," Maggie said darkly, disliking the guy more every time she heard his name.

"Yeah. Like I said, Zig was really good-looking, you know? All the waitresses were hot for him, but I was the one he wanted. I guess that made me feel important. I let him move into my apartment for a while and even paid his bills." Her lips tightened. "One thing about Ziggy—he taught me how to take care of myself. If the creep who's been bothering you comes around, he'll get more than he bargained for."

Maggie grinned. It was beginning to seem there was a lot more to her sister than just a rebellious nature and a penchant for getting into trouble.

"Trace's people changed the locks and installed an alarm system. We should be safe enough inside the house."

"I'd like to stay, Maggie, if you'll let me."

Maggie reached over and caught her sister's hand. "I'd love for you both to stay."

Ashley's eyes glistened. "Thanks. Want to hold him? He's ready for his nap so he won't wiggle around too much."

Maggie swallowed and stood up. "I've never held a baby. I really don't know how."

"It's easy." Fussing with the blanket, Ashley gently settled her son in Maggie's arms. "Just make sure you keep his head supported."

She did as Ashley instructed, nestling the baby against her shoulder, feeling the warmth of his tiny body seeping into her. Something softened inside her, made her heart swell.

"Are you nursing him?" she asked.

Ashley shook her head. "I wanted to, but I couldn't make enough milk. The doctor said Robbie wasn't getting the nutrients he needed, so I stopped. He's doing a lot better now."

Maggie gazed down at the infant in her arms. "He seems really happy."

Her sister smiled. "He almost never cries. He's such a good baby."

Maggie moved a little, gently swaying, watching as the baby's big blue eyes slowly began to close. "I'm an aunt," she said, feeling a ridiculous smile spread over her face. "It feels kind of funny." She looked at Ashley. "And kind of wonderful, too."

The girl wiped a tear from her cheek. "I wanted Mom to love him. But she hated Ziggy so much she couldn't get past it."

"Well, I love him already," Maggie said. "And we're going to make sure Robbie has everything he needs."

Ashley's shoulders seemed to relax, as if some of her burden had been lightened. "Thanks, Maggie." Her lips firmed. "And in the meantime, we're going to help Trace catch the creep who's been harassing you."

Maggie gazed down at the tiny baby in her arms and worry filtered through her. What if something happened? She only hoped that in letting Ashley stay she was doing the right thing.

Trace called Mark Sayers about the conversation he'd had with Emily, then arranged for Rex Westcott to handle surveillance on Maggie's town house that night. He knew Westcott was completely reliable, that he would be watching for anyone hanging around the condo, and he wouldn't be spotted.

Still Trace worried. There was something about

Maggie's stalker that had his instincts on alert, something that warned there was more going on here than it seemed. The guy might just be a loony, like most of them. Or he might be extremely dangerous, as Trace's gut continued to insist.

And now there was a young girl with a baby in the house.

Of course, the stalker's obsession was with Maggie. He wouldn't be interested in the girl, but there was always the risk of collateral damage. Trace didn't want Maggie's sister and her baby caught in the crossfire.

After a restless night, Trace drove to the office Sunday morning. The sun wasn't quite up, but it was already warm. In another month it would be full-blown summer.

Trace brewed a pot of strong coffee, filled his mug and sat down at his desk. He returned to Maggie's list of names and continued digging, looking for anything interesting he might find on the internet.

A little after eight, Rex Westcott walked in. He was not quite six feet tall, late thirties, slim with medium brown hair and intelligent hazel eyes. A slight limp from an old army wound caused a subtle hesitation in his gait.

Trace left his office and walked out to greet him. "Everything go all right?"

Rex yawned. "A little too all right. It's such a quiet neighborhood I had a helluva time staying awake."

"Coffee?" Trace asked with a smile.

"I'd kill for a cup."

The men walked back to the kitchen area and Trace poured a mug for Rex. "No sign of the guy, then?"

"No, and I looked pretty hard for any indication he'd been there the nights before. No cigarette butts, footprints in the flower beds, broken shrubbery, nothing."

"We'll try it again tonight. After that, we'll wait and see."

Rex finished his coffee in a few big gulps. "That'll keep me awake long enough to drive home. I'll get some sleep and be ready to go out again."

"Sounds good."

Rex left the office, and a few minutes later, Alex Justice walked in. He sniffed the air and flashed a grin that cut a dimple into his cheek. "Coffee! Thank God."

"Long night?"

"Early morning. I'm working that security breach on the Consolidated Boatyard. I need to get down there, take another look around."

"No rest for the weary."

"You got that right."

Alex stayed only long enough to check his phone messages, his email and whatever might have landed on his desk, then he was gone.

Trace called Maggie, relayed Rex's boring night, went back to his digging, came up with nothing, then went home. What he really wanted to do was see Maggie.

Which was exactly the reason he didn't.

Monday went much the same, except that the hum of people working in the office eased his nerves. That and hearing from Rex that again Sunday night he had seen no sign of Maggie's stalker. Trace had spoken to the phone company and they'd set up the trap, which would be operational beginning tomorrow. He needed to speak to Maggie, remind her that if the stalker phoned or she got any more hang-up calls, she needed to write down the time and date. Until that happened, all they could do was wait.

Trace checked the clock, decided that with a baby in residence, it was probably too early to call. Since he had plenty to do just running the business, he figured today would be a good time to play catch-up, so he settled in to work.

At ten o'clock he phoned the town house. Ashley answered.

"Hi, Ashley, this is Trace. I need to speak to Maggie."

"She isn't here, Trace. She said she had some work to do for her book. She took off about fifteen minutes ago."

He clamped down on a thread of anger. Dammit, he'd told her to check in with him before she left the house. "You know where she went?"

"Down to the shore. She wasn't sure where she was going to wind up. Wherever the shots looked promising, she said."

His temper began to heat. He remembered the young woman in the newspaper who had recently disappeared. Her body had washed up on the beach, and he had heard on the news that the police believed she had been murdered.

"I'll try her cell," Trace said, thinking of Maggie's stalker and worrying the same kind of thing could happen to her. "If she calls, tell her to phone me right away. Tell her I need to talk to her."

"Okay."

Ashley hung up and Trace clenched his jaw. What the hell was Maggie thinking to go off on her own that way? He worked hard at staying calm, but Maggie had a way of stirring him up. He told himself it was just that damned red hair, but he knew it was more than that. Knew he was beginning to care way too much.

He dialed her cell number but the call went straight to her voice mail.

Worry tangled with anger. He wanted to strangle her. Dammit, he thought he'd been clear. He didn't want her out there where the guy might be able to get her alone.

He stood up and went for more coffee, though he'd already had more than his share.

Where was she?

Dammit to hell and gone.

For the first time in days, Maggie felt free. She'd awakened early, rode her stationary bike and worked out a little with her free weights, then showered and dressed for the day. She had left the house half an hour ago, just as Ashley was getting up to feed the baby. Late enough that Maggie figured her watchdog, Rex something-or-other, had already gone home.

There'd been no sign of her stalker again last night. She was sure he hadn't appeared, or Trace would have called. Or more likely, his watchdog would have called the police and had him arrested.

Still, the guy was out there somewhere, and just because he hadn't been at her house last night didn't mean he couldn't be waiting for her to leave this morning. With that in mind, she had backed her little Ford Escape out of the garage with an eye on her surroundings, passing Ashley's battered old baby-blue Chevy parked in the unit A guest space.

As Maggie rolled out onto the street and drove toward the freeway, she memorized the color and model of each car behind her, even noted some of their license plate numbers to see if they continued to travel the same route she did.

The farther she drove out of town, the easier it was

to keep track. By the time she was cruising Highway 45 twenty miles out of Houston, none of the cars she had seen earlier were anywhere behind her.

She was absolutely sure she wasn't being followed, which gave her a great sense of relief.

Galveston was her destination. A lot of reconstruction was still going on after the damage done by Hurricane Ike a few years back. Sometimes the men and machinery working against the backdrop of the sea made dramatic photos.

She prowled Galveston Harbor, then headed for the beach, stopping here and there for any sort of interesting shot. School was still in session. It was Monday, so the beaches were relatively empty. Always fascinated by the contrast between white sand and blue sea, she snapped a few shots, one she particularly liked of the beach patrol practicing their rescue procedures for the upcoming summer season.

When her stomach began to growl, she pulled into a parking lot in front of a little thatch-roofed restaurant called the Lunch Shack. Delicious aromas wafting through the order window drew her in that direction, and she snapped a couple shots of the Asian chef in his tall white hat working over the grill.

She ordered crispy, deep-fried fish and chips, blowing her calorie count for the next several days. As she licked the last bite of tartar sauce off her fingers fifteen minutes later, her cell phone started to ring.

Trace had been calling, but she hadn't picked up. She knew he was going to read her the riot act, but she'd simply had to get away. Ashley had called to tell her he was looking for her, and Maggie had promised to call him on her way back to the city.

She dug the cell out of her purse to see if he was calling again, recognized Roxanne's number and answered.

"Hey, stranger," Roxy said. She was still visiting friends in New York, a couple she had met in Rome and a gay friend she knew from Carnevale in Venice. "I've been meaning to call, but time just slipped away. I figured you'd let me know if anything happened, but I've still been worried."

Plenty had happened, but she didn't want to get into all that now. "Well, my sister showed up. That was a big surprise. She has a baby."

"Your sister? Ashley? The teenager who lives in Florida?"

"She isn't a teen anymore. She's moved in with me for a while. It's a long story. You can meet her when you get home."

"Well, that's certainly news. What about the stalker?"

"Oh. Trace is back on the case. We talked, got things straightened out."

"Talked, huh? That's all you did?"

"For the moment." She told Roxy about the break-in and the figurine, and generally filled her in.

"Listen, I'll come back early if you need me."

"I'm fine, really. I've got an alarm system now and Trace seems to know what he's doing."

"I'm here for you, you know. If something happens, you call me."

Maggie smiled. She could always count on Roxanne. "I will, I promise. Enjoy the rest of your trip."

Roxy laughed. "Are you kidding? I'm practically a fixture on Fifth Avenue. I do love New York."

Maggie grinned as she ended the call. Feeling better after the conversation, she wandered a bit with her camera, took a couple of seascapes she thought might have potential. She was smiling when she returned to her car.

The smile slid away at the sight of the brown scrap of paper stuck beneath the windshield wiper. The lunch she'd just eaten went sour and nausea rolled through her stomach. Her heart was pounding. Her hand shook as she reached for the note, carefully pulled it from under the rubber blade.

Beloved Maggie. It is almost time for us to meet. Not yet, but soon. Soon, my dear, dear Maggie.

Sweet God, how had he found her? She'd been so careful, so sure she hadn't been followed. She glanced wildly around the Lunch Shack parking lot, but saw only a brown-and-black dog sniffing for garbage and a Hispanic couple with two young children walking toward the food order window.

Her Nikon D3S hung from a strap around her neck. Lifting the camera with trembling hands, she fought to steady the big 28-300 Tamron lens, and began clicking shots of each car parked in the area, including the license plates. The effort was probably futile—undoubtedly, the man had left the note and driven away, as he had done before—but maybe not.

Maybe he was still somewhere nearby, watching her, waiting for her to leave. Her skin prickled. She told herself maybe this time she would get lucky and get a photo of his tag.

As soon as she finished shooting, she slipped the strap off her neck and packed the camera away, climbed into the little SUV and dug her cell phone out of her purse. She brought up Trace's number, then realized she had used the last of her battery power talking to Roxanne.

"Dammit…" Tossing the phone onto the seat beside her, she started the engine. Trace had very specifically told her not to go out without letting him know, but she was used to being on her own and there was only so much time she could spend indoors. She wondered if he would lose his precious self-control and let his temper show.

She might have smiled if the situation had been different. She would enjoy another glimpse of the man beneath the iron control, the hot-tempered male he worked so hard to hide.

But as she pulled onto Highway 45, she wasn't thinking of the angry man she'd be facing when she got back to the city. Instead, all the way back to Houston, she kept glancing in the mirror, searching for the man who was ruining her life.

Chapter 12

Cursing beneath his breath, Trace hung up the phone in his office. Maggie hadn't called, and she wasn't answering her cell phone. Ashley had spoken to her, given her his message, but still Maggie hadn't bothered to call.

Shoving back his chair, he got up from his desk and paced to the front of the office to stare out the window, as he had done a dozen times already today.

"You're gonna wear out the carpet," Annie said, peering at him over the top of the little half-glasses perched on the end of her nose.

"Dammit, the woman is nothing but trouble."

"According to you, they all are."

He shot a dark glance her way but the receptionist ignored it.

"She's a photographer, right?" Annie shifted in the chair behind her desk. "She's got a show coming up. That's what you said. The woman has work to do."

"Yeah, well, this guy is a real weirdo. So far we have no idea who he is or what he might be capable of doing."

"Then I guess you're convinced he's real."

"What?" Trace turned to face her.

"It wasn't that long ago you dropped the case because you thought she was making the whole thing up."

"That's not exactly the way it was. I thought she wasn't being completely honest with me, and she wasn't."

Annie scoffed. "Women are allowed to keep a few secrets, honey. It's a rule."

His mouth edged up but he refused to smile. "I'll be in my office, doing my damnedest to work." He started in that direction, trying to get his mind off Maggie, who was probably enjoying the day while he stewed and fretted.

"If I remember, she was driving a little red SUV the day she came to the office to hire you."

He stopped and turned. "That's right. Why?"

"She just pulled into the lot."

Trace felt a sweep of relief. Striding to the door, he took a calming breath as he stepped outside and spotted Maggie getting out of her car, looking sexy as hell with her fiery hair a little windblown and her cheeks slightly flushed. He tried not to remember the way she tasted, tried not to think of that kiss, willed himself not to get hard.

But as she approached him, the look on her face sent his worry spiking up again.

"Dammit, where the hell have you been? I've been calling your cell for hours."

"I needed to take some pictures. I thought maybe Galveston. I drove down this morning." She was wearing jeans and sneakers and a simple white shirt. How that outfit could possibly arouse him, he couldn't imagine, but it did.

He drew on his self-control. "That where you went?"

She nodded.

"Why didn't you answer your phone?"

"I know I should have. But I knew you'd be mad. I needed to get out of the house. I had work to do, so that's what I did." She held out a piece of rough brown paper. "Unfortunately, I found this on my windshield after I stopped for lunch."

Trace's stomach knotted. "Dammit, Maggie." He took the note from her hand, read the words and softly cursed. "Did you get a look at him?"

"No, but I took pictures of all the cars parked in the area, including their license numbers."

"Good thinking. Maybe something will turn up."

"The thing is, I was really careful, Trace. I watched every car behind me until I was miles out of town. If he followed me, I should have seen him. I don't know how I could have missed him."

"It isn't always that easy to spot a tail."

"I just... I'm telling you, I was careful. I can't figure out how he did it."

Maggie was no fool. If she had been that observant... An alarm went off in his head. "Stay here, I'll be right back."

He headed inside, went into the equipment room and picked up a handheld bug detector, which was small, but one of the best on the market. Returning to the parking lot, he went over the car front to back. As he neared the trunk, the red light began to flash, and he heard the warning sound of the beeper.

Cursing softly, he reached beneath the rear bumper and pulled off a little round circle of plastic with a shiny metal center.

He held it up. "This is how he found you—GPS tracking device."

"He bugged my car?" Maggie gasped. "Oh, my God!"

Trace looked at the piece of plastic in his hand. "Pretty sophisticated. It's motion sensitive. Only goes on when the car is moving. Saves the battery." He dropped the bug in his pocket. "This guy's not your usual nutcase, Maggie. This joker's got a brain. We need to check your house."

Her head jerked up. "My house? Oh, God, you don't… don't think he's put something like this in my condo?"

"If he had a key, he could have hidden a microphone somewhere inside before you moved in. Or on the day he went to the open house—assuming that was him."

"He…he couldn't have hidden a camera, could he? I mean, I would have noticed—wouldn't I?"

Trace didn't want to think about the bastard taking lewd pictures of Maggie. "Depends on the size of the device and how well it's hidden."

She shivered. "He could have been watching me for weeks."

Trace made no reply. They wouldn't know until they searched the condo. "I'll get my gear and follow you back to your house."

Maggie nodded, but her face was pale.

Trace returned to the equipment room for an even more powerful detector, one that could pick up video as well as GPS, audio and phone transmitters. Maggie was waiting in her car when he climbed into the Jeep, and they pulled out of the lot together.

At the condo, Ashley opened the door. "You're supposed to call Trace," she said. "He sounded pretty pissed."

Maggie flashed a sugary smile at him over her shoulder. "Trace is a man of iron control. He never gets pissed. Do you, Trace?"

He grunted as he carried his equipment into the house. "If anyone can make it happen, darlin', it's you."

Maggie smiled as if that somehow pleased her.

Women. He would never figure them out.

Maggie sat nervously on the sofa next to Ashley as Trace made his way methodically through the house with the equipment he had brought, a little silver box the size of a laptop computer. Terrified of what her stalker might have seen, she insisted he start upstairs.

"Nothing in your bedroom or bath," he called down to her. "No cameras, no listening devices."

She felt a rush of relief. "Thank God."

"I can't believe this," Ashley muttered. "Bugging your car? The guy's got some nerve." Dressed in a pair of khaki shorts that showed a long stretch of leg, and a pink midriff top, her short curls a little messy, she glowed with a vibrancy that had been missing when she had first arrived. Maggie felt good about that.

Trace checked the upstairs hall, began to scan her studio. When she heard the beeping sound, Maggie's stomach clenched. Jumping up from the sofa, she rushed for the stairs.

"Where is it?"

"Top of the closet door. With the door shut it's almost invisible. Even with it open, the thing is really hard to see." Trace showed her the tiny camera, then dragged a plastic bag out of the hip pocket of his jeans and slid the device inside.

"You think he could have left prints?" Maggie asked.

"I doubt it. But it's always worth a look." He headed downstairs, swept the guest bedroom using earbuds to hear the beeping, since the baby was asleep, then the guest bathroom and powder room. Finding nothing, he headed into the living room, and finally checked the kitchen.

He was almost finished when the beeping began again. Maggie's stomach sank. "Where?"

"Behind the decorative trim over the sink." He pointed upward. "Lens looks out through the ornamental holes in the design."

Maggie walked over to where Trace was pulling down the second tiny camera. "Why would he put them in the studio and kitchen instead of the bedroom?"

Trace slid the camera into the bag, his dark brows drawing together. He shook his head. "I don't think he wanted to interfere with your privacy. His notes sound old-fashioned, almost gallant. 'Dearest Maggie. Precious Maggie.' The song he played comes from *The Prince and The Maiden,* which is set during a more chivalrous time. Maybe that's the way he thinks of himself."

"Like some knight in shining armor?" She rolled her eyes. "Give me a break."

"Could be."

"That's creepy," Ashley said as she walked into the kitchen.

Trace's jaw hardened. "Yeah."

A sharp knock sounded at the door and a jolt of adrenaline shot through Maggie. She set a hand over her pounding heart and started for the entry, but Trace was already there. He looked through the keyhole, then pulled open the door.

"Jason. What the hell are you doing here?"

The man who walked in was over six feet tall, young and blond and extremely good-looking.

"You went to Emily's," he said hotly. "She wouldn't tell me what you wanted, but she's totally freaked out. I want to know what the hell you said to her."

Trace closed the door. "You need to take it easy."

"I'm not taking it easy. My father is dead. I don't believe he killed himself. I don't think you do, either. I want to know what the hell is going on."

Trace released a slow breath. "You're right. You deserve to know the truth. I should have followed my gut and told you last week. If you'll calm down, we can talk about it right now."

Maggie sensed that some of the fight went out of him. For the first time he seemed to realize the scene he was causing in someone else's home.

"Sorry," he said.

Trace turned. "Maggie, this is Jason Sommerset, Hewitt's son. Jason, this is Maggie O'Connell and her sister, Ashley."

Jason nodded at Maggie. "Nice to meet you." He was dressed in perfectly tailored tan slacks, a short-sleeved burgundy sweater and a pair of expensive Italian loafers. He turned to Ashley and opened his mouth to greet her, but no words came out. She was just that pretty.

"Nice to meet you, Jason," she said with a smile, which gave him time to find his voice.

"You, too, Ashley."

"How'd you know where to find me?" Trace asked.

"Annie told me. I kind of pressured her into it."

Trace chuckled. "Nobody pressures Annie. She probably figured you had a right to know what was happening." He tipped his head toward the door. "We can talk outside." He spoke to Maggie. "Excuse us a minute, will you?"

"The patio's nice and private. There are chairs out there. I'll bring you a glass of iced tea."

Jason was still staring at Ashley. They had the same crystal-blue eyes, which at the moment were locked together as if they were in combat and the first to look away would lose the war.

Trace clamped the younger man on the shoulder. "Come on, son. I should have listened to my instincts and told you the truth from the start."

Trace's words broke the spell and Jason's gaze swung back to him. "It's about damned time," he said.

The men walked out to the patio through the sliding glass door in the living room, and Ashley's gaze followed.

"So who is he?" she asked with an elaborate show of nonchalance that spoke louder than words.

"Jason's father was the late Hewitt Sommerset, founder of Sommerset Industries."

"Jason said something about his father...that he didn't believe he killed himself. Does Trace think he was murdered?"

"That's what he's trying to find out."

Through the glass door, they watched as Trace and Jason sat down around the umbrella table Maggie had purchased after moving into the house.

"Good-looking guy, huh?" Maggie said, keeping an eye on her sister.

Ashley shrugged. "I know all about good-looking men. Most of them aren't worth the powder to blow them up."

Maggie laughed. "There have to be a few good ones out there." Her gaze went to Trace, sitting on her patio as if he belonged there. If he was half the man he seemed, he was definitely a white-hat guy.

"I guess so," Ashley said halfheartedly.

"Jason seems nice enough."

"They all do," she said drily.

Maggie didn't pursue the topic. Clearly, her sister's experience with "Ziggy" was enough to sour her on men. At least for the moment.

Walking into the kitchen, Maggie took out two

glasses and filled them with ice. She leaned into the fridge for a pitcher of tea, filled the glasses and set them on a tray. As she started for the patio, she noticed Ashley looking through the glass doors at Jason.

More than once, she saw Jason glancing back.

Jason fisted a hand on the patio table. "You're telling me that my brother-in-law—my sister's husband—may have murdered my father."

"We don't know that. We know he was embezzling money. We know he was stashing it away in an offshore account. We know there's a chance your father confronted him. The rest is only conjecture."

"Parker was out that night, not home like he said. Emily told you that."

"That's what she said."

Jason shot up from the chair. "That bastard killed my father. I know it."

Trace stood up across from him. "You don't know anything—not for sure. And until you do, you have to hang on to that temper of yours. If you don't, you'll only make things worse."

"I'll kill him, I swear it."

"That's just great. You'll go to jail for the rest of your life—exactly what your dad would have wanted. That attitude of yours is the reason I didn't tell you in the first place."

Jason sank back down in his chair. His head tipped forward and he ran his fingers through the golden hair at his temples. Finally, he straightened. "I guess you're right."

"You guess?"

"Okay, you're right."

"That's more like it. If you're going to be the head of the family—and run Sommerset Industries—you're going to have to man up, make some tough decisions. This is one of them."

The sliding door opened just then and Maggie walked out carrying a pitcher and glasses. The sun flashed on her fiery hair and the muscles across Trace's belly clenched. She put the tray on the table and set a glass of tea in front of each of them.

"Thank you," Jason said.

She smiled. "It looked like it was getting a little heated out here."

Jason flushed at the innuendo. Trace figured the heat he was feeling had nothing to do with the weather and everything to do with how badly he wanted to take the woman in front of him to bed. She turned and went back inside, and he watched the way her jeans cupped her sweet little ass. For an instant, he wished he could turn himself into a piece of denim.

"So what do we do?" Jason asked, forcing Trace's thoughts in a safer direction.

"We've done our homework. The police are all over this. They want Parker nearly as much as you do."

"Not even close."

"Maybe not, but the result is the same. Parker winds up in prison for the rest of his life."

Jason gritted his teeth. "He deserves to fry."

"Yes, he does, but maybe this is better." Trace's smile was grim. "You ever think what a nice little play toy Parker will be for some big roughneck bastard inside those walls? Parker's cushy days are over."

Jason's smile looked equally grim. "I guess maybe I could live with that."

"That's better. That's the attitude your dad would expect from you." Trace took a sip of his tea, tasted the sweetness, felt the chill slide through him. He flicked a glance toward the door, wishing the drink could cool his blood.

Jason's gaze followed his. "The redhead…she your girlfriend?"

"My client," Trace said.

"She's hot."

Trace took another cooling sip. "Yeah."

"What's the, um, story on the blonde?"

He'd been waiting for the question. The attraction between Jason and Ashley had hummed clear across the room. "I don't know too much about her. She's Maggie's half sister. Had it rough, I guess. But seems to have gotten herself pretty well squared away now. She has a baby."

Jason's head came up. "A baby? She's just a kid."

"She's old enough, only a few years younger than you. Maggie says she recently turned twenty-one."

Jason took a drink of his tea. "So she's married."

Trace shook his head. "Nope."

"Where's the kid's dad?"

"Blew her off, I guess. Or maybe she blew him off. He was kind of a no-good, I think. Makes you appreciate the father you had."

Jason looked back at the house, to where Ashley stood near the sliding glass door. She was as beautiful as Jason was handsome, Trace noted.

"When all this is over, maybe… Would you mind if I asked her out?"

"Up to you. Just be careful. Ashley doesn't deserve to be hurt any more than she has been already."

The younger man nodded.

Sensing their conversation had come to an end, Maggie appeared at the door, slid it open and stepped out on the patio. She turned and smiled, and Trace felt as if he'd been sucker punched. He cast a glance at Jason, wondered if the kid's momentary loss of speech when he'd met Ashley meant he'd felt the same thing.

Whatever it was that the two women shared seemed to run in the family.

Trace found no prints on the bug or the video cameras. He hadn't expected he would. On Tuesday, a crew installed surveillance cameras at the front and back of Maggie's town house.

Trace also called Mark Sayers to tell him about the cameras hidden in Maggie's condo and the GPS tracking device on her car.

"She's not making this stuff up," Trace told the detective. "Whatever she might have done as a kid, this is no joke. Maggie's got a serious problem."

"Yeah, well, sounds like you might have one, too. You'd better be careful, buddy. You don't exactly have a sterling record where women are concerned—especially redheads."

Trace clenched his jaw. "Just do your job, Sayers. Make sure the department knows what the hell is going on."

"She needs to file a report."

"She's already filed a report. I'll be happy to file another one if that's what it takes."

"Okay, okay, take it easy. I'll put out the word."

"Thanks." Trace hung up the phone and sat there thinking about the department and Hoyt Varner, wondering how far the captain was willing to go to get revenge for his son after all these years. Far enough to put Maggie's life in danger? The guy was a police officer. Trace had trouble convincing himself he would go that far.

At least the trap was up and working. He didn't have much faith in it, especially not after seeing the sophisticated equipment the stalker had installed in the house and car. Still, maybe the guy would call, and they would get lucky and be able to trace it back to the point of origin.

The week slid past. There weren't any new incidents and nothing showed up on the outside video cams. Trace's biggest worry was Maggie's upcoming gallery show.

The Friday night opening, which was also a benefit for a local children's shelter, had been featured in the newspapers and on TV, a very exclusive, invitation-only preview of Maggie's latest work. That much publicity could mean trouble.

It also gave them the best opportunity they'd had so far of catching the stalker.

Surveillance equipment didn't come cheap, especially not the quality that had been used on Maggie's car and in the apartment. That meant the guy had money. At five hundred dollars a ticket, the average Joe wouldn't be at the gallery opening. But the stalker could likely afford it.

The only possible description of the stalker they had came from the Realtor, Jim Brewer: big, in his forties, distinguished-looking, with silver-streaked dark hair. Unfortunately, that description fit a lot of men.

Trace would be watching, ready for any sort of trouble. But the guy was smart and he wouldn't want to give himself away. There was a good chance he wouldn't show up and the evening would go off as smoothly as planned.

If that was the case…

Trace thought of the weekend ahead. He wanted Maggie O'Connell. He was tired of playing the gentleman.

Unless work interfered, on Friday night he intended to do a helluva lot more than just be her escort.

Chapter 13

The weather changed later in the week, turning overcast and cloudy. By Friday evening, big black thunderclouds hung over the city, the harbinger of a heavy spring storm.

Maggie thought there might be fewer people at the opening, but maybe not. Since the ticket proceeds were going to the Weyman's Children's Shelter, publicity for the show had been overwhelming. It had become a who's-who-in-society event.

Wearing a long, slender, emerald-sequined gown with narrow rhinestone straps, Maggie paced from the living room to the front door and back.

Ashley sat on the sofa watching the Food Network, to which she seemed addicted. Nestled in her lap, the baby made soft little sucking noises as his mama gave him his bottle.

Ashley grinned at the show on TV. "Isn't she great?"

"Who?" Distracted as she waited for Trace, Maggie looked over at the screen.

"Giada De Laurentiis. Not only is she beautiful, but she's a really terrific cook." Her dream, Ashley had confessed, was to work in one of the nicer restaurants in town. Eventually, she hoped to attend one of the exclusive culinary schools in Houston and become a chef.

"She certainly has a following," Maggie said, thinking that Ashley had chosen a fine ambition. And since she loved to experiment with new recipes, Maggie was reaping the reward. Which meant she needed to get out on the racquetball court and burn a few calories.

She checked her watch, made another quick trip to the powder room to check her lipstick, then returned to the living room and began to pace again.

"Don't you know you're supposed to keep a man waiting?" Ashley said from the sofa. "You're at least fifteen minutes early."

"I know, I know. I'm a little nervous about the show."

"Oh, and here I thought it was because that hot cowboy of yours was going to be your date."

Maggie cast her a glare. "He's not my cowboy, he's my bodyguard. That was made perfectly clear."

"Okay, but if you don't come home tonight, I'm not going to panic, okay? I'll set the security alarm when you leave, and if the creep calls, I'll write down the time and date."

Maggie thought of the night she had found the porcelain figurine on the counter, and worry filtered through her. "You've got my cell number. If something happens—"

"I've got it. Stop worrying."

Maggie walked into the kitchen. She didn't feel quite right about leaving Ashley and the baby alone. But the alarm was working, and half of Houston knew she would be at the opening. If the guy was truly obsessed with her, surely he would show up there.

Maggie hoped so. She hoped she would be able to figure out who he was, get him to stop his harassment and get her life back in order.

She looked out the window over the kitchen sink. "Oh, my God, he's here." But she wasn't exactly sure the long white stretch limo that pulled up in front of the condo wasn't there for someone else. Not until the driver opened the rear door, and Trace set a hand on the crown of his hat, ducked his head and stepped out.

A gold box glittered in his hand as he walked toward the town house, and Maggie hurried to let him in. Her heart was pounding. It was ridiculous, but she couldn't stop a little thrill of anticipation.

"Don't act so eager," Ashley called out from the living room. "You're supposed to play hard to get."

Maggie grinned. "I am hard to get, but thanks for the advice." She took a deep breath and pulled open the door the instant Trace knocked, stepping back as he walked in.

Except for his crisp white shirt, he was dressed all in black: black Western tuxedo, black ostrich cowboy boots, black felt hat with a silver concho band. He looked like the Marlboro man on the way to a White House dinner, and he looked delicious.

A little curl of heat settled low in her stomach. "A limo? You didn't have to do that." But she loved that he had been so thoughtful.

"You're the star tonight. You ought to get star treatment." He handed her the gold box. When she lifted the lid, a gorgeous purple-throated, white-ruffled orchid nestled in gold-flecked tissue.

"It's beautiful," she said a little breathlessly.

"So are you." Those whiskey-brown eyes slid over her, moving from the loose red curls on her shoulders, pulled up on one side to show off her diamond earrings, to the soft cleavage the dress exposed, all the way to the rhinestones on her strappy high heels. "You're gonna knock 'em dead tonight, darlin'."

A rush of pleasure poured through her. Trace took out the corsage and slipped it on her wrist, and unexpected moisture stung her eyes.

"I never got to go to the prom," she said. After the incident with Josh, she'd been forced to hide out at home. Then she had moved to another school and none of the boys had asked the new girl to go. She smiled softly. "I feel like a prom queen tonight."

Something moved across his features, something hot and fierce. He understood, she realized, and her heart squeezed a little.

"Night's just gettin' started, darlin'." The words and the smoldering look in his hot, dark eyes made her breath catch.

"Have a good time, kiddies," Ashley called out from the living room. "I promise I won't wait up."

"Smart-ass," Maggie called back with a smile, and Trace laughed.

"You remembered to put my cell number in your phone, didn't you?" Trace asked Ashley.

"I've got both your numbers in my phone. Just go!"

His hand settled at Maggie's waist, guiding her toward the door, then outside to the car. Dressed in full chauffeur apparel including a jaunty little short-brimmed cap, the tall, slim, very efficient looking driver held open the door.

Maggie slid into the car, sinking into the deep red leather seat, and Trace slid in beside her. Tiny white lights lit the interior, which was partitioned off from the front. A silver ice bucket in the mahogany bar on one side held a bottle of Dom Pérignon.

"You thought of everything," she said, properly impressed.

"I guess we'll see." Trace's eyes touched hers as the car eased out of the parking lot. Reaching for the bottle, he unwired and popped the cork, poured the bubbling liquid into a crystal flute and handed it over, then poured one for himself. "I'm on duty, so this is all I'll have for now."

"Same here. I need to be at my best tonight."

"Honey, there's no doubt of that." He lifted his glass. "To the most successful opening you've ever had."

Raising hers, she silently added, *and to catching the maniac who is destroying my life.* She clinked her glass against Trace's, praying her stalker would be there. Hoping he would say or do something that would give him away.

"Your sister seems to be settling in okay," Trace said, resting his broad shoulders back against the seat.

"She wants to be a chef." Maggie smiled. "She's already a darned good cook."

"Sounds promising."

"I really like her. She's funny and smart. She's a great mother. She really loves that baby."

"How about you?" He took a sip of his champagne. "You like kids?"

Maggie shrugged, felt the slight friction of the rhinestone straps against her bare shoulders. "I've never had time to really consider having a family. Being a successful photographer meant everything to me. Making that happen took up most of my time."

"And now?"

"Now I have time to consider what's really important to me." She studied him from beneath her lashes. "How about you?"

He didn't answer right away, just took another sip

of champagne. "I got married, planned to have kids. It didn't work out."

She could tell it was a touchy subject, but she was curious. "That was then. How about now?"

Beneath the brim of his dressy, black felt hat, his eyes cut toward the window. "I've still got a bad taste in my mouth."

Maggie didn't press for more. She wasn't looking for a long-term relationship. Apparently neither was he. She told herself a no-strings affair was exactly what she wanted. That things might just work out. It could be good for both of them. Couldn't it?

It didn't take nearly long enough for the limo to turn onto Westheimer Road and pull into the line of cars arriving at the Twin Oaks Gallery. A red carpet stretched from the curb to the etched-glass front door, and valets parked the vehicles that pulled up to the curb.

A slew of reporters, both newspaper and local TV, took photos of the glamorous attendees making their way up the velvet-roped walkway.

Not exactly the Academy Awards, but an event like this was a first for Maggie and she was excited, and more than a little nervous. It occurred to her that she was glad Trace was with her, bodyguard or not. He had a way of steadying her, keeping her calm.

Well, at least until she looked at him. Then her mind shot off in the direction of sex, and she had to rein in her thoughts.

"We're almost there," he said, sitting forward in the seat to peer outside. Just ahead of them, a shiny red Ferrari and two big black SUVs with dark tinted windows pulled up to the curb.

"The Ferrari…that's Matthew Bergman," she said. "His father's a big patron of the arts and a well-known philanthropist. Matthew's a photography buff."

"I've done some work for the father," Trace said, causing Maggie to speculate on the endless number of business contacts he seemed to have. It occurred to her that Trace was a very well respected man.

The first SUV pulled up to the curb. "That's Senator Logan and his wife." Maggie watched as a man with silver hair stepped out of the car, followed by an attractive woman in a long, beaded, burgundy gown. "The second car is probably his aide, Richard Meyers, and his publicity spokesman, Duncan Ross. Now that Logan's running for governor, he rarely travels without an entourage."

It was their turn next. The limo rolled to a stop and one of a swarm of red-vested valets opened the door. "Welcome to the Twin Oaks Gallery," the young man said.

"Here we go," said Trace, and Maggie took a steadying breath. As she slid out of the limo, camera lights came on and several microphones appeared in front of her.

"This is quite an event, Ms. O'Connell." A short, slightly overweight reporter leaned toward her. "The proceeds from the tickets go to charity. Have you done this kind of thing before?"

"I've donated photos to help raise money for various nonprofit organizations, but nothing like this. The Weyman's Children's Shelter is a very good cause. When they approached me with the idea of combining the benefit with the gallery opening, I was happy to agree."

"Who's your escort?" one of the female reporters asked. Her gaze swept over Trace as if he were a juicy piece of meat, and her red lips curved in a smile of female awareness.

"Just a friend," Trace replied, before Maggie could answer. Not that it would stay secret for long.

They walked up the red carpet and went into the gallery, which was beginning to fill with guests. Soft music played in the background while waiters in short white jackets hurried by with flutes of champagne on silver trays.

Standing just inside the door, Faye Langston, the owner of the gallery, spotted Maggie and approached, a glass of champagne in her hand. She was tall and svelt, with heavy dark hair cut in a straight style that framed her face. Her nose was too long, which made her striking instead of beautiful.

Faye bent and kissed Maggie's cheek. "We sold every ticket," she said proudly. "The shelter will come out with a nice bit of money. Now all we have to do is sell some of your work."

Maggie hoped they would. Faye and Maggie were both donating a percentage of their profits to the shelter, which they hoped would help increase sales.

"Faye, this is Trace Rawlins. He owns Atlas Security. Trace, this is Faye Langston, the owner of the gallery."

"A pleasure to meet you, Ms. Langston," Trace said, removing his black felt hat. One of the waiters appeared out of nowhere to take it, and Trace ran a hand through his thick dark hair, which settled neatly in place. Maggie felt an urge to reach over and do the same.

Faye smiled up at him. "It's nice to meet you, Trace, and I hope you'll call me Faye." A slow, knowing smile curved her lips. "I'm sure you'll take good care of our guest of honor tonight."

Trace's dark gaze drifted over Maggie. "That's my plan," he drawled, with such an undercurrent of heat, Maggie's stomach contracted.

"Oh, look, there's Senator Logan...." Faye waved and smiled. "If you two will excuse me..." With a wink at Maggie, she silently slipped away.

Now that Maggie was actually there, she was beginning to relax. Dozens of her photos hung on the walls around her, each framed in a way that best displayed the work. Color and light, background and subject matter all came into play.

She had chosen the frames herself, and Faye had hired a calligrapher to make the delicate signs below each picture that included the title Maggie had selected, the date and place the photo had been taken. Each shot was limited to a certain number of prints that could be made and sold—an edition of twenty-five for this particular show—and each framed photo was personally signed. Looking at them now, she felt pleased and proud of the job she had done.

"You take beautiful pictures, Maggie," Trace said, his gaze fixed on a shot of the harbor during an approaching storm, a piece she had titled *Ferocity*. The shadowy light of day was fading as a seething wall of vicious black clouds rolled ominously toward shore. In the distance, a tiny sailboat raced frantically against time and weather to reach the safety of the harbor before the storm swept it away. "There's something special about each one, something that makes it unique."

Maggie smiled, appreciating the compliment a little more because it came from him. "I remember that day very well. The scene was so compelling I had to stop and take the shot, but at the same time it was frightening. I was afraid for the little boat. I stayed to watch until I was sure it reached the harbor."

Trace cast her an assessing glance, but made no comment. People began to approach her, the crowd growing, surrounding her, wanting a piece of her time.

"I'm gonna wander a little," Trace said, giving her room to do what she was there for. Be the celebrity of the evening. And help Faye sell her work.

* * *

"Hello, Trace. It's good to see you."

He turned at the sound of a female voice. "Mrs. Logan. It's always a pleasure." At fifty, Teresa Logan was beginning to show the strain of life as a senator's wife. Fine lines marked the corners of her eyes and settled around her mouth. Her blond hair had begun to thin. There had been a time when she had been as beautiful as her daughter.

Cassidy appeared just then, looked up at him and smiled. "Hello, Trace." They had dated the summer after Cassidy's graduation from high school. She had just turned eighteen, a feisty little auburn-haired girl with big, innocent blue eyes. Trace had just finished two years at community college.

Cassidy was married to a prominent surgeon now, her hair now blond and swept up in a sophisticated style.

"It's good to see you, Cassidy."

"It's certainly been a while." She smiled. "I hope you're doing well?"

"Business is good. Life is good. How about you?"

Before she could answer, her father, the senator, appeared at her side. "Trace. It's good to see you." Reasonably tall, with a solid build, and at sixty still setting women's hearts aflutter, Senator Logan was all smiles tonight, though when Trace had been dating his daughter, the man had done everything in his power to end the relationship.

He needn't have worried. It was never serious between them. Cassidy had bigger fish to fry and Trace had been set on a career in the army. Still, they had liked each other, which was enough to worry a man with the kind of political ambitions Garrett Logan had, even back then.

"Trace, this is my aide, Richard Meyers." Slenderly

built, Meyers was dressed in expensive clothes and gold aviator-style glasses. He was vain, Trace guessed, with plenty of ambition.

"And this is my media coordinator, Duncan Ross, and his wife, Elaine." Duncan was a balding man in his forties, with sincerity stamped all over his face. Elaine was short and plump and looked like a well-dressed housewife, which only added to her husband's credibility.

"Nice to meet you," Trace said.

"Trace is an old friend of Cassidy's."

Cassidy rolled her pretty blue eyes. "Not that old, Daddy, please."

The senator laughed. His expensive black tuxedo fit him perfectly, the ideal contrast to his leonine mane of silver hair. "Trace and Cassidy dated for a few weeks one summer."

"We were just friends," Trace said. "At the time, her father was terrified his little girl was going to run off and marry some cowboy with horse manure on his boots. But Cassidy was a lot smarter than that."

Everyone laughed.

"Trace joined the Rangers and I went off to college," Cassidy explained. "That's where I met Jonathan."

Trace smiled and shrugged. "And the rest, as they say, is history."

"I'm sorry Jonathan couldn't be here tonight," Cassidy said. "I would have liked for you to meet him."

"I'd have liked that, too."

They chatted for a while. Trace had never been a fan of Garrett Logan or his politics; in the last election, he had voted for the other candidate. But Logan was a smooth talker with the good looks and style that won voter confidence. Now, tired of the D.C. scene, he was running for governor. Odds were he'd win that, too.

The conversation waned and Trace excused himself. He started toward Maggie, who had never been completely out of his sight, and saw that she was still in conversation with a group of admirers. He flashed her a glance, caught one in return and began to make his way around the room. He was looking for anyone who fit the description the Realtor had given them, or anyone who seemed to be taking more than a casual interest in Maggie.

There were only a few big men in the right age bracket, with salt-and-pepper hair. Trace made a point of introducing himself to each one and getting his name, but none pushed any of his hot buttons. Though there was always a chance something would turn up when he plugged their identities into the computer.

On the other hand, there seemed to be an endless number of men who took a more than casual interest in Maggie.

One was there now, good-looking, late thirties, dark hair and blue eyes. He had managed to separate her from the other guests vying for her attention. Trace felt a shot of adrenaline that tested his careful control. He told himself it wasn't jealousy, and headed in Maggie's direction.

Chapter 14

Maggie noticed Trace bearing down on her, and darted a glance around, expecting to see the stalker. Then she realized he was glaring at Roger, and relaxed. The photography instructor was hardly a threat. He was the man responsible for a good deal of her success.

"Trace, I'm glad you're here. I'd like you to meet Roger Weller. I told you about him. I worked for Roger when I was in college. He was my mentor and I owe him a great deal."

Roger gave her a lazy smile. "And I've been trying to collect for years." His gaze ran over her, leaving no doubt as to what he meant. "So far it hasn't worked."

Maggie felt Trace stiffen beside her. "Is that so?"

"Roger and I are just friends," she said firmly. "He doesn't even live in Houston anymore, he lives in L.A." She cast Roger a warning glance. He had always seemed to want more from their relationship than Maggie was willing to give, but he had never really pressed her. "I was his assistant. Roger taught me everything I know about photography."

"I would have taught you a whole lot more, honey, if you'd just given me the chance," he teased.

"Roger, please." She looked up at Trace, saw his jaw clench. "He's kidding. We've always had a very professional relationship."

"That's right. Maggie didn't believe in mixing business with pleasure."

Trace pinned him with a glare. "Too bad for you, I guess."

"It's nice seeing you, Roger," Maggie said, taking hold of Trace's arm. "Now, if you'll excuse us, I'm afraid I need to mingle."

"I'm in town for a while before I head back," Roger told her. "Maybe we can have lunch."

Maggie tried not to look at Trace, knew the temper she would see in his eyes if she did. Clearly, his disposition wasn't nearly as calm as he liked to think.

She managed to smile. "I'm awfully busy, but maybe we can work something out."

Roger's mouth faintly curved.

Maggie turned and led Trace away before his testosterone got the best of him.

"Maybe you can work something out?" he said darkly.

"I was just trying to be polite. Besides, it isn't as if we're involved. You're here as my bodyguard, nothing more. It really isn't any of your business."

"Oh, we're involved. As soon as we get out of here, I'm going to show you exactly how involved we are."

Maggie's breath stalled. When she looked into those hot brown eyes, her heart skipped several beats. "You... you what?"

"One more word about *Roger* and I'll haul you into the back room and show you right now."

Maggie's eyes widened. Dear God, he meant it! She could tell by the way his teeth were clenched, by the muscle that worked in his jaw. He was jealous, and more than a little aroused.

"We…we can't leave—not yet."

Trace took the words exactly as she meant them. She wasn't going to stop him. She wanted him to kiss her, touch her, make love to her.

Beneath his tuxedo jacket, his broad shoulders relaxed. "That's all right, darlin'. We've got all night."

Her pulse started racing even faster than it was before. And now that she knew his intensions, knew what was going to happen after they left the gallery, she didn't want to waste any more time than she had to.

The hours seemed to drag after that. Champagne flowed and trays of sumptuous hors d'oeuvres were devoured, refilled and greedily consumed again. More guests arrived. The police chief, Charley Benton, a stout man with a receding hairline, stopped by. Maggie spotted him talking to Senator Logan, their heads bent close together, Benton laughing at something the senator said. The newspapers had mentioned their close relationship and that Benton was backing the senator's bid for governor.

"You're selling a lot of pieces," Trace said as a framed photo titled *Taste the Wind* was tagged with a red sticker to indicate it was sold. It showed a deserted stretch of shore, palm trees bent like ballet dancers, their fronds moving gracefully to the wind's relentless song.

A framed O'Connell photograph, depending on its size, went for as much as twenty-seven hundred dollars. Of course, there were a lot of expenses, and the gallery took a hefty share of the profit.

Trace's attention turned to the photograph beside it.

"I'm partial to this one, *Harbor Sunset*. Makes me want to go sailing."

Maggie had taken the picture at dusk, a snapshot down a long row of gleaming white powerboats docked in the Blue Fin Marina near Seabrook. People, just small specks in the photo, sat on their decks sipping icy drinks, mesmerized by the sunset casting soft, red-gold light over the bay. "Someone else must have liked it, too," Trace added.

Maggie smiled at the Sold sticker. "I guess your champagne toast worked. This was definitely the most successful show I've ever had."

His gaze sharpened. "Was? Past tense? Does that mean you're ready to leave?"

His dark eyes glinted. She read the heat, the promise. "Yes…" was all she said.

Trace made a brief call on his cell, and a few minutes later the limousine appeared in the alley behind the gallery. Just as Maggie had done several times during the evening, he checked his phone to be sure no message had come from Ashley. Then he waited as Maggie said a quick goodbye to Faye Langston and disappeared quietly out the back door.

He took off his tuxedo jacket and tossed it onto the seat, then helped her in and climbed in beside her. They both leaned back with a sigh. "You did good, kid," Trace said.

Maggie grinned. "I did, didn't I?"

She turned toward him, removed his hat and set it up in the rear window behind the seat, then ran a hand through his hair, setting the heavy dark strands back into proper position. "I've been wanting to do that all evening."

"That so? Well, this is what I've been wanting to do."

Catching her chin, he tilted her head back and settled his mouth over hers. Soft, moist lips. Warm, sweet breath. Instantly, he went hard.

"Damn, I want you," he said between nibbling kisses, slow, easy ones that had them both breathing faster. His control slipped a little as her lips parted and his tongue slid in to taste her. Maggie kissed him back and the kisses he'd meant only as a prelude deepened, turned hot and fierce. His insides tightened and his groin throbbed.

One of the rhinestone straps on her gown slipped off her shoulder. Trace pressed his mouth against her bare skin, inhaled the floral scent of her perfume. Maggie made a soft little sigh as he slid the second strap off, eased the gown down to her waist, leaving her breasts exposed. Her nipples were big and pink and pretty. He took one into his mouth, suckled, tasted, felt it harden against his tongue, and heard himself groan.

"Trace…" she whispered, arching upward, urging him to take more of her. Her breasts were full and tilted slightly upward. Her skin was pale and as soft as the petals of a rose. He took what he wanted, took his fill, and reveled in her sweet little mews of pleasure.

He wanted more.

He told himself he couldn't take her, not here. Not in the backseat of a car. But his hands gripped the hem of her sequined gown and shoved it up to her waist. She was wearing a tiny black lace scrap of a thong. He pushed it aside and his gaze fell on the tangle of ruby curls between her legs. The elastic snapped in his fingers as if it wished to do his bidding, and he eased her thighs apart and began to stroke her.

She was wet and slick and he ached to be inside her. Lust clouded his senses, a red haze that blinded him and urged him on. He could hardly breathe, hardly think.

"I need you," he said, kissing her again, plundering her mouth, inhaling her scent. His hands found her breasts, teased, caressed them. "I don't want to stop."

"Don't...don't stop, Trace, please."

Insanity took over, destroying his resolve. All he knew was heat and driving need. When he felt her unbuttoning his pleated white shirt, felt her fingers gliding over the muscles of his chest, he hardened to the point of pain. When she tugged the shirt from the waistband of his slacks, began to work his zipper, he nearly came.

"Maggie... God..."

"I want you, Trace. I can't wait any longer."

He knew better. Tried to fight for control. He had planned to take her back to his house, seduce her slowly, properly. Instead, he stroked her, felt her tremble, heard her moan. He didn't remember opening the condom, sheathing himself. He just felt the swift, hot burst of pleasure as he thrust himself deeply inside.

He tried to slow down, give her time to adjust, but when she moved beneath him, when she whispered his name with a sob, he completely lost control.

Long strokes claimed her. Deep, hard, penetrating strokes made her his. He wanted more. He took her and took her, made her come and then come again before he allowed himself to take his pleasure.

His pulse still thundered as he slowly spiraled down. Beneath his hand, the beating of her heart matched his own. He had told the driver to take his time, and thank God, the man had listened. It wasn't until Trace heard the deep male voice over the intercom telling him they had almost reached their destination that his thoughts began to focus and he realized what he had done.

Silently cursing, he eased himself from the soft warmth beneath him, got rid of the condom he barely remembered putting on.

"Dammit, I didn't mean for that to happen."

She adjusted her position on the seat, pulled her skirt down and the narrow rhinestone straps back into place. She looked up at him, and in the glow from the tiny white lights illuminating the interior, he saw her smile.

"That was some ride, cowboy."

Heat rose at the back of his neck. "I was planning a more subtle seduction."

Maggie reached out and cupped his cheek. "Were you?"

He turned his head, kissed her palm. "Don't think for a minute we're done here. I'm not through with you, lady. Not by a long shot."

She smiled as if that had been her plan all along. "Ashley said she wouldn't wait up."

His mouth faintly curved. "I'd kiss you again, but if I do, I'm afraid of what the driver might see when he opens the door."

Maggie laughed.

They climbed out of the car and he led her up the walk. He turned off the alarm, then lifted her into his arms and carried her inside. He heard his high-tech doggy door squeak, knew Rowdy had trotted into the kitchen from the backyard. Trace kept walking. Inside the master bedroom, he closed the door.

It was getting late but he wasn't the least bit tired. He was taking Maggie O'Connell to bed, and sleep was the last thing on his mind.

The storm had politely waited to break until they'd reached the safety of Trace's house. Maggie lay snuggled against him, his solid length and hard-muscled body a comfort as lightning flashed and thunder rumbled outside the bedroom window. Inside, she lay warm and content in his big king-size bed, beneath the soft breeze of a ceiling fan, and a lightweight down comforter.

They had made love twice since he had taken her to bed. The first time was the slow seduction he had promised, a melding of mouths and bodies, the soft give-and-take of a leisurely joining. The second time was more fierce, more demanding. Her cowboy had a sexual appetite as strong as she had suspected. He liked making love and he wasn't shy about taking what he wanted.

But his loving wasn't one-sided. Trace gave as much as he demanded.

As she curled against him in the darkness, one of his hard arms draped over her waist, she listened to the sound of his breathing, mixed with the heavy rumble of rain on the roof and the fierce sighs of the wind outside the window.

She thought of the pleasure he had given her, deeper, more consuming than anything she had experienced before. She thought of the way he had kissed her, caressed her, and a thread of desire curled through her.

Nestled spoon fashion against him, she felt his body begin to stir, felt the heavy length of his building erection. She could hardly believe it. Surely he couldn't want her again so soon.

"I can feel your heartbeat," he whispered against her ear. "I know what you're thinking." He bit down on the lobe. "I'm thinking it, too."

He moved a little, prepared himself. Maggie moaned as he entered her, began the rhythmical movements that aroused her, made her ache with yearning. He was big and hard, his strokes long and deep, quickening her blood and overwhelming her senses. Her body contracted around him, gloved him, milked him as he rode her. Pleasure rolled through her, dense and fierce, deep and drugging. Her climax hit hard, sucked her in and wouldn't let go. Her body was beginning to attune itself to his, to anticipate, to crave his invasion, relish it.

Trace groaned as he followed her to release, held her as she waited for her heartbeat to slow. Seconds ticked past. His muscles relaxed. His breathing went deeper and she knew he had settled back into sleep.

Maggie closed her eyes, weary and spent and wonderfully sated. But she didn't fall sleep. Instead, she listened to the heavy fall of rain and the wind whistling through the trees, her mind spinning back through the weeks since that day at the Texas Café. She had convinced herself what she felt for Trace was merely physical. He was really a hot guy and she was wildly attracted to him. That kind of desire was new to her and she wanted to experiment, find out what it was all about.

In college, she'd been attracted to Michael Irving's intelligence. Sex had been sort of a personal challenge, something to do to overcome the trauma after her night with Josh Varner. She'd met David Lyons and been attracted to his steady nature, his comfortable companionship. But she had needs, she had discovered during the time she had been with him. Sex was usually more her idea than his and never truly satisfying.

What she felt for Trace was different. Deeper, more alluring. Worrisome.

She didn't know what she wanted from him aside from more of his mind-boggling, incredible lovemaking.

She told herself that was enough.

Chapter 15

Maggie watched Trace step out of the shower, rubbing his hair with a fluffy white towel, another riding low on his hips. With those long legs, impressive pecs, six-pack abs and wide shoulders, he was gorgeous.

"I'll be dressed in a minute," he said.

"Okay, but I get to watch."

He just smiled and began to search through his underwear drawer. She'd already had coffee and fresh-baked Pillsbury orange-frosted breakfast rolls, courtesy of her host. He had let her shower first, and she was dressed and ready, wearing a pair of gray, lightweight drawstring sweatpants and a black T-shirt with a gold eagle on the front with the words Ranger Up printed underneath.

As bad as she looked, it beat the heck out of arriving home in a long green evening gown.

While Trace pulled on a pair of jeans, she used the rubber band on the newspaper she'd found in the kitchen to pull her hair back in a ponytail. All the while, she watched him, enjoying the play of muscle, the movement of crisp dark hair on his chest, the gleam of smooth suntanned skin.

"Keep looking at me that way and we aren't getting out of here for at least another hour."

Maggie laughed but her stomach dipped. After last night and this morning, sex should be the last thing on her mind.

"Okay, I'm going. I need another cup of coffee, anyway."

She made her way back to the kitchen, which was homey for a guy's, kind of a 1950s retro look with a chrome, Formica-topped table and red vinyl chairs, and red-and-white-checked curtains at the windows. The appliances, top of the line, were white. So were the cabinets and countertops.

Trace had given her a tour that morning. Three bedrooms, two baths and a powder room he had added himself. There was a dining room with a mahogany Duncan Phyfe table and six matching chairs.

"It belonged to my grandmother," he'd explained. "My dad and mom used it before I was born. I ended up with it. I guess I kind of like the way things were back then, you know? A quieter time and all. So I kept the stuff Dad had, and just worked around it, made it more my own."

One of the bedrooms had been converted into an office, with equipment as modern as money could buy: an iMac, a laptop, a printer that copied, faxed and scanned. A row of built-in mahogany file cabinets ran along one wall, and his matching desk was wide and fairly neat.

In the living room, a big flat-screen TV, at least fifty inches, was hidden away in a built-in mahogany cabinet so it didn't dominate the room. The sofa and chairs were burgundy, overstuffed and comfortable, the beige carpet a high-quality deep pile. Some nicely framed artwork hung on the walls, mostly Texas landscapes done in an impressionist style.

He'd done a good job. It was the kind of place a man would want to come home to. Or a place a young couple might raise a family. He'd told her he had wanted that once.

"I guess we'd better get going," he said as he walked into the living room. Along with his usual blue jeans he had on a light blue knit shirt and a pair of brown Rockports.

No hat today. Trace was a man of many facets. Maggie was coming to like each one.

A thought that got her moving. She didn't want to like him *too* much.

"I'm supposed to be at the gallery by noon," she said. "Faye and I plan to go over the sales, see which pieces were sold and have to be replaced. I need to get them reprinted, matted and framed. I only do them one at a time. Less chance of being damaged."

"There's something I'm going to ask you to do."

She looked up at him. "What's that?"

"Get me a list of your clients, people who've purchased your photos. You have one, right?"

"I do. But if you count the sales off the internet, you're talking about a lot of people."

"We don't have a choice. I'm running out of airspeed and altitude here. We can limit the time frame, go back just a couple of years. We're looking for collectors, people who purchased, say…at least three pieces."

"All right. It'll take me a little while to get the list into some kind of workable order. And some of my clients buy through art brokers. It'll take longer to run those names down."

"Do the best you can."

"Okay."

"I've got to stop by my office, check on a couple of things. It's right on the way to your house and it won't take a minute."

"That isn't a problem," Maggie said.

A few minutes later, Trace pulled the Jeep into the lot and turned off the engine. "You can come in if you want. Doesn't look like anyone's around."

She glanced down at her borrowed clothes. No way was she going anywhere but home. "That's okay, I'll just wait for you here."

He nodded, climbed out and disappeared inside the building. He had been gone only a few minutes when a sassy little silver BMW convertible pulled into the parking lot. Maggie watched as a petite redhead slid out from behind the wheel. She wore snug designer jeans, a crop top and high-heeled sandals. With her endless curves, brilliant blue eyes and straight, silky red hair, she wasn't just pretty, she was beautiful.

The office door opened just then and Trace walked out. An instant later, the gorgeous redhead threw herself into his arms.

Trace inwardly groaned as he spotted Carly sashaying toward him, hips swinging, a smile on her perfectly made-up face.

"Good morning, sugar." Before he realized her intent, Carly arms went around his neck and she kissed him full on the mouth. "Don't you look handsome today?"

He caught her wrists and set her back down on her feet, his gaze shooting to the Jeep, where Maggie watched from the passenger seat.

Carly reached up and undid a top button on his shirt.

"There, that's better. Mustn't hide all those pretty muscles."

Trace refastened the button. "I've got a friend with me, Carly. Is there something you need?"

"My, aren't we in a testy mood?" She turned and looked over at his Jeep. "Who is she? Do I know her?"

"No. Look, I've got to go. What is it you want?"

"I just happened to be driving by. I saw your car and thought maybe you'd buy me breakfast."

"I ate breakfast hours ago. You were probably still asleep." He glanced over at her little sports car. *Or maybe not.* "I thought you were seeing someone. I'm sure he wouldn't be too happy to know you were hanging around your ex-husband."

"I don't think of you as an ex, sugar. And who cares what Howard thinks? It's not like we're living together or anything."

"That's his car, isn't it?"

She gave him a kitty-cat smile. "It's *my* car. Howard bought it for me."

"I've gotta go, Carly. Take care of yourself." Trace started walking. He must have been completely insane to marry her. Jesus, what was he thinking? With his little head, obviously, instead of his big one.

He opened the door of the Jeep, climbed in and cranked the engine.

"Old friend?" Maggie asked. He didn't miss the sharp edge to her voice.

"My ex-wife."

Her eyes widened. "*That's* your ex-wife?"

"I would have introduced you, but Carly isn't someone you really want to meet."

Maggie sat up a little straighter. "She didn't look like an ex-someone. Looked more like a present-tense someone to me."

He turned, cast Maggie a look. "If you knew her, you'd understand. Once Carly gets her hooks into you, she doesn't let go. I've been trying to get rid of her for the last four years. So far it hasn't worked."

"How often do you sleep with her?"

The wheel jerked. Trace stepped on the brake, slowed the car and pulled over to the curb. "I don't sleep with Carly. Half the men in Houston have been in her bed, but in the past four years, not me."

Some of the fight went out of Maggie. "Look, it's none of my business. Last night was just a lark for both of us, anyway."

A muscle ticked in his cheek. "A lark? That's all it was to you?"

She shrugged.

"That's bullshit, Maggie. It was more than a lark and you know it." His temper was heating. Damn, the woman knew how to fire him up. He leaned over, caught her face between his hands and crushed his mouth down over hers. It was a hard, dominating, possessive kiss that told her exactly how he felt.

When he let her go, Maggie blinked up at him.

"It wasn't a lark," he said.

She swallowed.

"Say it."

"All right, it wasn't a lark. I'm not sure exactly what it was, but it wasn't that. Not to me."

He felt himself relax. "I don't know where this is going, Maggie. Apparently you don't, either. But we're going to find out. Okay?"

She just nodded. "Okay."

Trace put the car in gear, eased into traffic and drove on. All the while he was thinking that Maggie O'Connell was nothing at all like Carly.

Or at least he didn't think so.

* * *

As soon as Maggie got home, she dashed upstairs to change out of her borrowed clothes. Ashley was waiting in the entry when she came back down.

"Everything okay last night?" Maggie asked. "I didn't get a call, so I figured nothing happened."

"Nothing happened." Her sister flashed her a knowing grin. "Have fun last night?"

She felt the pull of a smile. "Actually, it was pretty amazing. At least until his ex-wife showed up this morning."

Ashley's grin faded. "He's still seeing her?"

"Says he isn't. The thing is, Carly's a redhead, just like me."

"So…?"

"So the first time I met him, the woman at the café said Trace had a thing for redheads. Maybe that's the only reason he's interested in me. Maybe he has some kind of hang-up about it or something."

"If you were a blonde and he had a blonde ex-wife, you wouldn't think anything about it."

That was true and it made her feel better. And Carly didn't really look that much like her. Carly was shorter, curvier. Even her hair was a lighter, more coppery shade of red. She was prettier, but there was nothing Maggie could do about that.

"Maybe you're right." She glanced toward the guest bedroom. "Robbie down for his nap?"

Ashley nodded. "Listen, I need to talk to you."

Maggie started walking toward the kitchen. "Okay, so talk." Ashley fell in beside her. "I need some tea," Maggie said. "Want a glass?"

"That'd be great."

She leaned into the fridge and took out the pitcher of sweet tea she usually kept there.

"There's leftover pot roast with a burgundy demi-glaze sauce left over from supper last night."

"Wow. Sounds good." Maggie had been eating like royalty since her sister arrived, a perk she hadn't expected. "But I've got to get down to the gallery. Save me enough for a sandwich when I get home."

Maggie filled a couple glasses with ice and poured the tea, handing Ashley a glass and filling one for herself. "So what's up?"

"I don't exactly know how to say this. It's not that I'm ungrateful or anything, but I've been living here, sponging off you for a couple of weeks now. It's time I got a job. I need to make some money to take care of my son."

Maggie took a sip of tea, giving herself time to think. The truth was she was beginning to like having her sister and little Robbie around. "You don't have to worry about that. I've got plenty of room."

"That isn't the point. I spoke to Mrs. Epstein. She says she hasn't met you yet, but she's your neighbor in the unit next door. I saw her out working on her patio and we got to talking through the fence. She's really nice and she loves kids, especially babies. Her husband died four years ago. Her son and daughter are grown and married, and she even has a couple of grandkids. I think she'd be great to watch Robbie while I'm working."

"I hate to point this out, but you don't have a job."

"I know, but it's time I started looking. I'm a really good cook, Maggie. Not a chef yet, but good enough to work the lunch shift or something at a restaurant. That way I'd be home most of the time, and Mrs. Epstein could take care of Robbie while I was on the job."

It sounded logical. If the situation were reversed,

Maggie wouldn't want to be dependent on a relative to take care of her and her child.

"All right, why don't we do this? I'll ask around, ask Trace to ask around, see if we can find something without you having to knock on doors."

"That'd be great, and I can keep watching the paper, see if there's anyplace that needs cooking help."

"Okay, then. Looks like we've got a plan." On impulse Maggie reached over and hugged her. "I'm glad you came here."

Ashley hugged her back. "So am I." They sat down at the breakfast counter and Ashley sipped her tea. "I know you didn't feel that way when I first showed up at your door."

Maggie shrugged. Denying it wouldn't help anything. "We didn't really know each other. And the truth is, I was always jealous of you. I guess you probably figured that out."

"Jealous? Why would you be jealous of *me?*"

"Because Mom loved you. She barely knew I existed."

"Are you kidding? Mom bragged about you all the time. The people at her bridge club used to watch for stories about you in magazines. They'd cut them out and give 'em to her."

Something eased in the area around Maggie's heart. "Really?"

"I was nothing compared to you. I was a total loser. That's hard on a kid, you know."

Maggie's throat tightened. "You weren't a loser. You were smart and beautiful. You had a lot of friends."

"Would-be friends. Not worth spit when it came down to it."

Back then, Maggie hadn't realized what a difficult time her sister was having. "It was different for me. I always missed having a mother, but at least I had a dad who loved me." Even after her Great Shame, he had forgiven her, stuck by her.

"In their own way, Mom and Dad loved me," Ashley said. "But they fought all the time and they mostly ignored me. In a way, you were the lucky one."

Maybe she was. Maggie had never considered that before. She reached out and caught hold of Ashley's hand. "You know what I figured out?"

"What?"

"I like you, Ashley Hastings. I really do."

Her sister laughed. "And besides that, I'm a really good cook."

Chapter 16

Maggie started working on the client list for Trace. She kept both email and snail mail addresses as a means of promoting her shows and the release of her new photo collections. It was all on computer, which was a major help. She went back two years, looking for anyone who had purchased two or more pieces, but the list was too long and unwieldy. She narrowed it to three purchases, then to four.

Each effort took a while. Eventually she checked her watch, saw that she needed to leave in order to make her appointment at the gallery and closed down the machine.

When Maggie arrived, Faye was busy with customers picking up framed photographs they had purchased at the gala.

"The walls are practically empty," she said, beaming as she met Maggie by her car. "What a terrific show."

Maggie made a mental note to get the new buyer information from Faye to add to her client list. Then she leaned into the back of her Escape and pulled out the first of five pieces from an earlier show she planned to put on display until she'd had time to print and frame more pictures for the new collection.

"Here, let me help you." Faye reached for another of the 24 x 36 photos, which were bubble-wrapped for protection.

"I can do this," Maggie said. "You're hardly dressed for it." The gallery owner wore a tailored blue skirt with a light blue silk blouse and low-heeled sandals.

"I'm fine," Faye said. "Faster if we both carry them in."

Working together, they got them inside and unwrapped. "I hope you can get the replacements done fairly soon. I'll have to hang something else until I get them. I'd like to have them up no later than week after next."

"That shouldn't be a problem." She would have to get in touch with the company that did the prints, but Fine Art Photo Imaging had always been prompt. The framing was another matter, but she worked closely with Frontier Framing and because she gave them a lot of business, her jobs got top priority.

For the next half hour, Maggie worked with Faye, climbing ladders and carefully hanging photos in the empty spaces left by those that had sold, adding some other photographers' pieces Faye had in the other room, then adjusting the spotlights to show off each work to its best advantage.

"The opening was such a success the Weyman people have already been calling to set up a date for a benefit next year," the gallery owner said as she climbed down a ladder. "I hope you'll be able to do it again."

"I don't see why not."

She smiled. "Your pieces really made the show a hit. People loved what they saw. There's such a poignancy about your work. You've got a wonderful talent, Maggie, for catching exactly the right shot at exactly the right moment."

"Thanks, Faye."

The dark-haired woman reached up and adjusted a smaller photo along the wall. "So…what about the cowboy? Half the women at the opening were swooning over him."

And I was one of them, Maggie thought. *The one who wound up in his bed.* The notion didn't sit as well as it might have.

"Actually, he was here as my bodyguard."

One of Faye's dark eyebrows went up. "Do tell."

Maggie filled her in on the stalker and the notes and phone calls she had received. "I thought maybe it was one of my clients. I was hoping he might show up last night, but I don't think he was here, and neither does Trace."

"Is there anything I can do to help?"

"Just keep an eye out. We have a description of someone who could be him, but no way to know for sure. A big guy in his forties, with silver-streaked dark hair. If someone fitting that description, or anyone else comes in wanting an unusual amount of information about me, let me know."

"Don't worry, I will. I hope you catch the sick bastard."

"So do I."

"In the meantime, bring me those photos as soon as you can. I can't sell them if I don't have them."

Maggie smiled, enjoying the momentary high from her success. Like everything in life, she knew it could end in a heartbeat.

* * *

"Magnificent photograph." Richard Meyers stepped back to admire the framed picture *Harbor Sunset* he had been instructed to purchase last night and pick up this morning. *Harbor Sunset* was an amazing shot of the Blue Fin Marina awash in the red-orange light of a flaming sunset. "Too bad it'll have to be destroyed."

Garrett Logan stared down at the picture on the table in his study. "You had just better hope we get our hands on that…what is it? The negative, but they don't call them that now."

"Memory card. We've got to get rid of everything Maggie might have photographed that day. That means we need to get hold of the card she used in her digital camera." Richard walked over to the wet bar in the corner, poured the last half of a can of Diet Pepsi into his frosty glass. "I talked to Faye Langston last night. Maggie prints and frames each picture one at a time. She works out of the studio in her home. If we move on this, we should be able to make the entire collection disappear before it becomes a problem."

Garrett looked down at the information card that had come with the purchase, the words elegantly drawn in calligraphy. The date of the photo was April 20.

His stomach clenched. "It's already a problem." He raked a hand through his thick silver hair. "Of all the bad luck."

Picking up the magnifying glass he had been using to examine the shot, Garrett leaned over to study the photo again. The names of the expensive white yachts lined up along dock B weren't apparent until he looked through the glass. Once he did, there was no doubt that the plush, fifty-one-foot Navigator, *Capitol Expense,* was his personal yacht. There was also no doubt he was the man sitting at the table on deck.

And the woman across from him…

He felt a wave of nausea. Thank God for Richard. He could count on him to handle this problem the way he did everything else. The man had become indispensable. Which worried Garrett a little, since he knew that was exactly Meyers's plan.

"Once we get rid of the memory card," his aide said, "there'll be no proof the two of you ever met. This'll all go away."

Annoyance filtered through the senator. Richard had a way of making everything sound so easy. "That's all well and good, but how, exactly, do you intend to make that happen?"

"I'm not quite sure yet. We'll need to do a little digging, find out everything we can about Maggie O'Connell—where she lives, where she works. We'll figure out where to find the card and get rid of it."

Garrett felt a trickle of his old self-confidence returning. Getting information out of people was his long suit.

"I heard a little gossip last night," Richard continued. "Just a whisper, but apparently, Maggie's been having some problems. Claims some guy has been stalking her, even broke into her house. I thought maybe you could use your connections with the police department, see what's really going on. Might be something that could work to our advantage."

Garrett started nodding, his confidence growing. "I'll handle it. I'll get on it right away. I'll let you know what I find out."

Richard smiled. "Perfect."

Trace adjusted his phone against his ear. "Thanks for letting me know," he said to Mark Sayers, the man on the other end of the line.

"Hey, no problem. We appreciate your help on this."

Trace hung up and leaned back in his chair, a smile of satisfaction on his face. On Monday afternoon, Parker Barrington had been arrested for embezzling funds from Sommerset Industries. Since the money ran into the tens of millions, the D.A. was able to convince the court that Parker was a flight risk, and the judge refused to set bail. At least the bastard was in jail. Which was a damned good start, but still not enough.

After Emily had amended her statement, refuting Parker's alibi for the night of Hewitt's murder, the police had gone back and done a more in-depth autopsy on the body. The results were not yet in but were due any day. Trace hoped the coroner would find something that would prove the shot that had killed him was not self-inflicted.

The office was humming, Annie working away up front. Through the glass wall in his office, he could see Alex Justice leaning back in the chair behind his desk, his feet propped up, his cell phone pressed against his ear. Ben was staring at his computer screen as if it held infinite secrets, working the keyboard and mouse. Rex had come and gone. He'd been making daily stops at Maggie's, picking up video cards from the wireless cameras aimed at her front and back doors, looking for anyone who might have approached the town house aside from neighbors and the kids playing in front. No one seemed out of place or looked suspicious.

Trace got up and walked into the office next door. Sol looked up from the computer screen, sat back and pulled off his horn-rimmed glasses.

"What's up, boss?"

"I've got some names I need you to run. I want to know if any of these guys have a connection to Maggie O'Connell."

Sol rubbed the bridge of his nose. "You think one of them might be her stalker?"

"They fit a possible description, but I talked to them at her opening on Friday night and I didn't get any vibes. Doesn't mean something can't turn up." He set the brief list down on Sol's desk. "And while you're at it, take another look at the first list of names I gave you. Go a little deeper, see if we might have missed something."

They had both done a search of the personal acquaintances Maggie had listed for Trace that first day. So far neither of them had come up with anything.

Maybe the third time would be the charm.

"I'll give it a shot," Sol said, which meant he might have to cross a legal line or two, but both of them would pretend he hadn't. Turning back to the computer screen, he started pounding away on the keyboard, and Trace returned to his office.

Roger Weller's name was on Maggie's original list, but sometimes the most interesting information couldn't be found on the net.

Last night Trace had phoned Johnnie Riggs, a good friend and ex-Ranger buddy who lived in L.A. Riggs made a living by digging up information—the kind people wanted to keep hidden. Mostly he worked nights, hanging around bars and nightclubs, talking to people on the street, working his contacts. If you wanted to know about someone in Southern California, Johnnie Riggs was your go-to guy.

Trace hadn't connected with Riggs last night, but he had left a message. When the phone on his desk started to ring, he wasn't surprised to hear his friend's husky voice on the other end of the line.

"Hey, man, glad you called," Johnnie said. "I was beginning to think you'd cocked up your toes."

Trace chuckled. "Still alive and kickin'. Hard at work, just like you. I need you to do a little digging."

"Yeah? Got a name?"

"Roger Weller. He's a celebrity of sorts, fairly famous photographer. My client used to work for him. Says he taught her everything she knows."

"That right?" Johnnie said, a suggestive note in his voice.

"According to her, not that kind of everything. She's fairly well known in the business herself. From what her photographs sell for, she makes more than a decent living, and Weller's a far bigger name."

"So the guy's got bucks."

"I did a preliminary search on the net. He's got a house in Laguna Beach. Owns his own gallery there."

"Not a cheap place to live."

"I want to know his off-the-record story, not just what the magazines say about how talented he is. And I want to know if he had more than a mentor-student relationship with Maggie O'Connell."

"That your client?"

"That's her."

"Redhead?"

Trace felt a trickle of annoyance. "As a matter of fact."

Johnnie chuckled.

"She's got a stalker, Hambone." It was Johnnie's Ranger name, well deserved since the man could eat his weight in food and never gain an ounce of fat. "This guy put cameras in her house, bugged her car. He isn't kidding around."

"Not good."

"No, it isn't. Let me know what you find out."

"Will do. I'll get back to you soon as I have something." Johnnie hung up the phone and so did Trace.

He needed to know about Weller, but it bothered him to be checking up on Maggie. He wanted to trust her. For the most part, he did.

But marrying Carly proved he couldn't trust his instincts with women. He needed to be sure Maggie was telling him the truth.

Ashley swung her racquet at the ball, slamming a return her sister missed, and scoring the final point in the game. It was over at last—thank God—since after having the baby, she was way out of condition.

"That was fun," Maggie said, walking toward her.

Ashley took the towel she handed her, wiped her face and neck. Both of them were perspiring and panting. Mrs. Epstein, the next-door neighbor, was watching Robbie while they played. Ashley looked down at her cheap, pink-and-silver plastic wristwatch. Robbie had been sleeping when they'd dropped him off, but he was probably awake by now.

She bent at the waist, bracing her hands on her knees and sucked in a final deep breath. The pounding of balls in the neighboring courts echoed around them. "I am so out of shape." Which was why her sister had won the first two games, then let her win the third.

"Give yourself a break," Maggie said. "You just had a baby."

Ashley straightened, blew out a breath. "I haven't played in ages."

"I try to play a couple of times a week. I don't always manage."

Ashley grinned. "It felt really great, even if you did let me win."

Her sister laughed. "Next time you'll beat me fair and square."

Ashley glanced back down at her watch. "We've been gone almost two hours."

Maggie walked over to the bench against the wall and began to stuff her gear into a blue-and-white gym bag. "I know you're nervous. It's the first time you've ever left Robbie with someone else. I'm a little nervous myself."

"We should get back." Ashley handed her the racquet she had borrowed, and they headed for the door. All the way to the town house, she worried, which she guessed all new mothers did. But when they knocked on Mrs. Epstein's door and the older woman pulled it open, everything seemed to be fine.

Doris was giving the baby the bottle Ashley had prepared before they left the house, and he was making those joyful little sucking sounds that meant he was happy.

"How's he doing?" Ashley asked.

"Just great." With short, slightly wavy, iron-gray hair, Mrs. Epstein was robust though a little stoop-shouldered, and she always seemed to be smiling. "He's a lovely little boy. Such a pleasure to watch."

"Looks like he's had enough," Maggie said, when the bottle was almost empty and Robbie no longer seemed interested.

The baby grinned and waved his chubby little arms as Mrs. Epstein handed the bottle to Maggie and the baby to Ashley. Robbie gurgled a laugh. Obviously he and Mrs. Epstein were getting along just fine.

"Well, we'd better get going," Ashley said.

"Keep track of your hours," Maggie told the older woman. "We'll write you a check once a week if that's okay with you."

Their neighbor straightened the paisley blouse she wore belted over a pair of navy pants, and gave them one of her warm, grandmotherly smiles. "Why, yes, dear, that's just fine."

"Thanks, Mrs. Epstein," Ashley said, hoping she would find a job soon so that she could pay the woman's meager wages herself instead of relying on her sister.

The baby's eyes began to drift closed. Inside the town house, Ashley went into the bedroom and put him down in the crib Maggie had bought for him. Ashley smiled as his little mouth parted in sleep.

The phone rang in the kitchen just then and she turned and started back out the door. So far there hadn't been any more calls from the stalker, but every time the phone rang, both she and her sister jumped.

Maggie walked to the breakfast bar and picked up the receiver. She listened for a moment, smiled and looked over as Ashley approached down the hall. "It's for you," she said.

"Is it Mom? She and Dad are the only ones who know I'm here."

Her sister just grinned and handed her the phone.

"Hello?"

"Ashley? This is Jason Sommerset. We met the day I came over to your house to talk to Trace."

As if she could forget Mr. Tall, Blond and Handsome. "I remember. Hello, Jason."

"Listen, I was thinking… Things are starting to smooth out a little for me. I was wondering if you would like to have dinner sometime."

Dinner? She hadn't dated since she had dumped Ziggy—or he had dumped her, depending on how you looked at it. "I'm a mother," she blurted dumbly, as if that meant she couldn't have supper with a man. "I have a baby, Jason."

"I know. Trace told me. I like kids. I don't see what that has to do with our having supper."

She scrambled, searched her brain, trying to think of an excuse. She wasn't ready to date. Was she? "Babies take a lot of time. It would be hard to get away."

"But not impossible," he said.

She drew a steadying breath. "Well, um, how would you feel about coming to dinner over here?" She looked to Maggie for approval and saw her sister nodding vigorously.

"Are you sure it wouldn't be too much trouble?" Jason asked.

"I love to cook. It wouldn't be any trouble at all."

She could hear the smile in his voice. "That'd be great. I'd love a home-cooked meal. What night?"

Ashley turned, mouthed, "What night?"

"How about tomorrow?" Maggie mouthed back.

No way, she thought, needing time to work up her courage. "How about Wednesday?" Maggie kept nodding. "Around seven?"

"That works for me. Anything I can bring?"

Just your gorgeous self, Ashley thought. "Maybe a bottle of wine."

"That's a given," he said. "I'll see you Wednesday night."

The call ended and Ashley set the receiver back in its cradle. "I've got a date," she said, still feeling shell-shocked. "With Jason Sommerset. He knows I have a baby."

Maggie ran over and hugged her. "Trace says he's a really nice guy."

Some of Ashley's excitement slipped away. "They all seem really nice in the beginning." Turning, she walked back to the bedroom to check on her little boy.

Maggie worked on her client list, but her concentration was wearing thin when the phone rang down-

stairs. Ashley had taken the baby and driven her old
blue Chevy down to the library. She needed to find
a cookbook—Italian, something special to make for
Jason. Recipes off the internet just weren't the same,
she said.

Wondering if it might be Trace, Maggie hurried to
the breakfast bar, smiling as she picked up the phone.
The sound of music floated over the line and her stomach instantly knotted.

"I…saw…you… I knew you would be my one true
love. I…saw…you…a vision so pure and sweet, my only
true love…."

Her heart was thrumming. Her palms grew damp
as she checked the time of the call on the kitchen clock
and jotted it down on the pad beside the phone. *Hang
up,* she told herself as the song continued to play. *You
have the information they need to track the call.* But
her fingers refused to obey.

Then he began to speak. "My dear…dear Mag-gie…"
The same electronically distorted voice, the same eerie
chill racing down her spine. "I've missed see-ing you,
Mag-gie. I've missed watch-ing you…. Soon, my prec-
i-ous dar-ling. Soon it will be time for us to be together."

Fear coursed through her. "You bastard! Leave me
alone!" She slammed down the receiver, getting a vicious thrill at the thought of the noise ringing in his ear.
She was breathing hard, her whole body shaking. She
hadn't seen Trace since the morning after the gallery
show when he had brought her home. He had called several times, but after their night of lovemaking, both of
them seemed to need a breather, time to sort things out.

Earlier, he had phoned to tell her he was checking
on the men at the opening who fit the description of the
stalker. So far nothing of interest had turned up.

She dialed his cell number with a shaky hand, and Trace answered on the second ring.

"Maggie," he said, recognizing her caller ID.

"He phoned again, Trace. It was…it was just like before."

"Where's Ashley?"

"At the library."

"Check your doors. I'll be right there."

He didn't have to come over. He could have gotten the time of the call, dialed the phone company from his cell and started them working on whatever it took to implement the trap.

But she was glad he was coming. She wanted to see him. Needed to see him.

A few minutes later he banged on the door. Maggie opened it, saw the handsomest cowboy she'd ever encountered and walked straight into his arms.

Trace held her tightly. "You're shaking." He ran a hand through her hair, smoothing it back from her face. "That bastard. I swear when I get my hands on him…"

He didn't say more. Didn't need to. She could think of a dozen things *she'd* like to do if she ever got her hands on him.

Trace caught her shoulders, eased her back to look at her. "You okay?"

She nodded, released a shaky breath. "I'm okay." She smiled. "Better now that you're here." She went over to the breakfast bar, hit the button on the recorder they had set up to catch the calls. Trace followed. Pulling his hat off, he set it on the counter.

The recording began. The song played as it had before. The distorted voice came on: "I've missed see-ing you, Mag-gie. I've missed watch-ing you…."

"Jesus," Trace said when the call came to an end. "He's missed seeing you." The creep's video cameras were gone. The GPS gone from her car. "I'll just bet he has."

Trace reached for the phone, dialed the phone company, a special number set up as part of the trap. He gave them the information they needed, then hung up.

"They'll call us right back. If they get a location, I'll phone the cops, have them meet me there."

He and Maggie waited anxiously. Fifteen minutes later, the phone rang and Trace picked it up. He listened, started shaking his head. He hung up and turned to face her.

"It was worth a try," he said, his features grim. "Call came from a cell phone. Disposable, with no way to track the owner or the address it came from. Just as I figured."

Maggie closed her eyes as despair settled over her. She fought an overwhelming urge to cry.

Trace eased her back into his arms. "We're gonna get this guy. Everything's gonna be all right."

She nodded, though she wasn't completely convinced.

"Since the trap didn't work, you'll need to change your phone number."

Maggie started shaking her head. "No way. I work out of my house, Trace. This is my business number. It's on my website, on my business cards. I'm not changing it. I'm not letting that creep control my life."

Trace blew out a slow breath. "If you feel that strongly, at least hang up when you realize it's him. Your calls are all being recorded. There's no reason to let him upset you."

Maggie nodded. Trace was right. There was no reason to let this guy have that kind of power over her. "All right, I'll hang up. I should have done it tonight."

"Good girl. I know how hard this is for you."

"I don't suppose you've come up with anything useful."

Trace shook his head. "Nothing's turned up on the outside cameras. I don't think he was one of the men at your show. So far he's covered his bases, but sooner or later he's going to make a mistake."

"I hope so."

"They always do. In the meantime, you need to play it safe, keep doing what you have been. If you leave the house, you need to take somebody with you."

Maggie's shoulders tightened. "I have to work, Trace. I have lots of things to do."

"This guy could be a serious threat, Maggie. And he's not going to be patient much longer."

She walked to the kitchen sink and stared out the window. Just the empty street, a lone streetlamp and a cluster of trees on the opposite side of the road… She wondered if the man might be somewhere out in the darkness right now. Watching. Waiting.

She turned back to Trace. "Maybe you're right. Maybe he's getting impatient. If he is, maybe we can force the issue, set some other kind of trap. He's after me. Let him come and get me."

Trace ran a hand through his hair. "I've considered it. I don't like it. I don't like the idea of using you as bait. I was hoping we could find a better way."

"Well, so far nothing's worked, and I'm tired of feeling like a prisoner in my own home."

He left the counter and walked up beside her at the window. For a moment, his gaze traveled from the lighted front porch into the darkness across the road.

"What about your client list? How's that coming along?"

"I'm working on it, but so far nothing stands out. No one's bought an extravagant number of photos, at least not that I've found so far." Maggie looked up at him. "I want this over, Trace. We've got to do something to catch this guy."

Trace's glance went back out the window. For several long moments he said nothing, then murmured, "We took the GPS off your car, so he can't track you from a distance. That means if he wants to see you, he has to follow you. Maybe we *can* draw him out."

Excitement replaced Maggie's despair. She liked the idea—more than liked it. She wanted this to end.

"I'll plan a trip. Go down to the shore like I always do. Last time, he bugged my car to find me. He can't do that now, but if I let it be known I'm going—tell Faye down at the gallery, mention it at the photo processing shop I use—maybe he'll find out and come after me."

"It might work. He's been keeping pretty good tabs on you somehow."

"For all we know he could be out there right now. Maybe he'll be watching that morning when I drive away."

Trace's jaw went hard. "If he follows you, we'll be ready."

They laid out a plan, a photography expedition to Kemah. They both knew the area, and *Ranger's Lady* was docked there, which would give them a base of operations.

"I'll have a couple of my guys in place before you get there. They'll know what to look for. He shows up, we'll have him."

They decided to make the trip next Friday. There would be less people milling around than on the weekend, fewer folks to worry about if things went south.

"Waiting is good," Trace said. "Give him a little time to cool his heels, get anxious, maybe a little careless."

Maggie's excitement built. "You really think it might work?"

"I think there's a chance."

She relaxed for the first time that evening. Trace reached for her, captured her face between his palms. His hands felt warm against her skin, then his lips brushed lightly over hers, settled, melded, and soft heat expanded inside her.

"God, I've missed you." He kissed her softly again. "Now that I've had a taste of you, I want you more than ever."

Her pulse kicked up. He was a strong man and virile. She could feel the control he used to hold himself back, and it made her want him more. Maggie gave herself up to a series of soft, seductive kisses that melted her insides and turned her whole body hot and liquid. Deep, wet, openmouthed kisses. Long, heart-stopping kisses that seemed to have no end. Dear Lord, the man could kiss.

Sliding her arms around his neck, she pressed herself more fully against him, felt the thick ridge of his sex, hard beneath the fly of his jeans. He cupped her bottom, lifted her against him, let her feel his need.

"Damn, I want you." Another deep kiss and he turned his attention to her breasts, palmed them, teased her nipples through her light cotton T-shirt. He caught the hem and drew it off over her head. She wasn't wearing a bra and those whiskey-brown eyes darkened.

"So pretty," he said, running a finger around the tip of one breast, bending to take the fullness into his mouth. Maggie's legs went weak. She made a little mewling sound as he lifted her into his arms and turned toward the stairs. There was purpose in those dark eyes, and remembering the last time he had made love to her, her body began to throb in half a dozen places.

He took the first stair, then another. At the rattle of a key in the lock, he jerked to a halt.

"Ashley!" Maggie said. "Oh, my God."

Trace set her on her feet, and she raced back down the stairs, grabbed her T-shirt and pulled it on just as the door swung open.

Her sister set the baby carrier down on the ceramic tile floor. "I found just the thing! Jason is going to love it." Then she spotted Trace and the excitement in her face changed to an expression of concern. "Did something happen while I was away?"

"I got another call," Maggie explained, casting a look at Trace, her body still thrumming with desire for him.

"We're going to catch him," he declared. "It's only a matter of time. Until then, you keep an eye on your sister, okay?"

"I will, don't worry," Ashley replied.

Trace's gaze locked with Maggie's and his look said he wanted to take her home with him, finish what they had started. "Probably not a good idea to leave your sister here alone tonight—not after telling the SOB to bugger off. You never know how some of these jokers will respond."

He was right, of course. She couldn't leave Ash and the baby, not tonight. Still, she was aching for more of those hot, wet kisses, more of his amazing lovemaking, and the smoldering look he gave her said he felt the same.

"I'm as close as my phone. If anything happens— anything—you call me. And the police. I talked to Detective Sayers. He's put them on notice this isn't a drill. They'll come if you need them."

"All right."

Ashley carted the baby carrier down the hall to their bedroom and Maggie walked Trace to the door.

"Best laid plans and all that," he said, settling his hat on his head.

She just shrugged.

"I hear Jason's coming over for dinner. Kid called to tell me. Kind of thinks of me as Ashley's protector, I guess. He promised to be on his best behavior."

"Good for him."

"You'll want to leave the lovebirds alone, so why don't I make dinner for you at my place that night?"

One of her eyebrows went up. "You can cook more than Pillsbury breakfast rolls?"

He grinned. "Quite a bit more." His gaze ran over her, as hot and sexy as before. "You might want to bring your toothbrush."

Her stomach contracted. Maggie smiled. "Sounds like a plan."

Chapter 17

Richard Meyers stood in the darkness behind the abandoned warehouse. Though it was well after midnight, the temperature was warm, the air damp and heavy. Only a sliver of moon lit the black sky. The property around the old metal building was littered with trash and rusty pieces of iron. A rat scurried into an overturned garbage can, and Richard shivered against an edge of fear.

A place like this was the last spot he would have chosen. He didn't know the man who had set up the meet, just a voice at the end of a telephone line, someone who knew the right people—for the right price.

Yesterday, Senator Logan had spoken to a contact in the police department, who had talked to a friend, a captain in the vice squad named Varner. Varner knew all about Maggie O'Connell and her possible stalker. He'd had a run-in with the woman years ago. The senator had gotten all the lurid details of the false rape charges and the fact that Varner had a long-standing grudge against Maggie.

According to Logan, at first the captain had believed Maggie's 911 calls were nothing but a publicity stunt. Lately, he had come to believe that "some kook," as Varner had put it, was obsessed with her. After the trouble she had caused his son, Varner figured it was poetic justice.

As far as Richard was concerned, the important point was that Maggie O'Connell had an enemy. If that enemy happened to break into her home and destroy her studio, well, one just never knew what a creep like that was capable of.

A noise in the darkness drew his attention. Footsteps crunching on gravel. A shadowy figure in a long coat with the collar turned up, and a narrow-brimmed fedora, appeared around the corner of the warehouse.

Right out of a spy movie. Richard bit back a laugh. He wondered how badly the guy was sweating inside the coat.

"You bring the money?" the man asked as he approached.

"I brought it," Richard said. "Half tonight. The rest when the job is finished."

The stranger nodded. In the darkness, with his hat brim in the way, it was impossible to see his face.

"There's a security alarm in the house," Richard told him. Another little tidbit the senator had uncovered. The man was a genius at getting people to spit out whatever he wanted to know. "Can you get past it?"

The man chuckled, a raw sound in the darkness. "Unless the place is protected like Fort Knox, it won't be a problem."

"There may be surveillance cameras outside."

"I'll find 'em, take 'em out."

"The residence is a town house. There's another property attached, to one side. They said you could do the job without destroying the neighboring condos. We don't want anyone getting hurt."

"I can't make promises, but there are ways to handle it. I'll do the best I can."

Logan had been adamant. But the senator was Richard's meal ticket and unless the problem was taken care of, both of them were in serious trouble. He wasn't about to let all his years of hard work go down the drain. Besides, there were certain risks in everything.

"The woman's sister is in the house. She's got a baby."

"I'll keep that in mind." But he didn't sound particularly concerned. "Now, do you want this done or not?"

Richard drew in a slow breath. He was already in so deep he had no real choice. "Go ahead and do it." Reaching into his pocket, he handed over an envelope containing fifteen thousand dollars.

"I'll be in touch," the man said, stuffing the envelope inside the pocket of this of his coat. Turning, he walked back around the corner of the warehouse.

Richard watched until he disappeared. Only then did he realize he was sweating as much as the man in the trench coat.

Trace got a phone call from Johnnie Riggs on Wednesday morning. He was sitting behind his desk, trying not to think of Maggie and the dinner he was cooking for her that night, trying not to get carried away as he imagined all the ways he meant to have her.

The phone call saved him, but just barely.

"Hey, buddy, how's it hangin'?"

Trace almost laughed. If his friend only knew. Johnnie's image appeared in his head, six feet of solid muscle, thick dark hair and dark eyes, a five o'clock shadow that was there by ten in the morning. "Hey, Hambone. Hangin' in there. Whatcha got?"

"I got a line on your guy Weller. Interesting stuff."

"Yeah, like what?"

"Like the fact he's in the closet. So deep not even his friends know the truth. He pretends to be a player. Likes the image of being a lady's man, likes the attention from all the women. And it keeps him from having to explain why he isn't married, isn't involved with a particular female. Fact is the guy prowls the gay bars down in the district, picks up male prostitutes, gets his rocks off, then goes back to his straight life as a hotshot photographer. Sex with a woman doesn't interest him. Looks like your lady was telling you the truth."

"My client, you mean."

"She's a redhead. Six to one, you're sleeping with her."

Annoyance filtered through him. Johnnie knew him too well. "As I recall, you've got a penchant for blondes."

Johnnie chuckled. "Point taken. Anything else you need?"

"Not at the moment. Send Annie your bill."

"Hope the info helps."

"Helps my peace of mind," Trace said and hung up. He'd needed to know about Weller, he told himself. He was just being thorough. And though he felt a little guilty for doubting Maggie's word, he also felt relieved to know she'd been telling him the truth.

He was smiling, thinking of the night ahead, when the phone rang again. This time it was Mark Sayers.

"Coroner's report just came in," the detective said. "Thought you'd want to know."

"Tell me." Trace picked up a pencil, wrote the words *Coroner's Report* on the pad next to the phone.

"They found a needle mark in Sommerset's neck. Missed it the first time because they figured him for a suicide. The puncture convinced them to look in a different direction, and guess what they found?"

"Tranquilizer of some kind."

"That's right. Ketamine. It's used in darts to sedate animals—deer, bear, dogs, monkeys, a lot of different stuff. You can get it from a veterinarian or over the internet."

Trace's fingers tightened around the pencil. "What do you bet Parker's computer turns up an internet search for animal tranqs?"

"Department's on it as we speak."

"If they find it, you'll nail the prick." He penciled *ketamine* on his scratch pad, a reminder to look it up. "You told Jason yet?"

"No, but he'll get an official call sometime this afternoon."

Trace grunted. "Good thing good ol' Parker's in custody."

Mark chuckled. "Might just be. But near as I can tell, Jason's a good, solid kid. He'll handle it."

Trace could almost see the fury in Jason's eyes. He'd handle it because he had to, but he wasn't going to take the news well.

The call came to an end and Trace leaned back in his chair. Parker had been so cocksure he could get away clean.

It wasn't going to happen.

Hewitt deserved justice. It was beginning to look like he was going to get it.

"I got a job!" Ashley burst into the condo and began to dance around, holding a brown paper bag of groceries as if it were her imaginary partner. "I start Friday night!" She shuffled her feet, twirled dramatically as Maggie descended the last few stairs.

"You got a job?"

Ashley grinned. "Yup!"

"I think I missed something," Maggie said. "Maybe you'd better start at the beginning." For the last couple hours she'd been upstairs going through her photography files, sorting memory cards, getting ready to take the pertinent ones to the photo imaging shop to have the pictures reprinted. As soon as they were ready, she would deliver them to Frontier Framing, get them matted and framed, then get them to the gallery.

Ashley carried the groceries into the kitchen and set them on the counter. "There was this ad in the paper, you know? I've been reading the Help Wanteds every morning. The job's only for a couple of weeks while Eddie—that's the cook—looks after his mom, but it's working in a restaurant and I have to start somewhere."

Maggie began to smile. "Congratulations. That's wonderful, Ash. So where exactly is it you'll be working?"

"The Texas Café." She began pulling groceries out of the bag, the ingredients she needed to cook supper for Jason Sommerset. Maggie had a hunch it had taken the last of the meager savings Ashley had brought with her from Florida.

"I'll be working for a woman named Betty Sparks. I told her I was living in Houston with my sister, Maggie O'Connell, and she said she knew you."

Maggie thought of Trace's fight in the café with Bobby Jordane, and inwardly winced at her shabby attempt to grab a paparazzi-style photo. "We met a few weeks back."

"She asked me if you were dating a guy named Trace Rawlins, and I said it looked that way, and she laughed."

Maggie felt a trickle of irritation. "I'm sure she did." But Maggie had a hard time seeing the humor. Betty had warned her Trace had a weakness for redheads. Apparently, she was just another one of them.

The thought did not sit well. She told herself her interest in Trace was also strictly physical, and managed a halfhearted smile.

"So you got a job at the Texas Café, and...?"

"And I start Friday night. I really liked Betty and I think she liked me. She said as long as I could cook, she'd teach me the rest of what I needed to know. I'm really excited about it."

"That's great. I'm so happy for you." Maggie shot a quick glance at the groceries spread out on the counter. "I take it Robbie's at Mrs. Epstein's?"

"I took him over a little early, since I had to go to the job interview, and cooking this stuff isn't easy. I really need to concentrate."

"You seem excited about seeing Jason."

Ashley pulled the cellophane off a package of cut-up chicken, set it in the sink and turned on the water. "I'm not sure. I'm kind of nervous. I know he's out of my league. There's only one thing he could possibly want from me. I don't know why I said yes."

Maggie rounded the breakfast bar and walked into the kitchen. "That is so not true. You're beautiful and you're smart. You have goals and you're willing to work hard to reach them. You have a lot more to offer a man than just your body."

Ashley looked up and her features softened. "That's really a nice thing to say. Thanks, sis."

She drew her into a hug. "I mean it. Jason's lucky to get a shot."

Ashley shook her head. "He isn't getting a shot. He's getting dinner. That's all."

Maggie smiled. "He's getting your wonderful company for the evening. That's worth a heckuva lot."

Her sister grinned. "He's getting chicken cacciatore with prosciutto tortellini gratinato. And lemon mousse with raspberries for dessert. That really is worth a lot."

Both of them laughed.

"So what about you?" Ashley asked as she began retrieving various pots and pans for the meal she was preparing. "You're going over to Trace's, right? Are you guys getting serious?"

Maggie scoffed. "Are you kidding? We hardly know each other. We're strictly in lust."

"I'd say you know each other pretty well. He always seems to be there when you need him. That's more than you can say for most men."

She pondered that, and how Trace had a way of making her feel safe and protected. "Not most men," she corrected, "but a lot." She smiled. "I never thought I'd have the hots for a cowboy, but I have to admit I do."

"But it isn't anything serious," Ashley said with a hint of amusement.

She shrugged. "I like him. I think he likes me. In bed, he's amazing."

Ashley had started to reach for a bowl, but stopped and turned.

"What is it?" Maggie asked.

"I've never felt that way about sex. You know, having the hots for a guy? Ziggy…well, he wasn't my first, but there were only a couple others, and none of them were amazing."

Maggie reached up and looped a curl of her sister's hair behind an ear. "You're young. You've got lots of time. You can wait until just the right man comes along."

"Is Trace the right man for *you?*"

Maggie ignored a funny little quiver in her middle. "When it comes to sex, he sure is." Grinning, she turned and headed back upstairs.

Her grin slowly faded. She just hoped her attraction to Trace didn't go a whole lot deeper than she wanted to admit.

Chapter 18

Everything was ready. The dining table was set with the white linen cloth Ashley had purchased at Bed Bath & Beyond when she discovered Maggie didn't have one. She had also purchased four place settings of white porcelain dishes, the kind the chefs used on TV. Thankfully, Maggie had decent flatware and a set of expensive crystal wineglasses.

"I saw them and I just had to have them," her sister had said with a smile and a shrug. "I have no idea why, but wine always tastes better in a pretty, long-stemmed glass."

Which, oddly enough, seemed true. Jason was bringing the wine, so the rest of Ashley's money went to buying the actual food. Except for the small bouquet of mixed spring flowers she had bought at the grocery store and arranged in a clear glass vase she had found beneath the kitchen sink.

Supper was simmering on the stove, the chicken,

tomatoes and spices bubbling in the skillet. The pasta was finished and covered to keep warm, the arugula salad crisp and chilled, just waiting for her to add her special oil-and-vinegar dressing. The lemon mousse was in the fridge.

She turned at the knock on the door, took a moment to catch her breath and slow her pounding heart. She smoothed the long skirt of the white piqué, sleeveless summer dress she was wearing with a pair of strappy silver sandals, and headed for the door.

When she opened it, Jason Sommerset stood before her. For several seconds she just stared. He looked like a movie star, only more masculine, and for an instant she considered just closing the door and pretending she wasn't there.

"Can I come in?" he asked, a smile of amusement on his lips.

"Oh, yes, of course. I just… I haven't dated in a really long time and… Well, to tell you the truth, I was never any good at it."

His smile widened. "Then we'll pretend this isn't a date, just two friends getting to know each other."

She felt a little of her tension ease, returned the smile. "Okay."

Jason handed her the bouquet she had only just noticed. She took it with a trembling hand. "Pink roses. They're gorgeous, Jason. Thank you."

"You're welcome." He walked past her into the house and set the bottles of wine he had brought on the kitchen counter. "I didn't know if you liked red or white so I brought both."

"Either is great with me, although red would probably go better with dinner."

She carried the flowers to the breakfast bar. They were neatly arranged in a pretty pink vase, so she wouldn't have to stop cooking to take care of them. She had never been given roses before. It made her feel feminine and kind of soft inside. She wondered if he had chosen them especially for her or if roses were what he usually brought a woman.

He turned toward the stove, sniffed the air. "Oh, boy, that smells delicious."

She grinned. "Chicken cacciatore with prosciutto tortellini gratinato. Lemon mousse with raspberries for dessert."

His blond eyebrows went up. "I guess you really do like to cook."

"I really do. Eventually, I'm hoping to get into a culinary school. I want to be a chef."

"Wow, I'm impressed."

"Too soon yet to be impressed, but maybe someday…"

"Definitely. You'll do it. I can see the determination in your eyes."

Something warmed inside her. He was taking her seriously, something few of the men she'd known had ever done. They talked while he opened the bottle of red, a French wine—a Rothschild Bordeaux, the label said, expensive she was sure. Ashley got the pair of Maggie's good glasses she had put on the table, and he poured wine into each.

"Where's your little guy tonight?" Jason asked, handing her one of the glasses.

"He's staying with the lady next door, Mrs. Epstein. Robbie really likes her. So do I."

"That's great. You know you didn't have to get a sitter. I wouldn't have minded if he had been here with us."

Ashley glanced at him, a little surprised. Ziggy had no patience with kids. Even if he'd stuck around, he would have been a terrible father.

The delicious aroma of simmering chicken, tomatoes and herbs filled the air. Jason lifted his glass. "To new friends."

She lifted her own. "New friends." They clinked the glasses together and each took a sip. She was no wine connoisseur, but it really tasted good.

"I like it," she said. "I don't know much about wine but I need to learn if I want to be a proper chef."

"I could teach you the basics," Jason offered. "For instance, this is a French Bordeaux. That means it's from the Bordeaux region. The date, 1999, is the year it was released for sale."

He told her a little about the white wine he had brought, which was a California chardonnay from the Napa Valley. "The truth is, almost all the modern French wines come from California stock. The original vines were destroyed by the Phylloxera virus in the early 1900s. Healthy vine stock had to be imported back to Europe."

Ashley smiled at the interesting little tidbit. It was nice to talk to someone who treated her as if she had a brain. "That's cool. I had no idea. I bet the French do their best to keep it a secret."

"I'm sure they do."

She smiled again. "You know they're starting to make wine in Texas. I don't know if it's any good."

He grinned. "Hey, if it's from Texas, it's got to be good, right?"

She laughed. So Jason thought like a true Texan, not just some jet-set rich boy. He continued to surprise her. She liked that about him.

"Are you hungry yet?" she asked. "The chicken looks like it's ready."

"Oh, yeah." He helped her carry the chilled salad plates from the fridge to the dining table, returned and retrieved their wine, while Ashley dished up the supper she had prepared, plating it prettily as she had seen chefs do on TV.

Jason held her chair as she sat down, then took his seat across the rectangular table.

"Everything looks great," he said, surveying the colorful spring bouquet and the elegant place settings she had taken such care to arrange. "You've done a beautiful job, Ashley. I feel like I'm eating in a gourmet restaurant."

She felt a rush of pride. "I hope the food is up to your expectations."

Jason surveyed the steaming plate in front of him, a hungry look in his eyes. He decided to try the salad. "This is really good. What's that spice in the dressing? I don't quite recognize it."

"Curry powder. It just gives the oil and vinegar and other spices a little extra zing."

Jason lifted his glass, then set it back down without taking a sip. Instead, his eyes remained on her face. "I almost called today and canceled our dinner. I got some bad news earlier. I wasn't sure I would be very good company."

She had noticed he seemed slightly distracted. "What happened?"

"You know my dad died. I mentioned it when I was here before, and it was in all the papers."

She nodded. "I saw it on TV. After you left the day you were here, Trace told us you didn't believe it was suicide, and neither did he."

Jason swallowed, the muscles in his suntanned throat going up and down. "The coroner's report came in today. They found small amounts of a drug in my dad's system. Something called ketamine, a tranquilizer they use to sedate animals. That bastard married to my sister drugged him and murdered him and made it look like he killed himself."

Ashley's heart went out to Jason. Believing a trusted member of the family was responsible made his father's death even more painful. "Are you sure he's the one who did it?"

"He was stealing company money. He did it, all right. If he wasn't in jail, I swear, I'd kill him." Jason glanced away, his jaw tight. When he looked at her again, he seemed so haggard, so defeated, that Ashley reached out and put her hand over his where it rested on the table.

"I don't think your father would want that, Jason, not for the son he loved. He would want justice. That's something you can make sure he gets."

She caught a quick flash of moisture in Jason's eyes, then it was gone. He turned his hand over, laced his fingers with hers.

"That's what Trace said. No matter how long it takes, I'll make sure my dad gets the justice he deserves, and Parker Barrington spends the rest of his life in prison."

He didn't let go of her hand, just gave it a gentle squeeze. "I'm really glad I came. You're not like the other girls I know. I think you really care about people. Most of them only care about how they look and how much money I spend on them."

Ashley eased her hand from his, then missed the warmth. "I'm glad you came, too." She smiled. "And I have a feeling my chicken cacciatore is going to make you feel even better."

Jason laughed, and she thought it sounded a little lighter than it had before.

"I haven't had a home-cooked meal in ages. Even when my mom was still alive and we had a chef, we mostly ate catch as catch can."

Ashley could hardly image a life like that.

"But next time it's my treat," he insisted. "If you still don't want to go out, we'll go to the store together and I'll buy the groceries."

Ashley looked at Jason and soft heat curled in the pit of her stomach. It wasn't lust. It was scarier than that. Jason wanted to see her again. They had more in common than she had believed.

She hadn't thought past tonight, but she wanted to see him, too.

Now she just hoped he liked the chicken cacciatore.

Trace opened the door and stepped back, welcoming Maggie into his house. He was dressed in dark blue jeans and a crisp white shirt, his black boots polished to a sheen. His hat was missing, his dark hair neatly combed, and he looked gorgeous.

A little thrill of excitement slipped through her. He was so damned sexy, so damned male.

"You look good enough to eat," he drawled, his golden-brown eyes going over the yellow sundress she wore. It was printed with miniature peach daisies that matched her lipstick, and his gaze settled on her mouth. Bending his head, he kissed her, a brief melding of lips as he led her into the house and closed the door.

His mouth found hers again, long enough to stir the heat beginning to curl low in her stomach.

"Peaches," he whispered, the flavor of her lipstick. "Darlin', you taste as good as you look." He moved closer, sank his fingers into her hair and tipped her head back, holding her in place as he ravished her lips.

She could taste his desire for her, thick and strong, feel the heat of his skin, the mounting tension in his body.

He started to pull away, save making love for later, but her heart was pounding, her insides quivering.

Going up on her toes, she slid her arms around his neck and pulled his mouth down for another kiss. It turned deep and erotic and left no doubt as to what she wanted. When she opened for him, his tongue slid inside to tangle with hers, and arousal trembled through her. She heard Trace groan, and his whole body tightened.

"If we don't stop now," he whispered, kissing the side of her neck, "we aren't going to make it through supper."

Maggie made a soft little purring sound, let her head fall back as he rained kisses over her neck and shoulders.

"You started this, cowboy. Now food is the last thing on my mind."

He growled low in his throat and captured her mouth in another burning kiss. She hadn't expected the evening to go quite this way, but at the feel of all those hard muscles pressing against her and the heavy, demanding length of his erection, all she could think of was making love. She wanted more of his burning kisses, wanted him to touch her, do the things he had done the last time they had been intimate.

His mouth claimed hers as he backed her up against the living room wall—thank God, the curtains were closed—slipped down the straps of her sundress and peeled off the top.

For several long moments he just stood there, his gaze hot and fierce as he drank her in. Then he bent and took the fullness of her breast into his mouth, and Maggie swayed against him. Her nipples were diamond hard, and beneath the fly of his jeans, so was he. She clung to his neck, slid her fingers into the hair at his nape, marveling at the silky texture. She arched her back, giving him better access to her breasts, and he didn't waste time accepting her invitation.

Her stomach contracted. She loved the feel of his mouth against her skin, the rasp of his strong white teeth on her nipple. Maggie closed her eyes as he shoved her skirt up above her waist and reached for her, skimmed a hand over the flat spot beneath her naval. She was wearing only a pair of white thong panties. She gasped as he caught hold of the narrow strap between her legs and ripped it away, tossing the scrap of white satin over his shoulder.

"I'll buy you some new ones," he murmured, his mouth coming down over hers again.

Maggie whimpered as heat scorched through her. She caught the front of his white Western shirt and jerked it open, the snaps popping as she bared his chest and ran her hands over the bands of muscle, which bunched wherever she touched.

Heat scorched through her, so strong her legs felt weak. Trace kissed her again, long and hot and deep. Her hands shook as she unfastened his silver buckle, then tugged his zipper down.

"I want you," she whispered. "You make me crazy."

His jaw clenched as if he was in pain. "Jesus God, lady."

She was in a fog of lust when he found her center and began to stroke her. Heat and pleasure rolled through her, need and sweet desire. She held on as he lifted her, wrapped her legs around his waist, freed himself and drove deep inside her.

Maggie moaned. He was big and hard, and every time he moved, pleasure swept through her. He took her with long, heavy thrusts that had her trembling, making little mewling sounds in her throat. She tightened around him, knew she was going to come.

With a wild, keening cry, she spoke his name and

collapsed against his shoulder. When she looked up at him, she caught the gleam of male satisfaction in his eyes.

"Better hang on, darlin'. We aren't done yet."

Oh, my God. Maggie's eyes widened as he started all over again, slowing his rhythm as he regained control, giving her time to catch fire again.

They came together in a blaze of heat and passion like nothing she had experienced before, the pleasure so deep and sweetly erotic she felt the sting of tears.

Trace held her for several long moments, then kissed her softly. "You okay?"

She just smiled and nodded.

He carried her into the bedroom and set her on her feet in front of the bathroom door. "You probably need a minute."

She looked into those fierce brown eyes. "What is it about you?"

He chuckled. "I don't know, but I'd better go check on dinner before we decide to do a little more research on the subject." His gaze raked her in a way that meant he was ready all over again. "Unless you want to skip dinner altogether."

Maggie grinned. "Tempting." More than tempting. "But suddenly I discover I'm starving. I'll be right out." She gave him a last seductive smile, darted into the bathroom, closed the door and leaned against it, feeling boneless and pleasantly sated.

Until tonight, she hadn't realized what a hussy she was.

Maggie grinned.

Trace released a slow breath. He couldn't remember a woman who turned him on the way Maggie did. He drove her crazy? The woman was driving him completely insane.

For an instant while they were making love he'd felt a rush of lust so fierce he'd thought he was going to lose it. *Not gonna happen,* he'd told himself, determined that pleasuring Maggie was more important that pleasuring himself. At least for the moment.

He smiled as he walked into the kitchen. His willpower had paid off a thousand times over. Damn, he liked making love to her.

Trace heard her moving around in the bathroom and his smile slipped away. There was no doubt the sex was great. Better than great. But after Carly, he wasn't ready for a serious relationship. When he'd discovered the truth about his marriage, discovered what a fool he had been, he had sunk to an all-time low.

He was never really in love with Carly, and yet it had taken him months to get past his doubts and regain some of his old self-confidence. He didn't want to go through anything like that again.

Maggie came wandering in, interrupting his thoughts. She'd done a nice job of putting herself back together, but there was no way to hide it. She looked like a woman well loved.

He wanted to turn off the stove and carry her back to bed.

The night is young, he consoled himself, thinking of all the ways he meant to have her.

"What's for supper?" She sniffed the air as she poured herself a glass of white wine. "Something sure smells good."

"Spaghetti and meatballs, salad and French bread. That okay with you?"

"You bet." She lifted her glass. "Want one?"

"Does a jackrabbit like to run?"

She laughed, poured more wine and handed it to him. She stood close enough that he could smell her perfume, and his body stirred. Maggie went up on her toes and kissed him full on the lips, and his erection returned.

"Food and then sex," she said. "Sounds good to me."

Trace kissed her back. When Maggie moaned into his mouth and her nipples went hard, his decision was made. *Sex and then food.*

Maggie didn't protest when he carried her into the bedroom again.

Chapter 19

Maggie woke up at two in the morning. She'd always had a reliable mental alarm clock and it served her well tonight. She needed to get home. Jason would be gone by now and she didn't want Ashley staying in the town house by herself. It was too soon after her telephone run-in with the stalker. What if the creep tried to break into the house?

She looked over at Trace, who was sleeping on his stomach, the sheet riding low on his hips. Lord, the man was gorgeous. A wide back ridged with muscle, smooth, suntanned skin and a tight little round behind... He attracted her as no man ever had, satisfied her as no man ever had, and yet she felt something deeper than just sexual desire.

Something she refused to think about with so much going on in her life.

Instead, she quietly put her now-wrinkled sundress

back on and headed for the door. She left a note on the pad by the phone, wrote "Enjoyed the meal and everything that went with it—not necessarily in that order" and headed out to her car. She couldn't lock the house up tight without a key, but pushed the button on the doorknob so no one could just walk in.

Her car was parked in front. She drove the little red SUV toward home and had almost reached the turn onto Broadmoor Street when her cell phone rang. She smiled as she recognized Trace's number.

"Hey, cowboy."

"I thought you were staying for breakfast," he growled. "I had a lot more plans for you."

She laughed, felt a little quiver of desire, which was ridiculous, considering. "I was worried about Ashley. I didn't want her there by— Oh, my God!"

"What is it?"

Maggie made a strangled sound into the phone.

"Maggie! For chrissake, what is it?"

"The house…the house is on fire!" Her throat closed up. "Oh, God, Trace, it's on fire!" She tossed the phone down on the passenger seat and stepped on the gas, fishtailed around the corner and shot down the street.

Orange and yellow flames roared into the air through the roof of the town house. Smoke billowed in thick, gray plumes into the ink-black sky. Her heart was hammering, trying to pound its way through her ribs. Her throat was as dry as the timbers going up in flames.

The first fire truck was already there, and another careened around the corner right behind her. Maggie jerked the wheel, forcing the car to the opposite side of the road and jumped out without closing the door. Her pulse was racing; tears blurred her vision.

Dear God, Ashley and Robbie! She started running

across the street, heading straight for the front door, but stumbled and nearly fell when a fireman stepped in her way, blocking her path.

"You can't go in there, miss."

"That's my house! My sister's in there—my sister and her baby!"

The fireman's big gloved hands settled firmly on her shoulders. "They're okay," he said gently. "They're safe. They're right over there." He tipped his head toward the street, angling his wide-brimmed helmet in that direction.

Maggie's heart squeezed. She sagged in relief. Drawing in a shaky breath, she brushed the tears from her cheeks, changed course and hurried toward the slender figure huddled in a blanket on the curb, little Robbie tight in her arms.

"Ashley! Ashley, oh, God, are you all right?"

Her sister stood up, holding on to the baby, and Maggie wrapped her arms around them both. She was shaking all over, her legs weak with leftover fear and relief.

"We're okay," Ashley said. "We're both okay."

Maggie's throat clogged with tears and she started crying. "I shouldn't have let you stay with me. I was afraid something would happen. If you and Robbie had been hurt or—or…" She swallowed, unable to complete the awful thought.

"We're all right, Maggie, truly. This wasn't your fault."

She looked over at the row of town houses. None of the other units were burning. So far the firemen had been able to keep the blaze contained to her house alone. All the other owners seemed to have been evacuated, and small groups milled around in the darkness, watching the firefighters battle the fire. Mrs. Epstein sat on a lawn chair someone had been thoughtful enough to provide, and was talking to some of the neighbors.

Maggie watched the flames leaping into the air, the dense streams of water shooting toward the roof from three different hoses, the wall of smoke slowly changing from black to white, and her throat clogged even more.

A noise caught her attention. She turned at the sound of boots ringing on asphalt, and spotted the tall, familiar male figure. *Trace.*

"Maggie!" He strode toward her, his hat missing, his hair still rumpled from sleep. His eyes were dark and filled with concern, his forehead lined with worry. His glance went from her to the fire. Then he spotted Ashley and Robbie, and some of the tension drained from his features. "Everybody get out okay?"

Maggie nodded. "Everyone's all right." She started crying again, shifted so that Trace wouldn't see. She felt his hands settle gently on her shoulders. He turned her toward him, drew her into his arms and just held on.

"It's okay," he said softly. "Your sister and the baby are safe. The other residents got out okay. Everything's going to be all right."

A little sob escaped. "This is my fault." She swallowed past the lump in her throat. "I shouldn't have made him mad. Oh, God, Trace."

His arms tightened around her. "This wasn't your fault. None of this is your fault." He eased her a little away, brushed a light kiss over her lips. "You scared the holy bejeezus out of me, darlin'."

The soft drawl rolled over her like a warm caress. She knew she had frightened him, and the worry in his eyes made her heart twist. She sniffed, accepted the handkerchief he pulled out of the back pocket of his jeans and blew her nose.

"I shouldn't have gone to your house tonight. I should have stayed home."

"I don't think that would have pleased your sister and Jason very much, and it wouldn't have changed anything anyway." He turned his attention to Ashley, who stared at the fire as if she were in a trance. "Tell me what happened, honey."

Ashley turned to look at him. Beneath the blanket, she was wearing her shortie, pink flowered robe, and her feet were bare. "I don't exactly know. After Jason left, I went over to Mrs. Epstein's to pick up Robbie. I brought him home and put him in his crib and we went to bed. I was sleeping pretty hard until something woke me up. I don't know exactly what it was, some kind of noise, I guess. I got up to check things out, and when I reached the kitchen, I saw this bright yellow glow over the yard. I didn't realize the house was on fire until one of the neighbors started banging on the door."

She took a shaky breath. "I grabbed Robbie, my purse and the diaper bag, and ran out of the house. People were streaming out of the other condos. Someone had already called the fire department."

"The fire started upstairs?" Trace asked.

Ashley nodded. "In Maggie's studio, I think. The door was closed and I didn't see any flames until I got outside. Then I saw the whole roof on the back side of the town house was on fire."

Maggie looked at the flames chewing through the space where all her pictures were stored. Weeks of work, hours of effort. Her computer destroyed, along with the files that held all her photographic memory cards, as well as the list of buyers she had been compiling. Her stomach rolled with a combination of nausea and anger.

"He destroyed my studio," she said, fighting not to cry again. "He was mad because I hung up on him."

"I'm so sorry, darlin'. All your hard work gone because some lunatic wants you and can't have you." Trace gazed back at the town house, which was mostly smoking now, though flames still burned in part of the upper story.

Maggie followed his gaze. "Do you think maybe the security cameras might have picked up something?"

"There's a chance. Stay here. I'll be right back." He crossed the small grassy area in front of the condo and walked up to one of the firemen, the one who appeared to be in charge. They spoke for a while. Trace pointed toward the camera mounted under the eaves beside the front door. The man replied, Trace nodded, then turned and started walking back in Maggie's direction.

"The arson squad's already here," he said. "See that red Suburban? They'll be doing some preliminary work tonight, asking questions, taking pictures. They'll come back tomorrow after the debris cools down, bring the dogs in maybe, examine the interior. They'll be able to tell us how the fire started and whether or not it was arson."

"*He* did this. You know he did."

"Whoever did this knew a lot about electronics. We installed a good system. He had to be damned good to get inside without setting it off."

"He put cameras in my house. He knew enough to do that."

"This would be a whole lot harder."

"Could you get in?"

He frowned. "Yeah."

"I guess he could, too."

Trace's jaw hardened.

"So what about the video cameras?" Maggie asked.

"If they're intact, the arson guys will take a look at them, let us know if they find anything." He pinned her with a hard, dark glance. "You're not gonna like this, but you and your sister are coming home with me. You'll stay there until we get all of this figured out."

"Why? So he can burn your house down, too?"

"Trust me, he won't get into my place. Protection is my business. The only way he gets inside is if I invite him in."

Maggie didn't argue. She would rather have checked her weary little family into a motel, but clearly, the stalker was dangerous.

Maybe he figured if he couldn't have her, he might as well kill her.

Early-morning sunlight streamed in through the kitchen windows. The weather was heating up. Ninety degrees predicted, and the humidity wouldn't be any fun, either.

Trace poured himself a cup of coffee and carried it over to the kitchen table. Rowdy trotted up beside him, dropped down on the floor next to his chair and rested his muzzle on Trace's boot.

"Well, boy, we've got company, like it or not."

Rowdy's ears perked up and Trace chuckled. "What was I thinking? Of course you'd like it. Two pretty females lavishing you with attention." He set his cup on the red Formica tabletop next to the *Houston Chronicle* he'd carried in off the front porch. On a lark, or maybe in a moment of nostalgia, he'd remodeled the kitchen to look like the 1950s kitchen his grandmother had in the old farmhouse out on the ranch. White and red and chrome. He still liked coming home to it.

He flicked his gaze to the hallway off the living

room that led to the bedrooms. His unwilling houseguests were asleep in one of them, exhausted after the fire last night.

Leaning back, Trace combed his fingers through his hair. Maggie felt responsible for the fire, but it wasn't her fault. If anyone was responsible, he was. She was paying him to protect her. He had failed.

Trace blew out a frustrated breath. He needed to talk to Anthony Ramirez, captain of the Arson Investigation Bureau. Tony was a straight shooter, and he and Trace had worked together before. Tony could confirm what Trace's gut had already told him—that the fire had been purposely set.

In return, he needed to bring Ramirez up to speed on the threats against Maggie and what little he had found out about her stalker. Until he talked to Ramirez, he couldn't be sure it was arson, but his instincts, bolstered by his brief conversation with a couple of the fire boys last night, were saying chances were nearly a hundred percent.

He had underestimated this guy at every turn. The last thing he'd expected the bastard to do was set Maggie's house on fire. The guy was obsessed with her. In some sick fashion, in love with her. Even if he'd been pissed, angry enough after the phone call to do her physical harm, a guy like that would want a face-to-face confrontation. He'd want to get her alone, have her all to himself when he meted out whatever punishment he believed she deserved.

Hell, she wasn't even there last night—which, since he had to have gone inside to start the blaze, he must have known. He had set the fire anyway, putting Ashley and her baby at risk.

Trace sipped his coffee, trying to get inside the guy's

head. Trying to make sense of things. Coming up with a big fat zero.

Again.

Talking to Ramirez came first and foremost, but he also needed to talk to Mark Sayers. The cops had shown up last night and taken a preliminary statement. Mark wasn't officially involved in the case, but he was a friend and a detective, and Trace wanted him kept in the loop.

He glanced at his watch, saw it was still too early for Sayers to be at the station, looked back down the hall to the guest room door. He had a dozen things to do, but didn't want to leave without making sure Maggie knew how to operate his alarm system. He wasn't taking any more chances.

He got up and poured himself another cup of coffee. As much as he wanted to leave, he didn't want to wake her. She was exhausted and worried. She'd been terrified last night and he didn't blame her.

He'd been damned terrified himself.

With her cell line open and connected to his, he could hear her crying as she'd raced like a madwoman toward the fire that threatened her family.

Maybe it was realizing how much she cared about them.

Maybe it was realizing how much he had come to care for her.

Whatever it was, his stomach had been churning as he struggled to drag on his clothes, shove his feet into a worn pair of boots and get the hell on the road. His heart had thundered as he'd raced to the condo. All the way there, all he could think of was Maggie.

He wanted her safe. He wanted her out of danger.

Hell, he just plain wanted her.

And he was beginning to realize he wanted her for a lot more than just sex.

The thought scared the hell out of him.

A memory stirred, of Maggie and their heated love-making last night, and his blood headed south in arousal.

The worst possible punishment he could inflict on himself was having Maggie O'Connell sleeping in his house—and not sleeping in his bed.

Chapter 20

A knock sounded at the door and Trace rose to answer it. Rowdy padded along beside him as he crossed the foyer and looked through the peephole, to find Mark Sayers standing beneath the wide, overhanging porch roof.

"I was just getting ready to call you," Trace said. "Come on in." He stepped back and Sayers walked into the living room, his light brown hair neatly combed, his cheap suit already rumpled.

"Listen, I heard what happened last night. Unofficial word is arson. I guess I owe you an apology. Looks like Maggie's troubles are bigger than I thought."

"Apology accepted. But I'm still gonna need your help."

"Hey, I'm a cop. It's my job to protect and serve. I don't want to see anybody get hurt. Just tell me what you need."

"You want a cup of coffee?"

"Love one."

Trace led the detective into the kitchen, took down a a mug and filled it with the steaming, dark Colombian brew.

"Thanks," Sayers said, accepting the cup. "So what's your take on the fire?"

"Well, that's the thing." Trace led him over to the kitchen table and both men sat down. Rowdy returned to his place on the floor at Trace's feet. "This guy's a whack job, for sure. That being said, I still can't get a handle on him. Maggie wasn't even home last night. Her younger sister and her baby were there."

"Jesus."

"This creep gets past the alarm system and gets into the house, so he has to know Maggie wasn't there. But he lights the place up, anyway. It doesn't add up."

"He wanted to punish her, maybe, for something he believes she's done."

"She hung up on him a few days ago," Trace said. "Maybe he was mad enough to kill her sister to punish her, but in my book it just doesn't wash."

"You never can tell, I guess, but it woulda been a major overreaction."

"From the notes he's left, he's got some kind of sick infatuation with Maggie. Killing her little sister and her infant child would hardly endear him to her."

Sayers started frowning. He looked at Trace over the rim of his coffee mug. "You aren't thinking this might be just a coincidence? Some lunatic firebug torches her place and the police and everyone else jump to the conclusion the stalker's to blame?"

Trace shrugged. He hadn't put the thought into words, but it had been lurking at the back of his mind.

"I don't buy it," Mark said.

"I'm not much on coincidence, either. We'll know

more after the arson guys finish their job. Tony Ramirez is a good man. He'll find the dots and string them together."

"You'd installed security on her place, if I remember."

Trace nodded. "And cameras front and back. He bypassed the alarm system as if it wasn't there. No word yet on the cameras, but odds are he took them out."

"You think her stalker is capable of that? You said he bugged her car, set up video surveillance inside the house."

"Like I said, I'll know more after I talk to Ramirez."

Sayers rose from his chair. "Let's meet again after. I'm not supposed to be involved in this case—so I'm not. Got it?"

"I got it. Thanks for coming by, Mark."

Just then the bedroom door swung open and Maggie walked out. She was wearing the bathrobe he'd loaned her, red hair in a sexy tangle around her shoulders. Trace felt that punch in the gut he'd felt before.

"I hope I'm not interrupting. I didn't know anyone else was here," she murmured.

"Maggie, this is Detective Mark Sayers. He was just leaving."

"I'm sorry about the fire," Mark said. "We're gonna catch this guy. A man like that is a danger not only to you and your family but to everyone in the community."

"Yes, he is. And I appreciate any help you can give us."

Trace followed Sayers to the door and closed it behind him. He was halfway back to the kitchen when a second, more frantic pounding started on his door.

"I think I'm living in Grand Central Station," he grumbled, returning to the door, this time spotting Jason Sommerset on the porch.

"Did you hear about the fire?" Jason strode past him into the living room. "I saw it on the news this morning. Maggie's town house burned up last night. I can't find Maggie, or Ashley and Robbie. I'm worried sick. Do you know where they are?"

"Take it easy, kid. Both women are here and so is the baby. Everyone's fine."

The tension left Jason's shoulders.

"Hello, Jason," Maggie called out from the kitchen, wagging her fingers in his direction. Trace noticed his traitorous dog curled at her feet. "Ashley's still sleeping. It was a very long night."

"I was really worried," Jason said. "I'm glad everyone's okay."

Just then the door down the hall swung open and Ashley wandered out into the living room, rubbing her short, messy blond curls. She was wearing the pink flowered robe she'd had on last night and was barefoot, her long legs exposed to way above the knees. She spotted Jason and froze like a deer in the headlights.

"Jason…"

He strode toward her, reached out and took both her hands in his. "Are you all right? What about the baby? I was scared to death when I saw what happened on the news."

Ashley swallowed and her eyes welled. She'd been the strong one last night. Now she crumpled. "I was so scared," she said, and Jason pulled her into his arms.

"You should have called me. I would have come."

"We hardly…hardly know each other."

He tipped her chin up. "We're friends, aren't we?"

Ashley gave him a watery smile. "I guess we are."

"You bet we are. And I've already got a place figured out for you and your family to stay."

"What?"

Jason turned to Trace. "A friend of mine is in Europe. As soon as I saw the news, I called him." A faint smile touched his lips. "Lucky for him it wasn't the middle of the night in France."

"Go on," Trace said.

"Jimmy owns a condo over in the Galleria. It's not far from my place. I told him what happened and he said Ashley, Maggie and the baby could stay at his house until he got home. He said he'd be gone at least another four weeks."

Trace started shaking his head. "That's not gonna happen. Maggie's the target. Ashley and Robbie wouldn't be safe. Just think about what happened last night."

Maggie came forward, her borrowed terry cloth robe trailing on the floor behind her five-foot-four-inch frame. He hid a smile. Damn, she looked delicious.

"Trace is right," Maggie said. "Ashley needs to be as far away from me as possible."

Jason's clear blue gaze swung back to the younger girl. "Then you and Robbie can stay. The place has security guards 24/7. We'll let them know what happened, make sure they keep an extra-sharp eye out for trouble."

"Maybe she should just stay here," Maggie said, her big green eyes going to Trace.

"I'm not the one who's in danger," Ashley said. "The guy wasn't after me. He set the fire in Maggie's studio. He was mad at her. He wanted to hurt her. I just happened to be in the way."

"He could have killed you," Trace said softly.

Ashley shrugged. "That's the way crazy people are. They don't think about the consequences."

She had a point. And he agreed she would probably be safer somewhere away from her sister.

"I'd keep an eye on her," Jason promised, looking at Ashley as if she already belonged to him. "If she needs anything, all she'll have to do is call."

Damn, the kid had it bad. Trace almost felt sorry for him. "Let's see what the arson squad has to say. They might have information that will help us decide what to do."

"I'm not giving up my job." Ashley's slender hands slammed down on her hips, making the flowered robe creep higher. Jason looked as if he were going to swallow his tongue. Man, the kid was in trouble.

"You won't have to quit your job," Trace promised. "We'll work all of this out." Somehow.

Though, at the moment, he had no idea how he was going to make that happen.

Maggie showered and put on the same wrinkled sundress she had been wearing the night before, all the clothes she had left in the world. The dress smelled like smoke and dredged up memories of flames and fear she would rather forget.

She thought of the fire and hoped the downstairs area of the town house had fared better than the upstairs, and that her sister's clothes could be washed and cleaned. That what little Ashley owned hadn't been destroyed by the water and smoke. But there was no way the fire department was letting them back in the house today, not with smoldering debris and hot, charred wood still making it too dangerous to go inside.

Fortunately, in the University District there were a number of clothing stores. Deciding Mrs. Epstein needed a day or two to recover, Trace called his receptionist. Annie volunteered to babysit for a couple hours, time enough for an emergency shopping trip to nearby Rice Village. Maggie had met Annie at the office and Trace trusted her completely. Though Ashley worried about leaving the baby with someone new, Maggie was sure, once she met the lady, her concern would be assuaged.

Jason insisted on accompanying them. With their nerves still on edge after the fire, both women agreed. Of course he would have to drive Maggie's car, since his flashy silver Porsche wasn't big enough for all of them.

While they waited for Annie, Ashley changed into a pair of Trace's lightweight sweatpants and an olive-drab T-shirt, then sat down in the living room next to Jason to give little Robbie his bottle.

Trace reached out and caught hold of Maggie's hand, and she let him lead her into the kitchen. While she seated herself at the table, he poured her a mug of freshly brewed coffee, poured one for himself, then sat across from her. She couldn't miss the concern in his face.

"What is it, Trace? You're making me nervous."

"It's nothing like that. It's just that we've talked about the fire, but not about your work and what losing it must mean to you. It looks like your studio is gone, your pictures all destroyed. You'll have to start completely over. I just want you to know how sorry I am."

Maggie reached out and caught his hand. There was something about those strong hands that always made her feel safe. And she knew how talented they could be.

"I was frantic last night…terrified for my sister and Robbie. And I was furious about what that bastard did to me and my family. But my pictures weren't destroyed."

Trace frowned. "I thought you kept your memory cards in the studio. They weren't there?"

"They were there. For the past few days, I'd been making changes in my filing system. I was just about finished. The thing is, a year or so ago I decided to store all my work online. There's a service called Photodrive. It's a commercial file storage website designed especially for professional photographers. Once I finish a collection, I put every picture I've taken on the site, just in case something like this ever happened—though believe me, I never thought it actually would."

"My company uses online storage, too. At least for some things."

"Not everything?"

Trace chuckled. "I'm a little too paranoid for that. If you'd see some of these computer geeks at work you'd know that a guy with the right skills can get into almost anything. Hell, I'm pretty damned good myself."

"Ah…yet another hidden talent."

His mouth faintly curved. "I guess you could say that." He took a sip of his coffee. "So you're telling me you still have the original files."

"That's right. Everything's on Photodrive. All I have to do is retrieve the photos I sold at the opening, get them reprinted and framed, to replace the ones that were purchased, and I'm back in business."

His dark eyebrows drew together. "Besides you, who else knows you still have those pictures?"

"No one. Why?"

"No reason…at least nothing I can put my finger on. Just one of those funny hunches you get after you've been doing this as long as I have. I want you to hold off on reprinting the photos for a while. Don't tell anyone you still have them. Your friend Faye Langston, over at the gallery, isn't going to like it, but, hey, you had a fire, right? What can you do?"

"She isn't expecting me to have them until next week."

"Great. By then I'll have talked to Tony Ramirez. He's head of the arson investigation. I want to hear what he has to say before we make our next move."

"All right." She needed to get started. It took time to get the photos ready to sell, but she trusted Trace's judgment. And it would set her back only a few more days.

"My client list is also stored on Photodrive," Maggie said. "I'll have to start all over sorting them, and get the new buyers' names from Faye, but at least it wasn't all destroyed."

"That's great news. In the meantime, I guess you and your sister are going shopping."

Maggie grinned. "With Jason Sommerset acting as bodyguard."

Trace smiled, shook his head. "The kid's in big trouble."

"Nice trouble, though, wouldn't you say?"

Trace looked at her with those hot, golden-brown eyes. "I think I'm in the same kind of trouble."

Maggie laughed. "I think maybe I am, too."

"You realize if Ash and Robbie move to the Galleria, you'll be staying here with me."

Heat crept into her cheeks. "I'd probably be a lot safer."

"You also realize you won't be sleeping in the guest room."

Her pulse picked up. "No?" With his Western shirt open at the throat, his skin darkly tanned, she wanted to press her mouth there, just breathe him in.

"So you may not be as safe as you think."

She wished she could kiss him. "Maybe not. Then again, I've always believed in living dangerously."

Trace's gaze ran over her and his mouth curved in a slow, sexy smile. "Looks like I do, too."

* * *

Trace left the women with Jason. The kid was used to the good life, but he was also an athlete who excelled at tennis, had been captain of his college swim team and had learned how to handle himself. Trace chuckled as he remembered the story Hewitt had told him, how Jason had come home from high school wanting to learn to box. His mother had cried and begged her husband to forbid it. Being the ultimate negotiator, Hewitt had convinced their son to try martial arts instead. Jason discovered he had a knack for it.

He could defend himself if the need arose, and he stayed in shape. Jason could take care of the women, or at least knew what to do if they ran into trouble.

In the meantime, Trace had put in a call to Tony Ramirez, who had agreed to meet him at the Atlas office. He was waiting when Tony walked in. He wasn't a big man, but strong as a bull, with powerful shoulders and arms. He had short black hair and a Roman nose. And he was smart, which was why he was good at his job.

"Good to see you, Tony." The men shook hands and Trace led him back to his glass-enclosed office. "You want a cup of coffee or a Coke?"

"I just had lunch. I'm fine."

Trace closed the door and both men sat down. "I appreciate your stopping by. What can you tell me so far?"

Tony opened the file he carried, though Trace knew he kept most of the information in his head. "As you already know, the good news is no one was hurt. The bad news is it was definitely arson. The guy disabled the wireless alarm before he went in—probably used some kind of sophisticated software. Same with the cameras."

"I was afraid of that." Recently, Trace had used the

same technique in Mexico on a rescue mission he had undertaken with his friends Dev Raines, Johnnie Riggs and Jake Cantrell. The high-tech gear had gotten them inside a fortified compound and into the sprawling mansion where a missing little girl was being held. Unfortunately, they'd had to shoot their way out.

"The perp went in through the sliding glass door," Ramirez was saying. "Started the fire in the studio. Multiple points of origin. Gasoline used as the accelerant. He opened the windows for ventilation. He really knew what he was doing. The whole damn room went up all at once."

"Definitely a pro."

Tony nodded. "He's a professional, all right, and way better than most. And here's the kicker. From the looks of it, the fire couldn't have been burning more than a few minutes when the 911 call came in. The station's just a couple of blocks away, but by the time the first truck arrived, the caller was already gone. The way it looks, there's a good chance the caller is the guy who set the fire."

"He wanted the fire boys to get there. He wanted the studio to burn, but not the whole house. He wasn't after the woman and her baby."

"I think he went out of his way to keep people from getting hurt, or setting the other apartments on fire. The way the blaze was constructed, it was meant to flash inward, taking out the room but not immediately burning into the unit next door. It would have, sooner rather than later. And with fire, there's always a chance something will go wrong. There's no safe way to commit arson."

"So there was the risk of loss of life, but the odds were in his favor."

"That's about it. Like I said, this guy's really good at what he does."

Trace leaned back in his chair. "Doesn't read like Maggie's stalker. What are the odds some nut job who has the hots for her is also a high-dollar torch?"

"Could be her nut job put up the money."

Trace pondered that. "Could be, but I don't see it."

"So what then? Someone with a grudge against Maggie?"

"I've been working that angle. So far it's led nowhere. A lot of people know about the stalker. Police, friends, people we've questioned. Maybe somebody wanted to jump on the bandwagon. Destroy her work and let the stalker take the blame."

"I hear she's pretty successful. Maybe someone doesn't like the competition."

"Maybe."

Tony stood up and Trace did, too. "Thanks, Tony. I appreciate the information."

"Hey, we're both on the same side." Ramirez stuck out a meaty hand and Trace shook it. "Take care of Ms. O'Connell. This may not be over yet."

Trace clenched his jaw. It wasn't over. But he was determined it would be. And soon.

Their arms loaded with bags and boxes, Maggie and Ashley returned to Trace's house late in the afternoon. Carrying another load of packages, Jason walked them to the door, and Trace pulled it open.

He smiled. "Welcome home."

Maggie's eyes widened at the sight of him cradling little Robbie against his broad chest.

"What in the world…"

"Annie had some things to do at the office. I was heading home so we swapped places."

Maggie looked at Ashley, Ashley looked at her and both burst out laughing.

One of Trace's eyebrows went up. "What? You didn't think I could change a diaper?" His mouth quirked. "I managed to figure it out."

Dropping her package, Ashley reached for the baby, and Trace gently handed him over. "Thanks, Trace," she exclaimed. "You've really been terrific."

"Not a problem."

Maggie gazed up at her tough Texas cowboy, thought of the way he'd looked standing there with a tiny baby in his arms and felt a tug at her heart. She had never met any man like him.

Jason cleared his throat, making his presence known. "So what about Ashley using my friend's apartment?" he asked hopefully.

"I think it's a good idea," Trace said. "Until we know what's going on, Ashley and Robbie are safer staying somewhere Maggie isn't."

Jason grinned ear to ear. He turned to Ashley, who held her son in the crook of her arm. "I've got access to the key. I can help you move in whenever you're ready."

"The sooner the better," Trace said.

"I'm working tomorrow night." Ashley smoothed a hand over the sleeping baby's head. "I called Mrs. Epstein. She says her house is still a little smoky, but the fire department says it's safe. She's all set to take care of Robbie. I guess there's no reason for me to stay here." She held up one of the shopping bags, jiggled it and grinned. "Besides, I'm already packed."

Trace chuckled. "You and Maggie should be able to

get back in the town house in a day or two. Maggie can give you a call when we get the word."

"Great."

The women searched through the bags, separating the items they had purchased, the baby clothes, pairs of shoes, slacks, blouses, jeans and T-shirts. Then Jason carried Ashley's share out to his car and returned for her and Robbie.

Maggie hugged her sister goodbye. Swept by a sudden sense of loss, she felt tears burn behind her eyes. "Call me or I'll call you. We need to keep in touch."

"I'll call, I promise."

Another quick hug, then Ashley and Robbie were gone. Jason closed the door and followed them across the porch.

Maggie felt a wave of sadness. Everything seemed topsy-turvy, weirdly upside down. Her house was destroyed, her sister once more living out of a suitcase. She felt like sitting down and having a good, long cry.

She sensed Trace's presence behind her. His arm slid around her waist, drawing her against him. "She'll be all right. Jason's a good kid. He'll make sure she's got everything she needs."

Maggie turned, managed a smile. "I like him. I know Ash does, too."

Trace ran a finger along her jaw. "It's gonna be all right."

She nodded, but in her heart, she didn't really believe it.

"Come to bed with me," Trace said softly. "I promise to make you forget all this, at least for a while."

Her throat ached. She needed him and somehow he knew. Instead of a reply, she stood on tiptoe and kissed him. Trace kissed her back, lifted her in his arms and carried her into the bedroom.

True to his word, at least for a while, he made her forget.

Chapter 21

Richard Meyers stood in the shadows beneath the bridge. With the moon hidden beneath a layer of heavy black clouds, the darkness felt as thick as the humid air. Night sounds intruded: the rustle of leaves, a rodent scurrying through the dirt along the creek bed, the sighing of the wind through the branches of the trees.

He was a few miles out of the city on a two-lane road to nowhere, exactly the place the phone call he'd received had instructed him to be. Richard didn't mind the inconvenience. The job he had commissioned had been completed exactly as planned. The man he had hired was worth every penny.

He spotted the shadowy figure approaching out of the darkness. Same long trench coat with the collar turned up, same narrow-brimmed fedora pulled low across the face. Last time, Richard had fought not to laugh at the ridiculous costume. Tonight he felt like grinning in sheer relief.

"You got the money?" the man asked in a voice that sounded slightly rusty.

Richard handed him the envelope, the second installment of their arrangement, fifteen thousand more in hundred-dollar bills. Thirty thousand was a hefty sum, but he'd wanted to hire the best. Apparently, he had.

The man stuffed the envelope into the inside pocket of the trench coat. "Looks like our business is finished."

"Yes. Thank you." He couldn't believe he was thanking someone for committing arson. But since that night at the marina, everything in his life had changed.

The man made no reply, just turned and walked away, the bottom of his trench coat flapping as he headed into the night and disappeared into a copse of trees along the road.

It was over. They were safe. For the first time in weeks, he could look forward again, instead of backward.

Richard breathed a long sigh of relief.

Maggie heard the knock and hurried to the door. Trace's security system was activated. He had shown her how to use it and assured her that once it was set, no one would be able to get inside the house undetected. She wasn't expecting a visitor. Trace was working at his office. She and Rowdy were the only ones at home.

The dog stood beside her, his ears perked up, black-and-white head tilted toward the sound of someone on the porch. Only a little uneasy, she peered through the peephole and let out a little whoop of glee.

Punching in the alarm code, she hurriedly opened the door. "Roxanne! I can't believe you're here! Good Lord, when I called this morning, I didn't expect you to get on a plane and fly home!"

The tall, statuesque brunette walked into the living

room and drew Maggie into a hug. "Are you kidding? You didn't think I'd want to come back when I found out someone was trying to murder my best friend?"

Maggie sighed. "I don't think he was trying to kill me," she said, leading Roxy toward the kitchen. "I wasn't even there that night." She had called Roxanne in New York that morning. After everything that had happened, she found herself desperately in need of a friend.

"I hung up on him," she continued. "I guess it made him mad and he wanted to punish me."

"Punish you? You haven't done anything wrong! I hope they find the prick and somebody shoots him."

Maggie laughed. "I'm sorry you felt like you had to come back, but I'm really glad you're here."

Roxy smiled. "Me, too." She rolled those haughty blue eyes and fluffed the smooth dark hair curled under at her shoulders. "Besides, I was getting bored. How much shopping can one woman do?"

Maggie grinned, feeling better than she had in days. "Trace is down at his office. How about a glass of iced tea?"

Her friend scoffed. "I'd rather have a martini, darling, but at this hour, I suppose iced tea will have to do." While she sat down at the Formica-topped kitchen table, Maggie filled two glasses with ice and added sweet tea she took from the fridge. Then she carried the glasses over and settled across from her.

"I think it's time you told me what's going on," Rox said. She glanced around Trace's tidy, masculine home. "Looks like a lot has changed since I left."

Maggie took a sip of tea. "I guess you could say that. I've got a family I didn't expect, the second floor of my house is a smoking pile of rubble and whoever did it is still out there somewhere." They had talked on the phone, but now she went into detail, bringing her friend up to date on the stalker, her sister and the baby, Jason Sommerset, and the fire.

"You aren't talking about *the* Jason Sommerset, son of the late Hewitt Sommerset?"

"One and the same," Maggie said. "Jason's a friend of Trace's. He's taken Ashley under his protection. My sister is beautiful, Rox. And she's really sweet. Jason seems to have a terrible crush on her."

"Well, she could certainly do worse than the heir to Sommerset Industries."

"It's funny. I don't think my sister cares how much money Jason has. She's had some bad times. The baby's father was a real loser. She just wants someone who will treat her well."

Maggie went on to tell Roxanne about the apartment Jason had arranged for Ash and Robbie till things got back to normal. "Ashley called when she got there, all excited. I guess the apartment's a real showplace. She says it has marble floors, an entertainment room the size of a small theater and gold nozzles in the bathrooms— of which there are many. It's a nice treat for her."

And Ashley having a place to stay would give Maggie time to work things out. Rebuilding the town house was going to take weeks, maybe longer. She needed to find somewhere else for them to live until it was finished, but she couldn't even do that until they caught the stalker.

"Jason Sommerset has all the money in the world," Roxanne said, "but as far as I know he's stayed out of trouble. No drunk driving, no rehab, nothing like that."

"He seems really great. I'm not sure how Ashley feels about him. I guess time will tell."

"I guess it will." Roxanne sipped her tea and grimaced, clearly wishing it was alcoholic. "You've done a great job of telling me everything, darling, but you managed to leave one small thing out."

"What's that?"

"The cowboy. You're living in his house. You aren't going to tell me nothing's going on between you."

Maggie's face went warm. "We're, um, involved, I guess you could say. Mostly it's just physical."

Roxanne eyed her assessingly. "Really?"

"Well, mostly. You said yourself the guy was a major hunk."

"So I did and so he is, but doing the dirty just for the sake of it isn't your usual style. Are you sure there isn't more to it?"

Maggie drew a circle in the frosty wetness on her glass. "I hope not. I mean, getting seriously involved with someone is the last thing I want."

"Sometimes things just happen."

"I suppose. Trace is pretty amazing. To tell you the truth, I'm doing my best not to fall in love with him."

Roxanne cocked a dark eyebrow. "Where's the fun in that, darling? Falling in love is what life's all about."

"Maybe. But sometimes there are other considerations."

"Such as…?"

"Such as…what if I'm like my mother, Rox? Celeste's a runner, you know? Whenever things go wrong, she just up and leaves. She ran from my dad, ran from her second husband. Now she's run off and left Ashley's father. So far, that's what I've always done. I run whenever things get too involved. I'm afraid of what'll happen if I ever let myself truly fall in love."

Roxanne reached over and caught her hand. "I'm not the person to be giving you advice. I've been in love more times than I can count—which means I've never really been in love at all. But I believe if Mr. Right comes along, somehow you'll know. And you won't have any desire to run away from him."

Maggie made no reply. She had a history of hurting the men she cared about. First Josh, then Michael, then David. She didn't want Trace to be another casualty of her changeable affections.

On the other hand, Trace's sexual history included a failed marriage and a string of redheads he cast aside like worn-out boots.

She didn't want to suffer that fate, either.

"For the moment, we're just enjoying each other," she finally said.

"And he's keeping you safe."

"That's right." But her heart was definitely at risk. There wasn't the least amount of safety in falling in love with Trace Rawlins.

Roxanne stood up. "I guess I'd better get going. I'm beat and have lots of unpacking to do. If you need a place to stay, just let me know."

"Thanks, Rox."

"I expect to hear from you every couple of days. If you don't call, I'll be calling you. Just remember, I'm here if you need me."

Maggie walked her to the door and the women hugged.

"Take care of yourself, darling. Keep in touch."

Maggie managed to smile. "I will." But she was thinking of what Roxanne and Ashley both had said, and trying to convince herself Trace wasn't Mr. Right.

Ashley showed up early for work Friday night. The Texas Café was already full, customers laughing and talking in their pink vinyl booths, couples sitting at scarred wooden tables. Platters of spaghetti, burgers and fries, and homemade pie and ice cream slid out through the service window behind the long food service counter lined with pink vinyl stools.

On the way to the café, she had dropped the baby off at Mrs. Epstein's, whose house smelled a little like smoked sausage, but had suffered no real damage and was slowly airing out. Though her battered old Chevy sat in the underground garage of her borrowed apartment, Jason had insisted on driving her to work. He had dropped her off in front of the café with a promise to return at the end of her shift.

Ashley thought of him as she worked over the grill next to Betty Sparks, the gray-haired woman who owned the restaurant. Betty was instructing her on how to broil the perfect burger. Ashley was eager to learn.

"You have to start with good meat," Betty said. "That's the secret. Good meat cooked just right—not too done, not too rare. Then a good, sturdy sesame seed bun. Got to have the seeds to make it right."

She was learning to make chili, and how to deep-fry fish and chips. She could make gourmet meals, but was learning the basics of how to cook for a crowd, how to handle the pressure and make everything come off the grill at the right time.

"I gotta check on things out front," Betty said, wiping her hands on a dishrag. "Don't worry, you're doin' just fine."

Ashley nodded. Filling in for the regular cook while he was taking care of his sick mother, she was only a little nervous at being left on her own. It was hot and moist in the kitchen, with steam coming off the steam tables, smoke off the grill, but she loved being there, loved that she was turning her life around, working to-

ward her goals, making a future for herself and little
Robbie.

An order for chicken fried steak came in. Betty had
shown her how to use the café's premade flour. mix to
coat the meat patty. Ashley smiled when it came out of
the pan perfectly golden-brown. A ladle of thick white,
country sausage gravy went on top, a ladle of buttery
corn, and she slid the plate through the service window
for one of the waitresses to pick up.

She turned the stainless-steel wheel to check the next
order, made a pair of creamy chocolate shakes, then returned to the grill for two more medium-rare burgers.

It was almost the end of her shift when the bell above
the door rang and a new customer walked in. Ashley
started at the sight of the thin, exotically handsome
man with high cheekbones and thick black hair pulled
back in a queue at the nape of his neck and tied with a
leather thong. He wore black jeans and a leather vest
with nothing underneath but a string of silver beads.

He looked like a rock star and she knew him instantly
as the man who had fathered her baby.

Ziggy.

There he was, a vision out of her past who had stepped
into the new life she was building. She wanted to wring
his neck.

She leaned through the service window behind the
front counter and spoke to Betty. "Would it be okay if
I took a quick break? I've got a problem I need to deal
with."

"Why, sure, honey." Betty's sharp eyes went to
Ziggy, who sauntered over to the counter and sat down
on one of the round, padded stools. "I'll take over until
you get finished."

Ashley untied the strings of her white cotton apron

and drew it off over her head, then walked out of the kitchen, heading toward the man at the counter.

Ziggy stood up as she approached. "Hey, babe." His black eyes raked her. "You're lookin' fine. Never know you just had a kid."

"That was three months ago, Ziggy. What the fuck are you doing here?" She winced as she slipped into her old self and said a word she hadn't used in months.

"What do mean, sweetheart? I came to see *you*—and our son, of course."

"Bullshit, Ziggy. How did you find me?"

"I talked to Tommy. Megan said you called and told her about your new job."

Megan Wiseman had been her closest friend in Florida. They hadn't talked in weeks, but the day Ashley had gotten her job at the café, she'd been so excited she had called her. Now she realized her mistake. Megan's boyfriend, Tommy Jensen, was a good friend of Ziggy's.

"So is that it?" she said. "You found out I was working, so you came here to hit me up for money?"

He clamped his hands dramatically over his heart. "You wound me, babe. I was just worried about you, that's all."

"I'm fine, Ziggy. I'm working—as you can see—and I'm doing just great. Now go away and leave me alone."

"You don't mean that, sweetheart." He reached out and cupped her cheek. Ashley knocked his hand away. "I'm your child's father," he said. "And you know how much I've always loved you."

"The only person you love is yourself, Ziggy. That's the way it was. The way it always will be. Now get out of here. Get out of my life before I do something I'll regret."

A familiar blond head appeared over Ziggy's shoulder. He was taller by a couple of inches and, in a completely opposite way, even better looking. And unlike her ex-boyfriend's arrival, just seeing him made Ashley's heart swell.

"You heard the lady," Jason said. "I'd advise you to leave. Now."

Ziggy turned. "Who the hell are you?"

"I'm a friend. And I'm asking you to leave. If you don't go on your own, I'll make sure you do."

Ashley couldn't believe her eyes. Jason was defending her. And from the look on his face and the way he was standing with his legs splayed and his weight on the balls of his feet, he was capable of doing exactly what he'd threatened.

Ziggy must have realized it wasn't a bluff. He took a step backward, putting some distance between them. "Fine. You want her, you can have her. Her and that squalling brat she's got."

Jason's jaw hardened. The restaurant fell silent. He took a menacing step toward Ziggy, who turned and started rapidly walking toward the door. He gripped the handle and pulled it open, ringing the bell, then flashed a last look Ashley's way and stalked out into the night. The door closed with a whoosh behind him.

Ashley's eyes burned. She couldn't tear her gaze away from Jason.

People returned to their meals and conversations, laughing as if nothing had happened. In the Texas Café, maybe nothing had.

Betty appeared beside her. "You okay?"

Ashley swallowed. "I'm okay."

"It's gettin' near closing time. Why don't you and your fella go ahead and go on home?"

"But you said you wanted to show me how to close up tonight."

"You'll be workin' tomorrow. I'll show you then."

Ashley's chest tightened. She was making friends here, people she could trust. People willing to help her.

Betty smiled and sauntered away, and Ashley turned back to Jason. "Thank you. No one's ever been willing to fight for me before."

He reached out and touched her cheek. "I'll fight for you, Ashley. Anytime you need."

Her eyes filled. Jason had a way of cutting through her defenses. "Take me home, will you please?"

He just nodded. He waited for her to collect her purse, then led her outside. When they reached his vehicle, he paused beside the powerful sports car.

"You don't have to be afraid, Ashley. I won't let him hurt you."

Color washed into her cheeks. "I wish you hadn't seen him. Now you know how stupid I was to get mixed up with a jerk like that." She shook her head. "I feel so different now. I feel a thousand years older."

"You aren't the same person anymore. You're a mother now and that changes everything."

She looked into his handsome face. "Yes, it does."

Jason bent his head and very gently kissed her. It was the softest, sweetest kiss she had ever known.

"Let's go get Robbie."

Ashley nodded. Her throat felt tight.

Jason opened the passenger door, his gaze sweeping over the cramped interior of the Porsche.

"Looks like I'm going to need a bigger car," he muttered as he waited for her to slide into the seat.

Ashley couldn't tell if he was talking to her or himself.

Either way, it made her smile.

Chapter 22

Wishing he could spend Saturday morning in bed with Maggie, Trace showered and dressed to go to work. When he walked into the living room, he spotted her pacing the floor and grumbling, glossy red curls flying at every turn.

She whirled to face him. "So…you're going off to work, but I'm just supposed to stay here."

"I've got some things I need to do," he said simply. He had a business to run, people who depended on him, and he wasn't going to find Maggie's stalker by staying in bed—an idea he infinitely preferred.

"I can't stay locked up this way much longer, Trace." Dressed in jeans that cupped her pretty little behind and a T-shirt that fit nicely over her luscious breasts, she looked good enough to eat. His mind raced back to the bedroom. With Herculean effort, he reined himself in.

Maggie stopped pacing and stood in front of him. "I have a job, just like you and everyone else. Besides,

I'm used to being outdoors shooting. I've got to get out of the house, Trace."

He shook his head. "Not by yourself. It isn't safe and you know it."

Maggie blew out a breath. "We need to catch this guy. What about the trap we'd planned to set? Can't we go ahead and do it?"

He sighed. "We need to do something, that's for damned sure." He had told her about his meeting with Tony Ramirez, told her the guy who had lit up her condo was likely a professional torch. He hadn't mentioned his theory that there was a good chance more was going on than just some loony who was obsessed with her.

He still wasn't ready to break that little bit of bad news.

"It'll take me a while to get the word out," Maggie was saying. "But the fire might work in our favor. The story was all over the local TV news. I know Sally Grimshaw over at KGEO. I'm a local girl and fairly well known. I think I could get her to interview me about the destruction of my studio and what my plans are for the future."

It wasn't a bad idea. As long as Maggie didn't give out any personal details, just kept to the information they wanted the stalker to know. If they could catch him, at least one of Maggie's problems would be solved.

And the truth was, Trace might be wrong, and her stalker actually could be the one responsible. Hell, maybe the nutcase *had* hired a torch to burn up Maggie's studio. Crazy people were just that—crazy. There was no way to predict exactly what one of them might do.

"So what do you think?" she asked, pulling his thoughts back to the moment. "During the interview, I could mention how eager I am to get back to work.

I could say I'm planning a trip down to Kemah to do some shooting this weekend. We could set it up the same as we planned before."

"It might work," he finally said. "Long as we have time to get ready. I need to talk to Ben and Alex. I want them there if the guy shows up." So far Trace had managed to keep his two friends away from Maggie. He'd been oddly reluctant to introduce her to a couple guys who looked as good as they did, and had half the women in Houston falling at their feet.

But he'd talked about their competence, told her how lucky he was to have them working for Atlas, even in a freelance capacity as they did.

Maggie looked up at him and smiled. "Okay, then. While you're at the office, I'll make a list, see what I can do from my end to start things rolling."

"All right, but let's work out the details before you make any calls."

"Okay." He could read her excitement. Her face was glowing, her green eyes bright. After her arrival at his house, she had commandeered his laptop, and for the past few days had been keeping herself busy by working on her client list, sorting names and looking for anyone with what seemed an inordinate interest in her pictures. So far, she hadn't found anyone.

Aside from that, she'd been answering sympathetic emails from friends and clients who had seen the story about the fire, talking to the insurance company about payment for the damage and trying to find a contractor to get started on the major job of rebuilding the town house.

But Maggie wasn't used to sitting home, and her frustration was evident.

"I've got quite a bit to do," he said. "I won't be home

before supper. We can go out or I can pick something up and bring it back."

Maggie walked toward him, draped her arms around his neck. "Why don't I cook us something? I looked in the freezer. You've got a package of pork chops. I usually marinate them in a little teriyaki."

His mouth watered. "I thought you couldn't cook."

"Unlike my sister, my skills are fairly limited. But I can manage teriyaki pork chops and salad."

"Sounds great." And staying home with Maggie sounded a helluva lot better than going out to some restaurant and wishing he was home making love to her. "Try not to get cabin fever, and I'll see you tonight."

She gave him a soft, openmouthed kiss that made it hard for him to turn and walk away.

Hell, it just made him hard.

He chuckled to himself. His sex life had never been better. By now he should be ready for a change, but he was far from bored with the perky little redhead. In truth, he couldn't get enough of her. Sooner or later that would end, he was sure. As long as he didn't let his emotions get too deeply involved, he'd be okay.

Trace vowed not to let that happen.

Trace thought of Maggie all afternoon as he worked behind his desk. It was difficult to concentrate on the invoices Annie had asked him to review, to sign payroll checks or take care of the myriad other little details he had put off doing all week.

And another problem had arisen.

According to Detective Sayers, there was a chance Parker Barrington could get out of jail.

Emily Barrington had recanted her story, telling the police that she had been angry at her husband and coerced into saying he had come home late the night of the murder. According to her, the coercer, unfortunately, was Trace.

Parker's fancy lawyers were making hay with the tale of the repentant wife who had said those things only because her husband had been ignoring her. The attorneys also insisted that someone had tampered with Parker's computer, using it to go online to look up information on tranquilizing drugs, inferring it was Jason, who would have had access to the machine.

Jason was going to go off the deep end when he found out.

Fortunately, there was still the not-so-small matter of the money Parker had stolen. The prosecutor was still convinced he was a flight risk, and so far the judge agreed. Trace just hoped Parker's expensive attorneys didn't come up with some new tap dance that would buy him a get-out-of-jail-free card.

Trace was convinced if the man did get out, he would be gone. And he wouldn't be taking his adoring little wife, Emily, with him.

A light knock sounded at his office door and Trace looked up from his computer screen. Through the glass, he saw Sol Greenway's lanky figure and waved him into the room.

"I saw you come in a little earlier," Trace said, having noticed his youngest employee sauntering into the office next to his a little over an hour ago. "What's up?"

"I came in to dig up some info for Alex, but one of the names on your list kept nagging me." Sol sprawled in the chair beside the desk and shoved his horn-rimmed glasses up on his nose. "I hate to admit I missed this before—not once but twice. I don't know why I went back to look at the guy again…something about the timing, I guess. Until today, I didn't make the connection."

Trace leaned over to take the paper Sol held. "What's this?"

"David Lyons was hospitalized a week after Maggie O'Connell moved out of his house. It was supposed to be some kind of kitchen accident. He cut himself while he was cooking. Stuff like that happens all the time, but it just kept bugging me. I think it was the date, you know, being so close to her leaving. Anyway, I went back into his hospital files—" Sol broke off as if he had already said too much about his hacking technique, and shook his head. "You don't want to know."

"No, I don't. Just tell me what you found."

"Lyons tried to commit suicide. He was distraught over losing his girlfriend. Slit his wrists. Came real close to dying."

Trace let the news sink in. David Lyons had been so crazy-in-love with Maggie that when she left him, he had tried to kill himself.

Which meant maybe he was just plain crazy.

"It was buried real deep. Lyons went to a lot of trouble to keep it secret. Three days after it happened, I found a big anonymous contribution to the hospital wing they were building at the time. I can probably go in and find out who it came from, but…"

"But your guess is it came from Lyons."

"Him or his parents. His family's loaded. An emotional problem like that could have affected his career."

But Maggie must have known. She had cared about the guy. Obviously in some way still did. She would have gone to see him the minute she'd heard he was in the hospital. Maggie had known and yet she hadn't told him. In fact, she'd gone out of her way to keep him from finding out.

Anger began to simmer inside him. He wanted to trust her. He'd been letting down his guard more and more. Maggie's silence felt like a betrayal of the very worst sort.

His jaw ached from clenching it so hard. "Anything else?"

"I'll keep digging if you want."

"Oh, yeah. That's exactly what I want. Maybe Lyons still has the hots for her. Maybe his obsession is mixed with some kind of weird need for revenge."

Sol nodded, stood up from his chair. "I'll see what I can find."

"Call my cell if you come up with anything."

Sol left Trace's office, went into his own and sat down behind his computer screens. Trace grabbed his hat and tugged it over his forehead, picked up his brief-case and left the office. Outside, the Saturday evening traffic was beginning to build. He'd been looking forward to going home.

The muscles in his neck tightened. In hiding the truth about Lyons, Maggie had lied to him again. Trace had known better than to trust her. He wanted her out of his house, out of his life. But there was no place safe for her to go.

Worse than that, part of him wanted her to stay.

By the time he turned into the alley behind his house, he had worked himself into a simmering rage. He tried for his usual calm, but couldn't seem to find it. He couldn't wait to confront her. She would just give him more bullshit, he knew. And yet, deep down, he wanted her to convince him she hadn't meant to deceive him.

He parked the Jeep in the garage on the alley and

strode up the walkway to the back porch. Maggie turned off the alarm, opened the door and smiled as he walked into the kitchen.

"Hey, cowboy." She caught the brim of his hat, lifted it off and hung it on the rack beside the door. "I was beginning to think you'd forgotten our date." She was wearing a sexy little black dress that barely covered her ass, dangling silver earrings and silver bracelets that jangled whenever she moved.

The sound made his groin tighten. "I didn't know it was a date," he said darkly.

"It's always a date on the rare occasion I'm cooking."

He followed her into the dining room, saw that she had set the table with his grandmother's china and silver. The candles were lit and there was an arrangement of pink carnations and pretty white daisies in the center of the table.

It made him yearn for the things he'd once wanted, a home, a wife who loved him, kids one day.

It made the anger he was feeling bubble up inside him, twisting his stomach into a knot. He tried to clamp down on his emotions, but when she turned and slid her arms around his neck, when she rose up on her toes and kissed him, something inside him snapped.

He could feel every soft curve, the fullness of her breasts and the hardening of her nipples. "I guess we did have a date," he growled, and kissed her with an angry fire he could barely contain. His heart was pounding, his blood surging hot and fast.

Maggie deepened the kiss, sliding her tongue over his, sucking his lower lip into her mouth. Her fingers moved over the front of his shirt. She popped the snaps and ran her palms over the muscles across his chest. He was close to losing control, worried he might, but Maggie didn't seem to care.

"I guess you missed me," she whispered into his mouth, pressing herself against his rock-hard erection. He was throbbing with every heartbeat, infused with a furious heat that ached to be released.

"Oh, I missed you," he drawled, kissing her deeply as he peeled the narrow black straps of her dress off her shoulders, tugged the bodice down and filled his hands with her luscious breasts. They were plump and enticing, and he lowered his head and tasted them, circled her nipples with his tongue.

Maggie moaned. He could feel her trembling, could sense her arousal. She wanted him and, damn, he wanted her.

He drove his hands into her silky red hair, holding her immobile as he plundered her lips. Maggie had closed all the drapes in the living room, and a pair of candles burned on the coffee table in front of the sofa.

He thought of her deception, thought of David Lyons and how far she had gone to protect him, and his anger swelled. He shoved her short black dress up over her hips, kissed her deeply, felt the tiny triangle of satin that covered her sex, slid it aside and stroked her.

She was wet and ready, breathing hard, pressing herself against his hand, urging his fingers deeper.

Trace obliged, stroking her nearly to climax, then turning her toward the sofa, bending her over the padded arm. She parted her legs, giving him access as he opened his fly, found her softness and positioned himself.

He took her in a single deep thrust, paused for a moment to regain control. Then he was moving, plunging deeply, taking what he wanted, telling himself he was punishing her for deceiving him. But he was only punishing himself.

With every thrust, his desire for her strengthened. With each of her soft little cries, his need for her swelled. He gripped her hips, drove himself deeper, faster, harder.

He wanted Maggie O'Connell.

But as they reached the peak together and she cried out his name, he realized he wanted more from her than just her beautiful body.

He wanted her trust.

And maybe even her heart.

It scared him to death.

"You're angry," Maggie said as she returned from the bathroom, her tousled hair combed and her short black dress once more in place. "I knew it when you walked through the door."

She could feel his dark eyes on her, following her movements as she continued toward him. God, he looked good. The line of his jaw wasn't as hard as it had been, and the muscles across his shoulders were no longer tied in knots. And yet she could still sense the tension running through his body.

"I was angry," he admitted. "I still am. But I would have stopped if you'd wanted."

"I know that." She paused in front of him. "I didn't want you to stop. You're a different lover when you're angry. You set your passions free. I like it."

His jaw tightened once more. "Damn it, Maggie."

"Tell me why you're so upset."

Trace blew out a breath. He wandered over to the dining table, picked up one of the pretty silver forks beside a flowered porcelain plate, then set it back down and looked at her. "You lied to me again."

She frowned. "I don't think so. I told you I wouldn't do that and I meant it."

"I found out about David Lyons."

A little tremor of unease moved through her. "I told you about David. I told you we lived together for a couple of months."

Intense brown eyes fixed on her face. She felt the impact as if he'd touched her. "You didn't tell me he tried to kill himself."

Her stomach clenched. She should have known Trace would find out. Digging up information was what he did for a living, what she had hired him to do. But she'd felt she owed a certain amount of loyalty to a man who had loved her so much.

"David was ashamed of what he tried to do. I didn't think telling you was important enough to override the pain it was bound to cause him."

Trace straightened, seemed even taller. "Someone is angry enough to burn your house down with your sister and her baby inside, and you didn't think it was important enough to tell me?" His temper was rising again. She wondered if maybe they'd end up having another round of hot, steamy sex.

"David isn't the stalker."

Trace strode toward her, reached out and caught her shoulders. "You can't know that. Not for sure. The man is obviously unstable. Maybe something happened recently that sent him off the deep end. I need to talk to him. I need to be sure he's not our guy."

Trace was right, she knew. She should have told him in the first place. Certainly after the fire, she shouldn't have hesitated. She was just so sure it wasn't David.

"All right, you can talk to him, but I'm going with you."

"Fine, but we need to do it now."

"Now? Right now? It's Saturday night. He's probably out on a date."

"Call him. If he'll meet us, we'll put supper on hold and eat when we get back."

"I'm telling you it isn't him. He wouldn't know the first thing about planting bugs and setting houses on fire."

"Maybe not, but he's got plenty of money—enough to pay somebody to do those things. If he did, then we can't know what he'll do next—or when."

A shudder ran through her.

"We need to eliminate Lyons as a suspect. Once we do, we can move forward, look in other directions."

She studied Trace's face, which was now closed up, hiding whatever he was thinking. "There's something you aren't telling me."

He hesitated, took a breath and slowly released it. "Look, odds are it was the stalker who paid someone to set your place on fire. The problem is the arsonist went in specifically to take out your studio."

"Because he was mad at me for hanging up on him."

"It's possible." Trace's eyes shifted away for an instant.

"But you don't think so." And suddenly it was clear. "You're thinking the fire might have been set for some other reason altogether, something that has nothing to do with my stalker."

His expression gentled. "It's something we need to consider."

Maggie started frowning, mulling over the prospect. "If it's true, who would go to that much trouble just to destroy my work?" She glanced up. "Someone who is jealous of my success?"

Trace's gaze held steady. "Or someone who wanted to get rid of something that was in one of your pictures." He waited a moment for the thought to sink in. "Your memory cards were in the studio. No one but you knew your work is also stored in Photodrive. Whoever set the fire was a high-dollar professional. Someone paid him a pretty penny to do a specific job."

"Which means if you're right, it must have been really important to get rid of my photos."

"We need to talk to Lyons. Afterward, if we're convinced it wasn't him, that he didn't hire someone to set fire to your studio for some sick kind of revenge, then we need to broaden our thinking."

Maggie sank down on the sofa, feeling slightly ill. "Oh, my God."

"Look, let's not get ahead of ourselves. At the moment, I'm working on the theory that David Lyons hired a guy to burn up your house just to cause you grief. He could afford it, and if he blamed you for driving him to the point of suicide, he might think he had good reason. Call Lyons. We'll see where it leads."

But as Maggie got up to retrieve her cell phone, she was thinking two things: that she had lost a little of Trace's trust tonight, something she discovered she wanted very badly.

And that he might be right, and her problems had just doubled.

Chapter 23

David was kind enough to invite them to the apartment he had leased after the breakup. Number 7 Riverway was an exclusive, twenty-story building along Buffalo Bayou just west of the 610 Loop.

He answered the door, his blond hair neatly combed, his khaki slacks and polo shirt perfectly pressed, his eyes warm in greeting as Maggie came through the door. Trace walked in behind her.

"Thank you for agreeing to see us," she said. She glanced around the apartment, which was luxurious, ultramodern, done in dark brown and white, with brown marble floors and twelve-foot ceilings. Its Spartan design perfectly fit David's orderly persona, Maggie thought, though she preferred a cozier, less formal atmosphere. It was just one of a dozen reasons they had never really suited.

"I saw the fire on the morning news," he said. "I meant to call you, make sure you were all right."

"As it turned out, no one was hurt." She turned, inviting Trace into the conversation. "David, I'd like you to meet Trace Rawlins. He's a private investigator. He's looking into the fire and some other problems I've been having lately."

David's pale blue eyes ran over the man who stood at her side. They were about the same height, but David had a lanky build instead of Trace's solid, V-shaped body. They were perfect opposites—night and day.

"It's nice to meet you," David said. "Why don't we go into the living room? Would either of you like something to drink?"

"No, thanks," Trace said. Maybe David didn't notice the way he was sizing him up, the slight tension in his jaw, but Maggie did.

"We're fine, thank you," she said. "Trace has some questions he'd like to ask. We're hoping it will help the investigation."

"Of course." David led them into the living room with its high ceilings, brown marble fireplace and high-tech, built-in entertainment center. Intricate glass sculptures decorated the shelves and sat on the chrome coffee table in front of a plush brown sofa and matching chairs.

"At the moment we're just collecting information," Trace said. "We need to know where you were the night of May 13."

David frowned. "I was out to dinner with friends. Why?"

"That's the night someone set fire to Maggie's condo."

David straightened. "And you think I had something to do with that?"

"Someone was angry enough to destroy her studio. Her work was the target. After what happened between you, maybe you wanted some kind of revenge."

David's gaze darted to Maggie. His expression closed up as he looked back at Trace. "I'm afraid I don't know what you mean."

Maggie felt a rush of guilt. "He knows our relationship ended badly, David. He knows about your suicide attempt."

"You told him about that?"

"It happened," Trace said, interrupting before she could defend herself. "That's what matters. And your breakup with Maggie was the cause. The question is how far are you willing to go to make her pay for what happened?"

David slid onto the edge of his seat. "You're insane. I'd never do anything to hurt Maggie. I loved her." He turned in her direction. "Part of me always will."

Her heart squeezed. She had known how David felt before they had moved in together, known he was deeply in love with her and that she would never love him that same way. She hadn't meant to hurt him, but she had.

"You don't believe I set the fire, do you, Maggie? I told you I was out with friends that night, and I can prove it. Even if I couldn't, surely you don't believe I'm capable of something like that."

Maggie walked over to his chair, knelt down next to the arm. She reached over and gave his hand a gentle squeeze. "I don't believe you were responsible, David. I never did. I just… Trace needed to be sure." She rose, and so did the two men.

"The fire was set by a professional," Trace said. "Someone highly paid to destroy Maggie's work." He glanced around the fabulously expensive apartment. "You've got the kind of money it takes to do something like that."

"I had nothing to do with the fire. I've only seen Maggie once in two years—the night she went dancing at Galaxy. Now if you don't leave, I'm going to call the police."

"Maybe that's a good idea," Trace said darkly.

David sighed, made another attempt to explain. "Look, that night at the club… Maggie reminded me it would never work between us. Deep down, I knew she was right. It isn't her fault we're so different. It isn't her fault she never really loved me. It's just the way life is. I've accepted it. And I'd never do anything to hurt her."

Some of the tension went out of Trace's shoulders. He gave David a last perusal, then slowly nodded. "I appreciate your honesty. And your cooperation. Whatever we've discussed goes no further than this room."

David swallowed. "Thank you."

He walked them to the door. "So the two of you… Are the two of you…?"

Maggie tried to smile. "Trace is just—"

"Yes," he said firmly.

David smiled sadly. "I'm glad she's got someone looking out for her. Take care of yourself, Maggie."

Her eyes welled. "Goodbye, David. And thank you."

She walked out into the hallway. Trace followed, closing the apartment door behind them. She turned, lifted her chin. "So now are you convinced?"

"My job requires that I trust my instincts. I needed to see him, talk to him. It was clear he didn't know someone had been paid to set the fire. He's still half in love with you, but he isn't obsessed, he's just lonely. He isn't your stalker. And he didn't pay someone to destroy your house."

"That's what I told you."

The corner of Trace's mouth edged up. "I guess you've got pretty good instincts yourself."

Mollified a little, she let him guide her to the elevator. Moments later they crossed the parking garage to the Jeep.

"So now we set our trap?" she asked as he held the door while she climbed inside.

"Yeah. Now we set our trap. And just to be on the safe side, we take a look at your latest photos. See if there's anything in one of them that might have convinced someone to pay big bucks and risk killing somebody so that no one would see them."

Standing on the huge front porch in the soft yellow lamplight, Jason banged on the front door of the big white-columned mansion so hard his fist began to ache. Billings, the butler, in his usual black suit and white shirt, pulled open the door.

"Why, Mr. Jason. It's good to see you. Please, come in."

Though Jason liked the little man with the dark hair and ready smile, he found his brother-in-law's pomposity in hiring a butler ridiculous. "I need to see my sister. Will you tell her I'm here?"

It was almost nine o'clock. He'd told himself to wait until morning, but his anger kept building until he just couldn't stand it any longer.

"I'll tell her," the little man said. "Why don't you wait for her in the blue room?"

"Thank you, Carl." It was Billings's first name, though neither Parker nor Emily used it.

The butler led him down the hall to the drawing room and disappeared, leaving Jason to pace the pale blue carpet beneath a pair of crystal chandeliers. The house was overblown and far too fussy for Jason's taste, with velvet sofas and gilded chairs, and porcelain figurines on rosewood tables.

The house he'd grown up in had been extravagant, but more subtle and in far better taste. This was done to suit Parker, not his sister. Emily had never had the courage to say no to her husband—which was the reason Jason was there.

Appearing in the open doorway, Emily floated toward him in a pair of loose-fitting black pants and a flowing, pink silk blouse, her short, dark hair gleaming in the lamplight. Even at this hour her makeup was flawless, but underneath, her features looked pale and strained.

He took a calming breath, reminded himself of the stress she was under.

"Jason. It's wonderful to see you." She stretched up on her toes and kissed his cheek.

"I know it's late, sis. This couldn't wait. We need to talk."

She flicked a glance at the butler, who hovered in the doorway. "Shall I have Billings bring us some tea?"

Jason clenched his teeth, fighting to rein in his temper. "I'm fine."

Billings took his cue and closed the tall, wood-paneled doors.

"Why don't we sit down?" Emily took a seat on the blue velvet sofa while Jason sat down across from her.

"I got a phone call today," he began. "The police tell me you changed your story about what happened the night Dad was murdered."

Emily glanced away. "I didn't exactly change it. I just…clarified things a bit."

His control slipped a notch. "You lied, you mean.

Parker didn't come home until well after midnight and you know it. What's going on with you, Emily? How can you sit back and help a man like Parker get away with murdering our father?"

Emily's spine stiffened. "Parker didn't do it. He says someone is trying to frame him. He insists he's innocent. As his wife, it's my duty to believe him."

"Do you also believe he didn't steal millions of dollars from the company? That he didn't stash the money in a half-dozen offshore accounts? Your name isn't on any of those accounts, Em. Parker never meant for you to go with him when he left the country."

She swallowed, kept her eyes on Jason's face, though he could see the effort it cost her. "I know he took the money. He was tired of working for a pittance of what he was worth."

Jason shot out of his chair. "Those are his words you're spouting, Em, not yours. The man is a thief and a murderer. Dad let him keep his job only because of you! Parker doesn't care about you, Emily. He never did. He married you for your money. He stole from all of us and he killed our father! How can you be such a fool?"

Emily started crying. "He says he's innocent."

Jason walked over and sat down beside her, slipped an arm around her shoulders. "I know you love him. You've loved him since the first time you saw him. Parker's handsome and charming. He pretended to be exactly the man you wanted. But it was all an act, Em, and by now you know it. You deserve a man worth ten times what he is, a man who will love you as much as you love him. A man who would never do anything to hurt you or your family."

Emily started sobbing, and Jason drew her gently into his arms. "You've got to tell the truth, sis. No half-truths, no more believing what you want to believe instead of what you know in your heart is true."

"I still love him, Jason. I love him so much."

"But you loved Dad, too. Remember how he always said no matter how old you got, you'd always be his little girl?"

She trembled. "I remember. I miss him so."

"Dad deserves justice. You know that, Em. Do what is right for our father. Do what is right for yourself."

She took a shaky breath and wiped the tears from her cheeks with the tip of her finger. "I know you're right. I've tried to tell myself the things you're saying aren't true, but I know they are. Parker doesn't love me. He never did." She shook her head. "I know I have to give him up, but I don't know how I'm going to get along without him."

Jason squeezed her hand. "I'll help you, sis. I promise." He smiled at her warmly. "I never understood how you could be so blindly in love with Parker, but for the first time in my life, I'm beginning to see. I've met someone, sis."

She looked up at him and a sad smile curved her lips. "You've always had girlfriends, Jason. As many as you wanted."

"Ashley's different. She's sweet and she's smart. She works hard and she has goals."

"You're a Sommerset. Maybe her goal is to marry you and have anything she wants. Look what happened to me."

"I don't think Ashley gives a damn about my money. As far as marriage goes, I think she'd rather be a chef than a wife." He grinned. "I'm hoping if I take it nice and slow, I might be able to change that."

Emily studied his face. "I've never seen you this way."

"I've never felt this way. She has a son, sis. The cutest little boy. I want you to meet them."

Tears filled Emily's eyes. "Parker said he wanted children, but he never thought the time was right."

"Tell the truth, Em. Let Parker get what he deserves. If you do, I truly believe you'll find the kind of happiness *you* deserve."

The tears in Emily's eyes slipped onto her cheeks. She nodded. Jason rose and so did his sister, wiping away her tears as she walked him out to the foyer.

"I'll pick you up first thing in the morning," he said. "We'll go see the D.A. together. Changing your story back and forth doesn't exactly help their case, but at least this will straighten things out."

"All right."

"You're doing the right thing, sis."

Emily managed a wobbly smile as Jason bent and kissed her cheek. He left the house, a quick check of his watch telling him it was almost time to pick Ashley up after her shift. She was already becoming part of his life, and though he knew he should take things slow, make sure what was happening between them was real, deep down he was certain it was.

Jason smiled as he turned the key, firing the Porche's powerful engine, and reminded himself to start looking for another car.

Chapter 24

Morning sunlight poured through the kitchen window, warming the house. It wouldn't be long before the air conditioner kicked on.

Rowdy barked, alerting Maggie to the chiming of her cell phone. She patted his head, ruffled his fur, walked over and plucked her phone off the kitchen table. Though hearing from her mother was rare, she recognized the caller ID and pressed the device against her ear.

"Hello, Mom."

"Maggie—thank God you answered. I've been so worried. I ran into Megan Wiseman, one of Ashley's girlfriends, at the grocery store, and she told me that no-good Ziggy is in Houston. Can you believe it? Ashley hasn't started seeing him again, has she? Dear God, that girl hasn't got a lick of sense."

Maggie's fingers tightened around the phone. "Ashley isn't seeing Ziggy, Mom. She's way past a jerk like that."

"Well, you don't know her. She's weak where that

man is concerned. Look what he's done to her already—left her with a baby to raise and no father to help support it. If it weren't for your help, I don't know what would have happened to that girl."

Maggie clamped down on her temper. She and her mother had never gotten along. Why was it she always seemed to forget that? "Ashley's doing just fine on her own. She's got a job, Mom. Next week she's applying for admission to the culinary arts program at the art institute. She's hoping to get a loan for the tuition and I think she'll get it."

Silence fell. "You mean she's going to stay in Texas? She isn't coming back home?"

"She needs her independence, Mother. As I said, she's making her own way, and she's feeling really good about it."

"Well…"

"I'll tell her you called, Mom. I'll tell her you were worried about her."

"You just make sure she doesn't get tied up again with that good-for-nothing Ziggy."

Maggie fought for control. "Don't worry about it, Mom. Listen, I've got someone here," she lied. "It was really nice talking to you."

"Tell her to call me, will you?"

"I'll tell her." And Ashley would probably call. She didn't get along with their mother any better than Maggie did, but she wanted to change her life, do what was right. "Bye, Mom." Maggie ended the call.

"Who was that?" Trace asked as he wandered up beside her.

"My mother." She waved a hand. "Don't ask."

"From the look on your face, I don't think I need to."

"I've got to call Ashley, let her know Mom was worried about her."

"Was she?"

Maggie sighed. "In her own way, I suppose."

He walked to the counter and poured himself a cup of coffee. "When you're done, we need to figure a few things out."

She looked down at the short terry robe she was wearing, one of her recent purchases. "Can I shower first?"

Trace already had. His eyes darkened and his mouth took on a sensual curve. "I was waiting for you earlier, hoping you'd join me."

She wished she had, would have if the phone hadn't started ringing. "Next time," she promised with a mischievous grin. They had slept late and made love and slept a little longer. It was Sunday. It was okay to loaf a little.

She glanced at Trace and felt the same warm stirring she always felt when she looked at him. Dressed in jeans and a yellow short-sleeved shirt, freshly shaved, with his hair still damp, he gave her a look that said he had sex on his mind—which should be impossible after the night they had shared.

He'd started toward her, his intention clear, when a soft knock sounded at the door. With a last heated glance, he walked over and peered through the peephole. After a moment's hesitation, he lifted the latch and pulled the door open.

"Trace! Oh, thank heavens you're home!" His gorgeous ex-wife burst into the living room. Maggie ignored an unwelcome stab of jealousy.

"I've got company, Carly. What do you want?"

The redhead glanced toward Maggie, who fought the urge to run for the bathroom. She knew how she looked: still dressed in her short robe, her hair sleep-tangled, no makeup and her legs bare way above the knee.

Trace appeared resigned. "Carly, meet Maggie O'Connell."

"Hello, Carly," Maggie said, forcing a smile she hoped didn't seem like a sneer.

The other woman's full lips thinned. She made no reply, just returned her attention to Trace. "She was the one at your office."

"That's right. Now what do you want?"

"Howard and I broke up. He got mad over some silly notion about me and the pool boy, and now he won't pay my rent." She flicked a warning glance at Maggie, clearly wanting to speak to Trace in private.

"If you two will excuse me, I need to take a shower," Maggie said, glad for the chance to escape.

Angry for no good reason and embarrassed for some equally nebulous one, she walked into the bedroom and closed the door. After drawing a calming breath she dialed her sister's number, taking a moment to fill her in on the conversation with their mother, but giving an edited version. Maggie's cell rang just as she finished. It was Roxanne.

"It's me, darling. How are you?"

"Roxanne—I've been meaning to call, but it's just been so crazy. I'm all right. No more fires, no more notes on my car. Of course, I'm a virtual prisoner, but aside from that—"

Roxanne laughed.

"I don't suppose you can sneak out to go clubbing?"

"God, I wish." She hadn't been dancing since the night they had gone to Galaxy. With so much happening, Maggie felt guilty even thinking how much she'd like to go. "Listen, I've got to run. At the moment Trace's ex-wife is standing in the living room, and I haven't even taken a shower."

"I thought he wasn't seeing her anymore."

"He isn't. Or I'm pretty sure he isn't."

"Then get rid of her and take your shower with the Marlboro man."

Maggie laughed. "Good idea. Talk to you later."

As she headed for the bathroom, Maggie's humor faded. Maybe she was wrong and Trace was still in love with Carly. Maybe even seeing her on occasion. The woman was standing in his living room, wasn't she? That had to mean something.

Maggie turned the water on hot and high, hoping to distract her thoughts from the pair in the other room.

It didn't work.

Dear God, she had it bad.

"So you and Howard broke up," Trace said. "What's that have to do with me?"

Carly ignored the question. Her blue eyes traveled to the bedroom door. "Are you serious about her?"

He wasn't sure how to answer. He was attracted to Maggie, more than attracted. Sexually, she turned him on more than any woman he had ever met. Last night, he'd been jealous of her relationship with David Lyons. He'd been possessive as he never was with a woman— not even his former wife.

Yet something was missing. After being married to Carly, he had serious trust issues. Just looking at her reminded him of the pain he had suffered when he had discovered the trail of men who had been in her bed. Maggie's constant evasions made trusting her almost impossible, and without that, he didn't see a future for them.

"She's my client," he said, avoiding the issue, hoping Carly would let the subject drop.

Her gaze slid once more toward the bedroom. "Looks to me like she's a lot more than just a client."

Trace's jaw tightened. "We're seeing each other, all right? Now tell me what you want."

Carly moved closer. She rested her palms on his chest and gazed up at him. The top of her head didn't reach his shoulder. "I was hoping you would loan me some money. Just a little, enough to cover my rent."

Trace took hold of her wrists and eased her away. "What about the alimony I pay you? It's more than enough to pay your rent and whatever else you need."

"Well, something came up. I'm a little short this month."

He didn't have to ask what that something was— either an expensive trip with one of her friends or a shopping excursion. "How short are you?"

"A couple thousand would do."

"You want me to give you two thousand dollars," he said darkly.

"I told you it's a loan."

"Yeah, right. Okay, I'll give you the money. But don't ask me again. We're done, Carly. We have been for years. I'm not your husband. We aren't even friends."

"Don't say that!"

Ignoring her, he strode into the bedroom, where he kept his checkbook in the top dresser drawer. Trace took it out and wrote a check for two thousand dollars.

Just as he turned to leave, Maggie opened the bathroom door wearing only a fluffy white towel. Her glorious red hair curled around her face. The tops of her breasts rose enticingly, and her pale skin was moist and glistening. Little droplets of water beaded on her legs and he wanted to lick them off. He was hard, itching to pull away the towel and kiss all that bare skin.

"Don't bother getting dressed," he said gruffly. "I'll be right back."

Maggie opened her mouth, but he didn't give her

the chance to argue. Returning to the living room, he handed the check to Carly and hurried her toward the door.

"Remember what I said. We're done, Carly. Don't come to me again."

She pouted as she stuffed the check into her purse and he urged her out of the house.

Closing the door, he strode back to the bedroom. But when he walked in, Maggie was no longer naked. She was dressed in jeans and a T-shirt. He didn't try to hide his disappointment.

"What did she want?" Maggie asked, her arms crossed defensively over her chest.

"It's always something. Money this time."

She tossed back her hair, moving all those damp red curls. His fingers itched.

"You must still care for her if you keep giving her what she wants."

"I feel sorry for her. Her life is a mess. Until she finds some way to change, it's going to stay a mess."

"And you're going to keep letting her jerk your chain."

He shook his head, his eyes on her face. "No. That's finished as of today."

"Why today?"

"Because you're here and you're important to me. Carly isn't. Not anymore. I told her it was finished and I meant it."

Maggie eyed him a moment, assessing his words, deciding whether or not to believe him. She moved closer, looked him in the face. "Are you sure?"

Trace slid his hand into her silky hair and dragged her head back, claiming her mouth in a hard, possessive kiss.

"Damned sure," he said against the side of her neck. "I want you, not Carly."

When he kissed her again, Maggie didn't fight him. He might have doubts about their relationship, but this was one area in which they seemed to be in perfect agreement.

It wasn't long before both of them were naked and back in his bed.

Trace played bodyguard all week. Tony Ramirez called to let him know it was safe for the women to go back inside the town house. Mrs. Epstein looked after Robbie while the sisters poked and dug through the waterlogged, blackened interior.

Jason insisted on accompanying them, and when Ashley found her few worldly possessions mostly destroyed, Trace was glad the kid was there.

"Oh, no." Ashley sloshed through puddles of water to reach a soggy little brown teddy bear. One of its eyes was missing and the stuffing was coming out the seams in several places. The bear was in bad shape to begin with, but the fire hoses had finished the job.

"It's Brownie," she said. Hugging the bear to her chest, she started to cry. "I know it's silly, but I've had him since I was a little girl."

Jason walked up behind her, turned her into his arms. "It's okay, honey. You've got all those memories locked up in here." He smoothed a hand over her curls, then tipped her chin up so she would look at him. "Nothing can ever take those away from you."

Ashley clung to him and Jason held her until Trace found himself looking away, his own eyes a little misty. When he glanced at Maggie, his chest tightened. Hell, she was crying, too.

Damned women, he thought. But he didn't really blame them. Trace eased Maggie into his arms. "It's all right, darlin'. It's mostly just stuff. Stuff can be replaced."

"I know." She didn't move out of his arms, and he thought how right it felt to have her there.

Maggie finally took a breath and eased away, gazed wistfully up the staircase.

"It isn't safe to go up there," Trace said, reading her mind. "The second floor's pretty much destroyed and totally unstable. But we can poke around a little more down here if you want."

She nodded. He and Jason both wore rubber boots, and the kid had bought a pair each for Ashley and Maggie. The downstairs was intact except for the horrific water and smoke damage.

They tromped past the soggy sofa and chairs and went into the bedroom. Ashley was cheered a little when she discovered most of the clothes in her closet had survived the fire and just needed a good washing.

Trace followed Maggie down the hall to the linen closet. She reached up to a shelf overhead and took down a cardboard box.

"What is it?" he asked.

"Family pictures. Mostly me and my dad. There's a few old ones of Mom and Dad before she left, some baby pictures of me. Some photos of me and my college friends." Maggie hugged the box against her. "I was praying they wouldn't be destroyed."

"I guess your prayer was answered."

She looked into his face. "My prayer was answered when I saw Ashley sitting on the curb that night, holding little Robbie in her arms."

Trace knew exactly what she meant. He'd never felt such a rush of relief as the moment he had found them all safe.

"Have you hired someone to fix this place?" Ashley asked, sloshing toward her sister.

"I've been talking to a guy named Will Jacobs. He was recommended by a friend of Trace's in Dallas."

"Gabe Raines. He's a developer," Trace explained. "He says Will is one of the best. He's honest and he won't charge an arm and a leg."

"When's he going to start?"

"First of next week," Maggie said. "Will says it's at least a two-month job."

Ashley surveyed the water creeping into the wallboard, making it swell, the wet drapes sagging from their rods. "You know, sis, this place could have used a little decorating, anyway."

Maggie looked at her sister, thought of the odd pieces of junk she'd used to furnish the town house. She surveyed the destruction around them, the puddles of grimy water, the soggy furniture that would all need to be replaced. A giggle escaped, turning into full-blown laughter.

Ashley laughed, too. Trace chuckled and pretty soon all of them were laughing.

Maggie wiped her eyes. "I guess you noticed I'm not much of an interior designer."

Ashley grinned. "I kinda couldn't miss it. When you get the place remodeled, I'll help you. I'm pretty good at that kind of stuff."

"I bet you are, and that'd be great."

Trace tried for a smile, but his thoughts had returned to Maggie and her stalker.

To the fire that could have been lethal—and what might happen next.

Chapter 25

The buzz of activity filled the white-walled interior of the Twin Oaks Gallery as Trace escorted Maggie inside. It was time to start moving forward with their plan to lure the stalker into the trap they were setting.

Trace had spoken to Ben and Alex, and both had agreed to help. On Friday, the men would arrive in Kemah before daybreak to stake the place out. *Ranger's Lady* would serve as headquarters for the operation.

"There's Faye," Maggie said, starting in the owner's direction. Trace was surprised to see spotlights shining on walls that were mostly bare.

"What's going on?" Maggie asked as the swanky brunette walked up to greet them.

Faye smiled. "I've been meaning to call. After the TV news broke the story of the fire, a rush of people poured in to look at your work. They were curious, I guess. People liked what they saw. The rest of your photos practically flew out the door." She laughed. "You just can't buy advertising like that."

Maggie glanced around at the empty spaces. "I guess not."

Two burly young men were busily hanging pictures, nicely framed black-and-white photographic portraits of interesting faces.

"Who's the artist?" Trace asked.

"Those belong to a guy named Zeke Meadows. I'm filling in with his work until Maggie can get me more pictures."

"I'm heading down to Kemah on Friday," Maggie said, spinning the story they had planned. "I'm starting to shoot again. I just need a little more time."

The brunette rolled her long-lashed blue eyes. "I guess there isn't any choice, but I can't sell—"

"What you don't have," Maggie finished for her. "Let my clients know I'm back to work starting Friday. Tell anyone who might be interested."

Faye cast Maggie a suspicious glance. She knew about the stalker, and the woman was clearly no fool. She turned to Trace. "So let me get this straight. You want people to know where Maggie's going to be this Friday."

"That's right."

"But you'll be there to make sure she's all right."

Trace smiled. "You can leave that part out."

Faye relaxed and returned his smile. "You got it, cowboy."

They talked a little while longer. Faye was upset that the fire had destroyed Maggie's latest collection, but as she had promised, Maggie kept silent about her Photo-drive storage. She did a bang-up job of convincing Faye not to do anything until they could work things out.

Which pleased Trace in one way, but reminded him how good she was at lying by omission.

Trace told himself she'd done exactly what he wanted. The trap would give them the stalker, and the stalker would be the guy responsible for the fire.

He wished he believed it.

On Wednesday morning, Maggie did a TV interview with Sally Grimshaw of KGEO TV in front of her burned-out condo. Again, she talked about her Friday morning trip to the shore.

"So you're going back to work," Sally said once they'd gotten started. She was blonde and petite, very attractive and extremely dedicated to her job as a journalist.

"That's right."

"I'm sure your fans will be delighted to hear it."

Maggie adjusted the mic pinned to the lapel of her pale blue silk blouse, which like all her clothes was a recent acquisition. "I certainly hope so."

"The fire was reported to be arson. Do you have any idea who might have set it?"

The question threw her. For a moment she wasn't sure how to respond. She glanced at Trace, who was standing nearby, then decided to roll with it.

"I've been having trouble with a stalker. Phone calls, notes on my car, that kind of thing. He's seems the mostly likely suspect."

"I see. Have the police made any progress in finding him?"

Maggie flashed a phony smile into the camera. "I'm sure they're doing their best."

They talked a few minutes about her upcoming trip to the shore, then the cameraman turned off the bright white light and the interview was over. The piece aired on the morning news, was shown again at noon and re-peated at five and eleven.

Word was out. Maggie hoped her stalker was still as interested in her movements as he had been before. If he showed up in Kemah—and she prayed he did—they would be ready.

There was just one last thing.

Trace wanted her to meet the rest of the team. He wanted her to be able to recognize the men in case there was trouble.

Alex Justice and Ben Slocum arrived at his house on Thursday night right after supper. Both in their early thirties, both over six feet tall, they were almost equally handsome. Alex, with his dark blond hair, blue eyes and dimples, had a lighter personality, charming and jovial, and yet she sensed an inner core of steel.

"It's a pleasure to meet you, Maggie," he said as he sauntered into the living room. No Texas drawl; instead there was a hint of refinement in his voice.

"You, as well, Alex. Trace has spoken very highly of you."

Alex grinned. "I'm amazed he mentioned me at all."

"Alex was in the air force," Trace added, tossing his friend a warning glance.

"Fighter jockey." Alex ignored him. "I hope Trace's been taking good care of you. The way he's kept you locked up, we figured we might have to stage a jail-break."

She laughed, wondering if Trace really had pur-posely kept her away from his two gorgeous friends.

Maggie turned to the more somber of the pair, a man with dark hair, ice-blue eyes and unforgiving features. "I gather you served with Trace in the army."

"Rangers. Yes, ma'am." The drawl was back, not as

slow and sexy as Trace's but with a slightly harder edge. Another Texan, she was sure.

Maggie smiled. "Looks like I should be safe enough with the three of you there to protect me. I just hope this works so I can get a place of my own and my life back to normal."

Both men glanced at Trace, but he made no comment. Once this was over, she would be moving out of his house, living again on her own. There was no commitment between them, no talk of the future. Both of them expected the arrangement to end.

Maggie told herself it was exactly what she wanted. They would still see each other, but they would be able to live their own lives. The thought made her stomach clench into a knot.

"Alex and Ben will be in place by the time you get to Kemah," Trace said. "You won't see them. But you can be sure they'll see you. I'll come in behind you. You'll be wearing a mic and an earbud so we'll be able to communicate. If you see someone you recognize, or something seems out of place, just sing out."

She nodded. "All right."

"This guy shows up," Ben said, "his ass is ours."

"Count on it," Alex agreed.

"I spoke to the county sheriff's office," Trace added. "They've been in touch with Houston P.D. and alerted their deputies. We'll have backup if we need it."

The men nodded. They finished the beers they were drinking while a few more items were discussed. The meeting ended on a determined note and the pair left the house. The sound of their footsteps crossing the porch faded away, then silence filled the living room.

Trace turned to Maggie, tipped her chin up and captured her lips in a soft, sexy kiss.

"Let's go to bed, darlin'," he said gruffly. "Forget all this for a while." The familiar heat was in his eyes, but there was something more. She recognized it as worry. He didn't like using her for bait.

But time had proved to be their enemy.

They didn't have any other choice.

Chapter 26

Maggie ignored the butterflies in her stomach. A heat wave had settled over the city. The day was hot and clammy, the dense, humid air sticking to her skin. She prayed her stalker had seen her TV interview or heard through the grapevine via Faye that Maggie would be driving to Kemah this morning.

She wondered if he knew where she had been staying since the fire, wondered if he had kept track of her somehow. She wondered if maybe he had seen her drive away from Trace's that morning, and a shudder of apprehension slipped down her spine.

She checked her rearview mirror. As she drove her little SUV down Highway 45, Trace followed somewhere in the traffic behind her. He was driving Alex's BMW in case the stalker had seen him in the Jeep. Alex and Ben were already in place. They would be watching for her arrival. None of the men were taking any chances, but she still she felt very alone.

The trip seemed to take forever, the road stretching endlessly ahead of her. Her neck ached from constantly looking in the mirror, or searching the cars ahead or beside her. Finally, the 518 exit to Kemah appeared and Maggie sighed with relief. She pulled onto the road that wound its way east toward Kemah and Galveston Bay. She didn't see Alex's silver-blue Beemer, but she knew Trace was back there.

She reached up and adjusted the seashell necklace she wore, which contained a tiny microphone. The men could hear whatever she said. She was also wearing an earbud, easily hidden by her heavy hair.

"I'm on the 518," she said, just to hear the sound of Trace's voice in return.

"Good girl. I'm a ways back, but I've got your GPS location." He had affixed a bug to her bumper just in case something went wrong and he needed to find her.

"Roger that," she said with a grin, beginning to get into the part.

She heard his deep chuckle, and warmth curled through her. It was amazing how sexually attuned she was to him. He was an amazing lover, intuitive in the things she liked, at times able to bring her to orgasm with only a touch. It was getting more and more difficult to imagine sleeping without him.

Maggie shoved the thought away. At the moment, she didn't have time to think of her sex life or her nebulous future. She needed to focus on the task ahead.

Winding through the traffic, she finally reached the 146 and found her way into the parking lot in front of the Kemah boardwalk. The plan was to start there, taking shots in the area, then wander over to the boardwalk marina, where *Ranger's Lady* was docked.

She turned off the engine and rounded the Escape

to the back. Opening the hatch, she grabbed her camera bag, pulled out her Nikon D3S, which had been in the back of her car the night of the fire, thank God, not in her studio.

She took her time getting ready, pulling on a yellow sun visor that matched her blouse, dusting off her white capri pants, lifting the strap of her camera over her head, attaching the Tamron lens.

If someone had followed or was already there watching for her arrival, she wanted to make it easy for him to find her.

She glanced around, looking for Alex or Ben, thinking maybe she would spot Trace, but saw no one. She ignored a moment of uneasiness and reminded herself the men were professionals. If they didn't want to be seen, they wouldn't be.

Sucking in a deep breath, she squinted, finding the sun bright even though she was wearing sunglasses and the visor. Then she pasted on a smile and started forward.

"I'm heading toward the entrance," she said into the mic.

"We've got you," Trace said into her earbud.

She meandered toward the red-white-and-blue arch, taking shots of kids and their parents, trying to look as if she was really interested and not just there as bait for a trap. She wandered awhile longer, careful to stay out in the open, making it easy to be seen.

A commotion to her left drew her attention. A man darted out of nowhere and ran toward her, and her heart jerked. Skinny black jeans, black T-shirt, long black hair tied back in a queue. He was lean-muscled and handsome. He was on a beeline course, headed her way, and she had never seen him before.

"There's a guy on your right moving toward you." Trace's voice held a note of tension.

"I see him."

"You're definitely his target."

"I don't know him, but—"

"I've got him," Alex said.

"On his twenty," said Ben.

The guy kept coming. He was young and nothing like she had expected.

"Hold your positions," Trace commanded. "Something doesn't feel right."

The man in black closed the distance between them. "Maggie? Maggie O'Connell?" He stopped right in front of her, his voice carrying into the mic.

"Yes? Do I know you?"

"I'm a friend of your sister's. Ziggy Murdock? I'm sure she told you about me."

The tightness in Maggie's shoulders relaxed. He wasn't her stalker, just Ashley's jerk of an ex-boyfriend. "I know who you are."

"Stand down." Trace's deep command came through loud and clear.

"I saw you on TV," Ziggy continued. "I thought if I could talk to you, maybe you could help me fix things with your sister."

Maggie glanced around at the tourists and locals, none of whom looked threatening. "I'm shooting, Ziggy. And even if I had time, I wouldn't help you. Ashley's life is on a different course now. She's over you and that's the way it's going to stay."

"Hey, she's got my kid, you know. That gives me some rights."

"Yes, it does. And I'm sure once she gets settled and you get your own life in order, Ashley will be willing to

make some sort of arrangement, if you're really interested in seeing your son. Until then, as I said, I'm busy."

She brushed past him, kept walking. Ziggy followed,
coming up beside her.

"You know what? You two bitches are just alike."

Maggie smiled. "I'll take that as a compliment."

"Yeah, well, fuck you." Ziggy turned and stomped
away, his long, thin legs carrying him off.

Trace chuckled into the earbud. "Guess he made a
long drive for nothing."

Maggie grinned.

"Nice work, ma'am." It was Slocum's hard Texas
drawl.

"Thanks," she murmured.

Maggie trolled for another hour, meandering past
the Saltgrass Steak House, circling the carousel, stroll-
ing beneath the Ferris wheel, taking photos along the
boardwalk out into the bay. She took dozens of shots,
but none were particularly good. Her mind wasn't on
work. It was on catching a stalker.

A string of musical chimes threw her for an instant—
a text message coming in on her cell phone. Maggie dug
frantically through her purse, pulled out the phone and
read the text marching across the bottom of the screen.

I didn't set the fire. I would never hurt you, Maggie.

Her insides turned to ice. She glanced frantically
around, but no one was looking her way, or seemed the
least bit interested. With trembling fingers, she reached
for the necklace, adjusted the mic.

"I got a text," she said, facing away from the patrons
on the boardwalk toward the open water, so no one
could see her lips moving. "I-it's from him. He says he

didn't set the fire. He says he would never hurt me." She took a deep breath. "Do you think he's here?"

"Could have come from anyplace," Trace's voice replied. "Forward the message and start walking. Keep your eyes open."

Maggie sent the message on to Trace. She knew he would try to find out where the text had come from. She steeled herself, forced herself to start again, to move at a leisurely pace.

The morning heated and the sun turned brutal, the humidity creeping higher and higher. Her skin felt sticky; her sunglasses slid down her nose.

"I'm going back to check the car, see if he might have left a note. Maybe he's somewhere nearby, watching for me to return."

"Roger that," Trace said. The others acknowledged the communication. Aside from Ziggy's brief appearance, and the text she had received, nothing had happened. And no one had seen anything out of the ordinary.

Maggie reached the parking lot, where the pavement was soft and hot beneath the soles of her sneakers, and heat rose in rippling waves. She wanted to climb inside the car and turn on the air conditioner, blast the icy coolness into her face.

At the sight of the empty windshield, she felt her shoulders droop. Unlike the last time, there was no note, no sign that her stalker had been there. Nothing but his eerie text message, which, like before, had probably come from a throwaway phone.

"Shall I head over to the marina?" she asked into the mic.

Alex and Ben had been aboard the boat that morning, she knew, a place to have coffee and wait for the sun to come up.

"Roger that," Trace said. "We'll rendezvous at the *Lady,* get out of the sun for a while, maybe try again a little later."

Though if her stalker was watching, he would see them all together, and any chance to make contact would probably be lost.

Still, getting out of the sun sounded like a great idea to Maggie. Imagining a cold drink and some time off her feet, she didn't notice the battered old Dodge van that was parked two cars down from her Ford on the opposite side. She didn't give it much thought when the driver backed the van out of its space and pulled up in front of her.

Then the van doors rolled open and two men in tank tops and camouflage cargo pants jumped out and shot toward her, their heavy lace-up boots clattering on the asphalt. One was white with curly blond hair, the other Hispanic with a do-rag tied around his head. Both were covered with tattoos and had solid, muscular bodies.

"Trace!" Maggie screamed as one of the men grabbed her camera and started trying to drag the strap off over her head. "Let go of that!" The heavy length of black nylon was looped around her neck. Maggie hung on tight, not about to let go. "Get away from me!"

"Get her purse!" the guy yelled to his friend, who grabbed her bag, which she was wearing secured across her body messenger-style. Even if she'd wanted to give it to him, she couldn't get it free.

"Goddamn it, lady!" He tugged on the strap, trying to jerk the expensive camera off over her head, while the other guy yanked on her purse, which held credit cards and several hundred dollars in cash.

Maggie dug her heels into the pavement and pulled back as hard as she could, at the same time twisting to get free. One of them shoved her and she went down, scraping her palms as she tried to protect the camera.

The second man pulled a knife out of nowhere, cut the strap on her purse and ran for the van. "Come on, Chaz!"

Maggie staggered to her feet, still gripping the camera, determined to hold out until Trace, Ben and Alex could reach her.

"I'm not giving it to you!" Her heart was pounding, slamming against her ribs, as she tussled with the blond man.

"You bitch!" A tattooed hand slapped her hard across the face and she stumbled but didn't let go. A red-and-blue serpent wound around the arm that fought for the camera, and a skull-and-crossbones gleamed on one shoulder.

"Stop it!" Her cheek burned, making her more determined than ever not to let him win. Then, suddenly, she was free, stumbling to keep her balance and not wind up on the ground again.

In a blinding rage, Trace grabbed the first guy by the back of the neck, spun him around and hit him so hard that his feet left the ground and his head cracked against the pavement. From the corner of his eye, he saw Alex grab the second guy, a muscular Hispanic with a faint mustache and deep-set black eyes. Alex slammed the gangbanger's head against the side of the van once, twice and again, and Maggie's purse tumbled out of his hands. Through the window, Trace saw Ben jerk open the driver's-side door, drag a second Hispanic guy out of the vehicle and smash a fist into his face.

Trace turned an instant too late. His opponent was on his feet, a tattooed arm swinging a punch that split

Trace's lip and sent blood flying across the front of his shirt. He rammed a fist into the thug's belly. A right, then a left, followed by third blow left the guy reeling.

Flicking a glance at Maggie, Trace saw the red mark on her cheek and punched him again, slamming him to the pavement. This time he didn't get up, until Trace grabbed the front of his tank top and hauled him to his feet, ready to hit him again.

"Trace!" Maggie's high-pitched shriek cut through the bloodlust, dragging him back to his senses. He shook his head to clear it and reined himself in, his fist shaking with his effort to stay in control. He'd known better than to make Maggie a target. The minute he spotted the van, he knew he had made a mistake.

Trace turned to see Alex mopping up the pavement with the gangbanger in the do-rag, then hauling him up beside the van. Ben goose-stepped the driver around the front of the vehicle, his arm cranked up behind him.

The guy with the serpent tattoo hadn't moved since Trace knocked him ass-over-tea-kettle onto the pavement. Trace stepped over the unconscious figure, checked the pulse beating at the side of his neck, found it strong and steady, and headed for Maggie.

She was trembling and pale, her hands scraped raw from her fall on the asphalt. Trace drew her into his arms.

"It's okay, honey, it's over. Everything's all right."

Maggie took a deep breath, but didn't let him go. All Trace could think was how glad he was that she was only scared and a little bruised, not seriously injured. She took another breath, managed to nod, and reluctantly, he released her.

A crowd was beginning to gather. In the distance, he could hear the wail of a siren.

Maggie gazed up at him. "I don't... I don't understand what's going on. Is one of these men my stalker?"

"No," Trace said darkly. "Maybe you ought to go sit
in the car, turn on the AC."

Maggie firmly shook her head. "No way."

The white guy was still unconscious. Trace turned
his attention to the driver of the van, who appeared to
be in his late twenties, with a shaved head and small
goatee. "Who hired you to follow the lady down here?"

"I don't know what you're talking about, man."

Ben whacked him on the back of the skull, summon-
ing a belligerent glare.

A few feet away, Alex shook his guy like a rat.
Trace had learned long ago that the jet jockey was a lot
tougher than his sophisticated appearance made him
seem. "You heard the man. Who paid you to follow
the lady?"

When the guy clamped his lips shut, Alex slid a hand
around his throat and hoisted him up against the side
of the van. "I asked you a question."

"Nobody paid us, man," he managed to choke out.

"Keep your mouth shut, Reggie," the driver warned.
Ben whacked him again and dragged him around to the
other side of the van, leaving his buddy at Alex's mercy.

Alex kept his hand around Reggie's throat, the threat
more than clear, and his tough-guy facade began to
crumble.

"You're going to jail for assault," Trace said to him.
"Do yourself a favor and cooperate."

"Nobody paid us," he said again. Alex released him.
"We just came down to drink some beer and have some
fun." Reggie rubbed his throat. "Then we seen her. She
was on TV so we knew she was some rich bitch photographer. We figured that fancy camera of hers had to
be worth at least a grand, so we went for it."

"I'm not rich," Maggie said fiercely. "I saved for a long time to buy that camera. I didn't steal it from someone the way you tried to do. And I didn't hurt anyone trying to get it."

Under his dark skin, Reggie's homely face went red. "Oh, yeah? Well, if you woulda just handed it over, you wouldna got hurt."

Trace's jaw went tight. "Since you and your buddies are going to jail, I guess your plan didn't work out too well."

A siren sounded a couple of times before a pair of car doors swinging open ended the conversation. Two deputy sheriffs rushed up from the patrol car that had stopped in front of the van. Another car rolled up behind the vehicle and a second pair of deputies shot out.

"The sheriff'll handle it from here," Trace said to Maggie. He walked over, picked up her purse and gave it back to her.

Her hand trembled as she clutched it against her. "But we didn't get the stalker."

Trace slid an arm around her, eased her against his side. "Maybe we'll get something off the text message he sent." Not likely, but possible. He glanced over at the men and deputies next to the van. "I want you to promise me something."

"What is it?"

"Next time some guy tries to steal your camera or your purse, you give it to him, okay?" He thought of the knife Reggie had been wielding and how much worse it could have been. "I don't care what you paid for it, nothing is worth your life."

She gazed up at him, her big green eyes searching his face. Damn, she was pretty.

"I knew you were out there. All I had to do was hold them off long enough for you to reach me."

Trace looked at her hard. "Promise me."

Maggie sighed. "Okay, I promise. I suppose you're right."

He walked her back to her car to wait for one of the uniforms to come over and take a statement.

"At least he called," she said, referring to the stalker. "He made contact. That could be good. Maybe we could try this again."

Trace forced himself to smile. "We'll have to wait and see."

But no amount of convincing was going to get him to risk Maggie's life again.

Chapter 27

"What are you doing?" Maggie walked into the living room to find Trace adjusting his big-screen TV.

"Getting ready to look at some of your photographs. The ones you stored in Photodrive."

"All my pictures are stored there."

"I'm just interested in the ones you showed at the gallery. The fire was set after the opening—before you had time to get the sold ones reprinted. I'm thinking someone who was there that night might have seen something in one of your pictures that he didn't like."

Trace had suggested the theory before. It seemed improbable. But the world was an improbable place and she had come to trust Trace's judgment. "I suppose it could happen."

"Since the gallery wasn't torched, we have to assume if there is something in one of the photos, it's in one of those purchased that night."

Going with the theory, she started nodding. "If some-one had something to hide, he would have bought the picture to get it out of sight. He would have needed to destroy the picture and the memory card and—"

"And hire someone to burn down your studio. That way the photograph couldn't turn up again."

"It makes sense—if I actually did take some kind of incriminating picture."

"We need to know which pieces were purchased and who bought them."

"The information's on your laptop." The one he had loaned her after the fire. "I had Faye email it to me again. I'll print us a copy." She smiled. "You'll be happy to know I'm almost finished with my client list. I need to integrate the stuff Faye sent, but once it's done, the list will be complete."

"That's great. The more information we have, the more likely we are to figure out what the hell is going on." He tipped his head toward the kitchen table, where his laptop sat open. "I want you to go online and down-load your latest photos onto a card. We'll bring the pic-tures up in high-def on the TV screen. That'll make them big enough for us to see in close detail."

"Great idea." Maggie walked over to the table and sat down. Trace had already plugged a photo card into the machine, so she was ready to go. Using his wireless connection, she accessed the internet, went to www. photodrive.com, put in her username and password and brought up her account.

The photos were listed by collection, her latest ef-fort entitled simply *The Sea*. It was the same name she was using for her coffee-table book—if she ever got it finished.

She downloaded the photos, which took a bit of

time. While she was waiting, she sent the file Faye had emailed of the buyers' names and the pictures purchased at the opening off to Trace's printer, which was down the hall in his office.

They were working a two-pronged approach, searching for her stalker, but also examining the possibility that the fire was set for an entirely different reason.

Maggie looked at the screen, saw the download of the photos was complete. Trace took the photo card out of the computer and she jumped up and headed down the hall. The printer was humming, spitting out pages of names when she walked in. She picked them up and returned to the living room.

"Let me take a look." Trace walked up behind her, his hard chest pressing against her back as he read the list over her shoulder. She smiled, feeling a little curl of heat.

"Looks like half the bigwigs in the city bought one of your photos. The mayor. The chief of police. Mrs. Robert Daily—she's chairman of the university board."

"I sold fourteen that night."

"Richard Meyers's name is here—Senator Logan's aide. Logan's daughter, Cassidy, too. I remember you mentioned Matthew Bergman, the guy in the Ferrari that night. I see his name here. I don't recognize any of the others."

Maggie looked down at the list. "Mr. and Mrs. Silverman have bought from me before. Mrs. Weyman's name is here, the founder of the children's shelter. I don't know the others, though I may have met them that night." She handed Trace the pages.

"Let's match the photos with the people who bought them, see if anything comes up."

But the idea that she could have taken a photo and

not noticed something important enough to drive a person to burn down her house seemed pretty far-fetched.

With a sigh, she followed Trace into the living room.

Trace stuck the photo card into the slot on the side of the TV. An instant later, the first picture popped up on the screen. This one he remembered from the gallery show, a photo of a deserted shore with palm trees blowing in unison as if dancing a ballet. He accessed the metadata, which told the time and date the photo was taken. He remembered the title: *Taste the Wind.* There were no people in it, nothing out of the ordinary. It was the print Mrs. Daily had purchased.

The next photo came up. *"Sands of Time,"* Maggie said. It wasn't on the purchased list. The next two pictures were beautiful, but when she and Trace cross-checked, neither were among the fourteen sold at the opening.

He smiled as the fourth picture came up, the tiny sailboat racing to escape the tentacles of a rapidly descending storm.

"Ferocity," Maggie announced.

He remembered her saying she had waited for the little boat to reach safety before she'd left the area, remembered how it had touched him that she had been so worried about the people on board.

"Looks like that's the one Mrs. Weyman bought." The woman was a heavyweight in high society, someone who would be concerned about her reputation.

"I don't see anything," Maggie said, carefully examining the photo.

"You said the boat reached the harbor. So nothing untoward happened to it."

"That's right."

He went to the next digital image, of surfers slicing

through a curl, the sun illuminating the wave from behind, making it look like glass.

"Color of Water," Maggie said.

He looked down at the list. "Cassidy Logan bought it."

Maggie smiled. "I took it when I was out in California. Down at Laguna Beach."

He raised an eyebrow. "Visiting good ol' Roger?"

Maggie didn't take the bait. "I stopped to see him. We're friends, remember?"

And nothing more, he knew with a smug sense of satisfaction. Since Roger was gay, he was one man Trace didn't have to worry about.

The next photo came up, a wide swatch of ocean stretching out from a sandy cove. An elaborate sand castle was slowly being washed away by the surf, the kids who had built it watching with solemn expressions. Clearly, they were proud and sad at the same time.

"I call it *Life and Death,*" Maggie said, and he got it. Like building a sand castle, life was bright and fun, and yet it was fleeting.

She looked down at the list. "Someone named John Andrews bought it."

Trace studied the photo. "Just a couple of kids. I don't see anything that might be a problem for Mr. Andrews."

Maggie's gaze followed. "Neither do I."

"Still, it wouldn't hurt to have Sol do a little digging, see if there's anything we should know about him."

"Sol's the computer whiz in your office, right?"

"That'd be him. I'll have him take a look at the buyers we don't know anything about."

They ran through the first half of the photos. Not wanting to miss anything, they spent longer than they had expected, and found nothing in the pictures that looked suspicious.

"My concentration is going," Trace said with a sigh. "We could both use a break, and I need to get down to the office for a while. How about we look through the next batch when I get home?"

Maggie glanced away from the last photo on the screen. "All right." He could read her disappointment. She was hoping that something in the pictures might help them find her stalker.

Trace caught her face between his hands and gave her a soft, reassuring kiss. "Maybe this whole idea will turn out to be a wild-goose chase. But we won't know for sure until we're finished. And we've still got your client list to work. Soon as you've got it done, we'll get started."

Maggie just nodded.

"I know it doesn't seem like it, but we're making progress, darlin'. Something will break sooner or later. It always does."

She sighed. "I hope you're right. I just can't…"

"You just can't what?"

She shook her head. "Nothing."

Trace kissed her again. "Get that list done for me."

Maggie's smile looked forced. "I will, I promise."

He turned, let out a soft whistle, and Rowdy shot out of the kitchen. A single bark said he was ready to go. Trace ruffled his coat. Rowdy loved to ride in the car. It didn't matter where. As long as it wasn't too hot, Trace usually took him along.

"Let's go, boy." He waved at Maggie as he headed out the back door, only a little concerned by the look he had seen in her eyes.

She'd be all right, he told himself. He would take

her out to dinner tonight, get her out of the house for a while.

Trace thought of the evening ahead and how they would make love when they got home, and he smiled.

True to her word, Maggie finished her client list. There were dozens of people over the years who had bought one or two of her photos. There were twenty people who had purchased three pictures, ten who had purchased four and two who had purchased five. Two different art brokers had acted on behalf of clients. She had gotten in touch with them, but neither had clients who had purchased more than two pieces.

Her work was finished.

She glanced around Trace's warm, cozy house and ignored a sharp little pang at the thought of leaving. It was past time to go. Whatever was going on in her life, she couldn't live in limbo any longer. Trace didn't believe her stalker had set the fire. She had received a text from him that said the same thing.

Oddly enough, she believed him.

It didn't mean he wasn't a danger.

It didn't change what she had to do.

Grabbing her purse off the table, she headed for the back door. She set the alarm as Trace had shown her, and made her way out to the garage. Her Escape was parked next to where Trace kept his Jeep. She backed into the alley and headed for the real estate office she had phoned yesterday morning after reading an ad in the paper.

Gallagher Realty handled apartment rentals in the area near where her town house was being rebuilt. Trace was going to have a fit, but it couldn't be helped.

Maggie glanced in the mirror, but didn't see anyone.

She hadn't heard from the stalker since the text she had received from him at the shore. Even if he continued to harass her, she had no choice but to move on. It was time to get back to reality, and that meant finding a place of her own.

She thought of the days and nights she had spent with Trace, and a soft ache throbbed in the middle of her chest. Both of them had known it would come to this, she told herself, known their little housekeeping interlude would have to end. She had hoped by now they would have found the stalker, but unfortunately, that hadn't happened.

It didn't matter. She had put her life on hold for as long as she could stand. It was time to take the necessary steps and move toward the future.

She swallowed past a sudden tightness in her throat. Living with Trace had been surprisingly wonderful. She could have guessed the sex would be spectacular, but hadn't expected the day-to-day living to go so smoothly, or expected how happy just being with Trace made her feel.

The trouble was, Trace wasn't looking for a long-term relationship. He'd had one failed marriage. He was gun-shy for certain.

And so was she.

She wasn't good at relationships. Sooner or later, things would go downhill, and the longer she stayed the more it would hurt.

She spotted the real estate sign, drove into the parking lot and turned off the engine. Fifteen minutes later, an agent named Mary Darwin was showing her a single-story unit on the third floor of a complex that looked out onto wide landscaped lawns dotted with huge, leafy trees. There was a single-car garage for each unit, a communal pool, and the entire complex was gated, which offered at least some sense of security.

An hour later, she walked out of the real estate office with a month-to-month lease in hand. She had rented a three-bedroom, two-bath unit so that once it was safe, there would be room for Ashley and little Robbie.

Maggie hadn't realized she would miss them the way she had. It was nice being part of a family. She hadn't foreseen how much that would mean to her.

She sighed as she leaned back in the seat and started the engine. It felt good to be out of the house and once more on her own. Instead of heading back to Trace's, she drove to the Galleria to do a little shopping.

She could easily imagine how angry Trace would be when he found out what she had done.

Maggie grinned. She definitely needed something sexy to wear when she told him.

Ashley sat hunched over the dining room table. Made of rosewood, it was elegant and gorgeous. Everything in the apartment was done in exquisite taste. French antiques were mixed with contemporary pieces; marble and glass and expensive oil paintings were everywhere.

She loved it here. Which was the reason she had to leave.

She was living on borrowed time, in a borrowed apartment, enjoying a borrowed life. She needed a life of her own and she would never have it as long as she was dependent on someone else.

So when Betty Sparks had approached her last night at the end of her shift, she had grabbed onto the opportunity the older woman had posed.

"We all know about the fire," Betty said. "I know you're okay for now, but sooner or later you're gonna need a place of your own. Me and Bill…we talked about it some." Her husband, Bill, sometimes cooked at the café. But he had a heart condition and Betty worried that he worked too hard.

"We got this place upstairs," the gray-haired woman continued. "Our daughter lived there when she went to college. Been empty since she graduated and moved off to Dallas. You been doing a real fine job here, honey. Me and Bill…we worked hard all our lives. Kinda come to us that maybe you could stay on after Eddie gets back to work. You could keep workin' nights, so we could take a little time off, and you'd have your days to go to that cooking school you've had your eye on. You and your baby could live right upstairs, you know. Just be part of the deal."

For a moment, Ashley was speechless. Then her eyes began to fill. "Oh, Betty, that would be perfect."

She had patted her on the back. "Don't cry, now. You ain't seen the place yet."

But it wasn't a bad place at all, and Betty said she was going to have it painted, and the carpet replaced, before Ashley and the baby moved in.

So she would be leaving the fabulous apartment Jason had arranged for her use, and striking out on her own.

And the first step was completing the paperwork lying on the table, an application for admission to the culinary school at the Houston Art Institute, along with an application for a student loan, a program Maggie had found for her on the internet.

Ashley filled in the last few blanks, smiled as she finished, then turned at the chiming of the doorbell. Her heart took a leap. Jason had phoned earlier. She was off work tonight and he was bringing Chinese.

She had been cooking so much lately she was looking forward to the treat.

The bell chimed again as she headed for the door. He was coming over early, as he often did. Time had slipped away while she was working on the applications, so she hadn't had time to change and still wore the jeans, flat leather sandals and a T-shirt with a bunny on the front she'd put on earlier. Funny thing was, Jason never seemed to mind.

She opened the door, excited to tell him all her news, and there he stood, handsome as a god with his gleaming blond hair and tanned skin, all warm smiles, and a soft look in his gorgeous blue eyes that seemed just for her.

"May I come in?"

She didn't realize she was staring. Warm color rushed into her cheeks. "Sorry." She stepped back and he walked past her, his arms full of brown paper bags. Ashley hurried ahead of him into a kitchen that was every cook's dream, waited as he set the bags on the long granite countertop.

Jason leaned over and pressed a light kiss on her lips. It made her stomach quiver. "Hungry?" he asked.

"Starving. I didn't realize it until I smelled that delicious food."

He opened one of the bags, inhaled deeply. "Pineapple sesame prawns and lobster dumplings." He looked into another bag. "Tea-smoked duck, steamed rock cod with ginger and scallions." He opened the last bag. "Bok choy with fresh pea leaves in garlic sauce—and fortune cookies, of course."

Ashley laughed. "The leftovers will feed me for a week."

Jason smiled. "Mike Choo down at the China Palace

cooks this stuff just for me. He knows how much I love Chinese."

Her smile slipped a little. Jason was used to the good life. Restaurant owners who catered to his every wish were nothing out of the ordinary. She wondered if he would still come around when she was living in a tiny apartment above the Texas Café.

She started taking down plates and getting out silverware. "I've got some news," she said as he pulled the cartons out of the bags and set them on the counter. "I just finished filling out my application for culinary school."

He looked up. "That's great, Ash." He glanced away, then back. "I know you don't have much money. I'd be happy to help you. You know I can afford it. Just tell me what you need and I'll take care of it."

She could feel her temper rising. She'd been afraid this would happen. She started shaking her head. "I don't want your money, Jason. My sister offered, too, but that isn't what I want. I'm applying for a student loan. I'm pretty sure I'll qualify." She looked up at him and managed to smile. "Besides, I'm keeping my job."

A frown appeared between his sexy blue eyes. "I thought you were just filling in."

"I was, but Mrs. Sparks wants me to stay. She says she'll work around my hours while I'm in school." She kept her smile in place. "And guess what? She's going to let me and Robbie live in the apartment upstairs. Isn't that terrific?"

Jason's frown deepened. "What's wrong with staying right here?"

"Nothing's wrong with it. It's the most beautiful apartment I've ever seen. But it isn't mine. Eventually your friend will be coming back. And the truth is, I need a place of my own."

"Jimmy's busy gallivanting all over Europe. He won't be back for weeks. I think you ought to stay here. I live close by in case you need anything and—"

"Please, Jason. Please try to understand."

He swallowed, took a deep breath. "I know how much you value your independence. It's one of the things I admire about you, Ash. But it just seems crazy when I have so much and you—"

"Don't say it! I know you want to help, but I just can't take your money!"

A lengthy silence followed. "Okay," he agreed with a sigh. "We'll do it your way."

Ashley looked up at him. "I just want to know one thing. If I move into a little apartment like that, will you still come and see me? I know you aren't used to that kind of place, but—"

He grabbed her shoulders, gently shook her. "Stop it! Stop it right now!" He bent down and kissed her, quick and hard. "I'm crazy about you, Ash. I wouldn't care if you lived in a doghouse. I'd still want to see you." And then he pulled her into his arms. "I just want you to be happy, honey. That's all I care about."

Ashley blinked back tears and clung to him. "Jason…" She loved the feel of him wrapped around her, the warmth of his body against hers. When he held her this way, it seemed as if nothing in the world could hurt her.

"It's all right," he soothed. "Everything's gonna be all right."

She nodded against his shoulder. She was falling in love with him. She had tried so hard to keep him at a distance, but he just kept breaking down her defenses. It couldn't possibly work out. Jason was a wealthy playboy and she was a working mother trying to scratch out a life for herself and her child. And yet when he held her like this, her heart swelled with love and hope.

He eased a little away. "Are we okay then?"

Ashley looked up at him and nodded.

Jason released a relieved breath, smiled and changed the subject. "So what are we doing tonight? I stopped at Blockbuster, got us a couple of movies."

Ashley smiled. "I got one, too. *The Prince and the Maiden.* I promised my sister I'd help her and Trace find the stalker. I thought if we watched it we might find a clue."

Jason grinned. "Sounds like fun." He glanced toward the bedroom. "Baby's asleep?"

"He'll probably wake up pretty soon."

"Then we'd better eat so you can give him his bottle."

He always considered Robbie. Jason smiled when he held her infant son, and Robbie always smiled back. She was afraid her boy was falling in love with him, too.

She didn't want to think about it. Jason was a man, and though he seemed to care about her, she knew she'd be a fool to trust him.

It made her heart hurt to think how sad she was going to be when he left her.

Chapter 28

Trace stomped the dust from his boots, turned off the alarm and opened the back door. Rowdy trotted in beside him.

"Maggie?" He hung his hat on the peg beside the door.

"I'm in here."

He walked in that direction, more eager to see her than he wanted to be. Damn, he liked having her around. Too much, he knew, but consoled himself that there was nothing he could do about it, not until they found her stalker.

"Hello, lover." She walked up to him, kissed him softly on the mouth. "I missed you."

His groin instantly tightened. "I missed you, too." He had called her earlier, told her he wanted to take her out to supper, and she'd seemed excited about going. She was already dressed to go in a short, sexy burgundy number. One more kiss like the one she'd just given him and he would have to change the time of their dinner reservation.

"So how was your day?" she asked, reaching up to run a hand through his hair. He resisted an urge to do the same to hers, to tangle a fist in all those glorious red curls.

"Pretty busy. I talked to Mark Sayers. He already knew how our little trip to the shore turned out—unfortunately. He did have some info. He managed to come up with the location of the cell towers the stalker's calls came through. Two from one location, one from another. It might be something we can use."

"That's good, I guess."

"Sayers mentioned Parker Barrington. Says the D.A.'s case is getting stronger every day. They think they can put him away for Hewitt's murder."

"That's great. From what you've said, it couldn't happen to a nicer guy."

Trace chuckled. "Jason was damned glad to hear it. I think the kid'll be able to move on with his life now." He leaned back against the kitchen table, settled her in front of him between his legs. "How about you? You get anything done?"

"I finished my client list." She tipped her head toward the kitchen. "We can go over it whenever you're ready."

"Good girl. But not tonight. Tonight I have a date with a beautiful woman."

She smiled. "I finished my work and then I went out and rented an apartment."

Trace frowned. "What are you talking about?"

"I rented an apartment over on Baylor. It's very nice,

and it's close to Broadmoor so I can keep an eye on the construction being done on my town house."

He took a breath and worked to calm his temper. "You can't do that, Maggie. You know it isn't safe."

"I already did it, Trace. I'm moving in the day after tomorrow."

He felt a growl welling up in his throat, told himself to stay calm. "What about your stalker? He isn't going to leave you alone just because you want him to."

"No, he isn't. But other people have problems like this and they don't just move in indefinitely with their bodyguard."

His temper heated. "Your bodyguard? That's all I am to you?"

"Of course not. But I have a life to live, just like you do, and it's time for me to live it."

He clamped down on his anger. "The man set your house on fire. He nearly killed your sister and her baby. What if he does something like that again?"

"You don't believe he set the fire. You think it was something else. The stalker says he didn't do it. He says he wouldn't hurt me, and as crazy as it sounds, I believe him."

"You believe him."

"That's right."

"These guys are unpredictable, Maggie. He might mean exactly what he says, but tomorrow something could happen that changes the way he feels. You can't take that kind of chance."

"It isn't fair to you, Trace. Can't you see that? Neither of us wants to make a commitment. When things don't work out, one of us is going to get hurt."

Some of his temper seeped away, replaced by a tightness beginning to build in his chest. "Is that what this is about? You and me? It's over for you and time to move on?"

"No! I mean... I—I don't know. I just think we'd both be better off if we put things back on an even keel."

But he wouldn't be better off without Maggie. Trace was only beginning to realize how deeply he had come to care for her. He liked having her there when he came home. He liked being with her, liked everything about her. Well, almost everything. He didn't like one damned bit that she was so willing to put herself in danger.

"This is a bad idea, Maggie. But if you want out that bad, I can make it happen. I'll set up security around your place. We've got guys who make regular rounds. I'll have them put your apartment on the route. We can do some kind of temporary alarm system until you get back in your condo."

He didn't say more. His chest was clamping down, making it hard to breathe. He should have known she was getting to him, should have backed off way before now.

It was his own damned fault, and he had no one to blame but himself.

Maggie walked up and looped her arms around his neck. "You're supposed to be mad."

"I am mad."

"We were supposed to fight and then have a round of wild, unbridled sex."

He eased her arms from around his neck. He felt sick inside, sick and angry with himself. "Sorry, I'm not in the mood anymore."

Tears welled in her pretty green eyes. "It had to happen sooner or later, Trace. We both knew that."

"Did we?" He turned and started walking. "I think you'd better call out for pizza. I'm not hungry anymore."

"Trace…"

He grabbed her client list off the table and kept walking. Carly had played him for ten kinds of fool. But Maggie O'Connell, with her soft smile and big green eyes, had managed to break through the wall he had built around his heart.

The following morning, Maggie knocked on the door to Ashley's fancy, borrowed apartment. She had been there with Trace a couple times to make sure Ashley and Robbie were settled in all right. In the lobby, the security guard recognized her and phoned upstairs to let Ashley know she was on her way up. It was all very classy and very secure.

She stepped out of the elevator and started down the ninth-floor hallway, her sandals slapping the marble tiles as she wearily approached the apartment. She was exhausted. Last night, instead of sleeping, she had tossed and turned and listened for the sound of Trace's boots when he came home, yearning to see him, afraid of the way she would feel when she did.

She took a breath and knocked on the apartment door, and a few moments later, Ashley pulled it open.

"Maggie! I'm so glad you're here! I was going to call you this morning. I was just waiting until I was sure you and Trace would be up."

The words made her stomach churn. The baby started crying somewhere inside and Ashley hauled Maggie into the massive entry and closed the door.

"Hold on, I'll be right back." Her sister darted off down a wide, marble-floored hallway and disappeared into the room she was using as a nursery.

A few minutes later she reappeared, little Robbie

wrapped in a soft blue blanket and nestled snuggly in her arms.

"Jason bought a baby monitor so I can hear him wherever I am. The place is so big it's kind of hard to keep track of such a little guy." She jostled him until he stopped crying, then rubbed her nose against his until he finally smiled. "Your aunt Maggie's here. She wants to hold you, sweetheart."

And as Maggie looked down at the baby, she really did. She needed the comfort and sweetness of the little boy's tiny body pressed against her. Needed someone who could cheer her up out of the terrible despair she had fallen into after Trace had gone.

He hadn't come home last night, though he must have stopped by sometime, since there was a note on the door.

Keep your cell phone handy and the battery charged. If anything happens, ANYTHING, call me. I'll help you move your stuff whenever you're ready.

"I have some really great news," Ashley said brightly, leading her onto the plush carpet in the living room.

Maggie cuddled the baby in her arms. "I could use some good news."

"I'm keeping my job at the café while I go to culinary school." Ashley grinned. "Mrs. Sparks has it all worked out. And she's got a place for me and Robbie to live, an apartment above the café. So you don't have to worry about us anymore."

Maggie reached up and pushed a shiny blond curl back from her sister's cheek. "I never worried about

you. I loved having you and Robbie with me. But I'm
happy for you, Ash. Really happy."

Her sister glanced around. "I'm really gonna miss
this place, but I'm excited, too, you know?"

"Yeah, I do. So is that why you were going to call?"

"No. Last night, Jason and I figured something out.
Come on, I'll show you." Ashley tugged her across the
thick carpet into a room with no windows. It was a giant
media space with a huge viewing screen, Dolby sound
and six wide reclining leather chairs.

"Jason showed me how to play this thing." She went
over and turned on the DVD player. "Last night we
watched the movie *The Prince and The Maiden*. That
was the song the stalker played for you over the phone,
right? We figured maybe we could find some kind of
clue."

Maggie kissed the top of the baby's head. One of his
tiny hands wrapped around her finger and she felt a soft
tug in her heart. She looked over at the massive screen.
"So you think you might have found something?"

"I'm not sure. We were thinking maybe it could be."
Her sister started the movie, zipped forward at high
speed, stopped a couple times until she found the place
she was looking for. "Here's where they sing the song."
The beautiful maid began to dance with the handsome
prince. The couple sang the verse together. "I…saw…
you… I knew you would be my one true love. I…saw…
you…a vision so pure and sweet, my only true love…."

"It's a lovely song," Maggie said wistfully, trying
not to think of Trace or recall the look in his eyes when
she had told him she was leaving. Trying to ignore the
grinding pain in her heart that she had destroyed a relationship that had become more precious than anything
she had ever known.

"You said the guy broke into your house, right? That night he left a porcelain statuette."

"That's right." She continued to watch the film until Ashley pushed the pause button.

"Well, here's the thing. The couple in the figurine were dancing, right? That's what you said."

"Yes." Maggie swung her nephew from side to side, watched his little hands fisting and his mouth working.

"Well, the song says, 'I saw you, I knew you would be my one true love.'" But in the movie, they aren't just singing, they're waltzing. Just like the couple in the figurine."

The truth hit her like a jolt of lightning, and chills rushed over her skin. She sank down in one of the leather chairs, clasping the baby in her arms.

"You're right. In the movie, they're waltzing. Just like the statuette." She looked up. "I love to dance. Until this started, Roxanne and I went all the time. That has to be it. I must have danced with him somewhere."

"I really think that's the clue. I think you danced with him and he fell in love with you."

She shook her head. "It isn't love. It's some sick infatuation."

"Not to him. He calls you, follows you. He thinks you belong to him, don't you see? Just like the maiden belonged to the prince."

Maggie's heart was pounding. She had to call Trace, tell him what they had discovered. Her palms began to sweat. She had to phone him, and half of her wanted that more than anything in the world.

The other half knew how difficult that call would be. Trace saw her actions as the end of their affair. He would be determined to get on with his life—just as she'd said she wanted to do.

Ashley reached for the baby, settled him back in the crook of her arm. "What is it, Maggie? Something's wrong. I saw it in your face when you walked through the door."

Sadness welled inside her. "I rented an apartment. I told Trace I was moving out tomorrow."

"You broke up with him?"

"I didn't break up with him. How could I? We were never really a couple. It was only a physical thing."

"That is so not true." Ashley settled into the over-size leather chair beside her. "He loves you. The way he looks at you…it's like he could just eat you up. Maybe he hasn't quite got it figured out, but he loves you."

Maggie's throat swelled. She only shook her head.

"You know what else?" Ashley gently pressed. "You love him, too."

"No…"

"You really don't think so? Look at you."

Maggie swallowed past the painful lump in her throat. "Even if I did love him, it wouldn't work. I'm really bad at relationships. I always run away when things get too involved."

"You mean like now?"

She closed her eyes. She was doing it again. Only this time, instead of escaping, feeling free, she felt as if she were falling into a deep, dark hole.

Ashley's hand settled gently on her shoulder, making small, comforting circles.

The tears in Maggie's eyes spilled over onto her cheeks. "I love him. I love him so much."

Her sister smiled. "Well, then, I don't see a problem. All you have to do is tell him how you feel."

A ragged breath seeped out. "You don't know him.

He had a really bad marriage. He was only just beginning to trust me. He won't do it again."

Ashley's smile faded. "Oh, Maggie."

She rose from the chair, bent down and kissed the
baby's forehead. "I have to call him. Tell him what you
and Jason figured out."

Ashley stood up, too, leaned over and hugged her.
"Do it. Call Trace. Don't give up on him yet. And don't
give up on yourself."

Chapter 29

Trace leaned back in the chair behind his desk at the office. He hadn't been home for two days. He and Rowdy had been sleeping on the sofa in the back room.

He rubbed the bristles along his jaw. He needed to shower and shave. But he was still on Maggie's payroll. He still had a job to do.

He sighed into the quiet. At least he'd been working on her client list. Sol had run the names of the people who had bought her photographs, but come up with nothing useful except the addresses of where they were employed.

Trace was working on a theory. He just hadn't had time to put it all together. He needed to talk to Maggie, explain what was going on. And he needed her help to finish going over the second half of the photos sold the night of the opening.

He didn't reach for the phone. Maggie was moving

out this morning. She hadn't called. Apparently, she didn't need his help.

At the sound of a knock on the door, he looked up, then rose to his feet as Jake Cantrell turned the knob and walked in.

"Hey, buddy, good to see you." Trace extended a hand. Cantrell gripped it and slapped him on the back.

"You, too, my friend." The former marine was six feet five inches of solid muscle, with dark hair and pale blue eyes. He and Trace had worked together off and on over the years, most recently with Dev Raines and Johnnie Riggs in Mexico on the child-abduction case.

"I thought you were south of the border," Trace said.

"Was. Just got back. Thought I'd take a week or two off, rest up a little before you put me back to work."

"If I don't have something by then, somebody will. There's always work for guys like us."

Men who knew how to handle themselves in tough situations, who put the job first and did whatever needed to be done to protect the good guys from the bad.

Jake sat down in the chair beside Trace's desk. His size made the office seem smaller. "So what's new around here?" he asked. "Anything exciting going on?"

Trace sighed. "I thought so for a while. It didn't work out."

Jake eyed the growth of beard along his jaw. "Another redhead?"

He nodded. "I must have a death wish."

His friend chuckled. "There's always next time."

But Trace was thinking, *not for me.* This was his last attempt at normal, his last stab at home and family. He hadn't said anything like that to Maggie. Hadn't realized it himself until it was too late. The pipe dream was over now. He wouldn't make the same mistake again.

"Unfortunately, she's still a client," he said. "Got a stalker. Maybe some other trouble, too. I can't just walk away—at least not yet." Trace filled Jake in on the fire and their failed trip to the shore.

"You need some help," he offered, "you know where to find me."

"Thanks. Alex and Ben have been pitching in. Rex did some recon. So far, nothing we've done has turned up squat."

"Like I said…" Jake stood up and headed for the door.

Trace walked him to the front of the office, watched him cross the lot and climb into his big black, open Jeep with its roll bar and oversize tires. The machine was beginning to show its age and the wear and tear Cantrell put it through.

Trace watched him drive away, the pipes rumbling a little louder than they should. When he turned, he found Annie staring out the window.

"That man makes my heart flutter, and I'm sixty-four years old."

Trace chuckled. "Well, obviously, you aren't dead yet."

She laughed. "I guess not." She turned her mother-hen glare on him. "You look like somethin' the cat dragged in. You know, I really liked this last one. I thought you two were getting along."

"I thought so, too. The lady didn't seem to agree."

"More fool she."

He released a tired breath. "I guess I'm not cut out to be a settled-down kind of guy."

"That is not true, Trace Rawlins. You were a great husband to that rotten little witch you married. I really thought this one was different."

"So did I. Shows how dumb it is to trust your instincts."

Annie opened her mouth to argue, but the phone rang, giving him a reprieve. He turned, headed back to his office.

"Line one," Annie called after him. "It's your lady. Maybe she's wised up."

He just scowled. As he sat down at his desk and reached for the phone, his stomach knotted. He pressed the receiver against his ear. "What is it, Maggie?"

"Jason and Ashley found something. I was going to call yesterday, but I…"

He didn't try to help her find the words. He knew why she hadn't phoned. The same reason he hadn't called her.

"So what did they find?"

"Maybe nothing. I'm not sure, but it might be important." She went on to tell him about watching the movie, about the prince and the maiden and how they weren't just singing the song, they were waltzing, just like the couple in the figurine.

"I love to dance, Trace. Before all this started, Rox and I went clubbing all the time. I think… I have a feeling I danced with him somewhere."

There was a long pause.

Trace leaned back in his chair. "I guess that means we're goin' dancin'," he heard himself say. "I'll pick you up at eight."

"I wrote down my new address and the gate code, and left it on your kitchen table. I'm borrowing your laptop for a few more days, if that's okay, until I can get my new computer hooked up."

"Like I said, I'll be there at eight."

"Trace?"

"Yeah?"

"Nothing… I'll see you tonight."

Trace hung up the phone. He didn't want to go. He didn't want to see her. He didn't want to feel worse than he did already.

Heading out of his office, he called to Rowdy, asleep in the back, heard his small feet padding across the carpet. Trace ruffled the dog's fur and adjusted his collar. "Come on, ol' buddy. We're going home."

He had almost reached the front door of the office when Annie's voice stopped him. "So what did she want?"

Trace grunted. "A dancing partner," he said, and closed the door.

Maggie was ridiculously nervous. As she waited for Trace, she paced back and forth across the living room. The rented apartment was furnished, but not with any sort of style, just gray carpet, a gray sofa and chair, a black coffee table and end units, and a couple lamps. The framed artwork on the wall looked like something from Walmart.

There was none of the warmth she'd grown used to at Trace's, nothing that made her smile. She missed the comfortable atmosphere. Missed hearing the thud of boots on the carpet. She even missed Rowdy.

The only thing the apartment managed to do was show her what a stupid mistake she had made.

Maggie sighed. She should have stayed, should have

talked to him, explained her feelings, found out what he was thinking in return.

But beyond the great sex they had shared, she had no idea what Trace's feelings for her actually were, and exposing herself that way just wasn't something she was ready to do.

Ashley said he loved her. But Ashley was young and inexperienced with men, no matter that she'd had a child. And Trace had never said anything remotely giving the impression that Maggie played any role in his future.

Nor had she to him.

She had hidden her feelings behind the incredible sex, hidden them from Trace—and also from herself.

Ashley was right about one thing: Maggie was madly in love with Trace Rawlins. She didn't want to run away from him—she wanted to run straight back into his arms.

But it wasn't going to happen. She knew what he would say if she told him how she felt. He wouldn't believe her. It was just that simple.

She had moved out of his house, basically told him she didn't think it would work between them. Saying she had changed her mind was just not going to cut it.

The doorbell rang.

She checked the time, took a deep breath, walked over and opened the door. Her heart lurched at the sight of him, standing there in his perfectly creased black jeans, a short-sleeved white Western shirt and black ostrich-leather boots. The ladies in the clubs were going to be drooling.

When he smiled, he looked so handsome Maggie's heart squeezed.

"I'm ready," she said, because if she said anything else, she was going to start crying.

His gaze ran over her. "You look nice."

She had taken extra care with her hair and makeup, tried on ten outfits before choosing a short red dress she had never worn, but which seemed to fit her nicely. She managed to smile. "Thanks, so do you."

His eyes fixed on her face. "I liked having you in the house, Maggie. I just wanted you to know."

Her eyes burned. "I liked being there. More than I realized."

He just nodded, then turned away from her toward the door. "Let's go catch a stalker."

She swallowed. He was all business now, the consummate professional. He was her bodyguard and nothing more.

And it was all her fault.

"We need to hit your usual places," Trace said. "Where's our first stop?"

"Galaxy. That's my favorite. Rox and I went there a lot."

"All right, Galaxy it is."

It didn't take long to reach the trendy nightclub in the Galleria district. He could hear the music throbbing out the front door as they drove up to the parking valet. Trace tossed his hat into the backseat and climbed from the Jeep, joining Maggie as a dark-haired young man helped her out onto the walkway. Trace raked a hand through his hair, settling it back in place, then rested a hand at Maggie's waist and guided her into the club.

Music thrummed inside. The place was high-tech, all brushed chrome and dark wood, with mauve and blue lighting. There was an empty stool at the bar. Trace guided Maggie in that direction. She was wearing a very short, sexy little red dress that showed way too much leg to suit him, and left her entire back bare. His jaw felt tight. She wouldn't lack for dancing partners.

"Order a drink," he said softly, clamping down on the jealousy he didn't want to feel. "Dance when you get asked. I won't be far away."

She nodded, ordered a cosmo. He had never seen her drink anything but wine before. He wondered if she was more nervous about the stalker or about being with him.

She looked pale, tired, and he might say sad. Maybe she regretted her decision. Or maybe that was just wishful thinking.

She took a sip of her drink, then slid off the stool to accompany a heavyset man onto the dance floor. The DJ was playing a fast song. The guy should have been clumsy, given his size, but he wasn't. They danced together as if they had done it a dozen times, and Trace made a mental note to get the guy's name.

A lot of people knew Maggie. She danced again and again, but none of her partners seemed overly possessive. They were just enjoying themselves, same as she was. A slow song came on as she headed back toward the bar. Trace told himself not to move, but all of a sudden there he was, taking her hand, leading her out on the dance floor.

He drew her into his arms and heard her soft little sigh. Maggie looped her arms around his neck and snuggled up to him, and though desire curled through him, mostly he just thought how much he missed her. He'd dated a dozen redheads. None of them made him feel the way she did.

None of them had the power to hurt him the way she did.

They danced well together. He wasn't great, but he wasn't all that bad. When the next song started, a Texas two-step, he couldn't resist hanging on to her hand.

"You know this one?" he asked.

Maggie grinned. "Just try to keep up, cowboy."

Guitars and fiddles, a good, fast Western song. He loved it. For a few short minutes, he forgot he was her bodyguard, forgot he was supposed to be watching for a stalker. For a few short minutes, like everyone else, he was just enjoying himself.

When the song ended, he walked her back to the bar.

"Thanks for the dance," she said, as if he was just another partner, but she was smiling.

"My pleasure, darlin'."

Trace went back to work then, waiting and watching every man who partnered her, telling himself it didn't bother him when she laughed or smiled at something one of them said. An hour later he came up behind her.

"I want the name of the first guy you danced with. He's the only one who comes close to fitting our possible description."

"That was Doug Winston. He comes in here all the time, but I don't think it's him. He just likes to dance. He's never even asked me out."

"We'll check on him, anyway." Trace urged her toward the door. "It's still early. We've got time to hit a couple more places."

She nodded and they headed outside. As the valet brought up the Jeep, Maggie's cell phone began to ring. She dug it out of her purse and pressed it against her ear.

She stiffened for an instant, then her face went pale.

"It's him," she mouthed as she walked farther away from the music so she could hear. Close beside her, Trace bent down so he could listen to the voice on the other end of the line. It wasn't distorted this time.

"I miss you, Maggie. I'm so lonely. Won't you come out and play with me?"

She swallowed, glanced up at Trace. He motioned for her to talk, whispered, "Try to get his name."

"I'd really like to," she said into the phone. "Tell me where you are and I'll come to you."

Trace nodded in encouragement, telling her she was doing the right thing.

The voice on the phone was deep and resonant, and yet it sounded oddly childlike. "Remember how perfectly we fit together, Maggie? I remember how you laughed, the way you smiled at me."

"That was a special night, wasn't it?" A faint tremor shook her voice. "I can't quite remember exactly when it was."

Silence fell over the phone. "You don't remember?"

"Not exactly. I need you to remind me."

He didn't reply. The silence stretched out. Then the phone went dead.

Trace clenched his jaw. Maggie's hand was shaking as she hung on to the phone. "He didn't try to disguise his voice this time."

"No. He thinks you know who he is. He's escalating. This isn't good." Trace dug his own phone out of his jeans pocket and dialed Mark Sayers, who sounded sleepy when he answered.

"Mark, it's Trace. I need you to track a call or at least find the cell tower it just came from."

"Maggie's stalker?"

"Yeah."

"Give me her cell number again. And give me the exact time of the call."

Trace reached out and Maggie handed him her phone. He checked the time and rattled off the information Sayers wanted.

"I'll get back to you," Mark said.

Trace clicked off and gave Maggie back her phone.

"He didn't disguise his voice," she said, tucking it back into her purse. "Maybe he wasn't using a disposable this time."

"Maybe. But even if he was, I've been working on an idea…"

He took her hand, led her to the Jeep and helped her climb inside. They had just pulled into the parking lot in front of his office minutes later when his cell started ringing.

"Disposable," Mark said simply. "But I got the tower location." Sayers gave him the address.

"So the three night calls came from one tower, the daytime call from another."

"That's right. Good luck with it."

"Thanks, Mark." Trace signed off and they started for the office. "I've been working on a theory." He unlocked the front door, led her inside, flipped on the lights and turned off the alarm. "Come on, I'll show you."

Maggie let Trace lead her into the conference room, where a map of Houston and the surrounding area was spread open on the table.

"The white stickpins mark the locations of the two cell towers where the calls originated." He pointed at one of the pins. "The night calls, including the one you got tonight, came from here. There were three of them. My theory is the guy was at home when he made the calls."

"That makes sense."

"The text message you got at the shore was a day-time call." Trace pointed to the second white pin. "It came from this tower here. I think the guy was at work."

Maggie studied the map. "And the colored pins?"

"Sol ran your main buyers and came up with a work address for each, their home addresses already being on the list. The yellow pins mark work and home data of anyone who bought five pictures. There were only two, and neither fell into either zone. The red pins are people who bought four pictures. There are ten of them, but some live out of the city, so aren't on the map. A couple live in an area serviced by one of the towers, but unfortunately, their work addresses don't fall in the daytime zone."

Maggie picked up the list. "Twenty people bought three pictures."

"That's right. I was just getting started on those when you called. We'll make those buyers green."

They worked together to place them. Locating the addresses through Google Maps using Alex's borrowed laptop, which Trace had brought into the conference room, they tried to find a person who lived in the night tower zone and worked in the daytime tower zone. Some people lived in other areas, and those names were discarded.

Maggie shoved the last of the green pins into the map. None were in both tower areas.

Trace blew out a breath. "Well, I guess my theory sucks."

She picked up the list. "You haven't located the ones that were purchased through art brokers."

"True, but those buyers bought only two pictures."

"I know, but he just started stalking me recently, so maybe time was a factor. And maybe he used a broker to keep his identity secret."

"Worth a try. We'll make them blue."

Maggie went back to work on the laptop. The first name was Maryanne Rosemore. "Doesn't sound too ominous." She typed the home address into Google Maps.

Trace located the area on the map and shoved in a bright blue pin. "Outside either zone," he said darkly.

"The last name here is Phillip Coffman." She frowned. "I don't know why, but it sounds familiar."

"Coffman… Coffman." Trace walked up beside her, typed in the name. "President of HTM Technologies." He looked at her. "Their offices are in the Park View Towers. That's right here." He found the location on the map and marked it with a pin. It was only a couple blocks from the daytime white pin.

Maggie's heart started pounding.

"What's the home address?" Trace asked, and she could tell he was trying not to get excited.

"It's 55556 Bayou Glen."

"That's in Tanglewood. Big money lives there." He stuck a blue pin into the map. It was inside the night zone. "Bingo."

Trace went back to work on the laptop, typing far faster than she could have, pulling up information on Phillip Coffman. "The guy retired six months ago after twenty years with the company." He glanced up. "He quit right after his wife died, but continued to do consulting work at the office on a part-time basis."

"Can you find a picture?" Maggie asked. Trace clicked on a couple more websites, found what he was looking for and turned the laptop around so she could see.

Big, forties, dark hair silvered at the temples. "Oh, my God."

"You recognize him?"

"He and his wife were known for their charitable contributions. Mrs. Coffman died of breast cancer. That's where I met her husband." Maggie looked up. "I danced with him at a breast cancer awareness fundraiser earlier this year."

Trace's voice was hard. "And let me guess…the band was playing a waltz."

Chapter 30

Trace phoned Mark Sayers, who sounded even grumpier than the first time he'd been awakened. "Sorry to bother you again, buddy, but I need your help."

Sayers grunted into the phone. "So you found him."

"Yeah, and I want to pay him a little late-night visit."

"What's wrong with tomorrow morning?"

"Nothing. If we had enough evidence to arrest him. We don't. All we've got are a couple of cell towers and a bunch of pins stuck in a map."

"But you're sure it's him."

"Everything fits, even the description, and Maggie recognized his picture. I'm certain it's him. We need to put the fear of God into this asshole. I need you to meet me at his house."

"I'm not supposed to be working this case."

"You aren't. The address is 55556 Bayou Glen. That's out in Tanglewood."

"Guy must have plenty of money."

"Enough to pay an arsonist to burn down Maggie's house." Seemed as if Trace had been wrong on that one. It would be interesting to see what Phillip Coffman had to say.

"I'll be there in twenty minutes." Sayers hung up, and Trace turned to Maggie. It was nearly two in the morning. She looked tired, but her eyes were bright and there was plenty of color her cheeks. She was fighting mad and he didn't blame her.

"I'm going with you," she said. "I want to talk to him."

Trace shook his head. "I'm taking you home." Back to her newly rented apartment instead of his place, which hadn't felt like home since she'd left. "We don't know how this guy is going to react when he finds out his dirty little secret isn't a secret anymore."

"Why can't they arrest him?"

"Where's the proof? We don't even have enough to get a search warrant. That's why I want Sayers there tonight. If we get any kind of probable cause, we can go in. Maybe we'll find what we need inside the house."

Maggie's chin came up. "I'm coming, Trace. You can take me home and I can drive myself, or you can let me ride with you." She gave him a sassy, belligerent smile. "I know the address, remember?"

"Dammit, Maggie!"

She didn't say more, just stood there glaring, making it clear she meant what she said.

"All right, you can come. But you have to stay in the car."

"Fine."

As he locked the office and led her outside to the Jeep, his gaze ran over her. The little red dress looked wilted, her fiery curls a little less tamed, but she was still the sexiest woman he had ever seen. And the most appealing.

They drove up in front of the house just as Sayers's dark brown unmarked police car pulled up behind them. Trace retrieved the Beretta 9 mm he'd stashed under the seat earlier, and stuck it into the waistband of his jeans, behind his back.

"Promise me you'll stay right here," he said.

Silence. "I'm in the car, aren't I?"

He didn't miss that she hadn't actually promised. He gave her a hard warning glare. "I should have hand-cuffed you to a chair and left you in the office."

Maggie just smiled.

Trace closed the door and walked up to Sayers, and the two of them approached the massive front doors.

"The way it looks, this guy's got money and power," Mark said. "He could cause a real shitstorm for me down at the department."

"If Coffman's as off the deep end as he seemed on the phone tonight, I don't think he'll go in that direction."

"I hope you're right. I think."

They reached the door and Sayers rang the bell. Then he started pounding. "Police! Open up!"

The residential lots in the area were huge. No lights went on, no neighborhood doors came open. Sayers pounded again and the front door swung wide, revealing Phillip Coffman, six-three, mid-forties and slightly overweight.

"Yes? What is it?"

"I'm Detective Sayers and this is Trace Rawlins with Atlas Security. May we come in?"

"I'm sorry, what is this about?"

Trace answered, stepping things up a bit. "It's about

your obsession with Maggie O'Connell. It's about stalking her, breaking into her home, putting a tracking device on her car, installing video cameras. It's about setting her house on fire and nearly killing two people."

Coffman started shaking his head. "I didn't set the fire. I would never do anything to hurt her."

Sayers glanced at Trace and then leaped into the fray. "But you admit to harassing her, breaking into her home?"

Coffman started frowning. He looked unsettled, but mostly just bewildered. "I don't know what you're talking about. Ms. O'Connell and I are very close friends. We…we're planning to be married."

Trace swore softly at the sound of Maggie's voice behind him. "We aren't getting married, Mr. Coffman! We don't even know each other! We danced together once—that's it."

Coffman smiled at her. "Maggie…my dear, sweet Maggie. I knew you would come to me. I knew it was only a matter of time."

"That's it," Sayers said. "Put your hands behind your back, Mr. Coffman. You're under arrest for violating section 42.072 of the Texas penal code. That's stalking, Coffman." Gripping the bigger man's arm, Sayers turned him around and snapped a pair of handcuffs onto his thick wrists. Coffman made no move to fight him, just kept staring at Maggie over his shoulder as if she had somehow betrayed him.

Sayers called for backup and a few minutes later a patrol car rolled up in front of the house. As the officers approached, Coffman turned a pleading look on Maggie.

"I don't understand, dearest. Tell them…tell them we're in love."

Maggie's cheeks flushed. "We aren't in love, dammit!"

"That's enough," Sayers said to Coffman, and started reading him his rights. The officers asked a few questions, then maneuvered the man down the walk to the patrol car and into the backseat. The cruiser rolled away and disappeared into the darkness.

"You'll both need to come down to the station in the morning to make a statement," Mark stated.

"No problem," Trace said.

Sayers blew out a weary breath. "I should have known after the first phone call that I wasn't getting any sleep tonight."

"Sorry about that." Trace glanced around for Maggie, but she was nowhere in sight. "Dammit!"

The front door stood slightly ajar. It was clear she had gone inside. Trace and Sayers followed.

"I was planning to get a warrant, go through the house with the detective in charge of the case in the morning."

"I guess not," Trace grumbled.

The house was huge, with very high ceilings and gleaming wood floors. The walls in the living room were covered in a silk brocade that matched the sofa. The entire house was spotless. Clearly, Coffman had a staff to take care of the place, though none of them appeared to be in residence.

Trace and Mark climbed the sweeping staircase and found Maggie in the massive master bedroom.

"For heaven's sake, don't touch anything," Trace said as he walked up behind her. She was standing there frozen, staring at a wall of photographs pinned one on top of another—all of her. Next to them were pictures of Angela Coffman. Pictures of Angela and Phillip together.

"Losing his wife was the stressor," Mark said.

"Maggie's about the same size," Trace said, "and both of them have red hair."

Maggie just stared. "I can't believe how many photos he took. How could I have not noticed him?"

"I have a hunch he had people working for him. That's how he got the bug on your car and the cameras installed in your apartment."

"Oh, my God, look at those." There was a whole wall of music boxes, all with dancing couples. Except that one had been broken and the dancing couple was missing. "That's where he got the figurine."

"Your guys should have a field day tomorrow," Trace said to Sayers.

When Maggie made no comment, Trace settled an arm around her shoulders. "Let's get out of here. Let the police do their job."

He led her back downstairs and they left the house, paused on the porch as Mark secured the property.

"We'll be down to make a statement in the morning," Trace said. "Thanks, Mark."

"I'm just glad it's over."

Trace nodded. Maggie was safe and his job was finished.

He should have been glad.

He wasn't.

"I can't believe I'm saying this, but I feel sorry for him." Maggie sat in the passenger seat of the Jeep as Trace wheeled the vehicle toward home. Well, not really her home. Maybe it would feel that way, eventually.

Maybe.

Besides, the apartment was only temporary. Once her town house was rebuilt, she and Ashley could decorate it, make it feel cozy this time. It wouldn't have a cheerful 1950s kitchen, but you couldn't have everything.

"The guy *was* kind of pathetic," Trace agreed. "He's obviously got mental problems. Losing his wife sent him over the edge. Somehow he identified you with her."

She felt a sweep of sadness. "He must have loved her very much."

Trace flicked her a sideways glance. "Doesn't change the fact he almost killed your sister and her baby."

Maggie caught his eye briefly. "He says he didn't set the fire, though. He admitted to everything else, so why would he lie about that?"

"The guy's a head case, Maggie. Probably hired someone to torch the place and doesn't even remember."

"I guess so."

Trace entered the gate code for the Baylor Apartments, drove into the compound and pulled up in her guest space. The sun was coming up, soft yellow rays shooting through the branches of the trees, the sky a pinkish orange. He walked her to the elevator and they made the short ride up to the third floor.

The closer they got to the apartment, the more her stomach knotted. She didn't want Trace to go. She wanted him to come inside. She wanted him to make love to her.

She wanted to tell him that she had made a terrible mistake and desperately regretted it. She wanted to tell him that she loved him.

One look at the set of his hard, bristly jaw, the distance he kept between them, and she knew it was too late.

She forced herself to smile as she used her key to

open the door. "It's been a long night. Thanks for everything."

"I just did what you hired me to do."

She nodded, felt a lump beginning to form in her throat. "I don't...don't suppose you want to come in."

He just shook his head. "Wouldn't be a good idea."

She didn't reply. She thought it was a great idea.

"I'll call you tomorrow," he said. "Take you down to make a statement. You'll need to get a restraining order. I can help you get things rolling with that, too."

She swallowed. "All right."

"Good night, Maggie."

She looked up into his face, so male, so ruggedly handsome, and her heart clenched. "Good night, Trace."

He turned and started walking, and Maggie just stood there, watching until he disappeared. Her chest was aching, her eyes wet with tears.

For the first time she knew how David Lyons had felt the night she had said goodbye and walked away.

Maggie rode with Trace to the station the following morning. He seemed so distant, so completely removed from her that she wanted to cry. When they were finished giving their statements, he drove her to Evan Schofield's office to sign the documents necessary to file a restraining order.

The law office was first-class all the way, with dark wood paneling, shelves filled with leather-bound books, and expensive bronze statues on the tables in the reception area.

The only attorney Maggie knew well enough to call was David, and she wasn't about to do that. Trace had suggested Schofield, and she remembered him being with Shawna Jordane during Trace's fight with her rap-star husband at the Texas Café. Schofield was well known in Houston for his wealthy clientele.

The hour in his office passed in a blur. The only thing she remembered aside from signing the documents was Schofield telling Trace the judge had ordered Bobby Jordane into rehab for the next ninety days.

"You don't think Shawna will take him back when he gets out?" she'd asked.

"Shawna's one smart lady," Schofield said. "I don't think she'll go down that road again."

"Let's hope Jordane learns something while he's in there," Trace commented.

"Most of them don't," Schofield had said.

Trace drove her home after that. They barely spoke on the way. He let her out in the parking lot of the Baylor complex.

"I need to return your laptop," Maggie said, wishing he would stay. "Do you want to come up while I get it?"

"I've got to get back. I'll pick it up some other time."

Her heart sank. "All right." And then he was gone.

Maggie trudged wearily along the corridor to the apartment. No matter what happened, she vowed, no matter the risk she would be taking, she was determined to talk to him, tell him how she felt.

She just couldn't seem to find the right time.

Jason carried the last cardboard box up the stairs and set it on the new beige carpet in Ashley's tiny living room. He had helped her get settled in. Mrs. Sparks had rounded up some furniture, and he had brought a few things over. Not too many. And he had purposely dinged up the ones he'd bought. He didn't want her to guess they were new.

The little place wasn't all that bad, small but kind of

cozy in a way he'd never known. All his life he'd rattled around in thousands of square feet of living space. He was so used it, he took it for granted. But he thought that spending his nights here cuddled up with Ashley wouldn't be all that bad.

"I need some green plants," she said, drawing his attention. "Soon as I get my next paycheck, I'm going down to Walmart to buy some."

He almost smiled. It was cute the way she was so thrifty. He'd never known a woman like that.

She turned to survey the placement of the sofa beneath the window, and the bookcases along the wall made out of Home Depot shelves and cement blocks she had spray-painted brown. She had a knack for decorating, he could see. Making a place as small as this look good with old, patchwork furniture was definitely a challenge, but she was doing a great job with the little she had.

"It's starting to look really good, Ash."

She came over to stand beside him. Her face was flushed from carrying the last few boxes up the stairs, her silky curls a little damp. "You really think so?"

"Yeah, I do. It's gonna be great when you're finished."

She smiled, reached up and brushed a lock of his hair back from his face. He felt that light touch like an electric shock to the heart, and all of a sudden the words just tumbled out.

"I love you, Ashley. I can't keep it bottled up inside anymore. I love you and I love Robbie and I want to marry you." When she just stared up at him as if he had lost his mind, he added, "We can live right here if that's what you want."

Her big blue eyes welled with tears. "Oh, Jason…"

He reached for her, gathered her into his arms. "I mean it. I love you so much. Say you'll marry me."

She clung to his neck and he could feel the wetness tracking down her cheeks. He prayed he hadn't rushed her too much, that in his haste to tell her how he felt, he hadn't driven her away.

"Ashley...?"

She eased back a little to look at him. "I love you, too, Jason. I've never felt this way about anyone. You're the sweetest man I've ever known."

He started shaking his head. "Don't say that. Don't say 'sweet.' Nobody marries a man who's sweet."

She smiled, reached up and touched his cheek. "You are sweet, but you're right, I won't marry you. Not now. Not until I get my life together."

A crushing weight seemed to settle on his chest.

"Besides," she continued, her moist eyes still smiling up at him, making him want to pull her back into his arms, "we haven't even made love."

She glanced toward the bedroom. "Mrs. Epstein is watching the baby. We have the apartment all to ourselves. I think...if it's what you want, too...now would be the perfect time."

His spirits lifted at the same instant his body went hard. "I want to make love to you more than anything in the world. I just... I didn't want to rush you."

She reached over and caught his hand. "We've waited long enough."

He let her lead him into the bedroom, his heart hammering away inside his chest. The queen-size bed he had told her came from a friend who was upsizing to a king had in fact come from Macy's. He hadn't dared buy her new sheets, so she was using some that Mrs. Sparks had loaned her.

He looked at the bed and then at her, saw that now she had made her decision, she was getting nervous.

"It's okay," he said, gently cupping her cheek. Leaning down, he very softly kissed her. "You don't have to do anything more. I can take it from here."

She smiled at him with such yearning his heart hurt. "I love you, Jason."

"I love you, too." And then he kissed her again and Ashley kissed him back, and everything seemed to fall exactly into place.

She was his, he knew. And no matter how long he had to wait, one day she was going to marry him.

Chapter 31

Trace sat at the kitchen table sipping a cup of thick black coffee. Unable to sleep, he had made the pot hours ago and now was brooding over the dregs.

He tried not to think about Maggie, but his mind kept going there. He kept wondering what would have happened if he had told her how he felt. He wondered if it would have made a difference. The problem was, until she was gone, he hadn't really figured out that he was in love.

By then it was too late.

It was never going to happen between them; he had to accept that. But there was this last nagging worry that wouldn't leave him.

He rubbed the bristles on his jaw as he walked into the living room and turned on the TV. The photo card with Maggie's latest collection was still in place. The list with the names of the photos sold the night of the opening sat on the end table. He picked up the list, then used the tuner to pull up the photo next in line from where they'd left off.

He recognized the picture, but didn't remember the title. He wished Maggie was there to help him.

Damn, he just wished Maggie was there, period.

He ran through the first few photos. Without knowing the names of the pieces, he couldn't compare them to the ones on the sold list, but he didn't notice anything incriminating. He went through a few more, not sure what he was looking for.

The police believed Phillip Coffman had set the fire. Coffman had admitted paying people to take photos of Maggie, to place the cameras in her house and the GPS on her car. But there wasn't anything to connect him to the fire, nothing in his house or garage, and his attorney had been adamant that his client was innocent of arson.

And the nagging suspicion Trace had had all along refused to go away.

The morning was slipping by. He needed to shower and get down to the office. He brought up another photo, tried to compare it to the titles and buyers on the list, then looked up at the sound of the doorbell.

Trace was wearing only his jeans, no shirt, no shoes; and smiled to think he couldn't get past the no-service sign on the door of the Texas Café. He looked through the peephole, saw Maggie standing on his porch, and his chest squeezed.

Dammit. He'd promised himself he would never let a woman make him feel this way again.

He opened the door.

"Good morning," she said brightly. Too brightly, he thought. "I took a chance you'd still be home. I brought your laptop back. I figured you might need it."

He stepped out of the way to let her pass, got a whiff

of her flowery perfume. "Thanks," he said gruffly, raking a hand through his sleep-mussed hair.

He took the laptop from her hand, but she made no move to leave, and he didn't want her to. "Listen, if you've got a few minutes, I could use your help." Damn, she looked pretty with her fiery hair loose. He tried not to think about how lonely he'd been without her. "I could make us a fresh pot of coffee."

"Yes! I—I mean, coffee sounds great." There was something in her eyes he had never seen there before. Something that made his pulse begin to hammer.

"So what kind of help do you need?" she asked, following him into the kitchen.

"I thought I'd finish going through those pictures you took. Just, you know, to satisfy my curiosity and tie up any loose ends."

"I think that's a good idea. What could it hurt, right?" She waited while he made the coffee, and he thought how good it felt to have her back in his house. How much more homey it seemed. Rowdy must have felt the same, because at the sound of her voice, he came trotting into the kitchen and made a beeline straight for her.

"Hello, boy." She petted his thick, black-and-white fur. "I missed you."

Trace wondered if there was any chance she had missed him, too. Wondered what would happen if he just blurted out that he was crazy about her. That he wanted her to move back in.

He didn't, of course. Common sense prevailed. If she wanted to be there, she would have stayed.

While the coffee was dripping, he went back to the living room and put the next photo up on the screen.

"That's called *Magnificent Storm*," Maggie said, walking up beside him.

He tried not to think of kissing her, lifting her up in his arms and carrying her off to bed. He focused his attention on the list.

"It was one of those sold that night, but it's a seascape. No people in it."

"No."

The next photo came up. *"Rising Tide,"* she said. People playing in the surf, some lying on beach towels in the sand. Most were too far away to see, but a young couple was kissing on a blanket closer to the camera, and there was such an innocence about them it made his chest ache.

"Plenty of people in that one but I don't see anybody doing anything wrong." He smiled. "Unless that couple has something to hide."

"They were newlyweds." Maggie returned the smile. "I talked to them, got them to sign a release, since they appeared so prominently in the photo."

"Probably not about them then, and no one else stands out." He clicked up another picture, the harbor shot he had liked the night of the show.

"I know this one. *Harbor Sunset.* I remember it made me want to go sailing."

"It was taken down at the Blue Fin Marina just as the sun was setting."

"That's near Seabrook. Lots of boats and lots of people."

"It was the end of a perfect day. Most of the boats were back in their slips and people were sitting out on their decks. You can see the names on the back of the yachts along the dock. The sun was coming in at just the right angle. The lighting was perfect. It made a great shot."

"Metadata says it was taken April 20 at 5:42 p.m."

"That sounds about right."

Trace looked down at the list. "Richard Meyers, Senator Logan's aide, bought it."

Maggie walked closer to the screen. "I wonder if Logan owns one of the yachts in the picture."

"As I think back, Cassidy said once that her dad had a really nice boat."

Maggie pointed to one of the expensive white yachts in the picture. "I bet that's his—*Capitol Expense*." It was big and flashy, something a guy like Logan would own.

She studied the photo, which was blown up to fifty-two inches, but in high-definition was relatively clear. "I think that's him—the guy with the silver hair sitting on the deck."

Trace moved nearer. "I think you're right." He studied the photo, beginning to get one of those niggling feelings at the back of his neck. "There's a woman sitting across from him."

"She's got really dark hair, so she isn't his wife."

"Then it's not his daughter, either. Both of them are blonde. Just for fun, let's find out who she is."

"How do we do that? Mainly, we just see her profile."

"We can tell one thing. She's wearing a bikini and she looks damned good in it."

Maggie laughed. "She looks young."

"Young and pretty. I don't think this is one of the senator's constituents."

Maggie looked up at him. "He's running for governor. It wouldn't help him any for word to get out he's having an affair."

Trace studied the photo. The woman was definitely not Cassidy or Teresa Logan. "Hard to believe he'd be willing to burn down your house, though, to keep it quiet."

"I guess it depends on how badly he wants to win."

Trace walked over and touched the screen. "There's something here, on the woman's shoulder. Some kind of colored mark. I can't quite make it out…"

Maggie leaned forward, close enough he could feel her warmth, breathe in that familiar perfume. His body tightened. Damn.

"Might be a tattoo," she said. "She's young. It's kind of the thing to do."

"Maybe." He pulled the card out of the slot in the side of the screen. "I know someone who can help us. He can give us a better look at the woman's face, and we'll find out what the mark is on her shoulder."

The coffee was done, the rich aroma filling the house, but Trace no longer cared. His instincts were screaming, telling him he had just hit the mother lode.

"Can I come with you?" Maggie asked, looking up at him with those pale green eyes that had drawn him in since he had seen her that day at the Texas Café. And though he knew he was being a fool, knew he would only feel worse when she left again, he opened his mouth and said, "Yes."

Maggie waited as Trace made a phone call. When he hung up, he led her out to his Jeep.

"Where are we going?" she asked.

"An old friend of my dad's. Pete Wilkinson. He's retired from NASA. Still does consulting work for them on occasion."

She snapped her seat belt in place, then sat back as Trace headed out of town, driving southeast, winding up in a subdivision in Pasadena. His father's friend must have been watching for them. A man in his late fifties, with iron-gray hair and a paunch around his middle, opened the door and stepped out on the porch as they pulled up in front of his single-story brick house.

"Come on," Trace said, leading Maggie up the walkway. The men shook hands. Introductions were made and Pete led them into his home.

"Thanks for seeing us, Pete. I have a feeling this may be important."

"Well, then, I hope I can help."

Maggie followed the men into Wilkinson's study, which was surprisingly high-tech, considering the rest of the house was simply furnished, with a dark brown overstuffed sofa, newspapers stacked on the coffee table and a dog bowl on the floor next to the kitchen counter. She could tell Pete lived alone.

In comparison, the office looked very space-age, with big screens filling the walls, and banks of computers. Photos of the space shuttle, pictures of the moon landing and impressive colored images from the Hubble telescope hung on what few walls were not otherwise occupied, next to an impressive array of gilt-framed awards.

"Pete worked on the software NASA developed to study the photos sent back to earth from space. They're still using a lot of it." Trace's mouth edged up. "Pete does consulting for the space center when they can't figure things out by themselves."

The older man just smiled. "Keeps me busy. I'm a widower, you see, and not the type to go out and play golf."

"Pete helped my dad with some of his tougher surveillance cases." Trace handed him the digital imaging card. "We're trying to identify a girl in one of the photos."

The photo expert stuck the card into one of his computers and used the keyboard to shoot forward through the pictures.

"There!" Trace stopped him. "That's the one we're interested in."

Pete shoved on a pair of thick-rimmed glasses and peered at the screen. "All right, let's see what we can see." He fiddled with the controls and the computer started enlarging then clarifying the image on the monitor. Enlarging, then clarifying. It didn't take long before they could clearly see Senator Logan's handsome, smiling face on the screen.

"That appears to be our illustrious senator," Pete said.

"That's right."

He went to work on the girl's profile, enlarging and clarifying until her image came sharply into view.

"Can't really see enough of her face to recognize her," Pete said.

Trace turned to Maggie. "Any idea who it might be?"

She shook her head. "No."

Pete went back to work, using his equipment to bring up the patchy image on the young woman's shoulder.

"It's a tattoo, all right," Trace said as the colored design came into focus. "Pretty fancy work."

"Looks like a small, extremely detailed fairy," Pete said, assessing the drawing, which was perfect in every way.

"Yeah. I don't think it's something you'd find in your average tattoo parlor. Guy's a real artist. This is extremely specialized work." Trace looked at Pete. "Can you get us some prints?"

"You bet I can."

A few minutes later, magnified photos of the senator and his lady friend buzzed out of the printer, followed by close-ups of her colorful tattoo. Pete plucked them out of the tray and handed them to Trace.

"Thanks, Pete."

"Let me know how it all turns out, will you?"

"You bet."

"Too bad about your dad," Pete said as he walked them back through the house. "Heart attack." He shook his head. "I always thought he'd go down in a blaze of gunfire."

Trace's smile was tinged with sadness. "I'm sure there were times he thought so, too."

Pete stopped at to the door. "Nice to meet you, Maggie."

"You, too, Pete. We really appreciate your help."

She and Trace left the house, enlargements in hand, and he headed the Jeep toward downtown Houston.

"Where to now?" Maggie asked.

"I've got a friend in the department. Danny Castillo. He's head of the Houston gang division and knows tattoos backward and forward. With a design as intricate as this one, he should be able to tell us who did the work. With any luck, the artist will be able to give us his customer's name."

"You think Castillo will be in?"

"We'll run him down sooner or later. My gut is telling me we're onto something here."

"Maybe the girl was just a friend of a friend."

"Could be. I have a hunch we're going to find out."

As they pushed through the glass doors, Maggie's nerves kicked in. She couldn't help remembering the night she had gone to the police station hoping to get help with a stalker. Instead, she had garnered snide looks and knowing glances, and very little interest in her troubles. She told herself this time would be different.

"He's here," Trace said, returning from a visit to the front desk. "He'll be out in a minute."

Maggie just nodded. Her stomach was in knots, though she told herself this had nothing to do with her, and was probably a waste of time. It didn't take long before a tall, good-looking Hispanic with short black hair combed straight back, and very black eyes, walked toward them.

"Hey, man, good to see you." Castillo shook hands with Trace.

"Danny, this is Maggie O'Connell. She's been dealing with a stalker. We're hoping you can help us run down a lead on something that might be pertinent to the case."

"Sure, whatever I can do. Come on back." Castillo led them down a long hall into a white-walled room that was worn and Spartan, the linoleum floors chipped in places, the baseboards scuffed with shoe marks. The wooden chairs around the battered table had seen plenty of wear. "You want some coffee or something?"

"Not for me," Maggie said.

"We're fine," Trace agreed. "We just need you to take a look at this picture. The tattoo is pretty impressive. Whoever did it knew what he was doing. We're hoping you can tell us the name of the artist."

Danny studied the photo and started to frown. "It was done by a guy named Caesar Hernandez. He's one of the hottest ink men in Houston. Caesar does one-of-a-kind tats. Designs the images himself by hand." Danny glanced up, his expression less friendly than it had been when they walked in. "Where'd you get this picture?"

"Maggie took it. She's a professional photographer. What you're looking at is a digital of a shot taken down at the Blue Fin Marina." Trace handed him the other close-up images.

"That's Senator Logan," Danny said.

"That's right. We're trying to locate the girl."

Danny's hard gaze zeroed in on Maggie. "When was this taken?"

Her shoulders tightened. The night she had gone to the police she had seen that same look on the detectives' faces. "I took it around sunset on April 20. The date and time is on the original photo."

"Stay right here." Danny left the room, closing the door solidly behind him.

"What's going on?" Maggie asked, looking up at Trace, a sick feeling curling in her stomach.

"I don't know. But it looks like Danny knows something that might help us."

"Or maybe he's figured out who I am, and he won't help us at all."

The door swung open just then and Castillo walked back into the small, suddenly airless room. Another man walked in behind him, stocky, balding, solid as a rock, his expression deadly serious.

"Ms. O'Connell, I'm Captain Roberts. I understand you took this photo April 20 of this year."

"That's right. Around five in the evening."

"The woman in the photo is Isabel Garner. You may have read about her in the papers. She went missing on April 20, but it wasn't reported till the next day."

"Oh, my God." Maggie remembered, all right. She had seen the report on TV.

"A week later, her body washed ashore. Cause of death was blunt force trauma to the head. I'm afraid Ms. Garner was murdered."

Maggie's gaze shot to Trace. His face appeared to be carved in stone.

"Then I guess you'll want to talk to Senator Logan," he drawled. "Since the senator appears to have gone to great lengths to keep this photo from being seen."

"Is that right?" the captain said.

"That's right. You might want to ask him about the man he hired to burn down Ms. O'Connell's studio— a torch job meant to destroy the photo you're looking at now."

The captain gave Maggie the first friendly smile she had received. "That sounds extremely interesting. I believe we'll do just that."

Chapter 32

It was over. Garrett Logan and Richard Meyers had been arrested for the murder of Isabel Garner—though they were already out on bail.

Maggie was back in her apartment. Trace was back in his house. She was taking photos again. She was living by herself.

And her heart was broken.

She'd never had the chance to talk to Trace, never summoned the courage to tell him how she felt. Instead, for a long, miserable week she had tried to pull her life back together, put things back the way they were, only to discover she wasn't the same person she had been before.

And she didn't want to be.

Sitting behind the new computer monitor in her half-baked, makeshift office, she thought of Trace and wondered for the hundredth time what would happen if she just drove over to his house, barged in and told him she was in love with him.

Maybe she would, she told herself. But then the telephone started to ring, another excuse that momentarily saved her. For an instant she thought it might be Trace, and she grabbed the receiver.

It was Ashley. "Hi, sis. I just… I wanted to check on you, make sure you were all right."

Things had slipped badly, Maggie realized, when little sister worried about big sister instead of the other way around.

"I'm fine."

"I guess, um, you haven't heard from Trace."

Maggie sighed. "I didn't really expect to. I'm sure he's busy. I'm not his client anymore. I'm sure he has other people to worry about now."

"I guess…."

She forced a little cheer into her voice. "How about you? Everything good with you and Jason? Are you still walking on clouds?"

She could almost see her sister's dreamy smile. "It's just like you said. Jason's amazing, Maggie. I finally found a guy I really have the hots for. I never thought it would be this way—not for me."

Maggie smiled into the phone. "That's wonderful, Ash. I'm happy for both of you."

"Listen, I gotta go. I'll be late for work. I just wanted to check on you."

"I'm fine, really. Call me when you have time to talk."

"I will." The line went dead.

Maggie wandered around the apartment, trying to get enthused about working. She had some new photos downloaded onto the computer. She told herself they were reasonably good, that with a little tweaking here and there she could use them in her coffee-table book.

She wasn't convinced.

A knock sounded on the door and she brightened at the thought of a distraction—Roxanne, perhaps. Or maybe it was Trace.

Her heart kicked up. She looked down at her T-shirt, which had a camera on the front and Flash Dancer printed underneath, and wished she had time to change. Instead, she hurried to the door.

She hadn't gotten around to upgrading the locks or installing a peephole, but it wasn't as important as it had been. Maggie turned the knob and pulled open the door, and the breath rushed out of her lungs.

"Hello, my dear. I've missed you."

Her chest clenched and for an instant she couldn't breathe. As Phillip Coffman shoved his way into her apartment, she thought of the dozens of photos of herself she had seen on his bedroom walls, and fear made her legs feel weak. She told herself to stay calm. Phillip had never actually hurt her. He hadn't set the fire, they now knew. Senator Logan was responsible for that. Phillip had mostly just spied on her and followed her and made eerie phone calls. And aside from his size, he seemed more pathetic than dangerous.

Still, she eyed the door, trying to judge whether or not she could get past him and make a run for it.

She might have tried—if he hadn't pulled a gun out of his jacket pocket. A big black semiautomatic, something like the one Trace carried.

"Phillip…" she said with a disbelieving breath.

"I've come for you, my dear. It's time for us to be together. Just the way I promised."

Her pulse raced. Her heart hammered so hard she could hear it.

"I thought… I thought you were in the hospital." In for psychic evaluation. Dear God, had they released him and not told her?

"My daughter, Susan, is such a good girl. She and her friend Clayton Arnold made arrangements for me to be released. Clay's a lawyer, you see."

Oh, she saw, all right. Clearly, Coffman had enough lucid moments or his daughter had enough money to pressure the right people into letting him go.

"I was feeling much better, so I came here first thing."

"Why…why did you bring the gun?" she asked.

Coffman looked down at the weapon as if he didn't know he held it in his hand. Then he smiled. "Because it's time, my dear, for us to fulfill our destiny."

Oh, my God, the guy was even further over the edge than he had been before. She started inching around him, moving a tiny bit at a time toward the door.

"I wouldn't do that if I were you." He swung the gun in her direction. "Don't you see, my love? I'm the only one who can save you." He leveled the weapon at her chest, freezing her where she stood. "But first we need some together time to talk about our future."

What future? she thought. *We won't have much of a future if we're dead!*

Phillip motioned with the pistol toward the living room. "Why don't we sit down and make ourselves comfortable? We don't have much time."

Maggie swallowed. If she ran, he might just shoot her, end things now. But maybe if she bided her time, she could talk him down, or find some way to distract him long enough to escape.

She forced herself to smile. "That's a good idea… dearest."

* * *

Trace's fingers felt damp where they held the bouquet of red roses. He hadn't been sure what to buy, but most women liked roses and red ones always seemed the most romantic.

He figured he needed all the help he could get.

For nearly a week, he had talked himself out of coming here, just showing up unannounced at Maggie's door. But the longer he stayed away from her, the more he realized how much he loved her. And he was afraid if he called, he would say the wrong thing.

He might do that anyway. He wasn't great at this love stuff. It had been easy to say the *L* word to Carly, because at the time he didn't really know what love was, and he just figured it was the right thing to do if he was going to marry her.

This time he meant it. He was in love, big-time, and he wasn't going to let this last chance at happiness slip away without a fight. He was a Ranger, wasn't he? At least he had been. Surely he was tough enough to fight for what he wanted.

The only trouble was, he had no real idea what Maggie felt for him, and the last thing he wanted was to marry a woman who didn't love him.

Been there, done that.

There was only one way to find out, he figured, and that was just to straight-out ask her. After all they had been through, he believed she would tell him the truth.

He stepped out of the elevator onto the third floor and started down the corridor to her apartment. Outside the door, he paused long enough to shine his boots on his pant legs. He'd reached for the bell when he heard voices. Maggie's he recognized, the other was clearly male. Trace's chest tightened. Maggie was in there with a man.

His hand squeezed around the stems of the bouquet. He considered tossing the roses away and just leaving, but he had come this far and he wasn't a quitter. Maybe the guy was a client or something. Trace couldn't hear what they were saying, but if that wasn't it, at least he would know the truth.

He reached out and rang the bell, and the conversation inside the apartment instantly stopped. No one came to the door, and he felt as if his heart had stopped, as well.

He summoned his courage. "Maggie?" He rang the bell one last time, knowing she was in there.

No answer. Clearly, she was too busy with her visitor to care if he had come. He dropped the bouquet beside the door and turned to leave, heard the crash of something breaking, then Maggie's high-pitched scream.

"Trace!" she cried out.

Adrenaline shot into every muscle in his body. He raised a booted foot and kicked as hard as he could, felt the door give way and knew a moment of gratitude that there wasn't a dead bolt. "Maggie!"

She stood in the living room, Phillip Coffman behind her with a big-ass semiauto pressed against her head.

"You need to leave," the man said. "This is a private conversation." Coffman's thick arm wrapped around her neck and dragged her more solidly against him. "Get out now."

"Take it easy," Trace soothed. "We're going to work all of this out."

"You aren't supposed to be here. You're interfering with our destiny."

"Put the gun down, Phillip, so we can talk."

The big man shook his head. "You're making this happen too fast. Maggie and I...we need time to make plans for our life together once we reach the astral plane."

She made a little whimpering sound in her throat. Trace wished he could look at her, try to reassure her, but he needed to keep his focus on Coffman. Sometimes he carried a little .25 in his boot, a habit that had served him well on occasion, but it hadn't seemed appropriate to bring it with him today.

"So that's your plan?" he asked Phillip, just to keep him talking. "You both die and go on to live in some other world? What about staying here? You and Maggie making a life together right now?"

Coffman frowned, seeming confused. "Could we do that?"

"I don't see why not. What do you think, Maggie? Don't you think that's a better idea?"

She swallowed, her fingers digging into the arm beneath her chin. "I think it's a fine idea. Phillip and I could get married. We could live right there in his house."

The older man stiffened. "That was Angela's house. We couldn't live there. We have to go somewhere else." He adjusted the gun, pressing it more squarely against her temple. "It's time for us to leave."

"Wait!" Trace moved closer. "If you stayed here, the two of you could go dancing. Remember that night? Remember the way you danced together? Don't you want to dance like that again?"

Coffman smiled. "I remember. Maggie looked so beautiful that night."

"And you...you were so handsome," she said. "It... it felt wonderful to be held in your arms."

Trace eased closer and Phillip's gaze sharpened. He turned the gun away from Maggie and pointed it squarely at Trace's chest.

"You don't belong here." Something hard and determined moved across his features. There wouldn't be any more words.

Maggie must have read his intent, for just as Phillip squeezed the trigger, she jerked away, knocking his gun hand sideways, destroying his aim. A shot went off with a violent roar. Maggie grabbed for the pistol at the same instant Trace leaped forward. The three of them went down in a heap. Maggie struggled with Coffman, the gun wedged between them. Trace fought to pull her out of danger, and the pistol exploded again.

"Maggie!" Blood poured onto the carpet. Trace heard her soft moan as he leaped to his feet. She lay motionless on top of Coffman. "Maggie!"

She moved just then and he saw it, realized the bullet hadn't hit her but had fired into Coffman's chest. That the blood soaking her clothes belonged to Phillip and not to her. Relief hit him so hard he swayed on his feet.

"Trace…?"

He pulled the gun from Coffman's limp fingers and tossed it away, saw that the shot had torn a ragged hole in the big man's heart. Trace drew Maggie to her feet and eased her into his arms.

"Easy, sweetheart, I've got you."

"Oh, God, Trace." She just hung on and so did he. He wasn't letting her go. Not this time.

"You okay?" he finally asked, though he could feel her trembling.

Maggie clung to him. "I'm okay."

Trace dug his cell phone out of his jeans pocket and

punched 911. He reported what had happened and gave the police the address.

The call ended. Maggie still held on to him and a faint sob escaped. "I thought I was going to die," she said. "I thought I would never have a chance to tell you how I feel." She looked up at him, her heart in her eyes. "I love you, Trace. I love you so much. I wanted to tell you, but I was afraid."

He clasped her closer. "I love you, too, Maggie, darlin'. And I'm an even bigger coward than you."

Her pretty green eyes sparkled with tears. "Can I… can I come home?"

His heart swelled with love for her. "That's what I'm here for, darlin'. I came to take you home."

Maggie packed an overnight bag, and once the police allowed them to leave, Trace drove her back to his house.

She had thought all this was finished, first when Phillip Coffman was taken into custody, then two days ago, when the police arrested Garrett Logan for the murder of Isabel Garner. Confronted with traces of the murdered woman's blood on the deck of his yacht, Logan hadn't denied his involvement with the beautiful young woman, but claimed her death was an accident.

His story was that Isabel, who had moved from Memphis to Houston only two months before she disappeared, had tried to extort him for money. Logan had overreacted, pushed her too hard, and she had hit her head on the railing of his yacht. He'd been frightened and confused, he had said. He had called his aide, and Richard had urged him to take the boat out to sea and dispose of the body.

Meyers had also been arrested.

Both men had denied any knowledge of the fire that destroyed Maggie's town house, though there wasn't much doubt who was responsible.

Logan and Meyers were going to stand trial, and Phillip Coffman was dead. Maggie felt sorry for Coffman's daughter. According to Detective Sayers, Susan Coffman had taken the news of her father's death extremely hard. She had blamed herself for what had happened. Considering Susan was responsible for her father's early release from the psychiatric ward, to some extent, Maggie agreed.

But all that was behind her now. Her life was her own once more, and this time she meant to make the most of it.

It was evening. A soft spring rain had started to fall, pattering softly against the roof. Maggie had showered away some of her fatigue, washed and dried her hair, and put on the white satin peignoir set she had bought after the fire to wear for Trace, but never got around to using.

As for Trace, he had been oddly quiet. Now, watching him walk out of the bedroom barefoot in just his jeans, she wondered what he was thinking. His dark hair still glistened from his recent shower. Drops of water beaded on his powerful chest and the six-pack muscles across his flat stomach.

She walked toward him, the peignoir floating around her ankles. The garment was almost virginal, and she felt that way tonight, as if this would be the first time they made love.

Trace reached out and ran a hand through her hair, pushed a curl behind her ear. "You look beautiful, darlin'."

She glanced away, feeling strangely shy. "Thank you."

He cupped her cheek, drawing her attention back to his face. "It feels different now, doesn't it?"

"Yes. Different in a wonderful way."

"I meant what I said. I love you, Maggie. I think I was attracted to those redheads over the years because I was searching for you."

Her eyes filled. "As soon as I moved out, I knew I'd made a mistake. I just didn't know how to undo it. By then I knew I'd found Mr. Right, but it was too late."

He kissed her softly. "Will you marry me, Maggie?"

Her throat closed up. She hadn't expected this, but she knew the answer, had no more doubts about what she wanted. The tears in her eyes spilled onto her cheeks. "I would be honored to marry you."

Trace kissed her again, tenderly at first, then more deeply. Lifting her in his arms, he carried her into the bedroom, her white satin robe spilling over his arm until he set her on her feet beside the bed. He eased the peignoir off her shoulders, leaving on the gown, then lifted and settled her on the mattress, following her down.

His mouth found hers and he kissed her once more, a slow, languid kiss that seemed to have no end. He smelled of soap and man, and tasted fresh and incredibly sexy. She ran her fingers over the muscles of his chest, thinking she would never get tired of touching him, of having him touch her.

Trace just kept kissing her, as if he had all the time in the world, moving lower, trailing hot, moist kisses over her throat and shoulders, down to her breasts. He kissed each one through the slick white satin, ran his tongue over the hardened crests, leaving them damp and aching when he peeled down the narrow satin straps, bent and took the nipples into his mouth.

Maggie arched beneath him, wanting more, wanting him naked and his hard length inside her. She had never desired a man this way, never trusted a man enough to give him her heart.

But she knew this man she loved, knew him to be honorable, caring and generous. Knew him to be truthful in his feelings. Knew that when he said he loved her, he meant the forever kind of love, the kind she was willing to give in return.

Trace eased her nightgown over her head, then left her long enough to dispense with his jeans. Naked, he settled himself between her legs, his beautiful whiskey-brown eyes on her face. He kissed the inside of her thighs and had her trembling. Her body wept for him and her heart ached with love.

There was something different in his lovemaking tonight, something that made her feel worshipped and adored. Something that told her she had found what she had been searching for so long.

Her body heated, turned hot and liquid. Trace knew exactly how to bring her to the peak and beyond, how to use his hands and mouth, just where to touch her to make her fly apart.

She cried out his name, but he didn't stop, not until he had carried her to the peak a second time. Then he came up over her, slid himself deeply inside. Slow and easy, propping himself on his elbows, kissing her and kissing her, stirring back to life the fires that he had so recently tamed.

Outside, the rain fell softly, pattering against the windowpanes. A slight breeze slipped through the trees. Inside the bedroom, the heat of their bodies increased with the friction of their movements. Maggie slid her hands into Trace's silky dark hair, gave herself up to the slow, tantalizing rhythm he set. Deep and penetrating, lazy, sensual strokes that had her moving beneath him, silently begging for more.

His rhythm increased along with his breathing, the pace spiraling upward, her need building. She was close, so very close.

Then she was there, crying out his name as she soared. Trace followed her to release and Maggie clung to him, feeling the rightness of it. The blazing joy.

They floated down together. Trace kissed her one last time.

"You said yes," he whispered against the side of her neck. "You can't change your mind."

Maggie smiled into the darkness. "I found Mr. Right. I'm not going to change my mind."

He rolled onto his back, taking her with him. "When, then?"

Maggie softly kissed him. "How about tomorrow?" she said, and heard a rumble of male satisfaction coming from Trace's hard chest.

Epilogue

They were married two weeks later. Trace didn't want to wait, and Maggie foolishly agreed to the hastily organized wedding that Annie and Ashley helped her arrange.

Damn, he loved her. And this time, he knew he had a woman who loved him in return. A woman he could count on, one who had stood up to a lunatic, put her own life at risk to save his.

The wedding was held in a chapel behind the Methodist Church, a place just the size to hold their small but valued group of friends.

Ashley was Maggie's maid of honor, Roxanne a bridesmaid. Trace asked Devlin Raines to stand as his best man, and Jake Cantrell partnered with Roxanne. Jason was there, grinning like a fool at Ashley, who had finally agreed to wear the beautiful, flawless but unpretentious diamond engagement ring he had bought her.

The rest of Trace's bachelor friends were there. Alex

and Ben, and Johnnie Riggs. Once Riggs and Cantrell had met Maggie and seen the two of them together, they resisted ragging him about marrying a redhead. Trace thought maybe they had fallen a little in love with her themselves.

Dev's two brothers, Jackson and Gabriel, flew in for the festivities with their wives, Sarah and Mattie. Evan Schofield was there and Mark Sayers.

Amazingly, Maggie's mom showed up for the wedding. It turned out to be a surprisingly touching reunion between a mother and her daughters.

The reception was held at the Texas Café, which they took over for the evening, and they partied there, dancing to the music of a country band until late into the night.

After the party, a limo took Trace and his bride out to the old family ranch house. He'd prepared it especially for their stay, with rose petals scattered over satin sheets on the old-fashioned four-poster bed, champagne and chocolate-covered strawberries on hand, and enough food laid in for a week.

They hadn't decided yet where they wanted to go for their real honeymoon. Italy, maybe, or Tahiti, or perhaps Australia. A trip Down Under might be an interesting place to visit, and provide some good photo ops for Maggie, give her what she needed to finish her coffee-table book. It really didn't matter as long as they were together.

This morning before the sun was up, he had saddled a couple horses, good, solid, easy-to-handle mounts he rode when he came out to the ranch. Maggie was excited. She hadn't ridden much over the years, she'd said, but she had always enjoyed it.

Most days they weren't doing much but making love, and whatever else hit their fancy.

"You know, darlin'," he said as he helped her swing up in the saddle, waited till she shoved the boots he'd bought her into the stirrups. She looked real good up there, in the white straw cowboy hat that went with the boots, her fiery hair tucked up under the crown. "We haven't talked much about kids."

Her head came up. "Kids? What about them?"

Trace swung into his own horse's saddle, tugged the brim of his hat down over his forehead. Rowdy sniffed the ground at the horses' feet. "You want some, right?"

Maggie grinned. "Oh, yeah. I want a houseful."

Trace hadn't noticed the tension in his shoulders until he heard those words. He relaxed and grinned right back. "Then I guess we'd better get started as soon as we get home."

Maggie laughed and nudged the little sorrel into a trot. "Looks like this ride is going to be shorter than I thought."

Trace's grin widened and Rowdy barked. As the morning sun broke over the horizon, he nudged his horse forward and came up beside her. Together they rode into the glorious future that dawned ahead of them.

* * * * *

Author's Note

I hope you enjoyed Trace and Maggie in *Against the Storm,* the fourth book in my Raines of Wind Canyon series. The novels, all tales of contemporary romantic suspense, began with the Raines brothers, Jackson, Gabriel and Devlin, in Against the Wind, Against the Fire and Against the Law.

In the next book, Against the Night, Trace's friend Johnnie Riggs, who first appeared in Against the Law, gets a chance to find love with a sexy little blonde schoolteacher posing as a stripper to find her sister, who has disappeared without a trace. Amy Brewer is willing to do whatever it takes to enlist John Riggs's aid—even if it means giving in to his determined seduction.

It's a tale of romance and high adventure that leads to true love. I hope you'll watch for Against the Night, the next book in the series.

Till then, all best wishes and happy reading.
Kat

Nicole Helm grew up with her nose in a book and the dream of one day becoming a writer. Luckily, after a few failed career choices, she gets to follow that dream—writing down-to-earth contemporary romance and romantic suspense. From farmers to cowboys, Midwest to *the* West, Nicole writes stories about people finding themselves and finding love in the process. She lives in Missouri with her husband and two sons, and dreams of someday owning a barn.

Books by Nicole Helm

Harlequin Intrigue

Covert Cowboy Soldiers

The Lost Hart Triplet
Small Town Vanishing
One Night Standoff
Shot in the Dark
Casing the Copycat

A North Star Novel Series

Summer Stalker
Shot Through the Heart
Mountainside Murder
Cowboy in the Crosshairs
Dodging Bullets in Blue Valley
Undercover Rescue

Visit the Author Profile page
at Harlequin.com for more titles.

WYOMING COWBOY BODYGUARD

Nicole Helm

For the female songwriters in country music
whose songs make up the bulk of my book soundtracks,
thank you for the inspiration.

Chapter 1

Tom was dead. She'd been ushered away from his life-less body and open, empty brown eyes thirty minutes ago and still, that was all she saw. Tom sprawled on the floor, limbs at an unnatural angle, eyes open and unseeing.

Blood.

She was in the back of a police cruiser, moving through Austin at a steady clip. Daisy Delaney. America's favorite country bad girl. Until she'd filed for divorce from country's golden child, Jordan Jones. Now everyone hated her, and someone wanted her dead.

But they'd killed Tom first.

She wanted to close her eyes, but she was afraid the vision of Tom would only intensify if she did. So she focused on the world out the window. Pearly dawn. Green suburban lawns.

She was holding it together. Even though Tom's life-less eyes haunted her. And all that blood. The smell of it.

She was queasy and desperately wanted to cry, but she was holding on. *Gotta save face, Daisy girl. No matter what. Never let them see they got to you.*

It didn't matter the name her mother had given her was Lucy Cooper. Daddy had always used her stage name—the name *he'd* given her. Daisy Delaney, after his dearly departed grandmother, who'd given him his first guitar.

She'd relished that once upon a time, no matter how much her mother and brother had disapproved. Today, for the first time in her life, she wondered where she might be if she hadn't followed in her famous father's footsteps.

She couldn't change the past so she held it together. Didn't let anyone see she was devastated, shaken or scared.

Until the car pulled up in front of her brother's house. He was standing outside. She'd expected to see him in his Texas Rangers uniform of pressed khakis, a button-up shirt and that shiny star she knew he took such pride in.

Instead, he was in sweats, a baby cradled in his arms.

"You shouldn't have brought me here," she whispered to the police officer as he shifted into Park.

"Ranger Cooper asked me to, ma'am."

She let out a breath. Asked. While her brother was a Texas Ranger and this man was Austin PD, Daisy was under no illusions her brother hadn't interfered enough to make sure it was an order, not a request.

When the officer opened the door for her, she managed a smile and a thank-you. The officer shook hands with Vaughn, then gave her a sympathetic look. "We'll have more questions for you, Ms. Delaney, but the ones you answered at the scene will do for now."

She smiled thinly. "Thank you. And if there's any break in the case—"

"We'll let you and your brother know."

The officer nodded and left. Daisy turned to Vaughn.

"You shouldn't have brought me here," she said, peeking into the bundle of blankets. She brushed her fingers over her niece's cheek. "It isn't safe having me around you guys."

"Safety's my middle name," Vaughn said, and there wasn't an ounce of concern or fear in his voice, but she could feel it nonetheless. Her straitlaced brother had never understood her need to follow their father's spotlight, but he'd always been her protector. "You didn't tell me you'd come back to Austin."

She'd thought she could keep it from him. Keep him and Nat from worrying when they had this gorgeous little family they were building.

Daisy had been stupid and foolish to think she'd be able to keep anything from Vaughn. She couldn't afford to be stupid and foolish anymore. Though she'd lived in fear for almost a year now, she'd believed it would remain a nonviolent threat. Her stalker had never hurt her or anyone she'd been connected to.

Now he'd killed Tom. The man Vaughn had hired to protect her. It wasn't her own failure. Rationally, she knew that, but kind, funny Tom, who'd done everything in his power to protect her, was dead.

"Come inside, Lucy." Vaughn slid his free arm around her shoulders and the first tear fell over onto her cheek. She couldn't let more fall, and yet her brother's steadiness, and the name only he and Mom called her, was one of the few things that could undo her.

Well, that and murder, she supposed. "Tom..."

"We'll handle the arrangements," Vaughn said,

squeezing her shoulders as baby Nora gurgled happily in her daddy's arms. "He was a good man."

"He shouldn't have died protecting me."

"But he did. He signed up for that job. You'll have time to mourn that. We all will, but right now we need to focus on getting you somewhere safe."

She wanted to say something snotty. Vaughn could be so cold, and though she knew it was his law-enforcement training, it grated. Except he held his baby like the precious gift she was, and Daisy had watched years ago as his voice had broken when he'd made his vows to his wife.

Vaughn wasn't cold or heartless. He just had control down to an art form. And his concern was her. Daisy felt like such a burden to him, and yet there was no way to convince him this wasn't his problem.

"Nat's got coffee on and Jaime is on his way over," Vaughn said, locking the door behind her then leading her up the stairs of his split-level ranch.

"What's Jaime got to do with this?" Daisy asked warily. "You can't get the FBI involved. I—"

"I'm not getting the FBI involved. I'm using my FBI connections to find a safe place for you while we let the professionals investigate."

"And by professionals you mean you."

"I mean anyone and everyone I can get on this case. With our connection, I'm not legally allowed to be part of the official investigation."

Which meant he'd launch his own unofficial one. No matter how by-the-book Vaughn was, he'd always break rules for his loved ones.

Nat came out of the kitchen as they crested the stairs. She pulled Daisy into a hard hug. "How are you?" she asked, brown eyes full of compassion.

Daisy had no questions about how Vaughn had fallen for Natalie, but she did have some questions about the reverse.

"Unscathed."

Natalie pursed her lips. "Physically. Which wasn't all I meant." She eyed her husband. "Coopers," she muttered with some disgust, though Daisy knew—for as little time as she managed to spend with her family here due to her crazy touring schedule—Nat spoke with love.

The doorbell rang, Nora fussed and Nat and Vaughn exchanged the baby and words with the choreographed practice of marriage. It caused a multitude of pangs in Daisy.

Her divorce had started the press's character assassination—thanks to Jordan's team, who were desperate to keep his star on the rise.

Then the stalking had started, and everything had become a numb kind of blank.

But she could still remember marrying Jordan with the hope she'd have something like Nat and Vaughn had. That had been a joke.

"Sit down. You want to hold Nora for me? I've got to go check on Miranda." Nat was maneuvering her onto the couch, placing tiny Nora into her arms and hurrying off to check on their other daughter as Vaughn and his brother-in-law ascended the stairs.

"Ah, the cavalry," Daisy said with a wry twist of her lips.

"Good to see you again, Daisy," Jaime Alessandro greeted. An FBI agent, married to Natalie's sister, Daisy had met him on a few occasions. He was more personable than Vaughn, but the whole FBI thing made Daisy uneasy.

"Let's get straight to it, then," Vaughn said, taking a

seat next to Daisy on the couch. Jaime settled himself on an armchair across from them.

"I'm sure you know how concerned Vaughn's been even before the murder."

Daisy eyed her brother. "No. You don't say."

Jaime smiled. Vaughn didn't.

"We've been looking into some options, along with the investigation. As long as the stalker continues to evade police, the prime goal is keeping you safe. To that end, I have an idea."

"That sounds ominous coming from an FBI agent."

"How do you feel about Wyoming?"

"Cold," Daisy replied dryly.

"I have a friend I was in Quantico with. He has a security business. I talked to him about your situation and he came up with a plan. It involves isolating you."

"I was isolated before. The cabin—"

"Is isolated, but not completely off the grid," Vaughn said of their old family cabin that had been vandalized during her last hiding stint. "It was traceable, and you've been easy to follow. We're going to take extra precautions to make sure you aren't followed to Wyoming."

Daisy wanted to close her eyes, but she shifted Nora in her arms and looked down at the baby instead. "So you want me to secretly jet off to Wyoming and then what?"

"And then you're safe while we find this guy. This is murder now. Things are escalating, which means everyone else's investigation is going to escalate."

"We can have you there by tomorrow afternoon," Jaime said. "They'll be ready for you."

Part of her wanted to argue, but Tom's lifeless body flashed into her mind. She didn't want to die. Not like that. And more, so much more, she didn't want Vaughn or his precious family in the crosshairs.

"Just tell me what I need to do."

Zach Simmons surveyed the town. It looked like every picture of a ghost town he'd ever seen. Empty, windowless buildings. Dusty dirt road that would have once been a bustling Main Street. You could feel the history, and the utter emptiness.

It was perfect.

He grinned over at his soon-to-be brother-in-law and business partner. "Still worried about the investment?"

Cam Delaney eyed him. "Hell yes, I'm still worried." He scanned the dilapidated buildings and the way the mountains jutted out in the distance, like sentries, in Zach's mind. This would be a place of protection. Of safety.

"This job's a big one for your first."

Zach nodded. He was under no illusions this wasn't a giant challenge. Tricky and messy and complicated. He couldn't explain to Cam, or anyone really, how thrilling it was to be out of the confines of the FBI's rules and regulations. He wouldn't take his time back as an agent for anything, but it had been stifling in the end.

So stifling he'd ended up getting himself kicked out.

This was better. Even if the first job was with some spoiled country singer star who'd gotten herself in a mess of trouble. Probably her own doing. But she was in trouble, and Zach and Cam's security company was getting paid, seriously paid, to keep her safe.

"Laurel come up with any connection to you guys?" Zach asked, hoping Daisy Delaney's last name was a coincidence. Not that he'd tell anyone, but all the Carson and Delaney coupling worried him a little.

He was technically a Carson, though his mother had run away from her family at eighteen and only started reconnecting this year. He told himself he didn't believe in curses or the Carson-Delaney feud the town of Bent, Wyoming, was so invested in.

So invested, Main Street was practically split down the middle—Carson businesses on one side, Delaney businesses on the other. Then there was the curse talk, which said if a Carson and Delaney were ever friendly, or God forbid, romantic, only bad things would befall Bent.

But over the course of the past year Carsons and Delaneys had been falling for each other left and right, and while there'd been a certain uptick in trouble in Bent, everything and everyone was fine.

Which his cousins and their significant others had turned into believing it was all meant to be, and went on and on about love solving things.

Zach didn't buy an inch of either belief—but still, the idea of a Delaney under his protection gave him a bit of a worried itch.

"She's still researching. It's giving her something to do now that she's on maternity leave. Baby should come any day, though, so I'm not sure she'll come up with any answers one way or another. You can always ask the woman."

Zach shrugged. "Doesn't matter either way."

Cam chuckled. "Sure. You're not worried about what might happen if she's some long-lost cousin of mine?"

"No, I'm not. I'm worried about keeping Daisy Delaney safe from her stalker, assuming there really is one." Because the Daisy Delaney case would set the tone for what he wanted to offer here. On the surface it would look like a ghost town. But below the surface it could be a place for people to find safety, security and hope while the slow wheels of justice handled things legally.

If he believed in life callings, and these days he was starting to, his was this. He'd been a part of the slow wheels of justice. He'd failed at protecting because of it. Now he'd do all he could to keep those entrusted to him safe.

"I should head off to the airport. You'll do the double check?"

Cam nodded. "Is turndown service offered as part of the package?"

"Up to you, boss," Zach said with a grin, slapping Cam on the back.

Cam eyed him, but Zach ignored the perceptive look and headed for his car. He didn't need Cam giving him another lecture about taking things slow, having reasonable expectations for a fledgling business.

Zach had endured a bad year. Really bad. His brother had been admitted to a psychiatric ward, and his long-lost sister had forgiven the man who'd murdered their father and kidnapped her. He'd been kicked out of the FBI—which meant no hope of ever getting back into legitimate law enforcement. And then he'd tried to help one of his cousins outwit a stalker-murderer and been hurt in the process.

In some ways all that hardship had brought him everything he'd ever wanted—his long-lost sister back in his life, a job that didn't seem to choke the very life out of him and some closure over the murder of his father.

Then there was this project. Ghost Town. He couldn't tamp down his enthusiasm, his excitement. He had to grab on to the rightness he finally felt and hold on to it with everything he had.

He didn't want to go back. He wanted to move forward.

Daisy Delaney was going to be the way to do that. He drove down deserted Wyoming roads to the highway, then to the regional airport in Dubois where his first client would be landing any minute.

Zach parked and entered the small airport, all the excitement of a new job still buzzing inside him.

He'd facilitated crisscrossing flights with his former FBI buddy, and only Zach knew the disguise she'd be wearing. Though he wondered how much a wig and sunglasses would do for a famous singer.

Zach liked country music as much as the next guy, so it was impossible not to know Daisy Delaney's music. She'd somehow eclipsed even her father's outlaw country reputation with wild songs about drinking, cheating and revenge. Country fans either loved her or loved to complain about her.

Of course, since her divorce from all-American sweetheart Jordan Jones, the complainers had gotten more vocal. Zach hadn't followed it all, but he'd read up on it once this assignment had come along. She'd been eviscerated in the press, even when the stalking started. Many thought it was a publicity ploy to get people to feel sorry for her.

It had *not* worked.

Zach couldn't deny it was a possibility, even if a man was dead—the security guard. A shame. But that didn't mean it wasn't a ploy. You never knew with the rich and famous.

Still, Zach was determined to make his own conclusions about Daisy Delaney and what might be going on with her stalker, or fictional stalker as the case may be.

The small crowd walked through the security gates. He'd been told to look for black hair and clothes, a red bag and purple cowboy boots. He spotted her immediately.

In person, she was surprisingly petite. She didn't exactly look like a woman who'd burn your house down if you looked at another woman the wrong way, but looks could be deceiving.

He'd done enough undercover work to know that well.

He adjusted his hat, gave the signal he'd told her people to expect and she nodded and walked over to him.

"You must be Mr. Hughes." She used the fake name Jaime had chosen and held out a hand. The sunglasses she wore hid her eyes, and the mass of black hair hid most of her face. Whatever her emotions were, they were well hidden. Which was good. It wouldn't do to have nerves radiating off her.

He took her outstretched hand and shook it. "And you must be Ms. Bravo." Fake names, but soon enough they wouldn't need to bother with that. "Any more bags?" he asked, nodding to the lone duffel bag she carried.

She shook her head.

"Follow me."

She eyed everyone in the airport as they walked outside, but her shoulders and stride were relaxed as she kept up with him. She didn't fidget or dart. If she was fearing her life, she knew how to hide it.

He opened the passenger-side door to his car. She slid inside. Still no sign of concern over getting into a car with a stranger. Zach frowned as he skirted the car to the driver's side.

But he wiped the frown into a placid expression as he slid into his seat. "We have about a thirty-minute drive ahead of us." He pushed the car into Drive and pulled out of the airport parking lot. "You could take your wig off," he offered. "Get comfortable."

"I'd prefer to wait."

He nodded as he drove. Tough case. A hint of nerves here and there, but overall a very cool customer. Cautious, though, so she clearly took the threat of danger seriously.

He drove in silence through the middle of nowhere Wyoming. He flicked a few glances her way, though it was hard to discern anything. He didn't get the impression she was impressed, but he hadn't expected her to be. He imagined she preferred, if not the glitz and glam of the city, the slow ease of wealthy Southern life she was probably used to.

Wyoming wouldn't offer that, but it would offer her security. He drove down the main street that was now his domain, this ghost town he and Cam had bought outright.

At some point they'd all be safe houses. Or maybe even a functioning town behind the facade of desertion and decay.

For right now, though, it was just the main house. He pulled up in front of the giant showpiece.

It had been built over a century ago by some railroad executive. From the outside the windows were all knocked out, the wood was faded and peeling paint hung off. Everything sagged, and it had the faint air of haunted house.

It made him grin every time. "Well, here we are."

For the first time he could read her expression. Pure, unadulterated horror. He'd be lying if he said he didn't get a little kick out of that. "I promise it's not as bad as it looks."

She wrenched her gaze away from the large house, then stared at him through the dark sunglasses. "Can I see your ID or something?" she demanded.

He shifted and pulled his wallet out of his pocket and handed it to her. "Have at it." He pushed open the door and got out of the car. "When you're ready, I'll show you where you'll be staying."

Chapter 2

What Daisy really wanted to do was call her brother and ask him if he'd lost his mind. Call Jaime and ask if she was sure this guy was sane. Call anyone to take her home.

But inside the wallet the man had so casually handed her was a driver's license with the name Jaime had given her. The picture matched the man currently standing in front of the horror-movie house outside the car. There were also all sorts of security licenses and weapon certifications.

Vaughn had said this place was isolated, even more isolated than their old family cabin in the Guadalupe Mountains. But she hadn't been able to picture how that was possible.

Oh, was it possible. Possible and horrifying.

She flipped the wallet closed and then looked at the giant, falling-apart building. If she didn't die because a stalker was after her, she'd die because this building was going to fall in on her.

It had to be infested with rats. And probably all other manner of vermin.

She couldn't get her body to move from the safety of this car, and still, the man whom she'd been assured would keep her safe stood outside, grinning at the dilapidated building in front of him.

He wasn't sane. He couldn't be. She was stuck in the middle of nowhere Wyoming with an insane person.

But Vaughn would never let that happen. So she forced herself to get out of the car and slung the duffel bag over her shoulder. She tried not to mourn that she hadn't been able to bring her guitar. This wasn't a musical writing escape. It was literally running for her life.

She stepped next to Zach. She still didn't trust him, but she trusted her brother. She looked up at the building like Zach Simmons did, though not with nearly the amount of reverence he had in his expression.

"I know it looks intimidating from the outside, but that's kind of the point."

"The point?" Daisy asked, studying a board that hung haphazardly from a bent nail.

"From the outside, no one would guess anyone's been here for decades."

"Try centuries," she muttered.

He motioned her forward and she followed him up a cracked and sunken rock pathway to the front door.

"Watch the hole," he announced cheerfully, pointing at the gaping hole in the floorboards of the porch. He shoved a key into the front door and pushed open the creaky, uneven entry. "Even if someone started poking around, all they'd see is decay."

Yes, that is all I see. She looked around. She had to

admit that although everything appeared to be in a state of decay, there were some important things missing. She didn't see any dust or spiderwebs. Debris, sure. Peeling wallpaper and warped floorboards, check, but it didn't smell like she'd expected it to. There was the faint hint of paint on the air.

He led her over the uneven flooring, then pushed a key into another lock. When this door opened she actually gasped.

The room on the other side was beautiful. Clean and furnished, and though there were no windows, somehow the light he switched on bounced off the colors of the walls and filled the room enough that it didn't feel dank and interior.

"This is the common area," Zach said. And maybe he wasn't totally insane. "Then over there past the sitting area is the kitchen. You're free to use it and anything inside as much as you like. Once we ascertain that you weren't followed on any leg of your trip, you'll be able to venture out more freely, but for now you'll have to stay put."

Daisy could only nod dumbly. Was this real? Maybe *she'd* gone insane. A break with reality following a stressful tragedy.

He locked the door behind them, which was enough to jolt Daisy back to the reality of being in a strange ghost town with a man she didn't know.

But he simply moved forward to a set of two doors. "Your bedroom and bathroom are through here." He unlocked the one on the right.

"What's that one?" she asked, pointing to the door on the left as he pushed the unlocked door open.

"That's where I'll stay."

"You'll... Right." He'd be right next door. This

stranger. Hired to protect her, and yet she didn't know him. Even Vaughn didn't know him, and Jaime hadn't known him since they'd trained together in the FBI. Why were they all so trusting?

He handed her the key he'd just used to unlock the door. "This is yours. I don't have a copy. The outside doors are always locked up in multiple places, so how and when you want to lock your room is up to you."

She knew he was trying to set her at ease, but she could only think of a million ways he could get into the room even without a key. Or anyone could.

People could always get to you if they wanted to badly enough.

He studied her for a moment, then gestured her inside. "You can settle in. Make yourself at home however you need to. Rest, if you'd like."

"Is it that obvious?"

"You've been through an ordeal. Take your time to get acquainted with the place. I'm going to do a routine double check to make sure you weren't followed from Austin. If you need me…" He moved over to the wall, motioned her over.

Hesitantly, she stepped closer, still clutching her bag on her shoulder. He tapped a spot on the wallpaper. "See how this flower has a green bloom and a green stem instead of a blue flower like the rest?"

She nodded wearily.

He pushed on the green flower and a little panel popped out of the wall. Inside was a speaker with a button below it. "Simple speaker to speaker. You need something, you can just buzz me through here. I can either answer, or come over, depending."

He closed the panel and it snapped shut, seamless with the wallpaper once again. How on earth had her life become some kind of…spy movie? "You've thought of everything, haven't you?"

He smiled briefly—something like pride and affection lighting up the blank, bland expression. Just a little flash of personality, and for one surprising moment all she could really think was *gee, he's hot*.

"That's what they pay me for." Then the blankness was back and whatever had sparkled in his blue eyes was gone. Everything about him screamed *cop* again, or, she supposed in his case, *FBI*. It was all the same to her. Law and order didn't suit her the way it had her brother, but she'd be grateful for it in the midst of her current situation.

She studied the room around her. Gleaming hardwood with pretty blue rugs here and there. Floral wallpaper and shabby-chic fixtures. The furniture looked antique—old and a little scarred but well polished. The quilt over the bed looked like it belonged in a pretty farmhouse with billowing lace curtains.

It was calming and comforting, and in a better state of mind she might even be able to ignore all the facades and locks and intercoms and the lack of windows. But she wasn't in the state of mind to forget that Tom, who'd been paid to protect her, was dead.

"Settle in, Ms. Delaney. You're safe here. I promise you that."

She carefully placed her duffel bag on the shiny hardwood floor. Exhaustion made her body feel as heavy as lead, and she went ahead and lowered herself onto the bed with its pretty quilt. "I'm not safe anywhere, Mr. Simmons."

He opened his mouth to argue, but she wasn't in the mood, so she waved him toward the door. "But I feel safe enough to take a nice long nap, if you'll excuse me."

He raised an eyebrow, presumably at her regal tone and the way she waved him off, but she was too tired to care.

He moved to the door, twisted the lock on the interior knob, then closed the door behind him as he exited.

Daisy took off the wig and then let herself fall into sleep.

Zach spent the afternoon going over the information he'd been given about Daisy's stalking, and the information he'd gathered himself in anticipation of her arrival.

The murder of her bodyguard while she'd been on stage was certainly the tipping point. The formal investigation had been lax up to that point. Except for the private one her brother had launched.

Zach appreciated the detail of Ranger Cooper's intel, and since he knew too well the stress and helplessness of trying to keep a sibling safe, Zach was grateful for his willingness to share.

Still, there were things that had been missed—well, maybe not missed. Overlooked. Probably still not fair. One of the things that had allowed Zach to do so well in the FBI was his ability to work out patterns, to find threads and connect them in ways other people couldn't.

The stellar way he'd handled himself as an agent prior to his brother's involvement in a case and Zach going rogue was what had kept him from having a splashier, more painful termination from the FBI.

He shrugged away the tension in his shoulders. He hated that it still bothered him, because even if he could rewind time, he'd do most things the same.

Daisy's doorknob turned, and she took one tentative step out. She'd finally ditched the heavy black wig, and her straight blond hair was pulled back into a ponytail.

She'd done something to her face—it'd take him a little more time to get to know her face well enough to know exactly what. If he had to guess, though, he'd say she'd freshened her makeup.

She'd changed out of the sleek black outfit into a long baggy shirt the color of a midsummer sky and black leggings. On her feet she wore thick bright purple socks.

She'd been in there for five hours, and from the looks of it, she'd spent most of the time sleeping—unless her makeup magically fixed the pallor of her skin and the dark circles under her eyes.

"Got any food in this joint?"

He stood and walked over to the side of the common area that acted as a kitchen. "Fully stocked kitchen, which of course you're welcome to. Tell me what you want to make and I'll show you where everything is and how to work everything."

"Coffee. Scratch that. Coffee hasn't been settling lately." She sighed, some of that weary exhaustion in her voice even if it didn't show in her face.

"My suggestion? Hot chocolate and a doughnut."

A smile twitched at the corner of her mouth. "That's enough sugar to fell a horse."

He scoffed. "Amateur hour."

She sighed. "It sounds good. I guess if I'm stuck with a crazed psychopath ready to kill those who protect me, I shouldn't worry about a few extra calories."

"I think you'll live."

She rolled her eyes. "You've never read the comments on photos of women online, have you? Still." She waved a hand to encompass the kitchen. "Lead the way."

"You sit. I'll make it. We'll go over where everything is in the kitchen tomorrow. You get a pass today."

"Gee, thanks." But she didn't argue. She sat and

poked at his stacks of notes. "That's a lot of paperwork for keeping me out of trouble."

"Investigating things takes some paperwork," he returned, collecting ingredients for hot chocolate.

"I thought you were just supposed to keep me safe while Vaughn and the police figured it all out."

He slid the mug into the microwave hidden in a cabinet and put a doughnut onto a plate. "I could, but that's not what CD Corp is all about."

"CD Corp sounds like the lamest comic villain organization ever."

"It's meant to be bland, boring and inconspicuous." He walked over and set the plate in front of her.

She smiled up at him. "Mission accomplished."

"And this mission," he said, tapping the papers, "is keeping you safe by understanding the threat against you." Not noticing the little dimple that winked in her cheek or the way her blue eyes reminded him of summer. "Anything I can do to profile or find a pattern allows me to better keep you secure."

"Can I help?"

He turned away, back to hot chocolate prep and to shake off that weird and unfortunate bolt of attraction. Still, his voice was easy and bland when he spoke. "I'm counting on it." He stirred the hot chocolate and then set that next to her before taking his seat in front of his computer.

"Have you noticed the pattern of incidents?" he asked, studying her reaction to the question.

With a nap under her belt, she didn't seem as cold and detached as she had on the ride over. But she also didn't seem as ready to break as she had when he'd shown her her room hours ago. As they'd walked through the safe house earlier, he'd finally seen some signs of exhaustion, suspicion and fear.

Now all those things were still evident, but she seemed to have better control over them. He supposed singers, being performers, had to have a little actor in them, as well. She was good at it, but it had frayed at the edges when he'd told her she was safe.

She'd shored up those edges, but there was a wariness and an exhaustion, not sleep related, haunting her eyes.

"The pattern that they always happen when I'm on stage? Yes, my brother pointed that out, but as I pointed out to him, that's just means and opportunity or whatever phrase you guys use. They know exactly where I'll be and for how long."

"Sure, but I'm talking about the connection to your songs."

She frowned, taking a sip of the hot chocolate.

"The incidents, including the murder of your security guard, always crop up in the few weeks after one of your singles drops on the radio. Not all of them, but I compiled a list of titles."

"Let me guess. The drinking, cheating and swearing songs?"

"No. There's not a thematic connection that I can find." Though he'd look, and would keep considering that angle. "But the connection right now seems to be that things escalate when the songs you wrote yourself do well."

She put down the doughnut she'd lifted to her lips without taking a bite. "That doesn't make any sense."

"Not yet. I figure if we pull on it, it will."

"How did you…"

He shrugged. "I'm good with patterns."

"Good with or genius with?"

He smiled at her, couldn't help it. He'd been trained as an undercover FBI agent. Took on whatever role he had to. He'd learned to hide himself underneath a million masks, but his personal attachment to this job and the safe world he'd created made it hard to do here. "Hate to bandy a word like *genius* around."

She laughed and for a brief second her eyes lit with humor instead of worry. He wanted to be able to give that to her permanently, so she could laugh and relax and feel *safe* here.

Because that was his job, his duty, what he was good at. Completely irrelevant to the specific woman he was helping.

He looked down at his computer, frowning at the uncomfortable and unreasonable pull of emotion inside him. Emotions were what had gotten him booted from the FBI in the first place. He didn't regret it—couldn't—but it was a dangerous line to walk when your emotions got involved.

"So, I think we can rule out crazed fan. It's more personal than that."

"Fans create a personal connection to you, though. They think they know you through your music—whether it was written by me or someone else doesn't matter to them."

"It matters to someone," Zach returned. "Or the incidents wouldn't align so perfectly with the songs you wrote."

She pushed out of her chair, doughnut untouched, only a few sips of the hot chocolate taken. She paced. He waited. When she seemed to accept he wasn't going to say anything, she whirled toward him.

"Look, I don't know how to do this."

"Do what?"

"Hide and cower and…" She gave the chair she'd popped out of a violent shove, then raked shaking hands through her hair. "A good man is dead because of me. I can't stand it."

The naked emotion, brief though it was, hit him a little hard, so he kept his tone brusque. "A good man is dead because good men die in the pursuit of doing good and because there are forces and people out there who aren't so good. Guilt's normal, but you'll need to work it out."

"Oh, will I?"

"I'd recommend therapy, once this is sorted."

"Therapy," she echoed, like he was speaking a foreign language.

"Stalking is basically a personal form of terrorism. You don't generally get through it unscathed. Right now the concern is your physical safety, but when it's over you can't overlook your emotional well-being."

"You spend a lot of time evaluating your emotional well-being, Zach?"

"Believe it or not, they don't let you in or out of the FBI without a psych eval. Same goes for in and out of undercover work—and a few of those messed me up enough to require some therapy. Talking to someone doesn't scare me, and it shouldn't scare you."

"That hardly scares me."

But the way she scoffed, he wasn't so sure. Still, it was none of his business. Her recovery was not part of keeping her safe, and the latter was all he was supposed to care about.

"Let's talk about the people on this list," Zach said, pushing the computer screen toward her. On the screen was a list of people she'd told her brother she thought might want to hurt her.

Daisy rubbed her temples. "Vaughn gave you this?"

He rose, retrieved some aspirin from the cabinet above the sink and set it next to her elbow. "Your brother gave me copies of everything pertaining to the stalking."

Daisy frowned at the aspirin bottle, then up at him. "Am I supposed to tip you?"

"Full service security and investigation, Ms. Delaney. Speaking of that, Delaney's a stage name, isn't it?"

"What? You don't have a full dossier on my real name and everything else?" She smirked at him.

He shook his head. The Delaney connection wasn't important. As unimportant as the way that smirk made his gut tighten with a desire he would never, *ever* act on.

What was important was her take on the list and what kind of patterns and conclusions he could draw. So he turned the conversation back to the case and made sure it stayed there.

Chapter 3

Sleep was a welcome relief from worry, except when the dreams came. They didn't always make sense, but Tom's lifeless body always appeared.

Even hiking up the mountains at sunset. It was peaceful, and Zach was with her, smiling. She liked his smile, and she liked the riot of sunset colors in the sky. She wanted to write a song, itched to.

Suddenly, she had a notebook and a pen, but when she started to write it became a picture of Tom, and then she tripped and it was Tom's body. She reached out for Zach's help, but it was only Tom's lifeless eyes staring back from Zach's face.

She didn't know whether she was screaming or crying, maybe it was both, and then she fell with a jolt. Her eyes flew open, face wet and breath coming so fast it hurt her lungs.

Somehow, she knew Zach was standing there. It didn't

even give her a start. It seemed right and steadying that he was standing in her doorway in nothing but a pair of sweatpants, a dim glow from the room behind him.

Later, she'd give some considerable thought to just how *cut* Zach was, all strong arms and abs. Something else he hid quite well, and she was sure quite purposefully.

"You screamed and you didn't lock your door," he offered, slowly lowering the gun to his side. He looked up at the ceiling, and gestured toward her. "You might want to…"

He trailed off and in her jumble of emotions and dream confusion, it took her a good minute to realize the strap of her tank top had fallen off her arm and she was all but flashing him.

She wasn't embarrassed so much as tired. Bone-deep tired of how this whole thing was ruining her life. "Sorry," she grumbled, fixing the shirt and pulling the sheet up around her.

"No. That's not…" He cleared his throat. "You should lock that door."

She wished she could find amusement in his obvious discomfort over being flashed a little breast, but she was too tired. "Lock the door to shield myself from lunatics with guns?" she asked, nodding at the pistol he carried.

"To take precautions," he said firmly.

"Are you telling me if I'd screamed and the door had been locked you wouldn't have busted in here, guns blazing?"

"They were hardly blazing," he returned, ignoring the question.

But she knew the answer. She might not know or understand Zach Simmons, but he had that same thing her brother did. A dedication to whatever he saw as his mission.

Currently, she was Zach Simmons's mission. She wished it gave her any comfort, but with Tom's dead face flashing in her mind, she didn't think anything could.

"You want a drink?" he asked, and despite that bland tone he used with such effectiveness, the offer was kind.

"Yes. Yes, I do."

He nodded. "I'll see what I can scrounge up. You can meet me out there."

She took that as a clear hint to put on some decent clothes. On a sigh, she got out of bed and rifled through her duffel bag. She pulled out her big, fluffy robe in bright yellow. It made her feel a little like Big Bird, which always made her smile.

Tonight was an exception, but it at least gave her something sunny to hold on to as she stepped out of the room. Zach was pouring whiskey into a shot glass. He'd pulled on a T-shirt, but it wasn't the kind of shirt he'd worn yesterday that hid all that surprisingly solid muscle. No, it fit him well, and allowed her another bolt of surprisingly intense attraction.

He set the shot glass on the table and gestured her into the seat. She slid into it, staring at the amber liquid somewhat dubiously. "Thanks." But she didn't shoot it. She just stared at it. "Got anything to put it in? I may love a song about shooting whiskey, but honestly shots make me gag."

His mouth quirked, but he nodded, pulling a can of pop out of the fridge.

"No diet?"

"I'll put it on the grocery list."

"And where does one get groceries in the middle of nowhere Wyoming?"

"Believe it or not, even Wyomingites need to eat.

I've got an assistant who'll take care of errands. If you make a list, we'll supply."

She sipped the drink he put in front of her. The mix of sugar and whiskey was a comforting familiarity in the midst of all this…upheaval.

"You don't shoot whiskey."

She quirked a smile at him. "Not all my songs are autobiographical, friend. Truth be told, I'd prefer a beer, but it doesn't give you quite the same buzz, does it?"

"No, but I'd think more things would rhyme with beer than whiskey."

"Songs also don't have to rhyme. Fancy yourself a country music expert? Or just a Daisy Delaney expert?"

"No expertise claimed. I studied up on your work, not that I hadn't heard it before. Some of your songs make a decent showing on the radio."

"Decent. Don't get that Jordan Jones airtime, but who does? Certainly no one with breasts." This time she didn't sip. She took a good, long pull. Silly thing to be peeved about Jordan's career taking off while hers seemed to level. Bigger things at hand. Nightmares, dead bodyguards, empty Wyoming towns.

"The police don't suspect him."

She took another long drink. "No, they don't."

"Do you?"

She stared at the bubbles popping at the surface of her soda. Did she think the man she'd married with vows of faith and love and certainty was now stalking her? That he killed the person in charge of keeping her safe?

"I don't want to."

"But you think he could be responsible?" Zach pressed. Clearly, he didn't care if he was pressing on an open, gaping wound.

"I doubt it. But I wouldn't put it past one of his people. After I filed for divorce they did a number on me. Fake stories about cheating and drinking and unstable behavior, and before you point it out, no, my songs did not help me in that regard. Funny how my daddy was *revered* for those types of songs, even when he left Mama high and dry, but me? I'm a crazy floozy who deserves what she gets."

Zach's gaze was placid and blank, lacking all judgment. She didn't have a clue why that pissed her off, but it did. So she drank deeply, waiting for that warm tingle to spread. Hopefully slow down the whirring in her brain a little bit. "I don't want to have a debate about feminism or gender equality. I want to be safe home in my own bed. And I want Tom to be alive."

"I'm working on one of those. I'm sorry I can't fix the rest."

He said it so blankly. No emotion behind it at all, and yet this time it soothed her. Because she believed those words so much more without someone trying to *act* sincere.

"What did you dream about?" he asked as casual and devoid of emotion as he'd been this whole time.

Except when he'd been uncomfortable about her wandering breast. She held on to the fact that Mr. Ex-FBI man could be a little thrown off.

"Hiking. You. Tom. It's a jumble of nonsense, and not all that uncommon for me. I've always had vivid dreams, bad ones when I'm…well, bad. They've just never been so connected or relentless."

"I imagine your life has never been so relentless and threatening."

"Fair."

"The dreams aren't fun, but they'll be there. Meditation works for some. Alcohol for others, though I wouldn't make that one a habit. Exercise and wearing yourself out works, too."

"Let me guess, that's your trick?"

He shrugged. "I've done all three."

"Your job gave you dreams?"

"Yeah. Dreams are your subconscious, the things you often can't or don't deal with awake. It's your brain trying to work through it all when you can't outthink it."

"You've given brains a *lot* more thought than I ever have."

"There's a psychology to undercover work. Your work deals with the heart more than the brain."

Because he cut to the quick of her entire life's vocation a little too easily, and it smoothed over jagged edges in a way she didn't understand, she chose to focus on the other part of the sentence.

"You went undercover? Yeah, I can see that. Bring down any big guns?"

He shrugged. "Here and there."

"What's the point if you're not going to brag about it?"

He pondered that, then gave his answer with utter conviction. "Justice. Satisfaction."

She wrinkled her nose. "I'd prefer a little limelight."

"I suppose that's why I'm in security, and you're in entertainment."

"I suppose." She finished the drink. She wasn't really sure what had mellowed her mood more—the buzz or Zach's conversation. She had a sinking suspicion it was both, and that he was aware of that. "I guess I'll try to sleep now. I appreciate the…" She didn't know what to call it—from responding to her distress to a simple drink and conversation—it was more than she'd been given in…a long time.

Well, if she was fair, more than she'd allowed herself. And that had started a heck of a lot longer ago than the stalking.

She stood, never finishing her sentence. Zach stood, as well, cleaning up her mess. For some reason that didn't sit right, but she didn't do anything to remedy it. She opened the door to her bedroom, took one last glance back at him.

He was heading for his own door. A strange mystery of a man with a very good heart under all that blankness.

He paused at his door. He didn't look at her, but she had no doubt he knew she was looking at him.

"Daisy." It might have been the first time he'd said her name, or maybe it was just the first time he'd said her name where it sounded human to human. So she waited, breath held for who knew what reason.

"You've been through a lot. It isn't just losing someone you feel responsible for losing. You've uprooted your life, changed everything around you. You might be used to life on the road, but this is different. You don't have your singing outlet. So give yourself a break."

With that, he stepped into his room, the door closing and locking behind him.

Zach didn't need much sleep on a normal day, but even with the usual four hours under his belt, he felt a little rough around the edges the next morning. He supposed it had to do with them being interrupted by Daisy's screaming.

It had damn near scared a year off his life.

Any questions or doubts he'd had were gone, though. Someone or something was terrorizing her. Didn't mean he wouldn't look at cold, hard facts. Hadn't he learned what getting too emotionally involved in a case got you?

Yeah, he was susceptible to vulnerability. He could admit that now. Being plagued by dreams, by guilt over the man who'd died only for taking a job protecting her, it all added up to vulnerable.

And he was *not* thinking about the slip of her top because that had nothing to do with anything.

He grunted his way through push-ups, sit-ups, lunges and squats. He'd need to bring a few more things from home. Maybe just move it all. He wasn't planning on spending much time back in Cheyenne with his business here.

His room still needed a lot of work, and he'd get to it once this case was shored up—as long as he didn't immediately have another one. Still, he had a floor, a rudimentary bathroom and a bed. What more did a guy need?

He knew his mother worried about him throwing too much into his job, whether because she feared he'd suffer the same fate as his father—murdered in revenge for the work he'd done as an ATF agent—or because she just worried about him having more of a life than work, it didn't matter.

He liked his work. It fulfilled him. Besides, he had friends. Cousins, actually. Finding his long-lost sister meant finding his mother's family, and he might get along more with the people they'd married, but it was still camaraderie.

He had a full life.

But he sat there on the floor of a ramshackle room, sweating from the brief workout, and wondered at the odd pang of longing for something he couldn't name. Something he'd never had until he'd met his sister—of course that had coincided with being officially fired from the FBI, so maybe it was more that than the other.

It didn't matter. Because not only was he *fine*, he also had a job to do.

He could hear Daisy stirring out in the common room. Coffee or breakfast or both, if he had to guess.

He'd hoped she'd sleep longer because there were some areas he wanted to press on today, and he'd likely back off if she looked tired.

Or he could suck it up and be a hard-ass, which was what this job called for, wasn't it? He knew what being soft got him, so he needed to steel his determination to be hard.

He ran through a cold shower, got dressed, grabbed his computer and stepped out to find Daisy in the kitchen.

She was dressed in tight jeans and a neon-pink T-shirt that read *Straight Shooter* in sparkly sequins on the back. On the sleeve of each arm was a revolver outline in more sequins. When she turned from the oven where she was scrambling some eggs, she flashed a smile.

Her hair was pulled back to reveal bright green cactus earrings, and she'd put on makeup. Dark eyes, bright lips.

The fact she'd made herself up, looked like she could step on stage in the snap of her fingers, he assumed she was hiding a rough night under all that polish.

But the polish helped him pretend, too.

"Want some?" she asked, tipping the pan toward him.

"Sure, if you've got enough." He dropped the laptop off on the table and then moved toward her to get plates, but she waved him away.

"You waited on me yesterday. My turn. Besides, I familiarized myself this morning. Thanks for making coffee, by the way. Good stuff."

"Programmable machine," he returned, not sure what

to do with himself while she took care of breakfast. He opted for getting himself a cup of coffee.

He didn't want to loom behind her, so he took a seat at the table and opened his laptop. He booted up his email to see if there were any more reports from Ranger Cooper, but nothing.

She slid a plate in front of him, then took the seat opposite him with her own plate.

"So, what's the deal? Play house in here until they figure out who did it?" she asked with just a tad too much cheer in her voice—clearly trying to compensate for the edge she felt.

"Partially. We're working on a protected outdoor area, but staying inside for now is best." He tapped his computer. "It gives us time to work through who might be after you."

She wrinkled her nose. "Believe it or not, sifting through who might hate me enough to hurt me isn't high on my want-to-do list."

"But I assume going home, getting back to your family and your career is. Lesser of two evils."

She ate, frowning. But she didn't try to argue, and he was going to do his job today. Nightmares and vulnerability couldn't stop the job.

"I want to talk about your ex."

"So does everyone," she muttered.

"Your divorce was news?" he asked, even though he'd known it was. Much as he didn't keep up with pop culture, he'd seen enough magazines at the checkout counter with her face and her ex's.

"Yeah. I mean, maybe not if you don't pay attention to country music, but Jordan had really started to make a name for himself with crossovers. So the story got big. And I got crucified."

"Why didn't he?" Zach asked casually, taking a bite of the eggs, which were perfectly cooked.

"Because he's perfect?"

"You wanted to divorce him," he pointed out. "He can't be perfect. No one is."

"Or that's exactly why I wanted to divorce him."

He studied her. The lifted chin, the challenge in her eyes. "Yeah, I don't buy that."

Her shoulders slumped. "Yeah, our families didn't, either. Neither did he, for that matter. I don't know how to explain… Do we really have to discuss my very public divorce?"

"Yeah. We really do. The more I understand, the better I can find the pattern."

"And if it's not him?"

"Then the pattern won't say it is."

"People aren't patterns, Zach. They're not always rational, or sane."

"Yeah, I'm well aware, but routine stalkers are methodical. It's not a moment of rage. It's not knee-jerk or impulse. It's planned terrorizing. Murder of your bodyguard? There was no struggle. It was planned. This person is methodical, which means if I can figure out their methodology, I can figure this out."

She heaved out a sigh. "You believe that."

"I know that."

"Fine. Fine. Why did I file for divorce against Jordan? I don't know. It's complicated. It's all emotions and… Did your parents love each other?"

Unconcerned with the abrupt change, because every thread led him somewhere, he nodded. "Very much."

"Mine didn't. Or maybe they did, but it was warped. It hurt."

He thought about his brother, alone in a psych ward,

still lost to whatever had taken a hold of his mind. "Love often does."

"You got someone?"

"Not romantically."

"Family, then?"

He nodded.

"I used to think loving my brother didn't hurt, not even a little—not the way loving my father did, or even my mom. Vaughn was perfect, and always did the right thing. He protected me and loved me unconditionally. But this hurts, thinking he could be in danger because of me."

"He's a Texas Ranger."

"That doesn't make him invincible. He also has a wife and two little girls and…" She swallowed, looking away from him. "I can't…"

"The best thing for 'I can't' is figuring this out. Looking at the patterns, and finding who's at the center."

"You really think you can do that?"

"I do. With your help."

She nodded. "Okay. Okay. Well, sit back and relax, cowboy. The story of Daisy Delaney and Jordan Jones is a long one."

He lifted the coffee mug to his lips to try and hide his smile. "We've got nothing but time, Daisy."

Chapter 4

"We met at a party." It was still so clear in Daisy's head. She'd stepped outside for air, and he'd followed. He'd complimented her on her music—never once mentioning her daddy.

She'd been a little too desperate for that kind of compliment at the time. She'd made a name for herself, but only when that name directly followed her father's.

"And this was before any of Jordan's success?"

Zach sat there, poised over his computer like he'd type it all out. Jot down her entire marriage in a few pithy lines and then find some magical *pattern* that either found Jordan culpable or...not.

"My brother looked into Jordan, you know."

"Yes, I know. I have all the information he gathered in regards to the...let's call it *external stuff.* But there's a lot of internal stuff I doubt you shared with your brother."

She laughed. "But you think I'll share it with a complete stranger?"

Zach blew out a breath, and though he had to be irritated with her, it didn't really show in the ways she was *used* to people being irritated with her.

"I know this is personal," Zach said, all calm and even and perfectly civil. "It hurts to mine through all these old things you thought were normal parts of a normal life. I'm not trivializing what you might feel, Daisy. I'm trying to understand someone's motivation for stalking and terrorizing you, and murdering your bodyguard."

"So you can find your precious pattern?" she asked, her throat too tight to sound as callous as she wanted to sound.

"Yeah, the precious pattern that might save your life."

She wanted to lean her head against the table and weep. Somehow, she had no doubt Zach would be kind and discreet about it, and it made her perversely more determined to keep it together. "He was sweet, and attentive. We had a lot in common, though he'd grown up on some hoity-toity, well-to-do Georgia farm and I'd grown up on the road. Still, the way he talked about music and his career made sense to me. He made sense to me. He asked me to marry him assuring me that it didn't have to change my career—because he knew where my priorities were."

"So you married for love?"

"Isn't that why people get married?"

"People get married for all sorts of reasons, I think. In your case, you've got fame and money on your side."

"Are you suggesting Jordan married me for my fame and money?"

"No, I'm asking if he did."

"I didn't think so." Even after she'd asked for a divorce, she hadn't thought Jordan could be that cold and manipulative, but after everything that had happened since the divorce… "He was so careful about any work we did together. Had to make sure it was the right project. He didn't insinuate himself into my career. So it didn't seem that way…"

"But?"

She didn't like the way he seemed to understand where her thoughts were going. She was clearly telegraphing all her feelings, and Zach was too observant. She needed to pull her masks together.

"He didn't fight me on the divorce. We'd grown apart. He'd thrown everything into his tour, his album, and I was touring and… We were both sort of bitter with each other but couldn't talk about it. I said we should end it and he agreed. He agreed. So simple, so smooth. Everything that came after was… calculated. Careful. He wanted us to split award shows."

"Huh?"

"Like choose which award shows we'd attend. If he was going to be at one, I wouldn't be. Like they were holidays you split the kids between. I don't know. I remember when my parents got divorced, it was screaming matches and throwing things and drunkenness. Not…paperwork."

"So it was amicable?"

Daisy hesitated. She'd dug her own grave, so to speak, with some of her behavior after she'd asked for the divorce. Because when he'd politely accepted her request and immediately obtained the necessary paperwork, she'd been...

Sometimes she tried to convince herself her pride had been injured, but the truth was she'd been devastated. She'd thrown out divorce as an option to get some kind of reaction out of him, to ignite a spark like they'd had before they'd gotten married.

But he'd gone along. Agreed. Wanted custody agreements over *award shows*.

So she hadn't handled herself well. At all. She'd never imagined *this*. She'd only acted out her hurt and anger and betrayal the best way she knew how.

Breaking stuff and getting drunk.

"*He* was amicable, I guess you could say. I was... less so."

"But you were the one who asked for the divorce."

"Yes." As much as she didn't want to get into this with Zach, she supposed she'd end up giving him whatever information he thought might help with his precious patterns. What else was there to do? How else did she survive this?

"Yes, because I wanted him to fight for me, or be mad at me or react to me in some way. But he didn't. I started thinking he'd never loved me, because he was so calm. If there'd been love, it would have gone bitter. Mine did. I think he just used me for as long as I'd let him, then was happy to move on." As if it had been his plan all along.

Even now, a year later, the stab of pain that went along with that was hard to swallow down or rationalize away.

There were bigger tragedies in the world than a failed marriage, including her dead bodyguard.

"So maybe it could be Jordan, but if it is him, it's not because I divorced him. Trust me, he got everything he wanted and *more* out of that situation. I don't think he'd sully his precious reputation by slapping back at me, when the press did all the work eviscerating me for him."

"Okay. What about other exes?"

"Because only a jilted lover could be after me?"

"Because we're going through the rational options first. We'll move to the irrational crazed fan angle after—" The sound of a phone trilling cut him off.

He pulled his cell out of his pocket, glanced at the display, then answered. "Yeah?" His face changed. She couldn't have described how. A tensing, maybe? Suddenly, there was more of an edge to him. The blandness sharpened into something that made her stomach tighten with a little bit of fear, and just a touch of very inappropriate lust.

If only she knew how to be appropriate.

He fired off questions like *when?* and *description?* jotting down what she assumed were the answers on the back of one of the many pieces of paper in the file.

"Get what you can for me," he said tersely and hung up.

He jotted a few more things down then got to his feet like he was going to walk off to his room without saying anything.

"What was that?" Daisy demanded, hating the hint of hysteria in her voice.

"Just some updates. Nothing to worry about."

She fairly leaped out of her chair and grabbed his arm before he could disappear into his room.

He clearly didn't know her very well because he

raised a condescending eyebrow, like that would have her moving her hand. But she'd be damned if she was letting go until she said what she had to say. "You want me safe? I have to know what's going on."

"That isn't necessarily true," he replied in that bland tone of his. "Knowing doesn't do much. All you have to do is stay put. I'll be back."

"You'll be back? You don't honestly expect me to—"

"I expect you to listen to the man currently keeping you safe. Do me a favor? Don't be cliché or stupid. Which means stay put. I'll be back." And then he walked out the front door.

And locked it from the outside.

Zach had no doubt he'd made all the wrong moves in there, but he didn't have time to make the right ones. He pocketed his keys, double-checked the gun holstered to his side and stepped out into daylight.

He took a deep breath of the fresh air, trying not to feel the prick of guilt at Daisy being locked inside for close to twenty-four hours. But it was for her safety, and Cam's phone call proved to him that he had to keep being excessively vigilant.

Which was why he scowled when Cam pulled up to the shack that disguised a garage behind the big house. Hilly was in the passenger seat so Zach tried to fix his expression into something neutral, but his sister being here complicated things.

Hilly was acting as their assistant. She ran the errands for groceries and the like, and she was helping with some of the paperwork while she went through nursing school.

Cam pulled his truck into the garage, then he and

Hilly exited. Zach pushed the button himself to close the door so it went back to looking like a falling-down shack.

Cam's expression grave and Hilly's suspicious. "I still can't believe this place," she said with a little shudder. "It's so *creepy* from the outside."

Zach smiled thinly. "And, as you well know, perfectly livable from the inside. So what's the deal?"

"Is she in there?" Hilly asked with a frown.

"Yeah."

"Well, let's go inside."

Zach rocked back on his heels. "Not a great idea right now. Besides, she doesn't need to know about this."

Hilly's frown deepened. Zach wanted to scowl at Cam for bringing her, but that would only make Hilly angrier.

Truth be told, he didn't understand the way Hilly got angry at all. It was sneaky, and came at you in new and confusing ways. Like guilt. He didn't care for it.

She glanced back at Cam. "I thought I was here to see what Daisy needed."

"You are," Cam agreed. "I just have some things I need to discuss with Zach about the case privately. I thought maybe I could do that while you talk to Daisy about anything she might need."

She looked back at Zach, her lips pursed, surveying him. An expression he never knew how to fully read. Judgment? Disappointment?

"I still think we can go inside and talk. There are rooms. Or you can let me go inside while you two powwow out here."

"Aren't you going to demand to know what's going on?"

"No. Cam and I agreed that there were certain cases

that required his confidentiality. I'm okay with that. So why don't you let me in?"

Zach nodded. He didn't particularly want to introduce anyone to Daisy, but she was likely tired of just *him* and walls for company. Hilly could talk to her about anything she needed, maybe make her feel a little more at home, and Cam could fill him in on the details in the privacy of his room.

They walked to the front of the house and Zach unlocked and relocked doors as they entered, and when he stepped into the common area he frowned at the absence of Daisy.

Then at the fact the door to his room was open. He stepped toward it, hand moving to his gun without fully thinking the move through.

He stopped short in the doorway, shock and irritation clawing through him at equal measure. "What the hell do you think you're doing?" Zach demanded from the doorway.

Daisy didn't even have the decency to jump as she sat there on his bed, rifling through his things.

"I can't say your room holds any deep, dark surprises, Zach. Bland guy. Bland… Oh, hello." Daisy leaned her head to the side to look around him.

"Get your hands off my stuff."

She blinked up at him oh so innocently. "Won't you be doing the same for me? Or have you already?" She got to her feet in a fluid movement and crossed to Hilly and Cam and held out her hand.

"Daisy Delaney," she offered with a sassy grin that likely served her well on stage.

"Hi, I'm Hilly," Hilly said eagerly, shaking Daisy's hand. "I'm Zach's sister."

"Zach's sister." Daisy looked at him and raised an

eyebrow before her smile sharpened. "Well, Hilly, you might be my new best friend."

"Sorry, if you're looking for dirt we only kind of found out about each other last year."

"Okay, so you can't give me the Zach dirt. How about you tell me what the hell is going on? I'm presuming you know." She moved her gaze to Cam. "Or you do."

"I, uh…" Cam cleared his throat, looking shockingly ruffled and uncomfortable.

"He's a big fan," Hilly stage-whispered.

"I am not," Cam retorted, sounding downright strangled. "I mean, I *am*, but not… Oh, hell."

Hilly laughed, leaning into Cam. They were more of a unit than Zach would ever be with his own sister, and he was never quite sure what to do with that sick wave of jealousy that swamped him sometimes.

Hilly had been kidnapped and raised as someone else. What would he envy of her life?

But when she linked hands with Cam and talked excitedly to Daisy, he knew exactly what.

"Hilly, why don't you take Daisy out to the kitchen and get her list. Hilly's our assistant. She can run any errands you need."

"Oh, he's dismissing the womenfolk," Daisy said with a sweetness that went bitter at the edges.

Zach could tell Hilly was trying to suppress a smile. But she didn't fight him. "I'm sure there are some things you'd like to have, Ms. Delaney. I can get you whatever you need."

"Call me Daisy," she replied, heading for the door with Hilly.

Zach *knew* he should keep his mouth shut, let it go.

But she downright needled him. "We'll talk about you going through my stuff later," he muttered as she passed.

"Ooh, shaking in my boots, baby cakes."

He sneered, as irritated with himself for letting her get to him as he was at her for being obnoxious as hell.

"Things are going well, then," Cam offered once Daisy and Hilly disappeared into the common room.

"Things are going fine. I want the full report."

"We didn't catch him at the airport, but a man was quizzing Jen at the General Store. Get many strangers, etc. She gave me a call and I ran him. Came in on a flight from Texas, but after Daisy's. No connections yet, but probably more than a coincidence. Someone's following her."

"I want to know *how*."

"Don't you want to know who?"

"Maybe. But if this is the stalker, they suddenly got so dumb they're sniffing around a small town thinking they won't make waves. My money's on a plant, or a hired hand. The *how* is more relevant than the *who*."

"He's rented a room in Fairmont, but I have some suspicions that's to throw us off."

"Does he know about *us*?"

"Unclear. As far as I can tell, he only has a vague idea of where she is. I assume he knows she's under some kind of protection, but he didn't make Hilly or me, and nobody followed us out here."

"We took every precaution." But something hadn't worked. Something had gotten through.

"It happens, Zach. Now we focus on protecting her. Jen's getting together her security footage and I'll work on an ID and any connections to Daisy. I'm sure you'll obsess over a pattern. Bottom line, we'll keep her safe."

Except hadn't he already failed at that? Maybe she was safe *now*, but the threat was at her door just like it had been back in Texas.

"Hey," Cam said. "Nothing's ever going to go according to plan. You know that."

Zach nodded at Cam. But a mistake had been made—plans or no plans—and that mistake had to be figured out before the consequences of his mistake started knocking.

Chapter 5

Daisy liked Hilly. She hadn't thought she would when the young woman had ushered her out of Zach's room with only a mild display of amusement.

But Hilly was sweet, a little heavy on the earnestness, which Daisy could only find endearing. The fact she'd ask for Daisy's autograph to give to the man huddled in Zach's room appealed to both Daisy's ego and the idea that love didn't always have to be messy. Hilly clearly loved her boyfriend and wasn't miffed that he'd gone a little tongue-tied over Daisy.

"So you don't know what's going on with the caveman clutch in there?" Daisy asked, scowling at Zach's door as Hilly finished up the list. It would be nice to have some *real* food in this place.

Hilly smiled. "They aren't really. Cavemen, that is. They're just…serious."

Which didn't answer the question. "No offense, Hilly, but one's your brother and one's your…" She trailed off, glanced at the rock on Hilly's hand. Not bad taste for a caveman, but Hilly could have picked it out herself. "Fiancé. You're not an unbiased observer."

"I suppose not, but they're good men. They both helped save me from people who wanted to hurt me."

"Really?"

"Zach's saved a lot of people, and gotten himself hurt in the process more than once. He's a good man. That I can promise you."

Hilly smiled as Cam and Zach stepped out of Zach's room, looking just as Hilly had described them: serious.

"I'll tell you about it sometime. Or ask Zach."

"Ask me what?"

Hilly shook her head and stood, slipping the list into her pocket. "I should head out to get the supplies so I can get them back to you before dinner."

"I'll keep in touch," Cam said to Zach.

"Aren't you going to say goodbye to Daisy, Cam?" Hilly asked sweetly.

He glared at her but then offered Daisy a smile and a nod. "It was nice to meet you, Ms. Delaney," he offered stiffly.

"Call me Daisy, sweetheart."

Cam made a little noise that might have been a squeak if he wasn't so tall and broad. Hilly ushered him out and that left her with Zach.

She scowled at him. Truth be told, she should be used to overly serious men worrying a little too much about her safety, but she'd always managed to keep Vaughn on the fringe of all that. Travel and no real trouble had helped until the past year.

But regardless of Vaughn's interference in her life, she wasn't used to someone being all up in her business. She wasn't used to someone getting under her skin in such a short amount of time.

And none of it mattered, because at the end of the day, her irritation with Zach didn't matter. Getting through this mattered. "I want to know what's going on."

"And I want to know why you were rifling through my stuff," he retorted, a slash of temper barely leashed.

Was it wrong she liked temper on him? That he wasn't all Mr. Bland Stoic? Because *this* was a lot more enjoyable than his pat, crap answers. So she grinned at him, since it seemed to make him grind his teeth together. "Show me yours, I'll show you mine."

"Someone followed you."

It took any and all enjoyment out of the moment. She sank into the chair when her legs went a little wobbly. "What?"

"Someone followed you here," Zach said, his voice flat but his eyes flashing with anger.

Was it at her or whoever was here? She wasn't sure she wanted to know.

"So I need a list of everyone who knew you were coming."

"You know the list," she replied, trying to keep the tremor out of her voice. "You, Jaime and my brother. Hate to break it to you, but they're not high on my suspect list. Well, I don't know you. It could be you."

"You didn't tell anyone that you were going out of town, or post a picture from the airport or—"

Injured pride reignited her irritation. "Oh, screw you."

"Hey, someone is *here*, and now I have to keep you safe under an even bigger threat, so a little truthfulness would be nice."

"Because I'm such a liar?"

"Get it through your thick, obnoxious skull that your

pride doesn't matter right now. One person, any person, who might have known you were leaving town, heading to the airport, anything. Because it matters. Clearly, if someone is here looking for you, it matters."

It was on the tip of her tongue to immediately dismiss him. But…it wouldn't be true, and she wanted to be safe more than she wanted to be righteous.

Just barely.

"I… I told my manager I was going to Wyoming, but—"

"Of all the idiotic bull—"

"I trust Stacy with my *life*," she shot back before he could finish. "I trust her with everything. It isn't her."

"Okay, great. So the three people who knew you were coming to Wyoming were your brother, an FBI agent and your manager. Who spilled the beans?"

"Maybe *you* did, jerk."

"Sure. I'm a security professional, but I bragged about bagging a big star client to someone who has a connection to you."

"I don't know you! You could have."

"But I know me, and I didn't. Stacy… Stacy Vine. That's your manager, right?"

"You cannot look into her."

"Can. Will."

She would not be so weak as to cry. She'd save that for when he couldn't see and lord it over her later. But her voice wasn't nearly strong enough. "You're asking me which of these people I *love* wants me dead."

He softened. She saw it all over his face and wanted to hate him for it. It would be easier if he was just the overbearing jerk, but he offered empathy far too often for it to be that simple.

God, she wanted something, anything, to be simple.

He took one of the chairs and moved it across from her. He sat, facing her, so that their knees were almost touching. He leaned forward, and she found herself wanting to lean forward, too. Wanting to be touched, comforted.

Wasn't that a joke? She knew better on a good day, with a man who actually liked her. This was neither of those things.

"It doesn't have to be that cut-and-dried. She could have mentioned it to an assistant. Written it down and someone read it. This is why the *who* is important, Daisy. If it's someone who's got a personal tie to you, they might be stalking people you know and love, too."

"How many ways do you want to hurt me, Zach?" She held up a hand before he could answer. He wasn't trying to hurt her. He had a job to do, protection to see to. Anything that hurt was all hers. "Sorry. That wasn't fair."

"You don't have to be fair. I'm going to do my job no matter what you are. Be mad, be unfair, but I need the truth. Always. It's the only way we get you out of this."

We. Like they were some kind of team. Which was too much the story of her life. Thinking some man was in it for her—Dad, Jordan—only to find all they cared about was their own bottom line. She didn't know how to weather that again.

What other option was there? She could lie to him, not trust him, and where did it get her? Nowhere. She was in the hardest lose-lose situation of her entire life, and boy, was that saying something.

"She's the only one aside from Vaughn and Jaime that knows. Nat—that's Vaughn's wife—might know, but Vaughn's pretty by-the-book. Even if he told her, he'd swear her to secrecy, and Nat would listen. You could always ask them, but I doubt they'd be careless."

"So we'll look into your manager."

"Yeah, sure. Fantastic."

Zach sighed, then rested his hand over hers. Warm, strong, capable. She really wanted to hate him, and he made it so dang hard.

"One thing at a time, okay? And eventually, we'll get there."

It was a cliché, and stupid, and worst of all, it made her feel better.

Zach spent most of his day looking into the manager, her connections and trying to figure out how anyone had followed Daisy here.

It couldn't be cut-and-dried because the person didn't know *exactly* where Daisy was, so that made any patterns sketchy at best. A frustrating point of fact Zach was having trouble accepting.

He also spent considerable time checking his security measures and watching the footage of the security cameras he had positioned on different places outside the house. When he was half convinced he saw a tumbleweed pass across his deserted Main Street he knew it was time to do something else.

Still, no matter what he did or how little he interacted with Daisy, he could practically feel the stir-crazy coming off her.

When Hilly returned with the groceries, and some updates on the tasks he'd asked her to accomplish, Zach thanked her and sent her away, though it was clear she wanted to stay and chat.

Much as Zach trusted Hilly and Cam to be aware of anyone following them, he didn't want to take too many chances on comings and goings being noticed—whether by the wrong people or even by locals who might talk.

Armed with the special item he'd tasked Hilly to find, Zach went to Daisy's room. She'd been inside with the door closed for about an hour. He knew she wasn't sleeping because he could hear her moving around.

He knocked, feeling stupid and determined in equal measure. It wasn't his job to set Daisy at ease or make her comfortable, but it wasn't *not* his job, either.

She opened the door with that haughty, bad-girl smirk, though it couldn't hide the wariness in her gaze. Still, both smirk and wariness softened as she noticed what he held in his hands.

"A guitar," she breathed, like he was holding a leprechaun's pot of gold.

"I don't know much about music, but there's a music shop in Fairmont and Hilly stopped in and picked one up. Probably not the quality you're used to, but—"

"Hilly stopped in and picked one up or you asked her to?"

"Does it matter?"

She tilted her head, studying him. In the end, she didn't say anything. She took the offered guitar and slid her fingers over the wood, the strings, the body and the arm.

There was something a little too erotic about watching her do that so he moved into the kitchen. It wasn't quite dinnertime yet, but they could certainly eat. If only to keep him from embarrassing himself.

But he couldn't quite seem to keep his gaze off the way she stroked the instrument, which meant he had to say something. *Do* something. Anything to keep his mind out of places he couldn't let it wander.

"I get a free concert, right?"

She grinned, turning the guitar over in her hands. She slid the strap over her shoulder, picked at the strings, fiddled with the knobs and whatever else.

"Ain't nothing free in this life, sugar." She said it, and then she sang it, noodling into one of her father's songs. The relaxation in her was nearly immediate. She softened, eased and lost herself in the song.

It was…enchanting, which wasn't a word he'd ever used or probably even thought, but she was mesmerizing. Like a fairy. With a dark, mischievous side. She moved seamlessly from one of her father's raucous drinking songs to one of her newer ones—the one she'd had some success with right before her bodyguard had been killed.

Sadness crept into her features, but not fear. She moved into a song it took him a few chords to recognize as one of the few duets she'd ever recorded with her father.

She stopped abruptly halfway through the song. "Hell, I miss that old bastard," she muttered.

That was a sadness he understood, and it made it impossible not to try and soothe. "My father wasn't a bastard, but I know the feeling."

"Not around?"

"He was murdered."

"Well. Hell, Zach, ease me into it, why don't you. Murdered?"

Zach raised a shoulder, no idea what prompted him to share that information. Soothing was one thing, but volunteering details was another. Yet, they piled up and fell out of him at a rapid rate. "Risks of the job. He was in the ATF, investigating a dangerous group. A long time ago. It happens."

"It shouldn't."

Why that simple phrase touched him was more than beyond him. He'd had a lot of time to deal with his father's death, accepting it and the unfairness of life. He'd investigated his father's murder, made sure it didn't consume him like it had his brother. He'd come to terms. He'd dealt.

But it shouldn't happen. No. It shouldn't.

"Is that why you do this?" she asked, still fiddling with the guitar.

"No, but it's why I went into the FBI. I'm assuming your father is why you went into music."

"Yes and no." She played a few more chords, humming with them. "He pushed me into it, and I did it partly for him, because of him, but I did it partly because it's in me. The chords, the stories." She pinned him with a look. "I'd say the same is true for you. Your father's life pushed you into law enforcement, but there's something in you that fits it."

"You'd be surprised," he muttered. "What sounds good for dinner?"

"Whatever," she said, taking a seat at the table and still playing random chords on the guitar like they were a link to safety or comfort. "I guess you didn't find anything with Stacy."

"No. Cam's working on the identity of who's here, and I'll have a report tonight, along with some video I'll want you to take a look at."

"Who's here. Why do you say it like that?"

"Like what?"

"Like who's behind this and who's here might be two separate people."

Her worry was back. She gripped the guitar hard enough her knuckles went white.

Part of him wanted to lie to her, but that wouldn't do.

That was letting himself get too emotionally invested. "It's certainly a possibility."

"So there could be two of them?"

"No, I'd say it's more likely someone hired."

"Like…a hit man?"

"Or just someone sent to find you. A lot of shady things are for hire out there. It'd be a way to ferret out your exact location without getting caught themselves."

"So even if you catch *this* guy, it won't mean you can connect them to the stalker?"

"Doesn't mean we can't, either. We don't know yet."

She rubbed at her chest. "I thought I knew how to deal with the unknown. You never know what's going to succeed or fail in music. I thought I would always just go with the flow, but if I hear you say we don't know one more time I might have a mental breakdown."

"Hey, this is the place for mental breakdowns. Creepy ghost town facade and all the modern comforts of home."

She laughed, but it faded quickly. "Home. Do you have a home?"

"I assume you mean home in the symbolic sense, not just four walls and a roof?"

"Bingo, cowboy."

Zach thought it over. Home to him was his grandparents' ranch they'd moved to after Dad had died. He'd never made one for himself. This place he was standing in meant something to him—bigger than just a building or a job—but it still wasn't…*home.*

"I guess not. I haven't really had anything permanent as an adult."

"I never had anything permanent."

"Do you ever wonder how you ended up the nomadic singer and your brother the stay-in-one-place Texas Ranger?"

"Are you just like your siblings?" she asked with one of her haughty raised eyebrows.

He sobered at the thought of his brother in a mental hospital, working through all the things that had twisted inside him since their father's death.

"You and Hilly seem similar," she offered as if *she* was trying to comfort *him*.

"Hilly and I only met just this year. I mean, I remember her when she was a baby, but—"

"She said the same thing. Add that to the murdered father and I'd say you've got quite the story, Zach."

"She was kidnapped by the men who murdered my father and raised under a different name."

Daisy blinked and opened her eyes wide. "I'm sorry, *what?*"

He shrugged, uncomfortable both with the subject and his idiocy for discussing it. "It's complicated, but... Well, it's all figured out now."

"Does the calm, bland, bored facade ever get exhausting?"

He didn't care for how easily she saw through him, so he did his best to raise his eyebrow condescendingly like she did. "Who says it's a facade?"

Her mouth quirked up at one side. "You weren't so bland or bored when I was rifling through your stuff."

Even now the reminder made his jaw clench, even more so when she full-on grinned and pointed at him. "See? Underneath all that robot exterior, there is a man with a living, breathing heart." She looked down at the guitar in her lap and frowned. "Believe it or not, Zach, I'd rather have a man with a heart on this case over a robot. That's why I was going through your things. I wanted to see if I could get to that heart."

"Believe it or not, Daisy, I do what I have to do to keep you safe. Robot exterior included."

She pursed her lips together as if she didn't quite believe him. As if she took it as some kind of challenge.

Lucky for him, he was not a man to back down from a challenge any more than he was a man to lose one.

Chapter 6

Zach was dead. Lifeless blue eyes. Blood everywhere. Just like Tom.

She turned to run, to save herself, but she tripped over another body and gasped out a sob.

Vaughn. *No.*

But even as she wanted to reach out, grab her brother, breathe some life into him, she ran. She didn't know how, because her brain was telling her running into the dark was all wrong.

But she kept running into the black. Into the danger.

"Daisy. Come on. Daisy." Zach's voice. But he was dead.

Still, she ran.

"Daisy. Stop."

She tried to speak, but she couldn't. She could only run and Zach swore viciously, the words echoing in the dark around her.

"Let's try this."

Why was Zach's voice haunting her? He was dead. She was alone. No, not alone. Running from... from who?

"Lucy?"

It wasn't immediate, but slowly she realized it wasn't totally pitch-black. A light glowed in the corner of the room. She smelled paint, not blood. And she could feel Zach there. Somehow she knew it was him, touching her shoulders.

"Lucy, wake up now."

Zach. Calling her by her real name. He was sitting on her bed. Twisted so that his hands gripped her shoulders, strong but gentle. He was using her real name and she was in Wyoming.

Dreaming.

"A dream," she muttered out loud.

"There now," he said, relief evident in his tone as he ran a hand down her spine. Weird to be comforted in a strange room with a man she barely knew touching her through the thin cotton of her pajamas.

But she *was* comforted. Enough that when he began to pull away she only leaned into him, ignoring the way his body stiffened. "You were dead. Vaughn was dead. And all I did was run."

His body softened against hers, and though his arms were more hesitant than take-control, he wrapped them around her.

A comfort hug. Maybe even a pity hug.

She didn't even care. She'd take comfort from pity if she had to. The images of that dream stuck with her, flashed in her head every time she closed her eyes. She focused on Zach instead.

He was warm with all that surprisingly hard muscle. He smelled like soap. She closed her eyes and breathed in deeply. She soaked in the warmth and rested her cheek against his chest, listening to his heartbeat.

A steady thump. As comforting as the rest of him.

She could feel his breath flutter the hair against her cheek. When he breathed, her body moved with the movement of his. Underneath her hands, splayed against his broad, strong back, she could feel his warmth seep into her.

What would all that muscle feel like without the Henley between her palms and his skin? To have her cheek pressed against his naked chest instead of soft cotton? She'd seen him with his shirt off. She could almost picture it.

So much better than the other pictures in her head.

It took her a minute to realize the buzz along her skin was pure, unadulterated *want*. And another minute to roll her eyes at herself for being so stupid and simple. She straightened, pulling away from him. His arms easily fell off her and he got to his feet quickly.

It amused her, soothed her a little, to think he might feel that bolt of attraction, too. What would be going on in that regimented brain of his?

"How about some ice cream?" he asked.

It made her smile. "Is sugar your answer to all of life's crises?"

"I wouldn't say sugar is the answer. Sugar is the… comfort. Besides, you had Hilly buy you some low-cal fruit atrocity kind. I figured you might be up for it."

"I'll take it." She slid out of bed. She'd learned her lesson that first night and had worn something acceptable to be seen in to bed.

Though, if she was honest with herself, she now regretted it. Thinking about an attraction to Zach, and what could be done about it when they were stuck in a weird safe house together, was far better than thinking about her dream or even her reality.

So she tried to decide what kind of come-on Zach Simmons, part robot, would respond to as she followed him out into the kitchen area. Nothing subtle. Being attracted to her was probably *very* against his personal code.

What would it take to make him break his personal code? She remembered the way he'd uncomfortably stared at the ceiling when her pajama top had been too revealing the other night. It made her laugh, which felt immeasurably good after the terror of that dream.

"Something funny?" he asked, looking at her with some concern—like maybe she'd lost it a little bit.

Maybe she had, but she figured she had a right to. "Just trying to think of things that make me laugh instead of cry or scream."

He frowned at that as he pulled out the carton of the frozen yogurt she'd requested. "I've been thinking about someone being here, and about what we can do."

"Thinking? Don't you sleep?"

He shrugged as he scooped the yogurt into the bowl. None for him, she noted. "When necessary."

When necessary. She had no idea why this man was such an endearing piece of work. Maybe it was because most of the men she knew pretended to have feelings when they really didn't, and Zach was the exact opposite.

"I think the leak is through your manager. It's what makes the most sense anyway. So we pull on that." He set the bowl in front of her, then went back to the freezer and pulled out a different carton.

She stared at the sad bowl of low-fat fro-yo that sometimes tasted good enough to make her forget about ice cream. Less so when someone wanted her dead or traumatized or whatever.

"What does *pull on that* mean in cop speak?"

Zach slid into the chair next to her. The bowl of dark chocolate, full-fat ice cream he set in front of him made Daisy's mouth water.

"Send a few fake messages, see which ones get followed. I haven't worked it all out yet, but that's my thought, and I'll need you to do it."

"You want me to lie to Stacy?" Daisy asked, her stomach turning at the thought. She was a decent enough liar, what with being a performer and storyteller and all, but the idea of lying to Stacy to prove someone she loved and trusted was part of this nightmare...

Yeah, fro-yo wasn't going to cut it.

"They don't have to be lies. They just have to be leads. Something we can follow and see who picks it up."

It still sounded like lying to her, and it sounded complicated. So she reached over and scooped a lump of his ice cream onto her spoon. Their eyes met as she slid the ice cream into her mouth.

It might have been funny if he didn't watch her so intently. If that direct eye contact didn't make her entire body simply *ignite*.

Under that stuffy exterior, Zach was proving to be a very, *very* dangerous variable in this whole mess. Because along with stalkers she didn't know what to do with, murder that scared her to her bones, and guilt that nearly ate her alive, she was still herself. Daisy Delaney. Lucy Cooper.

And she'd never been very good at pulling her hand out of the fire.

* * *

Zach needed more sleep. Clearly, a lack of it was the cause of his current lack of control.

Not that he'd done anything aside from watch her steal a scoop of his ice cream. And open her mouth around the spoon. And swallow the bite.

Then nearly spontaneously combust.

He looked down at his ice cream and tried to remember anything about what they were talking about. Anything that wasn't her mouth, or the way she'd leaned against him in the bedroom earlier.

He should cut himself a little slack. He was only human after all, and she was beautiful and engaging. She had that *thing* that made people want to watch her, get wrapped up in her orbit.

Maybe he'd like to be immune, but he was hardly a failure just because he wasn't.

But the one and only time he'd let his emotions get the best of him people had almost died. People he cared about. People he loved.

He couldn't—wouldn't—make that mistake again. No matter how tempting Daisy Delaney proved herself to be.

All his paperwork was in his room, as was his laptop. He had no shields to wield against her, and he had to think of this as its own version of war, even if it was only a war within himself.

"You could reach out and say you're willing to do a few shows," he said. He might not have his papers, but that didn't mean they couldn't talk through some options. When in doubt, focus on the task at hand. When tempted beyond reason, focus on what needed to be done.

"That'd go through my agent—the actual booking."

"Does your agent know you're here?"

"No. Not unless Stacy told him. I doubt she would have. She would have just told him I'm unavailable."

Maybe. The problem was, you never really knew what people told other people, and who those other people knew. There were so many fraying threads and he felt frayed himself. By her, by all this close proximity and by this damn dogged frustration that the case wasn't as simple as he might have thought.

"What about Jordan?"

She slumped, toying with her spoon. It amazed him the way she'd been mostly blamed and decimated in the press for being the instigator, the uncaring party, while Jordan poured his brokenhearted soul into his next album.

But every time Zach mentioned her ex-husband, she had a visceral reaction—in ways she didn't with other topics.

It twisted something inside him he refused to investigate, because emotions had to stay out of this. No more guitars. No more going into her room if she was having a nightmare. No more…

She took another bite of his ice cream.

Zach kept his gaze on his bowl. No more ice cream sharing, that was for sure.

"What *about* Jordan?" she asked, giving up on his ice cream and her own frozen yogurt.

"Would anyone have told him where you are? Does he have any connections to your manager or your agent?"

"He got a new agent when we got divorced. We never shared managers, though I guess Stacy was friends with Doug. In the way two people who sometimes have to work together are friends. She knows… Look, she was there through the divorce. She wouldn't give Jordan any information, and I don't think my agent is a fan of Jordan's after the way he was treated."

Or maybe he's not a fan of yours. Zach made a mental note to look deeper into the agent. "I don't really understand the ins and outs of your...what would you call it, staff?"

"Team," she replied emphatically.

"Let's go over the hierarchy there."

She shook her head. "I think I'd rather go back to bed and take my chances with nightmares."

"That's fine."

She eyed him. "It's fine, but be prepared to do it in the morning?"

Zach shrugged. "I have to dig, Daisy."

"No, you actually don't. You just have to keep me alive."

It was true. He hadn't been hired to investigate. He'd been hired to protect. But that didn't mean he couldn't or wouldn't do both. He needed her cooperation, though, which meant he had to go about getting the information a little more...strategically.

"You're right," he said, doing his best to sound like he agreed with her. "I don't have to poke into this or you. It's not my job." He stood, taking both bowls and walking them to the sink. "I'll butt out."

He turned, ready to head to his room. If temper flared a little unsteadily inside him, he snuffed it out. Emotions weren't his job, either.

Not investigating wasn't an option for him. But if she didn't want him digging into it, he'd do it without her.

She stood and stepped very deliberately into his path to his door. She cocked her head, studying him in a way that reminded him of being back in the FBI Academy—constantly being sized up for his effectiveness and usefulness.

He hadn't minded it then. He'd been full of the utter certainty that he belonged there, and that he was more than fit to be an agent.

Now, here, it scraped along his skin, unearthing too many insecurities he'd much rather pretend didn't exist.

"You did one hell of a job undercover, didn't you?" she murmured.

He was surprised at the change in topic, but he didn't let any of his unaffected poise loosen. "I suppose."

"The problem now is that you aren't undercover, so when you put on the act it doesn't add up."

"I don't follow."

"You don't care if investigating isn't your job. You're going to do it anyway. You don't let things go, and one way or another, you'll keep poking at me. There's something under this…" She waved her fingers in front of his face. "I'd say I don't understand it, but I do. I may not have grown up with my brother, but I recognize that cop thing—truth and justice above all else."

"So I remind you of your brother," he said flatly.

Her mouth curved, slowly, and with way too much enjoyment. The move so slow and fluid and mesmerizing he watched it the entire time—from mouth quirk to full-on sultry smile.

"No, I can't say you do, Zach."

He wanted to shift, to clear his throat, to do *anything* that might loosen all this tightening inside him. But it would be a giveaway.

Would it matter if you gave it away to her? She isn't your enemy.

"But what I will say is that if it wasn't for my brother, I wouldn't believe in the existence of good men with an inner sense of right and wrong and a deep-seated need to protect."

He held still. He met her gaze with all the blankness he'd honed in his time undercover. You made eye contact, but you didn't fall into it. You didn't get conned into believing you could act so well that someone saw what you wanted them to see.

So you gave nothing. You counted eyelashes or recited the Gettysburg Address. You didn't think over your plan, and you didn't give in to trying to analyze their thoughts or feelings—because thoughts and feelings couldn't be analyzed or predicted. They couldn't be patterned out.

Which, unfortunately for Daisy, was why he thought this whole thing was *personal*. Someone who wanted to hurt her for something more than her music or her reputation.

"So you can keep poking at me, and I'll keep poking back, but that doesn't mean I don't understand what you're trying to do. It doesn't mean I don't want you to do it. It means I'm frustrated and you're an easy target. All that rational, factual thought is the rock I can toss my irrational emotion against. And isn't that nice?" She patted his chest. "Maybe we'll even get to the point where we enjoy all the…poking."

He might have risen to the bait. Laughed or coughed or fidgeted at her overt sexual innuendo, but he knew that no matter how smart or worried she was, she was hoping whoever was terrorizing her was a random stranger and his investigation was pointless.

He couldn't let her think that by getting distracted over her purposeful baiting. Because it didn't fit, in Zach's mind. Whoever was doing this *knew* her, and it was very possible Daisy trusted them.

He didn't have to tell her that. He didn't have to poke at her—in any way, shape or form—though he might have wanted to rest his hand over hers...*just* to offer a little comfort.

Instead, he held still. Unearthly still. He kept her gaze, until that easy, flirtatious grin of hers faded.

"Your safety is my primary concern. However, it isn't my job or my aim to cause you undue emotional distress. Therefore, if my method of questioning is problematic, I can easily engage in other avenues of investigation that don't require any..." He desperately wanted to say *poking*. Wanted to smile and make a joke and ease all of that sudden tension out of her.

But maybe it would be better for everyone if there was a little tension that kept them from being too friendly.

"That don't require any avenues of questioning that might feel problematic on either of our ends."

She blinked. "Primary concern," she echoed. "Emotional distress." She shook her head and took a few steps back. The look she gave him was one of suspicion.

Since it wasn't his job to have her *trust* him, such a look couldn't bother him at all.

At all.

"Yeah, I bet you were a *hell* of an undercover agent, Zach," she muttered, but she was gathering herself. She was sharpening all those tools she so effectively used against him—an insightfulness, a confidence that she lashed against him like a weapon. "But news flash. You aren't anymore. Keeping me safe, investigating this thing, you can be regular old Zach Simmons, and it'll be more than enough."

How would that ever be enough?

But he couldn't say that to anyone, could he? So he merely nodded. "Noted."

Then, with absolutely no warning, she stepped forward again. She reached out and touched his face—a gentle caress one might bestow upon a loved one. She held his gaze with a softness he couldn't possibly understand.

Then she did the most incomprehensible thing he had ever in his entire life witnessed or been on the receiving end of.

She lifted onto her toes and pressed her mouth to his.

Chapter 7

It was wrong. Daisy had been well aware of that when she'd done it. Maybe she'd even done it because it was wrong.

But he'd laid down a challenge—whether he'd known it or not. He'd tried to turn off his personality, his entire essence. He'd tried to use the robot on her and that had only spurred her on to try to short-circuit the robot.

She would never again be told she didn't really mean anything, that she could be easily moved aside and closed off in a room without a second thought. No. Not for a man she'd been married to and not for a man who'd been tasked to keep her safe.

She would show *him*. She would get to him. And what better way to do that than to use her mouth?

His initial stiffness was shock, obviously, but when she didn't move away, changing the angle of the kiss instead, something shuddered through him.

Or maybe something broke inside him. *She'd* broken something inside him, because he didn't just return the kiss—he started one of his own.

Not a challenge or some kind of attempt at one-up-manship. This was...just a kiss, except *just* didn't fit.

It was real. It was Zach. As if a few days under the same roof could make you feel things for one another. But his mouth crushed against hers like they were long-time lovers, used to the act of kissing enough to have it practiced, but not so much that it didn't *melt*. A warmth that soaked into her bloodstream like alcohol, and a sudden weakness she knew she'd regret at some point.

But there was nothing to regret now with Zach's mouth on hers, his arms drawing her closer so that she was pressed against all that muscle and restraint.

Except there was nothing *restrained* about how he kissed her. It wasn't the explosion of lust she might have expected or understood. It was deeper, stronger. The kind of thing that didn't rock you for a moment, but forever. A kiss she'd remember *forever*.

Maybe because that thought horrified her enough to startle, Zach broke the kiss. He pulled his mouth from hers and nudged her back and away from him. Her knees might have been weak, but she saw a flicker of *something* in his gaze. Some kind of complicated emotion that disappeared before she could get a handle on what he might be feeling.

He fixed her with a gaze, and spoke with utter certainty. "This will never happen again."

She absolutely *hated* the way he said *never*, as if he were God himself and got to decree the way the world worked, the way *she* worked. So she smiled, all razor-edged sweetness. "Zach, don't you know better than to challenge me by now?"

"Do you want to *die*?" he asked with such a bald-faced certainty her insides turned to ice. Immediately.

"I don't know how a kiss is going to kill me," she managed, though she sounded shaken. She *was* shaken. Even with the ice of fear shifting everything inside her, her limbs felt like jelly.

She could still feel Zach's mouth on hers. He'd wanted her, or was it all another act? A mask?

No, he might be blank now but there was a kind of anger radiating off him. One she didn't understand because it didn't show up in any of the ways anger usually did. No yelling, no fisted hands, no threats or furious gazes. Not even the condescending sigh Jordan had perfected during their short marriage.

"You are in a dangerous situation," Zach said, and his robot voice was back but it frayed along the edges. "Potentially a life-or-death situation, and you're adding…" He sucked in a breath and then slowly let it out. His next words were no more inflected, but they were softer. "Listen to me, as someone who's been in a few life-or-death situations myself. The only thing that happens when you tangle emotion into dangerous situations is catastrophe."

"It was just a kiss," she managed, wincing at how petulant she sounded.

"It was a complication. One you can't afford."

That stoked some of her irritation back to high. She lifted her chin. "Don't presume to tell me what I can afford."

"Are you always so damn difficult?" he demanded, the slightest hint of a snap to his tone.

"If you have to ask that, you haven't been paying attention."

He rolled his eyes, and she had no doubt she was about to be dismissed. Part of her wanted to throw a

fit, make herself into more of a nuisance, but her surroundings were too much of a reminder of where her
fits and anger and *feelings* had gotten her.

A failed marriage *everyone* got to have a say about.
Isolation and loneliness that went deep because so many
people were willing to believe the worst about her and
think she deserved whatever she got.

Kissing Zach had been a mistake. She felt suddenly
sick to her stomach at how much of one. Thoughtless
reaction, plain and simple. When would she ever learn?

Mr. Control kissed you, too.

And since when did someone else's culpability matter to her end result?

His phone chimed in his pocket and he pulled it out,
clicking a few things. His expression never changed.

But it was something like four in the morning. Who
would be contacting him at four in the morning? Only
someone with bad news, and since she was his current
bad news...

"What is it? Is someone hurt? Is Vaughn—"

He shook his head sharply. "My cousin's wife had
her baby."

Zach didn't exactly strike her as the type to receive
middle of the night texts about a cousin's baby. "Don't
lie to me about—"

He held out the phone and on the screen there was
a picture of a red-faced baby wrapped in pink. Underneath the picture the text read:

Amelia Delaney Carson, 6 lbs 11 oz, 20 inches. Batten
down the hatches.

It was *odd* that a pang could wallop her out of nowhere, when she'd convinced herself that she wasn't
even sure she ever wanted babies. That she and Jordan

had come to the conclusion they wouldn't rush bringing *children* into the world when they had careers to build.

But her career had already been built, and what she hadn't admitted to herself was that she'd been hoping marriage would be a transition of sorts.

What she'd really wanted out of marrying Jordan had been a home. Full of music and joy and no tours or constant travel. Stability. She'd dreamed of a peaceful life. Not one devoid of performing, of being *Daisy Delaney*, but one where she got to choose when and where to play the role.

Daisy *was* her, and she loved that persona. But it had been her whole childhood and adolescence, and the older she got the more she felt like she'd earned a little time for Lucy Cooper.

Why she thought she'd be able to build that with Jordan, in that distant future he always talked about, was beyond her.

She handed the phone back to Zach. "Cute," she managed to offer. "I like the middle name."

He made an odd face. "It's the mother's last name," he offered, studying her warily.

"A Wyoming Delaney?"

He very nearly *winced*, which she couldn't quite figure though she decided to enjoy his discomfort anyhow.

"Do you know… Wyoming Delaneys?" he asked, failing at the odd casual tone he was clearly trying to maintain. "I mean, Daisy Delaney is a stage name, though."

He seemed a little too desperate to believe it was true. "Yes and no. Why does that weird you out? Worried we're related or something?"

"Carsons and Delaneys aren't related."

"I thought you were a Simmons."

He shook his head. "Anyway. We should try to get some sleep. We'll come up with some things to tell your manager and see if we can't get a lead."

She studied him. There was something weird about his discomfort over the shared name. Since she was more than a little irritated with him, she wanted to poke at it. "My legal name might be Cooper, but my stage name was my grandmother's name before she got married. Daisy Delaney. She was born in some little town in Wyoming. Something with a B? I'd have to text Vaughn. He'd remember. Oh, wait, it was Bent. That's why Daddy always used to wear his hell bound and whiskey *bent* shirt."

"Jesus," Zach muttered, looking so downright horrified she nearly laughed.

"What?"

"Nothing," he said far too quickly.

"Are we close to there?"

"Kind of. Anyway. Bed."

"Maybe I'm related to your cousin's wife. Wouldn't that be a trip?"

"Yeah, a real trip. Goodnight, Daisy."

Zach was tired of women. Particularly opinionated ones. Pretty ones. Infuriating ones.

He really didn't need his sister to add to it, but here she was, trying to tell him what to do.

"You have to come," she said, her tone something closer to a demand than he was used to hearing from her. Still, it seemed every day Hilly got a little more confident, a little more situated to life outside the isolated cabin she'd been raised in.

He stood on the dilapidated porch of the building

that usually gave him such satisfaction. After last night, not much did.

"I'm in the middle of a job. I can't just leave Daisy here locked up."

"You could bring her with you."

"Yes, that's genius. She has some kind of stalker snooping around Bent, so why don't I bring her to the hospital and potentially endanger every member of our family." *And hers, apparently.* Because Daisy Delaney's grandmother was from Bent, Wyoming.

He didn't believe in all the metaphysical nonsense spouted by his cousins—that the old Carson and Delaney feud had morphed into Carson and Delaney unions that were meant to be.

He didn't believe in meant-to-be.

"Are you okay?" Hilly asked.

The fact she even suspected he wasn't caused him to straighten, to remind himself he didn't have *time* for stupid worries over stupid nonsense.

"Of course I am. But this job is important. And we haven't found any solid leads. I can't leave her here, and I can't risk taking her somewhere else."

"She can't possibly still want to be cooped up in there."

"Hilly."

"I know. I know. Safety. Precautions. But…" She looked up at the dilapidated building. "How long can you feasibly keep her in this place? It's going to start to feel like a prison."

"Better a prison than a coffin, Hilly."

"Why do you have to be so *practical*?" she muttered.

"I believe it's in the job description."

"But your life isn't a job description, Zach. And neither is Daisy's."

Zach didn't know what other string of words would get her to stop this incessant merry-go-round. The flash of something far off in the distance put him on instant alert—enough so he no longer cared about words. Only getting her away.

"We're going to walk to your car. Once you're inside, I want you to call…" He racked his brain for someone who'd be able to help. Cam needed to watch the other guy. Most of his family was at the hospital with Laurel and Grady. Getting the cops involved would be tricky.

"What is it?" Hilly asked, her voice perfectly even, her expression still mildly bemused. But she understood.

He took her by the arm and they strolled back to her car. "Someone's out there."

He needed to make it look like he wasn't living here. He needed to lead the man somewhere else. And somehow, he had to get in contact with Daisy so she knew to stay the hell put.

"I couldn't have been followed. Cam's sitting on the guy." Hilly smiled brightly up at him as if he'd just said something hilarious.

"Well, then we have a second guy."

"All right. I'll call Cam and head his way. We'll come up with something. Don't worry about me. Keep Daisy safe."

"I don't want him following you."

"You can't want him staying here."

It was too close. Too dangerous. Unless he played all his cards right. "Go. Call Cam."

For the first time her cheerful, just-talking-to-my-brother facade faded. "I don't trust that tone, Zach."

"Trust the man who used to be the FBI agent, Hilly."

She hesitated, which cut like a knife even though she had every reason to doubt him. Hadn't Cam almost died because Zach had been too concerned about his brother's welfare to take care of business?

"I don't want you doing something on your own."

"I won't be on my own. I'll have you calling Cam for backup. But I need you to go on the chance he does follow you." Zach was counting on the former, but if it was the latter...

Well, he had a plan for that, too.

Eliminate the threat.

"Drive to Cam. Okay?"

"All right. Only because I can't think of a better plan. Do not do anything on your own, do you hear me?"

"I hear you."

She sighed disgustedly, presumably because she knew *I hear you* didn't mean he agreed to anything she'd said.

She reached out and took his hand, giving it a squeeze. She forced a smile for the sake of whoever might be watching them. "Just be careful. Because if you get hurt, I will have to end you." Her smile was a little more genuine at the end, and she turned and got in her car.

Zach couldn't spare a glance for the house, for Daisy. He stood exactly where he was and watched Hilly's car disappear.

Whoever was out there didn't follow.

Zach didn't head back into the house, and he didn't check on his sidearm or his phone, though he wanted to grab for both.

He didn't know who or what was out there. Someone could be watching, it could be a vehicle left behind as someone approached town on foot. It could be his eyes playing tricks on him, but the back of his neck prickled with foreboding.

Which meant taking every precaution necessary.

He walked down the dusty side of the road as if he

didn't have a care in the world. He even forced himself to whistle. He turned down the alley, keeping up the act of unhurried unflappability.

Once he was around the corner, he sprang into action. He'd been keeping his car hidden since that first day, just so no one happened upon it. He popped open the hidden keypad on the garage hidden in the building. He entered his code and moved as quickly as he could, watching for anyone who might pop into view. There was the possibility whoever had been watching was trying to break in the house, but that would take time.

He'd use it.

He drove the car out and closed up the hidden garage. When he pulled out of the alley, there was no sign of anyone trying to get into the house. So he took the opposite way out of his town at a slow pace.

He caught the flash again. This time he could tell it was a small compact car half hidden behind one of the far buildings in town. He couldn't make out the license plate—number or state—only the black fender glinting in the sun.

He kept his breathing in check and drove on, remaining slow and unhurried and looking around, pretending to smile as he enjoyed the beautiful Wyoming landscape.

When the car didn't follow after several minutes, he swore.

They suspected someone besides him was in town, and that was absolutely no good. So he swerved off the road and ditched the car. Since he wasn't being followed, he didn't worry about hiding it. Time was more important.

He ran back the way he'd driven, darting behind buildings on the opposite side of the car and mostly tried to keep out of sight of the car.

He stopped for a second on the opposite side of the road as the house Daisy was in. He stilled and listened.

No motor running, so they wouldn't have a head start on him. But he didn't like their proximity to Daisy. Because he couldn't even be sure someone was in the car. Whoever was watching could have gotten out to start snooping around the house.

He wished he knew how long they'd been there and that he could be sure the car had followed Hilly. Because if they hadn't followed Hilly, they had more information than Zach liked to consider.

Either way, Daisy had a leak and now she was in the direct line of fire.

Which meant Zach had to move. And fast.

Chapter 8

Daisy impatiently tapped her fingers against the countertop. Where the hell was Zach? It wasn't like him to stay holed up in his room with the door closed, though she supposed he might have had a break in the case or was making phone calls he didn't want her to hear.

Since *she'd* been holed up in her room strumming on the guitar he'd gifted her, it was more than possible he'd left. She couldn't fathom him doing that without telling her, no matter how irritated he was about the kiss.

She smiled to herself. Oh, the moments after hadn't been any fun, but the in-the-moment had been something she'd willingly relive over and over again.

It was the first time in a while where she'd felt…normal. Like Lucy Cooper, or even the Daisy Delaney from years ago when she hadn't had anything normal outside the music. There had been a simplicity in that time.

Of course, there was nothing simple about being either version of herself now, and certainly nothing simple about the aftermath of kissing Zach.

Still, she gave herself permission, here alone, to enjoy the memory of something she could pretend was simple.

The slight creaking sound brought Daisy out of the memory. She tried to shake away the wiggle of alarm. It was an old house—no matter what improvements Zach had made—of course it creaked.

But in the silence that ensued after, her heart beat harder until it became such a loud thud she knew she wouldn't hear the sound again even if it came from one of the walls.

She looked around, trying to remind herself she was safe. Locked and hidden away.

But someone knows you're nearby.

She marched over to Zach's door. She wouldn't tell him about the noise. She'd just insist he give her some information. Maybe she'd come on to him. Whatever it took so that he was around and making her feel safe.

She knocked. Harder than she should have.

He didn't answer.

Alarm went from a wiggle to a flop. She grabbed the knob and tried to turn it.

Locked.

The wiggles and flops turned into chains that restricted her breathing. "Zach," she croaked. She cursed herself for the nerves, the fear, the total ineffectuality of her voice. She breathed in and out, tried to use some of her old tricks for the occasional bout of stage fright.

"Zach," she repeated, louder this time but more firm. Surely, he'd hear it through the door.

Nothing happened.

She wouldn't panic. Couldn't. She pounded against the door for a while, but then she heard something else—a creak, a moan. Something definitely from the outside. Which meant if there was someone other than Zach outside, they could definitely hear the banging.

But he had to be in there. He was probably trying to teach her a lesson or something. Scare her so she'd stop hitting on him. Yes, that had to be what this was.

Well, wouldn't he be sorry? She marched to the kitchen, ignoring the way her hands shook and her heart beat a painful, panicked cadence. She grabbed a butter knife and marched back to the door and got to work.

It took longer than she would have preferred as she had to wiggle the knife in the slot, then between the door and the frame. She was shaking at this point. Where *was* he? She thought for sure he'd pop out if she started trying to break into his room. Surely, he'd only locked it to keep her out.

The door finally gave and she swung it open. "Aha!" she yelled, pointing the knife into the room.

But it was empty. She moved around, searching every corner and under the bed, even the closet.

No one. Not a soul.

"Oh, God. God. Zach, if this is some kind of joke or test, I'm over it."

But he didn't appear, and those *noises* kept coming from outside this hellhole disguised as a safe place.

Panic bubbled through her, paralyzing her limbs and squeezing her throat. Her heart beat too hard in her ears and she desperately wanted to scream.

But she'd been through worse than being left alone. Seeing Tom dead was the worst. No one had a right to make it worse than that.

Then something rustled in the closet. Something big. But she'd just been in that closet. How could—

A figure stepped out and she screamed before her

brain could accept that it was Zach *miraculously* show-ing up out of nowhere.

"How did you do that?" she whispered. He wasn't *magic*. There had to be an explanation.

"Tunnel. Shoes."

"Tunnel shoes? What does that—"

"Get some damn shoes, Daisy. Purse if it's handy. Ten seconds." Without further explanation he strode out of the room and into the kitchen. She scurried after him but stopped short when he pulled two guns out of the top cabinet above the refrigerator while she only stared.

Until he gave her a sharp look.

"Move," he ordered, snapping her out of her shock.

She had to move. Questions were clearly for later when he wasn't grabbing extra guns. She hurried into her room, shoved her feet into tennis shoes and looked around for her purse. Ten seconds. She had way less than ten seconds now and she was not the neatest per-son on the planet.

But she caught a glimpse of the strap under her duf-fel bag and lunged for it, tugged it from the haphazardly spilled-out bag and ran back to Zach. He held a laptop across one arm while he typed with the other, a huge backpack strapped over his back.

When she peered over his shoulder at the screen of the laptop—which had been full of pictures of the ghost town they were in—he snapped it shut. "The front is the best option. Follow me. *Stick* to me. Do whatever I say without question and everything will be fine. If something happens to me, no matter what, you run. You understand me?"

"Zach. I don't understand *anything*."

"We'll figure it out when we're safe." He took her by the hand and pulled her to the door.

Even as a million questions assaulted her, she understood Zach Simmons was not a man to overreact. If he wanted them to run, she'd run.

He pulled her out into the first room that looked as dilapidated as the outside. "Lock the locks," he said, handing her a key chain with three keys on it. They weren't labeled, but she didn't ask which one was for which—she just kept trying till she had all three locks locked.

He was peering at something through the wall. "See that picture frame on the ground?"

She looked down. There was an old, battered picture frame with a ripped piece of paper inside. "Uh, yeah."

"Hang it up on that rusty nail."

She did so, and blinked as it perfectly hid the key holes from view.

"Now, come hold my hand again."

She wanted to make a joke about hitting on her, but the words stuck in her throat. They were running, and that couldn't be good.

So she slid her hand into his and let him pull her along. He slid out the door, and she followed suit. He didn't lock this door, instead left a rusty-looking padlock hanging off the handle.

His gaze swept everywhere, and then he gave her hand a squeeze. "Now we run. I'm not going to be able to hold your hand without whacking you with the bag, so you'll just have to follow me. If you can't keep up—"

"I'll keep up." No matter what.

He nodded firmly. "Good. All right. Let's go."

He moved across the dusty road, and it was only then she realized he held the closed laptop in one hand and a gun in another. Still, she followed him, behind one building, and then through the alley between two even worse-off ones. Caved-in roofs, fire-scorched walls.

He reached the small ramshackle building at the end of the road and handed off his laptop to her while hanging on to his gun. With his free hand, he reached through a jagged break in the glass window of the back door, fiddling around until the door popped open.

He slowly pulled his arm out, and then opened the door just as slowly. It took her a minute to realize he was trying to mitigate the squeaking noise that echoed through the air as he opened it. When the opening was big enough, he gestured her inside.

Trying not to balk at the dark, or the spiderwebs, she stepped into the dank, smelly interior. Zach followed suit, pulling the door closed behind him before fishing a flashlight out of his pack.

He led her farther inside and she kept waiting for the nice part—the part that had been redone inside all the dilapidation.

But this one had no new pretty interior. No working kitchen. It was abandoned and untouched for years. "We're going to stay…here?"

Zach had put his pack on the floor and took his laptop back without a word. She was sure he wasn't paying any attention to her at all as he worked furiously.

When he finally spoke, she fairly jumped with adrenaline.

"*You're* going to stay here. I'm going to figure out what the hell is going on. You know how to shoot a gun?"

She blinked at the weapon he held out to her. Thanks to her brother, she'd had a few shooting lessons. She was even somewhat familiar with the kind Zach held out to her.

She nodded, and he handed the gun over.

"Anyone comes in here that isn't me or Cam, or doesn't say the code word *feud*, you shoot. Understood?"

She swallowed, and managed another nod.

With that, he got to his feet, strapped multiple guns to his person and strode for the door.

Zach slid out of the building, making sure no one was around to see him. It was painful to leave Daisy wide-eyed, scared and alone, but he couldn't hole up with her and hope the guys went away.

He'd learned, over and over again, that waiting in safety often caused more problems than it solved. Sometimes you had to act to keep people safe.

He hurried behind the buildings, keeping his body out of sight from as many angles as possible.

From what he'd been able to tell with his video surveillance, there were two men. One who'd been poking around the house, and the one who'd stayed in the car—presumably ready to drive off.

It turned his stomach to think he was ready to drive off with Daisy. Even more so that *two* men were here.

It had to be the manager leaking information to someone, whether maliciously or with an accidental slip to someone. He didn't have time to figure out the pattern, though. He had to stop those men before they had a chance to hurt Daisy.

He moved into a position where he knew he'd be able to see the driver of the car with minimal chance of being detected. He angled his body and his head, and managed to make out the car.

The driver was no longer in it, so Zach moved forward—until he saw both of them standing in front of the car, discussing something.

They had their backs to him, so descriptions would be hard, but it wouldn't matter. These weren't the masterminds trying to get to Daisy. Everything about them screamed hired muscle.

Which, again, in Zach's mind meant not a crazed fan, but someone with a personal connection. And someone with money.

Like Jordan Jones.

And if it *was* Jordan, he'd have endless funds to keep sending people just like this.

Zach moved back behind the building. Taking them out was only a temporary solution. More would come in their place. But if he could question them, he might be able to glean enough information to make the connection.

The only question was how to immobilize the threat of two men with guns who wanted the woman he was trying to protect.

He needed them to separate, and even then it would be risky. But it would be a risk he'd have to take. He examined the building he was hiding in. He needed somewhere he could isolate one man, without getting trapped by both.

He needed to get one headed in the other direction. He pulled the phone out of his pocket and pulled up the app he used to control security in the safe house. He poked around until he came up with an idea.

Have the back door alarm on the house go off. Once they started heading over, he'd make enough noise they'd feel like one of them had to come his way.

It took a few minutes—first the men headed toward the siren, alert and with hands on their weapons. Zach kicked at a board next to him, the hard crack of impact then splitting wood loud enough to hopefully get one's attention.

He couldn't watch for their approach. Instead, he

had to stay hidden and hope he was about to fight only one man.

He saw the gun first and immediately moved. He kicked the gun out of the man's hand. The man leaped forward, but Zach had better vision and grabbed him from behind. Zach managed to get an arm around the other man's throat. Zach was taller, though the man was thicker.

"Who are you?" Zach demanded in a whisper as the man struggled against him.

The man didn't answer, and no one came to his rescue. Elsewhere, the alarm continued to beep, which was a good sound cover for the fight Zach was about to have here.

"Who sent you?" Zach asked, tightening his grip and dodging the man's attempt at backward blows.

The response was only a raspy laugh as he twisted and nearly got free before Zach strengthened the choke hold.

They grappled, but Zach kept the choke hold. He asked a few more questions, knowing he wouldn't get an answer but hoping he might get *something* that would ID the man or give him a hint.

Over the sound of his alarm, he heard something else. Something just as shrill. Sirens in the distance. It was unlikely to be coincidence that sirens were closing in on the empty ghost town. Cam and Hilly must have decided to call the cops. Hell. Zach sure hoped they'd sent more than one because he had no doubt that the other guy was now on his way back.

"You think the cops will help you? Or her, for that matter?" the man rasped.

"Guess we'll find out." Zach managed to jerk one of the man's arms behind his back, but it left him open to an elbow to the gut. His grip loosened just enough to have the man slip out of his grasp.

The man tried to take off on a run, but Zach lunged, tackling him to the ground. They tussled, landing blows. The other man was bigger but Zach figured he could hold his own until the cop car actually got here.

The next blow rattled his cage pretty good, so much so that he thought he heard a dog bark and growl.

But then there really was a dog, growling and leaping. Zach had a moment of fear before he recognized the dog, and it jumped at his attacker. The man screamed, and Zach managed to wrangle himself free of his grasp.

A cop appeared, gun held and trained on the man on the ground—the man who was clearly scared to death as the dog growled and snapped right next to his face.

"Free. Sit," Hilly's voice called.

The dog stopped growling, planted its butt on the ground and wagged its tail before turning his head toward Zach.

"Thanks for the assist." He gave the dog a rubdown, wincing only a little as his face throbbed. He glanced up as Hilly, who'd given her dog the command, came running. He was a little surprised when she kneeled next to him instead of her dog, Free.

"You're bleeding." She ran her hands over him as if checking for breaks or injuries, but he held her off.

"It's just a split lip. Please tell me Cam is here and you didn't try to white knight this yourself."

"It wasn't just me. I had Free. Plus the cops."

Zach swore, but he couldn't muster up much heat behind it. "I've got to get to Daisy." He glanced at the Bent County Sheriff's Deputy who was handcuffing the man who'd attacked him. Deputy Keenland efficiently did the job and read the man his rights.

"There's another one," Zach offered.

"We've already got him," the cop replied.

"I want to talk to them."

Keenland gave him a raised eyebrow. "We'll be transporting them to the station, where *we'll* question them. We'll take your report, as well."

He didn't have time for this. He glanced at Hilly. He didn't even have to ask. She nodded.

"Far building on this side," he said quietly so Keenland, busy pulling the arrested man to his feet, wouldn't hear.

He'd have to entrust Daisy to Hilly while he took care of this. It bugged him, but it had to be done. He pulled out his phone and turned off the security so Hilly could get into his apps, and then handed her his phone and his keys to the building.

"Be careful." They all needed to be a hell of a lot more careful.

Chapter 9

Back in the fake nice house inside an outside dilapidated old house, Daisy couldn't find any of the calm or resignation she'd had in the days leading up to this.

Someone had found her here. Maybe they hadn't gotten to her, but they'd tried. In this place that was supposed to be a secret from everyone.

Which meant someone she loved and trusted was either out to hurt her, or close enough to someone who did to slip the information to them.

God, her head hurt. Almost as much as her heart as she went back over so many interactions.

Could Jaime be the bad link? She didn't know him that well, even if he was Vaughn's brother-in-law. He could have told anyone, couldn't he? But Zach trusted him. Surely, Zach would know…

Except Zach wanted her to believe Stacy was responsible. Could her manager harbor some secret hatred of her? Was it as simple, and heartbreaking, as that?

Or was it deeper, messier, more complicated?

Worse than the riot of emotions and fear and questions pulsing inside her, Cam and Hilly were being obnoxiously and carefully tight-lipped about what exactly had gone down after Zach had left her in the abandoned house.

Only that he'd be back soon to explain everything. But time kept ticking by as she sat at the table, watching Cam and Hilly.

Which was actually the worst part of all. Hilly and Cam moved around the kitchen and common area acting like the perfect unit. A team. A partnership.

She felt so completely alone. The separation of the past few years echoing inside her like she'd been emptied out—of love and companionship and hope. There was only fear left.

She rested her forehead on the table and did everything she could to keep from crying. No one was going to see her cry. Nope. She would brazen through this like she'd brazened through everything else in her life.

Maybe she was tired. Maybe she wanted *normal* for a little bit. Maybe she wanted a little house in the country and a nice man she could trust to build a family with.

And maybe Daisy Delaney and Lucy Cooper weren't made for those things.

Her phone chimed and she nearly fell over lunging for it on the table. Surely, it would have to be Zach. Everyone else had stopped calling and texting and surely—

She stared at the text message from Jordan. The first sentence made her uneasy, so she clicked it to read the whole thing.

I just heard you're out of town for a few days. Someone told me it might be rehab. I really hope you get the help you need. Peace to you.

Peace. Peace? Anger surged through her, and while some of it was prompted by all the fear and things out of her control right now, most of it was prompted by that *ridiculous* send-off.

Peace to you.

Peace.

She'd like to give him some peace. Right up his—

"Is everything okay?" Hilly asked gently, but with concern.

Daisy smiled up at Hilly, though she knew it came out too sharp when Hilly took a step back. "Yes. Just a text from an annoying…acquaintance. Apparently, the rumor is I'm in rehab." She wanted to bash the phone into little bits. "How do I respond to a text like that?"

"You don't," Cam said in a voice that reminded Daisy of Zach.

Where *was* he?

"You'll have to excuse me if I don't want the world thinking I'm in rehab. My reputation is in enough tatters."

"But if people think you're in rehab, they won't think you're *here*," Cam replied reasonably. Apparently, whatever trouble had happened had cured him of his slight starstruck nature. Or he was just getting used to her.

Daisy couldn't say she cared for it. "Whoever is after me already knows I'm here."

"But the fewer people who know, the fewer people your stalker can use to get to you."

It was so reasonable, really unarguable, and now she wanted to bash her phone against Cam. She was tired of being reasonable in all these impossible situations. She wanted to act out. She wanted to *fight*.

She wanted to tell Jordan to go jump off a cliff. Or

write a song about lighting all his prized possessions on fire.

One by one.

But Cam was right and Daisy's only choice was sitting here, not responding, not reacting. Just waiting for someone to succeed in hurting her.

"Did Zach okay the cell phone use?" Cam asked, his attempt at casual almost fooling her into thinking it was a generic question.

"Yes, thank you very much. He did something to my phone to block traces or something. But he wanted me to be able to email my agent from my phone and a few other things. I don't know. Techie stuff. But it's perfectly Zach-approved." Because everything in her life now suddenly was Zach-approved.

Except herself. She could still rile him up to the best of her ability. Assuming he came back and didn't abandon her here.

She closed her eyes, nearly giving in to tears again. Oh, God. That was what she was *really* afraid of. Not that someone had found her, but now that they had, Zach would leave her.

Hilly pushed a mug and plate at her.

"Drink some tea. And eat some cookies."

"You Simmonses and your ungodly sugar addiction." An unexpected lump formed in her throat. "Where *is* he?" she asked, hating that the emotion leaked out in her scratchy voice.

Hilly patted her hand. "He's safe, and he'll be back soon."

She didn't need him to come back. She didn't *need* Zach Simmons. At *all*. He was a bodyguard, more or less.

But God, she wanted him here pushing cookies on

her, telling her what the next step would be, and reassuring her he'd take care of everything.

"Five minutes."

The deputy didn't move, didn't even spare him another condescending look. "We've taken your statement, Mr. Simmons. You're free to leave."

"I need five minutes. Hell, I'll settle for two questions."

"Simmons."

Zach turned around and sighed. Detective Thomas Hart stood, plain-clothed, in the doorway, and Zach knew he was officially done.

He followed Hart out of the building and into the parking lot. It was dark now, and Zach wasn't all that sure he knew how much time had passed. But he hadn't gotten what he wanted yet.

"There has to be something you can tell me."

"There isn't. Sincerely. He's not giving us answers."

"I want a name, Hart. A last known address."

Hart turned, crossed his arms over his chest. "You won't get one. Stop harassing the deputies. Go home. Deal with whatever business you've got going down on your own."

"I can hack into your system in five seconds flat," Zach returned disgustedly.

Hart held up a finger. "First, I didn't hear you say that. Second, be my guest. Because I can't give you that information. Zach, you know as well as I do, whatever they're after—however it connects to your mysterious business—these guys are hired muscle. They're not going to tell you or me anything you really need to know."

"But you'll investigate who's paying them."

"If it's pertinent."

Zach swore. "You're killing me."

"Hey, it's my day off. You're killing *me*. The only reason McCarthy called me is because he knows we're friends. You better know you'd have been arrested for disturbing the peace and interfering with an ongoing investigation if not for your connection to Laurel."

"I'm a Carson. Doesn't that mean your kind is always tossing mine in jail for no reason?"

"No real Carson was ever an FBI agent, that I can tell you." At Zach's scowl, Hart grinned. "Want to go play darts? Take your mind off it so you can work out the knots?"

Part of him did. It was something he and Hart did often when Hart was stuck on a difficult case and needed something mindless to do. Maybe it was exactly what Zach needed. Maybe he could get somewhere on this whole mess if he just separated himself from it for an hour or so.

But Daisy was back there and something had to be done. She couldn't spend the night there. Even with these two guys locked up, more would be coming. More might be on their way, and while Zach could lock them up in that building pretty tightly— anything could happen.

Damn, but he needed some answers. "Can't. Got work."

Hart nodded. "I'll leave you to it. Just leave the deputies alone."

"You going to pass along whatever information you find out?"

"Night, Simmons," Hart said, opening his car door and sliding inside.

Zach sighed but he dug his keys out of his pocket and walked to his car. He *could* keep pounding at the deputies, but they wouldn't budge. And the more he did, the less chance he had of sneaking some information out of Hart later.

He didn't have time for either, though. Action was required. Cam wouldn't approve of the idea forming, which meant Zach would need to be especially sneaky.

He drove back to the house, watching for tails, taking the long, winding way and missing the turn off the highway twice and doubling back before he was satisfied no one had followed him.

He parked his car back in the hidden garage, though he wondered if it should be easier to access.

Well, not if he could get his plan wheels turning ASAP. He'd need to get rid of Cam and Hilly first.

He texted Cam that he was disengaging the security from the outside and coming in. Then set about to do just that. When he finally stepped into the common room, Daisy jumped to her feet from where she'd been seated at the table.

"Oh, my God. You're hurt."

It startled him, the gentleness mixed with horror in her tone. Like she cared. She even rushed over to him and touched the corner of his mouth, which was a little swollen from the elbow he'd gotten there.

"I'm all right," he managed, his voice rusty. "Just a tussle." He ste/pped away from her too soft and too comforting hand. "I need to get the security systems—"

"I'll get them running," Cam said, holding up Zach's phone. He went to work and Zach turned back to Daisy.

She looked pale. Exhausted.

"Thanks for your help, guys, but you should head home," he said to Cam and Hilly, keeping his voice neutral. "We'll all sleep and reassess in the morning."

Cam studied him, and Zach did his best to look blank. Cam couldn't know what he was planning. Not yet.

Cam handed the phone back and looked at Hilly. Something passed between them because Hilly nodded.

He'd never been able to communicate with anyone like that, and he wasn't sure if that was just the nature of never having been in a serious, committed relationship the way Cam and Hilly were, or some fundamental lack inside him.

Right now was certainly not the time to wonder about it.

"Show him the text message," Hilly said, laying a comforting arm on Daisy's shoulder before she passed by.

"What text message?" Zach demanded.

Daisy glared at Hilly, but Hilly and Cam slid out the door, clearly leaving Zach to handle it.

"Daisy. Show me the text message."

"It's nothing," she replied, but she picked up her phone, tapped a few things, then slid it his way. "Just Jordan being oh so very concerned."

Zach read the text message, scowled at the screen. "Where did he hear you're out of town?"

"Zach. I'm sure any number of people are saying that about me since I'm not home or touring or anything else."

But Zach didn't like it. For a wide variety of reasons he'd parse later, once he got his plan off the ground. "Does Jordan often contact you?" If this was out of the blue, it would give some credence to Jordan being involved.

"Not often. But a text message isn't out of the norm. Things like 'I'll be at x place on y date. I'd appreciate a lack of a scene.'"

Zach's mouth quirked, though he knew it shouldn't amuse him. "Let me guess. You caused three scenes."

She grinned at him, eyes sparkling. "How'd you

know?" But she sighed. "I don't let anyone tell me what to do, most especially some *man* who thinks he has a right when he gave that up. And trust me, I want nothing more right now than to show up at his door drunk as a skunk. But I've learned not to give in to the impulse *every* time—because half the time it's a publicity stunt. He wants a scene from me so he can play the injured, horrified party."

A publicity stunt. "He wants to ruin you," Zach said flatly.

"He wants to make me look bad. I think there's a difference." She shrugged jerkily, pretending it didn't bother her. But he could see the bother written all over her tense posture and the way she gripped the phone. "The more I think about it, the more I can't pin him for this. He's too much of a narcissist. Nothing he does to me is trying to ruin me—he's just trying to help himself."

But a dead ex-wife could be helping himself, making him a sympathetic figure once again. And being a narcissist didn't make a person less likely to exact revenge if they felt they'd been wronged.

But he didn't need to argue with her or convince her of anything. Jordan was as high on his suspect list as her manager. He'd find out the truth and she'd deal with that one truth, instead of all the possible ones.

Weary, aching body, Zach lowered himself into one of the kitchen chairs. "Then your response should really stick it to him."

She looked at him sideways. "Go on."

"Verbal judo."

"What's verbal judo?"

"I won't give you the whole spiel, but basically it's

a way of talking to people that neutralizes a confrontation."

"I don't want to neutralize it. I want to explode it."

"I know you do, sweetheart, but we're trying to give
you a low profile."

"He expects me to explode. Shouldn't I give him
what he expects? Just to keep him from looking too
deeply into things? Or maybe even salvage some piece
of my reputation."

Since Zach didn't believe Jordan was all that igno-
rant of what was going on, he merely shrugged. "You
could, but he knows *something* is up. This is his version of fishing. So instead of giving him the reaction
he wants, drive him crazy. Just say thank you for your
concern. It gives away nothing. It harbors no ill will,
and it admits no guilt. It'll probably eat him alive since
he was clearly fishing for a reaction. It's *that* part I don't
trust." Or the timing—reaching out just as two people
trying to get to Daisy were taken into custody by police.
Pretending he thought she was in rehab. Zach wasn't
going to trust any coincidences.

Daisy stared at her phone, contemplating. "You really
think a response like that will eat him alive?"

"He knows you, right? Understands that you'll do
the opposite of what he says, understands that any attempt at peace offerings will end with fiery explosions.
So you don't give him what he wants."

"You make me sound like a shrew."

"No, I'm trying to make him sound like a jerk. Because he could just not. He doesn't need to reach out,
doesn't need to poke at you. He could leave you be. But
he's trying to piss you off, and so much worse than that,
he's doing it under the guise of concern. Don't give him

the satisfaction, because trust me, he's getting some satisfaction over that or he wouldn't be reaching out."

She contemplated her phone, then she picked it up and began to type.

Thanks for your concern!

She angled the screen toward him. "Is the exclamation point too much?"

"I think it works."

"Send," she said, tapping the screen with a flourish. Then she sighed and stared at him, her eyes lingering on the split lip and the bruising along his jaw. "I thought you were convinced Stacy was the culprit."

"I'm not convinced anyone is the culprit. We're looking into any possibility." And they needed to find them sooner or later.

He opened his mouth to tell her the rest of his plan, but she moved over to him and touched the part of his cheek that throbbed. Everything inside him tangled tight. She studied him, her fingers gently tracing over the line of his bruised jaw.

If he'd known what to expect, he might have been able to ward it off, but her gentleness undid him. Magnetized him. He couldn't remember anyone… His life was taking care of people, finding out the truth, saving people when he could.

No one ever asked if it was a burden. He'd never wanted or needed anyone to comfort that burden. It was his.

But Daisy's touching him was being given a gift so perfect, he wouldn't have ever thought to ask for it.

She slid into his lap. He held himself still, even if with all that stillness a desperate desire rioted inside him. It wasn't like the other night, her trying to prove something, defuse something, or just forget her circumstances.

There was a sweetness to this, even as close as their bodies were. Even though she made him want her in totally unsweet ways. She was gentle. She was…caring.

"Daisy." It was a croak, but he didn't have the wherewithal to feel self-conscious over it.

"Shh." She pressed her mouth to the side of his, just the gentlest, featherlight brush. "Someone's got to kiss the hurts."

A breath shuddered out of him, and even though it was the absolute last thing he should do, he closed his eyes as she gently kissed all along the bruised portion of his jaw. It was comfort and it was relief, and he had no business taking it from her when he was supposed to be keeping her safe.

Safe. Not hiding in abandoned buildings while someone prowled *this close* to being able to touch her.

No, today he'd failed. There could be no more failure. Only action.

"We don't have time for this." Which wasn't precisely true, but it was a hell of an excuse because his willpower was fading.

"I think we have all the time in the world," she replied, pressing her mouth to his neck.

His vision nearly grayed before he had a chance to slide her off his lap. Dear *Lord*, was that hard to do. Harder to let her go after he nudged her back a pace.

But he did it. "Pack your bags, Daisy. We're headed to Nashville."

Chapter 10

Daisy felt…strange leaving Zach's little ghost town. Like she'd miss it. Which was crazy since she'd been cooped up in that odd little house, not out enjoying the blue sky or mountains in the distance or in this very early morning's case, the stars out in their full and utter splendor.

Nothing had been good here, and yet she didn't want to leave. Didn't want to face Nashville or the people she knew, even with Zach at her side.

Because facing meant accepting that someone she loved and trusted might be behind this.

But she didn't argue. She'd packed her bags like Zach had said. She'd enjoyed maybe thirty seconds of looking up at the vast universe before Zach had whisked her into his car and started the drive.

He'd said nothing about the kisses, but for a few moments he'd relaxed under her.

She smiled a little to herself. Well, not *all* of him had relaxed.

She gave him a sideways glance. He was driving to some tiny independent airport in some other part of middle of nowhere Wyoming, where they'd fly in some tiny little plane to a few airports all the way to Nashville.

Nashville. It wasn't home, because she didn't particularly feel like she *had* a home. She'd been touring since she could remember, only ever staying with Mom and Vaughn for bits of time. As an adult she'd bought a house in Nashville, but she'd sold it when she'd married Jordan.

Then they'd sold the house they'd bought together. The house she'd thought she'd start a family in, have a life in.

"You know, I don't have a place in Nashville," she said after a while.

"I do."

"You have a place in Nashville?" she asked incredulously. She'd believed he knew enough people to take a small plane halfway across the country, but this seemed far-fetched. And yet, she trusted him implicitly, regardless of what seemed believable.

"I know people, Daisy. I found us a safe place to stay."

She kept staring at him, because something about the split lip and the bruising on his face—even with the dark five-o'clock shadow over it, made her feel safe even when she knew she wasn't.

But Zach would protect her, no matter the circumstances. Even though she knew Zach was human and that anyone could reach her if they wanted to badly enough, someone would fight to keep her safe.

Take blows. Give blows. For her.

He could push her away or insist they didn't have time for more than a kiss, but one thing Daisy knew was that Zach wasn't stoic or unaffected. He was worried about getting emotionally invested because he was already on his way to getting emotionally invested.

The thought cheered her enough that she dozed off, until Zack was waking her up with her real name again.

"Sleepy you doesn't seem to answer to the name Daisy," he offered, his voice rough with exhaustion and yet his lips curved.

"That's because Daisy Delaney doesn't sleep."

"All right, Lucy Cooper. You should really talk to that alter ego of yours, because you could both use some sleep." He gave her head a little pat and then slid out of the car.

She could only stare after him. There was something about the way he said her given name. It slithered through her, a not totally comfortable sensation— because it was too big for her skin. It made her heart swell and her eyes sting.

Jordan had never called her Lucy, even after she'd asked him to. Because she didn't want to be Daisy Delaney to her *family*. She'd wanted to separate it all out.

He hadn't understood.

Zach probably didn't, either, but he still used her name as though it didn't matter what he called her— she was the same. Not two identities fighting for space.

He opened the passenger door and looked at her expectantly. Right. She was supposed to get out of the car, not get teary over something so stupid.

"You haven't told me what the plan is," she said as she got out of the car. He grabbed their bags out of the trunk and headed for a squat little building.

The sun had risen, but it was still pearly morning light. And they had a long way to go to reach Nashville.

"Well, first we'll go see your manager."

"Together?"

He shrugged. "I don't see why not. You'll just tell people I'm your bodyguard." He walked to the building and knocked on the door, waiting for an answer.

When a scrawny young man answered he greeted Zach by name. They conversed for a while and then the young man led them through the office and out a back door.

Daisy felt like she was in a dream, complete with a tiny plane that made her breath catch in her lungs.

It didn't look safe, and if she'd been with anyone else she would have brought that up. But Zach would never take risks with her—that she knew. It had to be safe.

For a tin can hurtling through the air.

Zach helped her up the stairs and gave her hand a squeeze. "Afraid of flying?" he asked empathetically.

"I never have been before." She looked around the tiny cabin. "This plane changes things a bit."

"We'll be fine," Zach assured, and she was sure he thought so. She wasn't sure he was *right*, but she knew he believed he was. He gestured her into a seat and she took it.

"Why are we going to Nashville now?" Because if he talked maybe she wouldn't feel like running screaming in the opposite direction.

"Waiting isn't working. We're not getting closer— the trouble is only getting closer to you, and without warning. So we go straight to the potential leaks. We ferret them out. Besides, this way the rehab rumor can't really get anywhere."

He fastened her seat belt for her as she only stared,

that same feeling from before—heart too big, skin too small.

She swallowed, trying to sound normal or just *feel* normal. "What does my reputation matter?"

"Jordan's taken enough from you, and whoever is behind this has taken even more. You don't need to give them pieces of yourself, too. We'll nip any rumors in the bud, and we'll find out the leak in one fell swoop."

No one had ever cared how many pieces she gave of herself as long as they got the pieces they wanted. Even Vaughn, for all his wonderful qualities, didn't understand her enough to do more than worry about her safety.

So she did the only thing she could think to do. She leaned over and pressed her mouth to his. She smiled against his mouth when he kissed her back for a brief second, then stiffened and eased her away.

Oh, he wanted her. She thought he might even *like* her.

"You have to stop doing that," he said sternly.

She did it again, a loud smack of a kiss, though this time he was tight-lipped and less than amused. Still, she flashed him a grin. "Stop kissing me back and maybe I will."

He didn't say anything to that, which made her settle back into her seat with a smile.

Shuttling on and off planes was exhausting. Add to that, Zach hadn't slept—not since the night before. But he drove the rental car through Nashville to the little farmhouse on the outskirts that one of his law-enforcement friends used as a safe house sometimes.

Daisy would like it. Somehow, he knew that. But he

hadn't been prepared for the way her delight wound through him.

"Oh, my God! A chicken coop!" She jumped out of the car and practically ran over to it, leaning over the fence around the fancy little coop. He didn't see any chickens, but the gray, cloudy skies were spitting out a drizzle that probably kept the animals safe in shelter.

"My friend says there's a list of chores to do, if you're into that kind of thing."

She turned to look at him, eyes bright and smile wide. "Are you kidding? Why didn't you bring me *here* in the first place?"

He didn't mention it had been because he didn't trust most of the people in Nashville who had any connection to her. Her brother had wanted to isolate her to keep her safe.

It had been a failure of a plan—Zach's own fault for not seeing the holes in it.

He shook that failure off—had to until the job was done—and focused on the new plan. "I do want you to give your manager a call and tell her you're planning to come into town tomorrow. Tell her you want a meeting, morning or afternoon doesn't matter, but I want her to believe you're leaving in the evening."

"And are we keeping this meeting?"

"Of course."

Some of her simple joy over the chicken coop had faded, but she didn't argue with him. Didn't try to tell him for the hundredth time she trusted her manager. "And…"

She trailed off, turning her gaze back to the chickens. He couldn't read her feelings from just looking at her back, but he thought the fact she was hiding her face told him enough to gather she wasn't happy.

"You'll be with me, right?"

"You aren't going any damn where without me, sweetheart."

She turned to face him again, lifting an eyebrow. "Oh, is that so?"

"You're not going to be contrary over that. Not right now. This isn't about telling you what to do. It's about keeping you safe. You and me are stuck like glue."

She smiled sweetly—which should have been his first clue something was off, but he was dead on his feet. She sauntered over to him, chickens forgotten. She reached out, and he stiffened against the touch.

Not that it didn't shudder through him as she playfully walked her fingers up his chest. He tried to ward it off, but then she looked up at him under her lashes.

"Like glue? What kind of sleeping arrangements were you planning?"

Lust jolted through him so painfully it was a wonder he didn't simply keel over. Or give up...and in to her.

But he wouldn't. He couldn't. "We'll figure it out inside."

"Don't tease, Zach." She sighed heavily, lifting her palm to his cheek.

It was becoming too common, too much of a want to have her hands on him. Still, he couldn't move away, could barely hold himself back from leaning in.

"You need to sleep."

"Safety first."

She looked around the picturesque yard. Even with the drizzle falling, it had a cheerful quality to it. Green grass and trees, red chicken coop and barn bright and clean in the rain. It was the complete opposite to the desolate, decaying place he'd originally taken her to.

It felt weirdly symbolic, only he was so exhausted he

didn't know if it was good or bad. He ushered her inside with the security information his friend had given him. He dropped the bags and followed the email instructions on how to set all the security measures for the house.

"What's the best way for you to contact your manager?"

She eyed him and he had to stifle a yawn, had to work to keep his eyes open.

"In this case I think I need to call her. She'll have to rearrange her schedule to see me, I'm sure. She'll do it, she'll want to, but we'll have to work out the when and where."

"Okay. So, you'll call and set up a meeting." There'd be security to worry about—if the leak was through her manager's office someone would know she was there and accessible. "Make sure she doesn't think you're getting in until tomorrow, and thinks you're leaving in the evening."

"Okay. Can I make the call in private or do you need to listen in and make sure I'm a good girl who follows instructions?"

He wasn't sure what that edge in her tone meant, so he decided to ignore it. He made sure he held her gaze and didn't yawn, though one was threatening. "I trust you. There are three bedrooms. Take your pick. Just give me the time when you're done."

She stared back at him for a few humming seconds. He thought about the plane, when she'd kissed him and he'd been stupid enough to kiss her back.

Even though intellectually he knew it was a failure to get emotionally tangled with her, that it would put her in danger—put them both in danger. Though he never forgot how emotional entanglements had almost caused so much loss last year, he couldn't seem to help it. He was emotionally tangled.

There had to be a way to block it off. He knew better now. His brother was in a psych ward, and Cam had almost died. There were *costs* to an emotional connection—and if he couldn't control the connection, he had to find a way to keep it separate and make sure it didn't affect the case.

He knew better now, didn't he?

"You don't want a play-by-play of the phone conversation?" she asked after a while.

"The time will be enough." Because he had to focus on the facts of the case. The facts of what it would take to protect her. Enough with his precious patterns and trying to understand her and her life. He had to focus on the *facts*.

If he'd pulled her into more danger by bringing her closer to her stalker, he didn't have room for anything else.

Eventually, she nodded, picked her bag up off the floor and went in search of a room.

Zach picked up his own bag and pulled out his laptop. Before he could fall into blissful sleep, he had some work to do.

He'd been ignoring his phone for most of their travel, so he turned that on while he booted up his computer.

He winced a little at the ping of voice mails and text messages that sounded a few times. Yeah, a couple of people weren't too happy with him or his disappearing act.

He didn't bother to read all the text messages, and he deleted all the voice mails from Cam and Hilly without listening. But he did read the most recent text from Cam.

I hope you know what you're doing, because your client—you know, the guy paying us—isn't too thrilled.

So Zach would tell Daisy to contact her brother. Except, Texas Ranger or not, couldn't the leak just as easily be on his side?

Better to play this out as secretly as possible even if it meant everyone was angry with him. He'd suffer some ire to keep Daisy as safe as possible, and the best way to keep her safe was to test every possible leak in isolation.

So he didn't respond to Cam's text and went ahead and turned his phone back off. He needed to outline a plan for tomorrow.

He'd just close his eyes for a second, recalibrate the plan in his head, then formalize his hazy plan into something more specific. More…something.

The next thing he knew, someone was taking his hand. "Come on, sleeping beauty," an amused voice said.

He couldn't manage to open his eyes, but he was being pulled to his feet. Everything seemed kind of dim and ethereal. It was probably a dream.

Yes, he was dreaming Daisy was taking him somewhere, nudging him onto a bed, slipping the shoes off his feet.

He really was dreaming that after a while she curled up next to him, rested her hand on his heart and brushed a kiss across his cheek.

And since it was a dream, he let himself relax into it. Place his hand over hers, pull her curled-up body closer to his and settle into sleep.

Chapter 11

Daisy wasn't sure what had compelled her to climb into bed next to Zach. He wouldn't appreciate it when he woke up. But she felt safer here, nuzzled against him, than anywhere else.

Talking to Stacy had been an exercise in torture. Daisy had wanted to tell her friend what was really going on, but all she'd been able to do was vaguely apologize for disappearing and ask for a private meeting, trying to evade Stacy's questions.

Daisy had read into every pause, every question. Was Stacy the one who wished her harm? Would this meeting end up being dangerous?

She swallowed against the lump in her throat and focused on Zach. The room was dark, but the glow from a bedside alarm clock was enough to illuminate his profile. His big hand over hers.

She felt safe with Zach. Not just the whole "in danger with a security expert and former FBI watching out for her" thing, but she felt…emotionally safe with him. Which was weird. She didn't even feel that with Vaughn or Mom. She felt she had to be careful around them, because she'd followed Dad's footsteps and they hadn't approved—even if they loved her, they didn't *understand* her.

She wasn't certain Zach did, but so far it sure felt that way.

And are you really stupid enough to think Zach is different than all the other men who've let you down?

Except she'd watched Vaughn fall in love with Nat, the way it had changed him, opened him up. Because good men existed. She just hadn't known very many. Could she really trust her own judgment that Zach was one?

Except here she was, curled up next to him, with none of those doubts that had plagued her with Jordan. She didn't doubt Zach. He didn't make her doubt.

She let that thought lull her to sleep. She awoke to the jerk of his body, and male cursing. She smiled before she opened her eyes.

"I fell asleep?" Zach demanded, practically leaping out of bed. Outrage and sleep roughened his voice. She tried to press her lips together so she didn't smile, but she failed.

"Yeah, you were kind of dead on your feet, cowboy," she offered, stretching lazily out across the bed. "I tried to wake you up, but the best I could do was half drag you to bed. I didn't take advantage, though."

He gave her a sidelong look. Then he scrubbed his hands over his face and through his hair. Her fingers itched to do the same to him, but she knew Zach would want to right himself and get to work.

And quite frankly her heart felt a little soft, waking up next to him—even with the jolting wake-up. She wanted to wake up next to someone, which was not a new dream or fantasy, but it was certainly even more compelling with Zach as that someone.

"The meeting with Stacy is at eleven."

"Eleven?" He swore again. "That only gives us about two hours to plan."

"Why don't you take a shower, and I'll make coffee. Then we can plan." She didn't wait for him to agree before she slid out of bed and started heading for the door. She needed…coffee. A little coffee would steady the fluttering feeling in her chest.

But Zach stopped her on her way out of the room— a hand to her shoulder—and the flutters only intensified. He stared at her for the longest time, his big, warm hand resting on her shoulder.

"Whoever is behind this is to blame for all of this, no matter how much you trusted them. You can worry about a lot of things, but I don't want you worrying that you should have seen through someone."

Was that the fear inside her? Maybe. Whether it was Jordan or Stacy, part of her didn't want to know because then it would mean she was wrong.

At least she already knew she'd been wrong about Jordan. Maybe she'd root for him to be the person who wanted to hurt her. Except… She'd still feel stupid. Stupid and guilty that Tom's life was lost over something so…

Zach pushed a strand of hair behind her ear, sending a shiver of delight down her spine. Easing some of that band around her lungs. "We're going to figure this out, and then you're going to go back to your life. I promise you that." He smiled, a small smile meant to reassure. "And now that I've actually slept, no one's about to stop me. Trust that."

"I do," she whispered with far too much emotion. More than the situation warranted. But he made her feel all of these things she'd yearned to feel her whole life. Only music had ever soothed her this way. Only music had ever given her a sense she deserved anything good.

Here was Zach. Good, through and through, standing there close enough to lean in to. To kiss. To believe in.

She cleared her throat and took a step away. It was one thing to kiss him when she was trying to get under his skin, or forget about all the things wrong with her life right now. It was another thing to kiss him when she felt this…vulnerable.

She turned and walked carefully to the kitchen. She poked around until she found the coffee. It was percolating when Zach came out of the room they'd slept in, showered and dressed. He'd shaved, and the ends of his hair glistened.

It wasn't just lust that slammed through her. It was something so much bigger than that. Which kept her from acting on the lust.

She cleared her throat and placed a full mug on the table. "Here. I already put way too much sugar in it."

"Thanks." He placed his laptop on the table, slid into the seat, drank a careful sip. "Perfect."

And this was far, far too domestic for her poor heart right now. "So what's the plan?" she asked, sliding into her own chair. She was in danger. *That* was a far more important, and in weird, emotional ways, safer, topic.

"We'll go into the meeting together. You can introduce me as your bodyguard. No names, that way we don't have to remember a fake one. You'll say you're worried about your safety, but you really think your reputation needs a few shows to prove you're not in rehab."

"Like I said before, that'd go through my booking agent."

"Right. We'll stick with a version of the truth. You don't trust anyone else right now. You want to work everything out through her. Maybe it's not her normal job, but she could do it with extenuating circumstances."

"I guess so."

"As casually as you can, mention how you're heading home tonight."

"I don't have a home," she returned, too soft to make a joke out of it.

But Zach didn't even blink. "Who knows that?"

"What do you mean?" she asked, trying to drink enough coffee to chase away her dogged exhaustion.

"I mean, who of our suspects would say you don't have a home? Would Jordan?"

"He'd probably say Nashville. Home is where the career is, after all."

"And Stacy?"

"She'd probably say Texas, since my brother is there and she knows how much he and his family mean to me."

"Okay, there's a flight to Austin at ten. So you mention you're heading home tonight. If Stacy or someone on her staff heads to Texas, we know it's her. If Jordan starts poking around Nashville, we have reason to suspect him."

"How will you know all that stuff?"

Zach shrugged, tapping away at his computer. "It's not a perfect plan, but I've got eyes and I've got ears." He took another sip of his coffee then looked over the table at her. "All you have to do is talk to her like you normally would."

"But I don't feel normal. The phone was bad enough. In person?"

"In person, I'll be there. I can talk for you if need be. Just pretend to be overwrought."

"I'm never overwrought," she replied, but she kind of wished she could be. Wished she could hand it all over to Zach and let him take care of it. But no matter what he'd said about it not being her fault, this was her doing. Some choice in her life had made this happen.

She had to stand on her own two feet to fight it.

Zach knew Daisy was nervous. It radiated off her as they slid out of the rental car, three blocks away from Stacy's office building.

Still, Daisy had that chin-in-the-air determination pushing her forward, and she didn't hesitate to walk with him. She didn't let those nerves overcome her.

Zach scanned the sidewalks, the buildings, the people who walked in front of them, as they zigzagged their way to the office building. He kept close to Daisy, hand always ready to grab his concealed weapon if need be.

But he didn't see or sense a tail. He'd expected to. It was a relief, though, and sadly not just for Daisy's safety. If he could scratch her manager off the suspect list he knew it would take a weight off her shoulders.

Zach opened the front door to the office building and gestured Daisy inside. For the remainder of the time he didn't walk by her side, but at her back, as most bodyguards would.

They rode the elevator in silence and walked down another hall without a word. Daisy's demeanor changed from vibrating nerves to cool determination, and that struck him as sadder somehow. How hard she was trying.

He noted every name on every door or sign, would write them all down after. Investigate any possible connections. Even though he shouldn't hope for any particular outcome because it would cloud his judgment, he hoped he could prove Stacy had nothing to do with anything.

As they entered the office labeled *Starshine Management*, a young woman behind a big desk immediately jumped to her feet with a bright smile. "Ms. Delaney! It's been so long."

"Hi, Cory. I've got a meeting with Stacy."

"Of course. Of course. Oh, my gosh, though, Ms. Delaney. I have to tell you, 'Put a Hex on My Ex' is getting me through a really tough breakup. I swear. I don't know what I'd do without your music."

Daisy smiled tightly. "You'd muscle through, but isn't it great we can have music to ease our hurts?"

"That's *exactly* right. I'll get Ms. Vine now." She grinned and bopped down the hallway before disappearing into an office with the blinds of the big glass front windows closed.

Daisy's expression melted into sadness. Worry.

"I'm not familiar with 'Put a Hex on My Ex.'"

Daisy's mouth quirked as he'd hoped it might. "Not many people are. It was on my first album after I stepped away from my dad's label and people didn't quite jump on the bandwagon right away. Not my most popular hour, though I love that song. Even more now."

He'd meant to change the subject, but it brought up an interesting point he'd overlooked. "Did you write your own music with your dad's record label?"

Daisy rubbed a hand to her temple and closed her

eyes. "A few songs, I guess. Though I had cowriters with all of them, I think."

It was an angle he hadn't looked into enough—that someone who might want to hurt her might have a connection not just to her, but to her father. "Did Stacy have any connection to your dad's label?"

"Yes. She was an assistant. I convinced her to leave and take me on as her first client."

Could that be the connection? But he didn't have time to press her for more details because a woman who didn't appear much older than Daisy stepped out with the perky secretary.

"Daisy! *God.* I've been worried sick." She engulfed Daisy in a hard hug before giving Zach a lifted eyebrow perusal.

"This is my bodyguard," Daisy said with a dismissive wave. "You know how my brother worries."

Stacy slipped her arm around Daisy's waist and started leading her down the hall. "Well, as he should. I'm so sorry this is happening to you, Daisy. What can I do?"

"I was hoping you'd ask that."

They were led back to Stacy's office, big and spacious, with a large window letting in a lot of light. Stacy didn't settle in behind the giant desk, instead taking an armchair that faced the one Daisy slid into.

They opened with small talk about mutual acquaintances, and Zach didn't notice anything odd about Stacy's demeanor. She acted like a friend, a concerned one, and a businesswoman invested in her client's career.

Daisy, to her credit, seemed perfectly relaxed, but there was just *something* about the way she held her purse in her lap that kept him from believing the act.

Daisy went through everything he'd tasked her with

bringing up. The potential of a small, intimate concert with lots of security to promote her next single, the fact she was going to go home to relax for a few days. Asking Stacy to keep that last part secret.

"Daisy. Are you sure everything is okay? You don't seem like yourself."

"Would you seem like yourself if you'd found your bodyguard dead?"

Stacy winced. "I'm sorry. I'm just worried." Stacy gave Zach a cursory glance. "Not just for your safety, but for *you*. Are you sure you want to do any kind of performance with this going on? We can't exactly background check fans. I know you want to promote the album, but—"

"Wait. Why do you assume the person who killed Tom is a fan?" Daisy asked, and there was dismay clear as a bell in her voice.

Stacy blinked, all wide-eyed innocence Zach didn't know whether or not to believe. "Who else would it be?"

A loud siren interrupted the conversation, making all three of them jump at the jarring blast of sound.

Stacy frowned, glancing around the office. "What terrible timing for a fire drill," she called over the blaring noise.

Stacy looked uneasy, Daisy even more so. As for Zach himself, he didn't trust the timing at all.

"We should evacuate," he offered, holding out his hand for Daisy to take. "What route would you normally take for a fire drill?"

Stacy shrugged helplessly, getting to her feet. "I... I don't remember. The stairs, obviously. Outside the doors. Then out the front? Or is it the back? Cory would know."

Zach nodded grimly, keeping his grasp on Daisy firm as he led her to the door.

Cory was standing in the middle of the office's waiting area, a bunch of things in her hands. She glanced back at them, worry and confusion replacing her previously cheerful expression. "I don't know what to grab and what to leave and—"

"I'm sure it's just a drill…" But Stacy's words trailed off as Cory pointed to the hallway outside the glass doors of the office. Smoke snaked across the floor.

"Come on," Zach ordered, pulling Daisy for the door. "Keep low. Evacuate the building in the most efficient way possible."

"Someone should call 911," Cory said, her voice trembling as Zach opened the door and pointed Stacy and Cory out, keeping Daisy next to him.

"We'll call when we're out. The most important thing is getting outside right now."

Stacy and Cory seemed totally helpless in the hallway, staring at each other as smoke continued to snake around them.

"Follow us. Form a chain," Zach ordered, keeping Daisy's hand in his as he led them toward the staircase he remembered seeing.

The stairs were worse when it came to the smoke, but there was no heat—no flame that he could see. There weren't sprinklers going off, and Zach had a bad feeling it wasn't a fire so much as a distraction. Or a diversion.

Once they made it down the stairs, the lobby was filled with even more smoke, thick and acrid.

Daisy was tugging against his grip. He looked over his shoulder, but the smoke was thick enough he could only barely make her form out behind him. He didn't want to speak, trying to avoid inhaling as much as possible. But she kept pulling, harder and jerkier.

He nearly lost his grip on her, squeezing it tighter at the last moment and giving her a jerk toward him. "Stay with me," he ordered, and began pulling her through the smoke.

"Wait," she croaked.

But they were wading through smoke in a dangerous situation and he would most assuredly not wait.

He got them out of the building, milling crowds pushing at them the minute they stepped outside. Still, he kept pulling her, weaving through the crowd and away from the building.

"Zach! I lost my hold on Stacy. We have to go back," Daisy said desperately, her voice raspy from smoke.

Zach didn't stop moving or pulling her along. "They're fine. I don't think it's a fire. Now, what the hell was that stunt? Pulling on me that way? If I'd lost my grip on you—" He glanced back when she hacked out a cough.

Tears were streaming down her face, and his heart twisted painfully in his chest at her misery.

"It was Stacy," she offered weakly. "She kept grabbing and pulling at me in the opposite direction. I think she knew a better way out."

Zach nearly stopped cold, but the smoke and chaos reminded him to keep moving—with Daisy firmly in his grasp. "She did what now?" he demanded. It was easier to move faster out here where there was less of a crowd, so he hurried.

"I'm sure it was an accident. She was panicking and thought we needed to go in the other direction. But when you pulled on me, she lost her grip. She and Cory went out the back way, I think."

Zach shook his head, pulling her toward where they'd

parked the car blocks away. He wanted to protect her from the truth, but he couldn't. It wasn't his job. "That doesn't look good for Stacy, Daisy. That wasn't a fire. It was smoke bombs, or something similar. Someone was trying to create a diversion. Someone knew you were coming and wanted to get to you, and it looks like Stacy was trying to help someone do just that."

Chapter 12

Daisy didn't talk on the drive home. The pretty little farmhouse didn't cheer her up at all. She went straight to the bathroom and got into a steaming-hot shower and cried herself empty.

She'd trusted Stacy with her *life*. Everything Daisy had built for herself had been done with Stacy at her side.

She wanted to believe it was panic that had made Stacy try to pull her in the opposite direction of Zach. Maybe there was some explanation, but they hadn't stuck around to get it. Maybe she could still believe Stacy only *looked* guilty accidentally. Nothing was proven. Nothing was sure.

Except Zach, who was most definitely sure Stacy was involved.

Daisy half wished someone would just *do* something to her. At least it would be over then.

But that thought made her feel sick to her stomach.

She didn't want to be harmed or worse, even if it ended this waiting game. Upset and alive was better than at peace and dead.

She got dressed in comfortable pajamas even though it was only late afternoon. Part of her wanted to sleep until this whole thing was over. It wasn't possible, but maybe for tonight while she came to grips with how bad this looked for Stacy's connection to everything.

She stepped out of the bathroom, tempted to head into the room she'd put her stuff in yesterday. Which was not the room she'd spent the night in with Zach.

Zach. She couldn't shut him out even though she wanted to. He was trying to keep her safe, determined to. It wasn't his fault she apparently had terrible judgment when it came to people. It wasn't his fault the people she thought were trustworthy and honest were potentially wishing her harm.

So she forced herself to walk back out to the pretty little living room. It reminded her of something out of *Little House on the Prairie*, but there was a sheen of cleanliness and chicness to it. It was its own little fantasy world, and boy, could she use a fantasy world.

Complete with hot protector guy standing in the kitchen cooking. No doubt making her dinner. No doubt he'd watch like a hawk to make sure she ate.

When he turned to glance at her, there was sympathy there. It made her throat close up all over again. She didn't want to cry in front of him, though, much as she knew he'd comfort her and be perfectly sweet about it.

She wanted to be strong, not to prove something to him, but to herself. That a fleeting thought about wishing someone would just end things didn't mean she particularly wanted to be ended.

"So that was more eventful than I thought it would

be." She settled herself onto a stool at the counter that separated the kitchen from the dining area.

"That it was. I know it's hard for you to think Stacy could be a part of this, but we have to accept that possibility."

Daisy nodded, spinning her phone in a little circle on the counter. "Yeah. I get that."

"If it helps, I don't think she's acting alone. The hired muscle back in Wyoming, smoke bombs. She doesn't strike me as someone who could run a demanding business and plan all this. I think she might be a pawn."

"Oh, gee, more people out to get me."

"She might be an unwitting one."

"Whatever she is, she's connected." Even saying the words made Daisy's stomach twist. She kept thinking she'd accepted it, and if she accepted it she could move forward.

Except she couldn't accept it. Even when Zach was calm and reasonable.

"All evidence points to yes." Zach drained pasta in the sink with a deft hand.

"Where'd you learn to cook?" she asked, wanting to talk about anything other than Stacy.

"My mother. She believed in raising boys who could take care of themselves." Something on his face changed.

"Boys. You have brothers?"

"A brother."

"You've only mentioned Hilly and your murdered father. I didn't know there was a brother."

He shrugged. "Did you want my life history?"

Because the honest question hurt her more than it should, she smiled sharply at him. "Well, we did sleep together, sugar."

His mouth quirked as if he almost found her funny. "Uh-huh. Well, I have a brother."

"Is he Mr. Protector guy, too? Or are you more like me and my brother?"

"What's you and your brother?"

"Opposites, through and through."

"But you love him."

"Of course I do. Vaughn was one of the very few uncomplicated relationships in my life. Well, mostly uncomplicated. I always knew he didn't really approve of me, but he supported me anyway." She hadn't always appreciated that support the way she should have, and she'd never thanked him for it.

Although he'd be horrified by a display of emotion, even if it was gratitude. The thought made her smile a little bit. But she realized, as Zach placed a bowl full of spaghetti in front of her, he'd very efficiently avoided the question.

"So what does your brother do?"

"He's done a lot of things."

She raised an eyebrow. "You know, when someone touches a sore subject with me I tell them to jump off a cliff."

"And I doubt it dims their curiosity regarding the sore subject," Zach replied.

"Avoiding the question doesn't dim my curiosity."

"Ethan's in a psych ward. He, in fact, nearly murdered Cam."

"Cam, your business partner, Cam? The man marrying your sister?"

"The very same."

He really, *really* never failed to surprise her. She might have thought him cold at the way he delivered that so emotionlessly, but his eyes didn't lie as well as the rest of him. The less sympathy she offered, though, the more he seemed to reveal to her. "Well. I can see why it's a sore subject."

"Dad's murder hit him particularly hard. He tried his hand at a lot of things, but the unsolved case was an obsession, one that became unhealthy and dangerous. I love my brother, even knowing his... I hesitate to call them faults. He's mentally ill. He's... Well, my attempts to protect him, to care for him, not only put the entire undercover FBI investigation I was a part of in jeopardy, but nearly got Cam killed, too. You learn from experiences like that. And, in my case, you get kicked out of the FBI."

"Which is why you shouldn't get emotionally involved," she said, remembering how seriously he'd asked her if she wanted to die after she'd kissed him that first time.

He tapped his nose, then focused on eating.

"It isn't the same," she said softly.

He raised an eyebrow, and somehow she'd known he'd give her that condescending look he thought hid all the turmoil inside him. Maybe he managed to hide it from other people, but not from her.

"You knew your brother had issues, and you kept protecting him until you didn't have a choice. That isn't the same as feeling something for me. Emotion didn't cause those mistakes. Underestimating your brother's illness and your power over it would have been the issue. It doesn't mean you'll make the same mistakes with me."

"Who says I won't?"

She blinked at that, more than a little irritated when her phone trilled. Downright furious when it was Jordan's number calling her.

"Why can't that bastard leave well enough alone?" she grumbled, reaching for the phone to hit Ignore.

"Take it," Zach said in that leader-ordering-a-sub-ordinate tone that would have angered her more if she wasn't so confused.

"Huh?"

"Take it. See what he wants. On speaker."

She didn't want to talk to Jordan, not when she was getting somewhere with Zach. Not when today was already in the toilet. But she did as Zach ordered her to do because she didn't know what else to do in the moment besides stomp her feet and throw a tantrum like a child.

"Jordan," she greeted as coolly as she could muster.

"Daisy. Thank God you're all right."

Fear snaked through her. While Zach had told her the smoke bombs at Stacy's office had made the news, people had been distracted enough not to notice she'd been in the building. So far. "Why wouldn't I be all right?" she asked, trying to keep her voice devoid of emotion.

"The attack on Stacy's office! They're claiming it was an innocent prank, but this is all too close for comfort. I'm worried about you, Daisy. What kind of trouble have you been getting yourself into?"

She glanced up at Zach, who had that icy law-enforcement scowl on his face. But again, in his eyes she could see the truth. Heat and fury.

"You know I'm in town?" she asked carefully.

"I keep tabs, Daisy. I've told you that before." He sounded so disdainful she wanted to punch him. "I have to know if you're going to show up and make one of your scenes."

"But you said you thought I was in rehab."

"No, I said that's what people were saying, and that I hoped you were getting help. You need help."

And you need a knee to the balls.

"We need to talk, Daisy. In private. No staff. No bodyguards. I have some important news for you and

I need to make sure you're going to handle it the correct way."

She opened her mouth to say she'd show him the correct way to handle something, but Zach reached across the counter and tapped her hand. He scribbled something onto a piece of paper then angled it toward her.

Take the meeting.

She jerked the pen from his hand and wrote her own note back.

Without you?

"Daisy? Listen. Meet me at our old lunch place. What do you say, eight o'clock before your flight?"

Daisy stared at Zach, who nodded emphatically. She let out a sigh. "Fine, Jordan. I'll be there at eight. Goodbye." She hit End on the call before he could say any more.

"Stacy had to have told him you were here. She's the only one who knew about that flight," Zach said, scribbling more things onto a new piece of paper. "There has to be a connection there."

"Between Stacy and Jordan? They didn't like each other. Trust me. Cory could have told him, too."

"Cory didn't know about your flight unless she was eavesdropping. Besides, Jordan and Stacy disliking each other isn't valid enough to disregard the potential connection. Because it doesn't have to be a connection of friendship, does it? The enemy of my enemy is my friend and all that—and before you say anything, I know Stacy isn't your enemy, but sometimes people harbor resentments we don't know about. You said she was at your father's label with you."

"No, she was my father's manager's assistant. We used to sit around and complain about what a smarmy old codger he was, so when I finally got the guts to go out on my own, I asked if she wanted to come with. We'd been friends, dreaming about futures where we didn't have to answer to anyone. Might have been tough work those first few years, but I'm pretty sure Stacy has been amply rewarded."

Zach paced. "None of this adds up," he muttered. "We're missing something." He tilted his head, clearly working something out in that overactive brain of his. "Or someone. What about someone who would know both Jordan and Stacy separately. Someone who who knows you well enough to use them both against you? Who in your life would know both Jordan and Stacy enough to understand their relationship to you?"

"My agent. Jordan's staff—his manager, his assistant—basically anyone on his payroll who would have worked with Stacy during one of our joint ventures before the divorce."

"I looked into Jordan's staff before, but we'll go through them again. See if we can find a specific connection to Stacy. And then triangulate it to your father."

"And while you're doing all that?"

"You better get ready. Because you're going to have to hide some of your fury toward Jordan. Just long enough to get us through this meeting and get what we want out of it."

The patterns didn't add up, but Zach was beginning to think he'd been looking at them all wrong. There were a lot of players, but no clear leader. No clear link.

If he could find the link, the pattern would fall into place.

Daisy didn't think anyone would have something against her writing her own songs, but Zach had to believe it was industry related. Jordan, the rising star.

Stacy, the star's manager—who came from her father's record label.

"What about this manager? The one Stacy worked for."

"What about him?" Daisy asked, staring out the window as Zach drove through drizzly downtown traffic to the restaurant Jordan had picked out.

"Could he have been angry at you for stealing Stacy away?"

Daisy snorted. "He didn't care about Stacy. He cared about power."

"What does that mean?"

"Look, he'd be like…eighty now. I doubt he overpowered Tom and killed him. I doubt he'd have the wherewithal to follow me around the country."

"*He* isn't. Whoever is behind this is sending people, Daisy. What would this guy be angry about?" He didn't add *and why the hell didn't you tell me*, which he considered a great feat of control.

Daisy shifted in her seat. "Nothing. He got away with it all. There'd be nothing to be angry about."

"Got away with what exactly?"

She sighed heavily. "He just said some kind of inappropriate things and I told my dad about it. But it's not like… There was nothing to be angry about. Nothing happened to him."

Zach parked in the lot in front of the restaurant, then looked over at her. "*Said* some inappropriate things, or *did* some inappropriate things?"

She waved a hand and pushed the passenger door open. "Doesn't matter."

"It *does* matter," he insisted, but she got out of the car and started walking toward the door—which was not the plan they'd agreed on. He hopped out of the car, stopping her forward progress. "Follow the plan, Daisy. And tell me about it."

"It doesn't *matter*. Trust me. Nothing bad ever happened to him. If he's angry with me, it's not enough to want me hurt. Why would he be angry? He's old and rich and retired, I believe. Hell, he might even be dead. Whatever he is—he's fine, and not out to get me."

"Name."

"Oh, for God's sake, Zach. Can't you trust me?"

"I trust you implicitly. I don't trust anyone who would say or *do* inappropriate things to you when you were a teenager."

They couldn't keep having this conversation in public, even with her big sunglasses and baggy clothes.

"He grabbed me. I told him no. He grabbed me again. I said I was going to go tell my dad. He laughed and said Dad wouldn't do anything. And guess what? He was right. *Oh, Don's just old guard, Daisy girl. Don't be alone with him.* Problem solved, right?"

"The hell it is."

She shook her head, wrapping her arms around herself. "It was forever ago. It's ancient history."

It wasn't. He could tell it wasn't, but she didn't want to discuss it and here wasn't the place. "What about Stacy?"

"What *about* Stacy?"

"Did he assault Stacy, too?"

"He didn't *assault* me, Zach."

"Grabbing is assault, Daisy," he returned forcefully. But he softened because even for all the difficult situations he'd been in, he'd never had to mine through his past. Never had to wonder who was against him. He placed his hands on her shoulders. "I know it hurts. I can't imagine how much it hurts to wonder about everyone you trust, or everyone you don't want to have to think about. I wish there was some other way, but we're missing a link and the sooner I can find it, the sooner whoever is torturing you can be brought to justice."

"I just want this to be over. I'm not even sure I care about justice," she said, looking teary.

He let her lean into him. Rubbed his hand up and down her back. "I know. I know. One link. I just need one link and then I can connect it all. I can make it over for you. Let me follow this lead. A name, and all you have to do is—"

She lifted her head off his shoulder, and nodded behind him. "Have dinner with my ex-husband?"

Zach didn't turn. Instead, he kept his arm around Daisy, kept looking down at her. "We're going to play this a little differently than we planned."

"Oh, really?"

He dropped his head and brushed his mouth against hers, inappropriately enjoying that for once he'd been the one to surprise her with a kiss. "Not your bodyguard this time."

Her mouth quirked up. "Well, this should be interesting."

He slid his arm around her waist and turned to face Jordan Jones, who did *not* look happy to see them.

Zach grinned. "Indeed it will."

Chapter 13

Daisy's whole life, she'd prided herself on standing on her own two feet. Even when her father had been taking her from show to show as a little girl, she'd understood that it was necessary to prove a certain amount of independence so she didn't turn into her father's toy or trophy. If she hadn't inherently understood that, her mother had made sure to remind her.

Daisy had wanted to be a singer, and she'd become one. On her own terms. But there had been things that had undermined that independence, that certainty. Her father ignoring the fact his manager had—as much as she hated it, she'd use Zach's word— *assaulted* her. Jordan being…well, self-serving, she supposed.

Could she hate him for that?

"I thought we were going to have dinner, Daisy. I don't appreciate—" he trailed off, looking Zach up and down "—whatever stunt this is."

Turned out, she could hate Jordan for a lot of things. "No stunt. My boyfriend refused to let me out of his sight with everything going on." She patted Zach's chest. "He's very concerned about my well-being."

Jordan sighed, all long-suffering martyrdom. "If that's supposed to be a dig against me, perhaps I should apologize for treating you like an independent woman?"

Perhaps you should apologize for being an emotionally abusive jerk wad. But she smiled sweetly. "Jordan Jones, this is my boyfriend..." She tried to come up with a fake name, but Zach intervened.

"Zach Simmons," he offered, holding out a hand for Jordan to shake. "I'm in law enforcement, so I understand just how dangerous this threat against Lucy is. Her going anywhere alone wasn't a great idea. I'm sure you understand her safety is paramount."

It...warmed her somehow that he was using her real name, and his. Jordan probably wouldn't notice or care, but it was...a gesture.

"Well." Jordan straightened his shoulders. "Of course. That's what I wanted to talk to Daisy about. Her safety."

"Great!" Zach said so genially Daisy wanted to laugh. "Let's head in." Zach kept his arm around her waist as he led them inside and told the hostess they had three in their party.

It was something to watch, how easily he could switch into someone else. A role. She understood that a little. After all, there was a certain amount of *role* she stepped into when she got on stage. Daisy Delaney was parts of Lucy Cooper carefully arranged into a different package.

But she'd really never expected too many other people to understand that. It had been part of the attraction of Jordan—that he understood the complications of being someone else at the same time you were yourself.

But she supposed there were all kinds of ways people put on masks every day, not just to go on stage.

The hostess led them to a dimly lit booth and Daisy had to fight the need to laugh hysterically. She was sitting in a restaurant with her ex-husband and her security expert slash fake boyfriend slash man she really wouldn't mind seeing naked.

While apparently, said man suspected both her manager and her ex-husband of stalking and murder.

Zach draped his arm over her shoulders easily, chatted with Jordan about the music industry. Daisy could hardly pay attention to Jordan's pretentious rambling about his career. Had she really been this *fooled*?

But she had been. Fooled or desperate or something. It made her feel sick and ashamed she hadn't seen through him—but he hadn't talked about himself back then. He'd talked about her. Flattered her—in just the ways she'd been desperate to be flattered.

A strange thought hit her sideways as Jordan nattered on. Could he have been coached? Told what would hit all her vulnerabilities, and then used them against her?

Oh, that was insane. Whatever was happening to her hadn't been going on for *years*. Her failed marriage was hardly some kind of convoluted plot to…hurt her or whatever. She was getting paranoid. Insane maybe.

"Which brings me to why I called," Jordan was saying, his gaze moving from Zach to Daisy. Pretty blue eyes the color of summer skies. She'd thought she'd seen love in them once, and she didn't know if she was just that delusional or if he had actually felt something for her and it had disappeared.

It made her unbearably sad. And then Jordan continued.

"The rumor *was* you'd disappeared to go into rehab,

and it got me thinking how great it would be if you just did that."

"What?" she replied, because surely he didn't mean what she *thought* he meant.

"You might want to work on your comedy, buddy. Because that isn't funny," Zach said, steel laced through his fake genial tone.

"Can I get y'all something to drink?" a perky waitress asked, clearly not reading the mood of the table.

They all ordered robotically, except Jordan, who smiled and flirted when the waitress recognized him and expressed her undying love for his music.

If she recognized Daisy, she didn't mention it.

When she disappeared to get the drinks, Jordan looked at them both with that patented *Jordan Jones* smile. It was charming, and he was handsome. She wanted to punch him in the nose, but Zach's arm around her shoulders had tightened as if keeping her seated.

"It seems to me a rehab facility would be safer than going around disappearing with—" he looked at Zach "—boyfriends. Especially the way your last one ended up."

"Tom was my bodyguard and he died trying to protect me, you inconsiderate—"

Jordan held up his hands, looking at Zach with a sigh as if to say, *What do you do with a problem like Daisy?* "I'm only suggesting a safe place for you, Daisy."

"You want me to fake going into rehab so I can be *safe*?"

The waitress put glasses in front of them, and this time she gave Daisy a much longer look. Though she was smart enough not to say anything.

Jordan sipped from his glass. "I mean, you could actually go."

"I'm not an alcoholic, Jordan. Contrary to your staff's attempts to make me out to be."

"Of course. Of course." He opened his mouth to speak, but the phone he held in his hand trilled. He glanced at the screen, a slight frown pulling at the corner of his lips. "I have to take this," he said, sliding out of the booth. "If you'll excuse me." He moved away from the table and Daisy couldn't hear what he was saying.

"I can't believe you married this joker," Zach muttered when Jordan was out of earshot.

"*That* is not the joker I married." No, Jordan knew how to slip into a role, too. Was she forever falling for men who acted one way, then turned out to be another? "You know a little bit about pretending to be someone else to get what you want, don't you?"

He looked at her, something like sympathy in his gaze that made her want to punch him, too. Or lean into his chest. She really wasn't sure.

He reached out and pushed a stray strand of hair behind her ear. "All I want right now is to keep you safe."

Which softened her up considerably.

"Which means I'm going to get my hands on his phone."

"Huh?"

"I don't trust this rehab thing."

"He's just trying to make me look bad, Zach. Ever since I asked for a divorce, that's his number one goal. Because if he can make *me* look bad, he can make himself look better."

"Maybe. Maybe that's all it is, but he doesn't strike me as particularly smart. Manipulative, yes. A good actor? Sure. But someone is pulling his strings, Daisy. I'm going to find out who."

"It's got to be someone on his staff."

"I agree. His manager, maybe? Was there anyone he was particularly…deferential to?"

Daisy tried to think back over her time with Jordan. "I think he's been through something like three managers. He used to talk about some uncle who was in the industry, but I never met him. If he mentioned him by name, I don't remember him."

"I need his phone. So when I give you the signal, you're going to spill your drink on him. I'm going to palm his phone and head off to the bathroom to wash up."

"You're going to palm his phone? How?"

"Trust me." He smiled, tapping her nose. "If you do, maybe I'll teach you a few things about going undercover."

It amused her, even though all she really wanted was to have her life back. "You better be quick, though. His phone is like an arm. He'll notice it's missing."

"You just spill his drink. I'll handle the rest."

She did so, and beautifully. Perhaps with a little too much enjoyment as the dark soda splashed across Jordan's white shirt, but hell, Zach enjoyed Jordan's outrage a little too much himself.

Zach immediately jumped to his feet, calling for the waitress and shoving napkins at Jordan. It gave him ample time to slip the phone out of the sticky soda and pretend like he was going to run to the bathroom for more paper towels even though the waitress was hurrying over with a rag.

Zach moved quickly to the bathroom, locked himself into a stall and went to work on Jordan's phone.

Zach didn't have time to try and figure out Jordan's passcode, so he used a quick hack to bypass the code and get into Jordan's home screen.

He pulled up the contacts list. The first fishy thing was the lack of names. Everyone was labeled with letters and numbers rather than anything that helped Zach identify who they were. Pretty confusing for a guy who had tons of contacts in his phone.

And pretty damn suspicious. Zach pulled up the recent calls. With his own phone, Zach took a picture of the screen. Of the eight calls on top, two were repeated three times each. It might be nothing. It might mean everything. Now that he had the numbers, he'd go from there.

Text messages didn't reveal anything of importance, and his apps were as run of the mill as any. Zach didn't have time to dig further. Hopefully, the phone numbers would be something to go on.

He stepped out of the stall, wiped off the phone with a paper towel and turned it off, ready to head back to the table. If Jordan had noticed his phone missing, Zach would just explain he'd gone to wipe it down and Jordan would be none the wiser.

But when he stepped back into the restaurant, the few patrons had their noses and phones pressed to every available window, and Daisy stood next to an empty table, hand to her mouth.

"What's going on?"

She gestured faintly at the window, but there were so many people crowded around it he couldn't see anything.

"The cops came and arrested him." Daisy looked up at him, searching for some kind of answer, but he was as confused as she was.

"The cops came in and arrested Jordan?"

She nodded. "A-at first it was just… They asked if they could speak with him outside. He looked so confused, but wholly unconcerned. I think he even thought maybe they were going to ask for his autograph or something, but instead… I looked out the window and he was being handcuffed. *Handcuffed.* Zach, it doesn't make any sense, and it's already being uploaded onto the internet in three million ways."

Zach looked down at the phone in his hand. "I guess I should give the cops his phone."

"Did you find anything?"

"I took some pictures of his recent call numbers, but if he's being arrested for something, the police should have it." He led Daisy outside through the small crowds of people, pushing his way through to the female cop holding the curious onlookers as far back as she could.

"Excuse me, Officer? I have Jordan Jones's phone right here."

The officer looked at him with a raised eyebrow as he held out the phone, but she didn't say anything.

"We had a little drink spill," Zach explained. "I cleaned off his phone for him. But figured you might want it."

"And you are?" the cop asked with no small amount of distrust.

Zach explained who he was, and the cop managed to escort him and Daisy to a slightly private corner. Zach showed the police officer all his identification and permits to prove he was Daisy's security, and gave an account of the drink spill.

The cop took and bagged the phone. "I imagine our detectives will be in contact with you, Ms. Delaney."

"Can you tell me what he's being arrested for?"

The cop looked at Daisy, then him. "The murder of Tom Perelli."

Daisy audibly gasped, and Zach might have, too. *Jordan* as murderer? Even though he'd suspected Jordan was involved, it was hard to believe the man he'd just had dinner with was capable of murder.

But he didn't have time to dwell on that. Some people were beginning to look at Daisy and murmur among themselves. Phones began to move from the cop car where Jordan was now loaded up, to the dim corner where he and Daisy stood.

He moved his body to shield her from the prying eyes and phones, then discussed the best way to get out of the parking lot undetected. As the cop began to instruct the crowd to leave so she could back up the patrol car, Daisy and Zach slipped around the crowd and into Zach's car.

Daisy didn't say anything as they drove back. Zach couldn't read her mood, but he couldn't concentrate on it, either. He paid attention to every car on the road with them.

Quite frankly, he expected to be followed. He expected…something. Surely, this wasn't *it*. It was too easy, too neat. Something else had to be at work here.

But in the end they made it back to the farmhouse without any tail Zach could see. Once inside, he made as many calls as he could to weasel some information out of a few overly talkative individuals.

Daisy sat on the couch, staring at nothing. During one of his calls he'd fixed her some tea. She hadn't touched it.

After he'd gotten the answers he'd wanted, or at least *some* of the answers, he sat down next to Daisy. She didn't move. Didn't say anything. He supposed she was in shock.

"The police received an anonymous tip, which allowed them to obtain a search warrant for Jordan's place. They found the gun used to kill Tom in a hidden safe in his bedroom closet."

"Anonymous tip," Daisy echoed. "Someone else knew he... He couldn't have..." She swallowed. "Zach, I don't understand. I really don't. Maybe I could believe he stalked me, or even threatened me all those months, but to kill Tom? I can't..." She shook her head. "But it's over, isn't it? If Jordan is the murderer, and he's in jail, this is over."

Zach didn't know how to tell her he didn't think it was over, that this was all too easy. And maybe it *was* over. Maybe it wasn't his gut telling him things were too neat. Maybe it was his desperate desire to be with her.

"Zach?"

She looked up at him, and in all that confusion and despair there was hope. Hope that this meant she got to go back to her real life and feel safe again. Hope that this could all be put away as some ugly part of her past.

For her, he wished he could believe it. Even if it meant their time together was up. She deserved to go back to normal, instead of living in fear.

"It's possible it's over," he said carefully, not wanting to burden her with his doubts. "Obviously, we'll want to see if they give him a bond. I'd hope not, but we want to make sure he's going to stay in jail before it's...fully over."

Daisy nodded, wringing her hands together. "I can't... I didn't know him. I thought I did. I loved the version of himself he showed me, but it wasn't him. I can't imagine him *killing* someone, but I certainly can imagine him wanting to hurt me."

She popped to her feet, began to pace. "He wanted me to go to rehab. He wanted me swept away so I wouldn't be credible. That's why he wanted to meet."

It was possible, Zach supposed. But the timing struck

him as odd, even more so with the arrest in front of Daisy. Zach had some research to do on those numbers from Jordan's phone before he fully accepted this version of events. And he'd want to read the police report and—

"What about you?"

He looked up at Daisy, his mind going over all the things he still needed to do to be *sure*. "What about me?"

"You'll have to go home, then, won't you?"

It felt like a slap, even as she watched him with wide, sad eyes. He cleared his throat. She might have kissed him a few times, he might have grown to like her quite a bit, but their odd relationship was a temporary one.

He pushed away all those conflicting emotions that were no doubt clouding his judgment about Jordan's guilt. "My job is to keep you safe. Until we're assured Jordan stays in jail, that means I'm still here."

She nodded, gave him a tremulous smile that just about cracked his heart in two. "Good." When she sat, she didn't sit next to him. Instead, she slid onto his lap, much like she had way back in Wyoming.

She cupped his face with her hands, looked right at him. "Then be with me. Really."

Chapter 14

Daisy poured everything inside her into the kiss. The pain, the uncertainty, the horrible sadness that swept through her at the idea Zach wouldn't be in her life anymore.

She wasn't sure if it was the kiss that finally broke through Zach's whole "emotions are distractions" thing—because it was one hell of a soul-searing kiss—or if it was as simple as he believed this was over.

She wished she could, but everything felt wrong and off. Maybe she couldn't believe Jordan was a murderer because it made her look like a fool, but there were all these wiggles of uncertainty inside her she couldn't quash—even with Jordan in jail.

Zach's kiss could eradicate it, and all the other painful things inside her. She could focus on pleasure and the absolute safety she found in him and leave everything else behind, even if only for a little bit.

She thought she'd have to convince him, but his arms

banded around her and his mouth devoured hers as if he hadn't rejected her attempts at this *routinely.*

He maneuvered her onto her back on the couch, sprawling himself over her so that she sank into the cushions. She reveled in that feeling of being covered completely, safe and complete somehow—like being in Zach Simmons's arms was exactly where she needed to be.

He kissed her like she was the same to him—the place *he* needed to be.

There were so many ways she'd been made to feel small and insignificant in her life by the men who were supposed to love her. Zach had never mentioned love, but he made her feel cherished and important more so than anyone else. He believed her, he trusted her, and time and time again he'd put her above his own interests.

She pulled his shirt off quickly and efficiently. She sighed reverently, tracing her fingers down his abdomen. "I've been waiting for this since I saw you shirtless that first night."

He muttered a curse and then kissed her again, a fervency and an urgency she appreciated because it seared away everything else—all those awful things in the real world out there. It was only him and her, perfectly safe.

His hands streaked under her shirt and then pulled her up into a sitting position, his body straddling hers.

"If this is a curse, I'll damn well take it," he said, his eyes bright and lethal.

"Curse?"

"Carsons, Delaneys, long story." He closed his eyes and shook his head as if he couldn't believe he'd brought it up. "I'll tell you later." Then he lifted her shirt over her head and let it fall to the ground. His mouth streaked down her neck as his hands made quick work of her bra and she forgot her questions as he kissed her everywhere.

His groan of appreciation as he tugged the button and zipper of her jeans made her feel like a goddess. "One favor. Don't call me Daisy."

He paused briefly, then met her gaze as he pulled her pants down her legs. "All right, Lucy."

It squirmed through her—somehow beautiful and uncomfortable at the same time. But she didn't want to be Daisy to him, not because she was ashamed of that part of her, but because Daisy had to keep people at arm's length from all the demands inside her—from her music, from her drive to succeed, from the chaos that sometimes existed in her head.

But if she was Lucy, just herself without the mantle of fame or curse of being a storyteller, then she could feel like she really belonged to *him*. Not something bigger than them. Just them.

Zach stopped suddenly, keeping his body ridiculously tense. "Wait. Condoms. We don't—"

She patted his cheek. "Never fear, sweetheart, condoms and booze are two things I never leave home without."

"Do I even want to know why?"

"Sometimes a girl has a rep to protect. Or destroy, as the case may be. I like to be prepared."

"Well, I won't look a gift bad girl in the mouth. Wow, that sounds wrong."

She laughed, and was surprised to find it made the moment that much more special. That she could want him and laugh with him and feel safe with him. She brushed her mouth against his as she slid off the couch. "Come to bed, Zach."

He followed her and she rummaged through her bag, in only her underwear and socks. She might have felt a little silly if Zach wasn't watching her as though he'd like to devour her from top to bottom, then bottom to top.

That made her feel powerful no matter what she had on. She found the old crumpled box of condoms, discreetly checked the expiration date and then pulled one out, holding it between her fingers. "Aren't you lucky?"

"Yes," he said reverently, so reverently her eyes actually stung. She tried to saunter over to him, keep it light—focused on the attraction and the laughter, not... not the way her heart felt squeezed so hard she could barely catch a breath.

But when she reached him, she didn't know how to keep it all together. All she could do was lean against the warmth of his chest. Try to find some strength of spirit against that strong, dependable frame.

"I don't want this part to be over. The us part," she whispered, listening to the steady beating of his heart. She'd never, ever revealed herself like that before, laid her emotions that bare.

But she'd never let herself be Lucy with anyone outside her brother and her mother, and even they still saw her as part Daisy. Why she thought Zach understood the dichotomy inside her, she wasn't sure. Maybe she was stupid—the kind of stupid who married a murderer and—

He swallowed and ran a hand over her hair. Sweet and full of care. "Lucy," he said raggedly.

She shook her head against that despair in his voice. "I know. It's impossible. And God knows I shouldn't trust my own instincts when it comes to men. Maybe you're a secret murderer, too. How would I know?"

She wanted to run away, but Zach pulled her back and took her face in his hands.

"Lucy," he repeated, quieting her. She still felt wound up and stupid, but his hands on her face were a balm.

She wanted to stay here—right here—forever. Safe with Zach, who was good, and understood her somehow. A man who cared, and not just for show. She kept trying to convince herself it was just her dumb brain fooling herself again, but looking at that steady gaze she knew. She *knew* Zach was different.

And she was head over heels in love with a man she couldn't have.

But she kissed him anyway, fell to bed with him anyway, and let the sensations overwhelm her so she didn't think about anything except pleasure. Except finding release with this man who meant everything.

This man she'd have to say goodbye to, and soon.

But he kissed her, filled her, and for sparkling minutes of ecstasy she forgot everything except them.

Zach wasn't sure he'd ever slept so soundly, or so long. He woke up feeling like a new man.

Of course, that might have been the sex.

Which really shouldn't have relaxed him considering it added quite a few complications to his nagging worry that Jordan's arrest was too easy. How could he tell the difference between what was true, and what his feelings for Lucy made him *want* to be true?

But facts were facts, right? There was evidence Jordan had done it. Why was he letting emotion sway the facts again? Didn't he know how that ended up?

He was almost grateful for the pounding on the door. If it didn't worry him. He slid out of bed as Lucy grumbled complaints.

Lucy. It was funny how easy it was to vacillate between the names. She seemed like both women to him,
but somehow it seemed more…meaningful that he'd
gone to bed with Lucy.

Possibly he was losing his mind.

He pulled on his pants and grabbed his gun that he'd
left in the nightstand. With the pounding continuing at
increasing levels, he didn't have time to strap his holster on, so he simply held it behind his back as he made
his way through the living room to the door.

He checked the security camera on his phone, but the
man on the stoop wasn't familiar. He was about Zach's
height, wearing jeans, an impeccably unwrinkled button-up shirt and a rather large cowboy hat.

Still, he was knocking. It could be information about
Jordan. Zach eased the door open, weapon at the ready.

The man's cool blue eyes took in Zach's shirtless
form and those eyes hardened.

"Can I help you?" Zach asked as he flipped the safety
off behind his back.

"Vaughn!"

Zach glanced back at Lucy, who pulled the bright
yellow robe she was wearing a little closer around her
as she stepped forward.

Zach was glad he recognized the name as her brother's or the hot burn of jealousy at the pure delight in her
tone might have had him acting stupidly and rashly.

"What are you doing here?" she asked, approaching
them. She looked like she was about to lean in to hug
her brother, but instead gripped her robe tighter. "I told
you everything was fine."

Yeah, it wouldn't exactly be rocket science to figure
out what they'd been doing together last night. And she
certainly hadn't told him she'd contacted her brother.

"I came to take you home," Vaughn said, his voice cool and detached. But the words made Zach's blood run cold even as he set the gun back down on the counter.

"You didn't have to come collect me like I'm a sheep to be herded," Lucy countered. She glanced at Zach, but he couldn't read whatever was in her expression when she quickly looked away again.

"Maybe not," Vaughn countered. "But I thought Jordan being the suspect might hit you a little hard and you'd want—" he looked Zach up and down "—a friendly face."

"Uh, right. Well. Vaughn, this is Zach. I don't suppose you two have met, though you know of each other."

"Of each other, yes. Jaime spoke highly of you." After another moment of cold perusal, Vaughn offered his hand. "I was impressed by the detail in your reports."

Zach shook it. "Same goes. It's good to meet you," Zach offered, trying to sound businesslike despite the general lack of shirt, socks and shoes.

Vaughn did not return the sentiment, though it was hard to blame him. Zach hadn't had a normal brother-sister relationship with Hilly since they'd grown up apart, and she'd come into his life already connected to Cam, so there'd been no big-brother suspicion to be had.

But that didn't mean he couldn't understand Vaughn's. Especially considering Vaughn had arranged for Lucy's protection.

"Why don't you go get dressed?" Vaughn said to Lucy. He gave Zach a sharp smile. "Zach and I will chat."

Lucy rolled her eyes. "Yeah, you're a real chatterbox. But I'll go get dressed since I'll be more comfortable, and since I have no doubt Zach can stand up to the likes of you." She gave her brother a little poke, and then drifted her hand down Zach's arm as she sauntered away.

Zach thought he could probably handle her brother—Texas Ranger or not—but he didn't quite need her stirring the pot on the subject.

Especially when it gave him a quick few minutes alone with her brother, which meant, even though he still had his doubts, he had to tell Vaughn he didn't think this was over. Somehow, he had to convince her brother that it wasn't Zach's heart doing the talking.

"I don't think she should go back home with you," he said when Lucy disappeared into the room, firmly and sure, but with absolutely no transition or finesse. He *could* have eased into it, but Lucy could also only take a few seconds to change. Time was of the essence.

Vaughn merely raised an eyebrow, reminding Zach a little uncomfortably of Lucy.

"I'm not saying Jordan isn't involved, but…" Zach knew he'd be shot down, but the incessant worry in his gut meant he had to say it. "There was evidence he's the murderer—I can't refute that. What concerns me are the loose ends. I'm not convinced this is it, or that Jordan's arrest means the danger to Lucy is over."

Vaughn studied him, and Zach braced himself for some kind of condescending lecture about being stupid.

It didn't come.

"I'm not, either," Vaughn said. When Zach could only stare at him, openmouthed, Vaughn continued. "Which is why I came out here. I didn't want her alone thinking she was safe, any more than I wanted to have to tell her she wasn't."

"Join the club," Zach muttered. He had to tell her. *Had to*. And yet, she was just accepting her ex-husband was a murderer. How could he add the fact it didn't make Stacy or anyone else less potentially involved?

"Should I ask your intentions when it comes to my sister?" Vaughn asked with a wry twist of his lips.

"Why? Did we fall back in time a century? I'm pretty sure Lucy can handle my intentions." Not that he knew what they were, or why he suddenly wanted the curse to be true.

Vaughn didn't smile, but Zach didn't get the impression Vaughn was a particularly smiley guy. Still, his mouth loosened in what Zach would term *amusement*. Maybe.

"Lucy," Vaughn repeated as if surprised Zach was using her given name. "Well, that's new."

"Is it?"

Vaughn shrugged. "I don't make it a habit to poke into my sister's personal life, but she isn't keen on letting too many people call her by her real name."

It was funny how Vaughn said *real* and it didn't sit well with Zach. They were both real enough—Daisy and Lucy—they were both her. He shook his head. "So how do we break it to her?"

"I'd like to not. To protect her on the sly until we figure out the whole picture."

Zach snorted his derision, unable to stop himself.

"I said I'd *like* to, not that it would work." Vaughn sighed heavily and scrubbed a hand over his face. He didn't appear mussed by travel or beset by fatigue or worry, but that simple gesture told Zach he was all of those things. Sick to death worried about his sister's safety.

Vaughn gestured Zach to sit down on the couch, so Zach did so, Vaughn taking a seat next to him. "Quickest version you've got of the loose ends you think still exist?"

"Two main ones," Zach returned, keeping one eye on Lucy's bedroom door. "One, how Jordan had enough information to know Daisy was going to be with Stacy—which to me points to a potential connection with Stacy."

"What about other people in the office?"

"I laid a little bit of a trap. We gave information to Stacy and only Stacy—of course she might have slipped and told someone, but I'm willing to bet Stacy told Jordan, or someone who knows Jordan."

Vaughn shook his head. "That's going to hurt—worse than Jordan—if Stacy's involved."

"Yeah. And I'll be honest—the second thread? I think there's someone else. Someone from her past, or maybe your father's. Someone who is using Jordan and Stacy and whoever else to exact some kind of… revenge."

"Why do you think that?"

"Patterns. Hunches. The way it's all played out."

Vaughn sighed. "You got notes?"

"You wouldn't believe the notes I have."

"I'll want some time to go over them." He glanced back at Lucy's still-closed door. "We don't have time."

"No. We don't. Look, why don't you let me tell her? That way she can be mad at me instead of her brother. We don't have to go into details. We can just say we're taking precautions until we're sure Jordan worked alone."

"How good of a liar are you, Zach?"

Zach's mouth quirked. "I've worked any number of undercover jobs for the FBI. How good of a liar do you think I am?"

"To her," Vaughn replied simply, which made Zach's

stomach lurch. "Believe it or not, I've…been where you're standing. At least, if my assumptions are correct—and they usually are. Protecting someone can lead to a lot of strong feelings."

"I don't think we're going to appreciate you warning me off. Grown adults. More important things at hand."

"The most important thing at hand is my sister's safety. Which you've been in charge of. Feelings—"

"Can complicate that. I'm well aware."

Vaughn gave him a look Zach couldn't read, then shifted uncomfortably in his seat. "Believe it or not, emotions aren't always the enemy when it comes to keeping the people you…care about safe."

"Not my experience, no offense."

"And yet in *mine*, I kept the woman safe, married her and have two amazing kids with her. So…you know. I guess it just depends."

Before Zach could say *anything* to that, because *marriage* and *kids* made his tongue stick to the roof of his mouth, Vaughn switched gears.

"Number one thing we should focus on?"

Zach forced himself to change gears, too. "Jordan was arrested over an anonymous tip, so someone out there knows something."

"It could be Stacy."

"It could be. No doubt."

But Zach was sure there was more, and that he was running out of time to find it.

Chapter 15

That was how Lucy found her brother and her lover, heads bent together going over the details of her case. She couldn't hear what they were saying in their low tones, but it made her realize Jordan had never really mingled with her family or her friends.

He'd never sat next to Vaughn on a couch and discussed anything with this kind of serious back and forth.

Of course, Zach and Vaughn weren't exactly arguing the finer points of the Cowboys' defense or the Astros' pitching staff. They were discussing Jordan or the case or something about her. Keeping her safe, while she wandered around wondering how many people in her life had betrayed her.

The second they noticed her there, Vaughn loudly mentioned something about the home value of a place like this. Lucy shook her head. "All right. Let's cut the crap."

Zach looked back at her, picture-perfect innocence. She couldn't understand why his ability to put on and take off masks with such ease didn't scare her, but it didn't. It was a part of who he was, and so far he hadn't used it for any negative reasons against her.

"Crap?" he asked cheerfully. But he watched her, steady and concerned, and maybe that was why she couldn't get uneasy about him. He never pretended about his emotions toward her. Oh, he might bottle them up, but he didn't try to fake any.

She moved into the living room, fidgety and desperately trying to hide it by perusing the books laid out on the coffee table. She wanted to be steady and calm like them, but she never could really get there.

"Did they give Jordan a bond?" she asked, hoping to sound casual and unaffected. Last night Zach had explained to her that when it came to murder most judges denied bond, but in cities like Nashville it wasn't unheard of to simply set the bond high.

And she knew no matter how high a bond, Jordan wouldn't just be able to pay it, he'd be certain to.

"No bond. He'll stay put in jail until the trial," Zach returned, watching her in that eagle-eye way of his. She might not have minded that too much, but her brother was doing the same thing.

It brought home how much she'd kept Vaughn at arm's length over the years, and how much he would have been there for her if she'd let him. She couldn't blame his stoicism or disapproval, because it had been she who hadn't wanted to give anyone that piece of her.

She hadn't even given Jordan any pieces of herself. She'd weaved dreams and fantasies about their future, but she'd never let Jordan in on any of them. He'd been more like a statue to build her fantasies around than a person to build a life with.

He might have manipulated her and taken advantage of her vulnerabilities, but he wasn't exactly the whole reason their marriage had fallen apart. Any more than she could really truly believe he was the full reason Tom was dead, no matter how much she desperately wanted it to be that easy.

"He's going to have himself a hell of a lawyer," Lucy replied, trying not to sound grim or resigned, but perfectly reasonable instead. "Money buys a lot. He could be out in no time."

"I imagine you're right," Vaughn agreed, devoid of emotion one way or another.

She wanted to scowl at the both of them, demand they *react* in some way, but they both looked at her. Concern and… Oh, she was stupid to think Zach was looking at her with love, but she'd already determined she was stupid, so why not just ride the wave?

"So when are we going to talk about the fact Jordan couldn't have known about the smoke bombs or to call to meet me without Stacy telling him?"

Vaughn sighed. "I'm sorry, Luce."

She tried to smile at Vaughn, though she knew it was weak at best. She perched herself on the arm of the couch on Zach's side. "I'm sorry, too, but…well, Jordan had a reason to hate me, I guess. Stacy didn't." No matter how many ways Lucy went back through the past few years, she couldn't even make up a reason.

Daisy Delaney could be prickly and difficult, but she'd always been those things with Stacy. Since those first days of stepping out of her father's shadow. Nothing about her behavior had changed. Except the addition of Jordan into her life and, in some ways, career.

If this had happened while she was still married to Jordan, she might have been able to blame that, but she'd divorced him.

What reason did Stacy have to hate her now that she'd dropped the demanding weight around both their shoulders?

"I just can't understand why she'd want to hurt me. I know, I *know* there aren't other explanations for how Jordan got the info, but I can't understand it. That weighs on me."

"I've been pondering another angle," Zach said in that gentle way of his, which meant it would not be a gentle angle *at all*.

She saw the warning look Vaughn gave Zach and shook her head. She couldn't bury her head in the sand and let these two men handle things, though they would have gladly done it and it might be easier on her emotional well-being.

This whole time she'd been holding back, hoping things would right themselves. Hoping it would be taken care of by someone else, and it hadn't been. Oh, she'd thought about her past, who might hate her, but she hadn't tugged on old hurts or scars, because she'd thought surely all the people paid to keep her safe would figure it out.

But that just wasn't going to work. She needed to be present. She needed to revisit those scars so they could end this completely. Vaughn and Zach could only do so much—she was the real center of this problem—which meant she had to center herself in the solution.

Tom was dead. Jordan was in jail. She suspected one of her oldest, closest friends of being part of it.

Now was not the time to hide. It was time to be the woman in her songs—not just in name but in deed. The kind of woman who went after what she wanted and got it no matter the consequences, no matter what she had to sacrifice or lose.

She leveled Zach with an even stare. "What's the angle?"

"Your father."

She hadn't braced herself for that. The flinch that went through her had to be visible, and if only Zach had seen, that might have been okay, but Vaughn being here for this...

Vaughn hadn't had much of a relationship with Dad, and she knew that Dad's dying with no reconciliation weighed on him.

She stood back up and headed to the kitchen. She started the process of making coffee in the hopes that having something to do would ease her tightly wound insides. "Well, Stacy has a connection to Dad, sort of, as an assistant to Don. It's an awful long game for her to want to hurt me over something a dead guy did. Especially now after so many years of opportunity."

"I want to go back to the conversation we had before the whole Jordan debacle. Your father's manager—Stacy's boss."

She stiffened again. She should have known Zach would come back to this, no matter how it didn't connect. "I don't see how this connects to Don."

"I don't, either, but we have the fact that he hurt you, which caused you to leave your father's fledgling label. After which, that label fell apart—if my research is correct."

"Don hurt you?" Vaughn demanded.

Lucy gave Zach a warning look not to say more. "It fell apart because Dad didn't know what he was doing. Excellent entertainer. Not so great on the business front.

Everyone knew *he* was the reason for the failure, not me leaving."

"How did Don hurt you?" Vaughn demanded again.

"It was nothing," Lucy insisted. It bothered her to realize so many years later Vaughn would have supported her and protected her no matter what if she'd told him about the incident. But she'd known it would have come at the cost of the career she wanted…so she'd just kept quiet. Better to keep what she wanted and ignore the hurts, right?

"Lucy, you will tell me—"

"I don't need a big brother!" she shouted, slamming the can of coffee against the counter. So much for being calm and collected—but who said calm ever got a woman anywhere? Maybe she needed to be *angry* and let it out. Maybe she needed to rage and act.

"I need this to be over," she said a little more evenly but with just as much emotion. "So look into Don Levinson, who is probably *dead*." She flung a hand toward Zach. "Look into anyone who might have hated my father. I'll give you every name I can think of. I just need this to *end*."

Zach stood, moving over to the kitchen. He didn't touch her, though she desperately wanted him to. Wanted that anchor to something solid and true, because no matter how she told herself to be strong, all her foundations were shifting under her. Zach seemed to be the one thing left that wouldn't.

"We all want it over, because we all want you safe," he said gravely.

She wanted to tell him she didn't know how to *deal* with that. Who had ever protected her? But that wasn't fair to Vaughn, who would have if she'd have let him. Because the real issue was, who had she ever *let* protect her?

Zach.

She didn't even have the good sense to question that because he stood there, handsome and sweet, and she'd never been so certain of Jordan. She'd convinced herself she was in love with Jordan, convinced herself to love him because of his act. But she'd never *felt* it wash over her as some irrefutable fact.

She'd had to work at loving Jordan and believing in that love. This thing inside her that waved over her whenever she looked at Zach was different, and it was real—no matter how little she understood that.

Zach wasn't an act. She'd *seen* him act. The real him was the man who'd made love to her last night.

She wished she could rewind time—stay right back there—where she didn't have to deal with loose ends or her brother.

But both had to be dealt with. Standing in this kitchen, looking at Zach, wishing this could be normal life without her safety in question—she realized for the first time in this whole nightmare year that at some point her life would be hers again.

She'd lived in the scary *now* for a year, most especially this past awful week. But it would have to end at some point and once it was over she'd have her life back. Completely. She'd be able to visit Vaughn and his family without worry. She'd be able to settle down somewhere and build whatever kind of life she wanted—including one with a partner, a real partner.

Maybe even in Wyoming. Maybe even with Zach. Why not? It was her fantasy life right now, so why not indulge in all those impossibilities?

"What about trying to ferret out the anonymous tip?" Vaughn asked, singularly focused on the task at hand. "Surely, the cops have some way of tracking it."

Zach turned back to his conversation with Vaughn,

so Lucy focused on the coffee and the nice little fantasy of settling down in a ghost town where no one could find her if she didn't want them to. Zach could protect people and she could write music.

She was brought out of the reverie that eased some of that tension inside her by the vibrating of her phone in her pocket.

Lucy slipped the phone out and looked at the message. From Stacy.

She glanced at Vaughn and Zach, but they were deep in computers and papers and theories, so she opened the message.

911. Call back. No ears.

The *no ears* made her uneasy, but what could Stacy do over the phone? Maybe she was calling to warn her about something. Explain something. Hell, maybe she was calling to confess all.

She looked at the two men in her life again. They certainly didn't need her for whatever it was they were doing, and she wasn't so sure she needed them for this.

Part of her knew she should tell them about Stacy's text *before* she made the call, but they were handling everything else. Why couldn't she handle a simple phone call?

She opened her mouth to make her excuses, then realized neither one of them would come up for air for hours if she left them alone.

She eased her way into the hall. Then toward the back door. Slowly and as quietly as possible, she undid all three locks. She hadn't been out here, but Zach had mentioned a back porch she could use. She just hadn't had a reason to yet.

She stepped out onto it. It was less of a porch and

more of a sunroom. The walls were made out of glass, glass she suspected was reinforced with whatever special security measures someone protecting people might use—if the giant keypad lock on the door to the outside was anything to go by.

Still, the day was sunny, and everything outside the glass was a vibrant, enticing green. God, she was tired of being cooped up, of feeling like she had to be in someone else's presence for every second. She hadn't realized how much she missed just stepping outside and lifting her face to the sun.

Which meant this had to end and she had to talk to Stacy. She dialed Stacy's number, staring at the green outside, trying to breathe in the sunshine to offset the nausea roiling around inside her.

"Oh, thank God, Lucy. I don't know what's going on. Everything is so messed up. Jordan's in jail? What is happening?"

Stacy only ever called her Lucy outside work, those occasions they interacted as friends. Stacy had never had any trouble keeping both names straight. Was it because she was a two-faced backstabber?

"I don't know what's happening," Lucy replied flatly.

"Jordan's team is trying to lay the seeds that you've framed him."

Lucy snorted, lowering herself into a cushioned wicker chair and pulling her legs up under her. "The police didn't seem to think that was a possibility." She closed her eyes, trying to ignore the seed of fear and worry that Stacy had planted. God, would he succeed at that, too?

No one could prove she was trying to frame Jordan. Of course that didn't mean the tide of public opinion couldn't turn even further against her. That was what

Jordan's team would try to do. Not just a wild, alcoholic cheater, but a murderer, too.

"I mean, Jordan's stupid enough to be set up," Stacy continued. "I'd certainly commend you for your creativity and for getting his big mouth out of the way."

"Are you accusing me of something, Stacy?" Lucy asked coldly, because an unforgiving chill had swept through her. Any conflict she had over not trusting Stacy was fading away with each statement. If Stacy was really worried about *her*, wouldn't this conversation go differently?

"No, God, of course not." Stacy sighed heavily into the receiver. "Everything is so messed up. So confusing. Can we meet for lunch?"

"Not without two bodyguards," Lucy retorted sharply.

"Two?" Stacy asked—the question one of confusion, or was it calculating the odds? Was it filing away information to use later?

It broke Lucy's heart to think Stacy was fishing. Broke Lucy's heart that she had to lie. "To start. You know how overprotective Vaughn is. I swear he's hired half the country to look out for my well-being and investigate what on earth is really going on." She tried to make herself laugh casually, but couldn't muster the sound.

"You don't think Jordan did it?"

"All evidence points to yes, based on what I've heard, but you know, some people are more concerned for my safety than how much information I've got."

"You know, don't you?" Stacy said, her voice hushed and pained.

Lucy had to swallow at the lump in her throat. She waited for the confession, but Stacy didn't speak.

"What do I know, Stacy? Why don't you go ahead and tell it to me straight for once."

"God." Stacy's voice broke. "Don't hate me, Luce. It was an honest mistake. They all were."

An honest mistake. Tom was dead and Stacy had made an *honest mistake*. Lucy couldn't speak past the lump in her throat.

"Okay, okay. Just hear me out, okay? I know I'm the reason Jordan knew you were in town. I would have told you, but I didn't even realize it until someone told me you'd been at dinner together when he got arrested. Then I pieced it all together and—I'm sorry, okay?"

Lucy frowned. That wasn't exactly the grand confession she was expecting, but it was something. "You gave him the information about me coming here? Or going to Wyoming?"

"Here! Of course. You were totally safe in Wyoming," Stacy returned, and it was too hard to try and decide if she was an excellent liar or simply telling the truth.

"Truth be told, I don't understand why you came home when no one knew you were there."

"Because someone knew I was there, Stacy. I wasn't safe there. Someone found me. Now, what exactly did you tell Jordan? This time and before."

"Nothing before! How can you think that of me?" Stacy muttered a curse. "Listen, listen, okay? I hadn't talked to Jordan in months, but he called me not long after the smoke bomb. He was fishing, I knew he was, but he knew all the right buttons to push. I didn't mean to tell him. I was… He was being irritating, and I was trying to one-up him. I said I'd seen you at my office and you were *fine*. It wasn't until long after I'd hung up that I realized he was goading me and I was just dumb enough to bite."

It sounded plausible enough. God knew Jordan could manipulate. But how had someone found her in Wyoming? And why had Stacy pulled her in the opposite direction of Zach at the office?

Stacy wasn't copping to any of that, so what on Earth was this 911 emergency all about?

"Were you the anonymous tip?" Stacy asked after some beats of silence.

Lucy's blood chilled. "Pretty sure if I had any tips they wouldn't be anonymous, and I would have handed them over when I found Tom dead in my dressing room."

"Jesus," Stacy said, sounding truly sickened by the thought.

"Someone knew I was in Wyoming. You were the only person I told."

"You really think I'm behind this," Stacy said, sounding so shocked and hurt Lucy's own heart twisted in pain. But she had to be strong. Because manipulations were apparently the name of the game, and she'd fallen for too many.

"You were the only one outside my immediate family who knew where I was going," Lucy said, doubling down.

"I didn't tell anyone. Not a soul. Not even Cory. Cory..." There was a long pause.

"Don't try to pin this on Cory. What possible reason would she have for being involved in this?"

"It wasn't me, Luce. Whatever you think. I haven't done anything. I swear to God. I made a mistake in talking to Jordan, but...nothing else. How is this getting so out of hand?"

"What exactly is getting out of hand, Stacy? Because I'm lost."

Stacy swore again. "I might know... I have a bad feeling I know who's behind all this. Jordan told me something a long time ago that I never told you. I know

I should have, but you were head over heels for him. If it didn't connect to some things with Cory lately, I might not have even remembered, but..."

"But what? What is it?"

The line was quiet except for Stacy's breathing. "Someone's here," Stacy whispered. "Oh, God, someone's in my house."

Fear bolted through Lucy sharply, and she forgot all of her suspicions at the sheer terror trembling through Stacy's voice.

"Stacy. Hang up. Call 911. Okay? Stacy?" Still shallow breathing. "Stacy!" Lucy yelled. "Hang up and call 911."

"Help m—"

The line clicked off.

Chapter 16

"Stacy's in trouble!"

Zach jumped to his feet, heart in his throat as Lucy ran into the living room.

"What?" he and Vaughn echoed in unison.

She waved her phone in both their faces. "I was talking to Stacy on the phone and—"

"Why the hell were you doing that?" Vaughn demanded. Which kept Zach from having to demand it.

"Zach," she said, turning to him, clearly thinking he'd be more reasonable than her brother. That wasn't the case, but he'd try to pretend. A sort of good-cop-bad-cop deal.

"She's at her house," Lucy said, panic in her voice and broad gestures. "She said someone was in her house and then the line went dead."

"Go back to the beginning," Zach said, trying to remain calm. "Explain everything."

She looked up at him helplessly. "There isn't time!"

"Lucy." He took her by the shoulders. "Just do it. Quickly, but from the beginning."

Lucy shook her head, still gripping the phone like it was a lifeline to Stacy. "She wanted me to call her. So I did, and she talked about Jordan being arrested, and said she accidentally told him about our meeting and me heading home."

Vaughn and Zach scoffed together.

"Look, I don't know. She seemed fishy and yet not and she was going to tell me something she thought I should know, then she said someone was in her house and her line went dead. She said *help*. Please." Blue eyes looked up at him, full of tears and fear. "Even if she's…part of this, she's in trouble."

Zach wasn't convinced that was true, but it was possible. It was also possible she was trying to lure Lucy to her house, and he'd use that if he could.

"Why didn't you tell us she was calling?" Zach asked, trying to be gentle.

"She wanted to talk privately," Lucy replied, sounding resigned. "But she was scared, Zach. That wasn't an act. I don't… It couldn't have been. I'm not saying it's on the up and up, but this is complicated and she's in *danger*."

Complicated was right.

"Call the cops," Zach instructed. He shook his head at Vaughn, who'd opened his mouth to speak. "Not you or me, her. She's the one who spoke with Stacy, so she's going to give them her account. You two stay put. But call the cops and tell them everything you remember about the phone call."

"You don't know that she's telling the truth," Vaughn said firmly.

"No, but I don't know that she's not," Zach returned,

moving for his gun, his holster, keys, wallet. "If this is some sort of plot to get to Lucy, she'll be here, protected by you and out of harm's way. If it's not, then I get close enough to see what she might be planning. I'll need her address."

"Wait, you're not…going," Lucy said incredulously.

"If she's in trouble, I'm going to help," Zach said, weapon already strapped to his body. "And if she's trying to lure you, I want to be there to figure out why."

"But the cops—"

"I want them to check it out, but I want to get there first in case something is off. The more information I can gather, the better chance we have of putting this away for good."

"But if it's a lure, it could be dangerous. You could be hurt."

"Not if you call the cops." He didn't like Lucy being out of his sight right now, but they were both going to have to deal with their worry. Vaughn would protect her. He was more than capable. "Make sure you tell the cops I'll be there and give my description and that I'll be happy to verify and ID who I am so they don't mix me up with anyone else."

He leaned forward to kiss her goodbye—just on the off chance this was dangerous and things went south—but the presence of her brother gave him pause.

Screw it. He kissed her. Hard. "Stay put. I mean it. Both of you." He didn't need to worry about Vaughn keeping an eye on her. There was no doubt in Zach's mind Vaughn would lay down his own life to save his sister's, just like Zach would do.

So Zach would go, no matter how much uncertainty plagued him. Because this didn't add up and if it was a lead, he'd darn well take it. "Text me the address."

By the time he was in the rental car, Stacy's address was plugged into his navigation system and he was on his way.

He wished he had more time to plan, but if Lucy sincerely thought Stacy was in trouble there wasn't time for plans. He had to act. Stacy might be involved, like Jordan, and about to be hurt to protect a killer's true identity. Stacy could be luring Lucy to her, or trying to get her alone.

Endless possibilities. So he had to be ready for anything.

He beat the cops to her house, which wasn't too far from the farmhouse. That certainly gave him some pause, but he quickly got out of the car and began moving toward the house.

It was quiet. Stacy didn't have the same amount of property as the place they'd been staying, but it was still secluded from the neighbors by a pristine lawn and thick trees around the perimeter.

Zach glanced into the garage through the windows. There was a car parked inside the tidy building. If someone was here, there was no evidence of a vehicle besides Stacy's own.

He didn't want Stacy to be guilty for Lucy's sake, but believing things for Lucy's sake was bound to get people hurt. He'd already let his emotions get too involved here even after promising himself not to.

That was… Well, it had happened. He couldn't change it.

So he'd have to do better for Lucy than he'd done for Ethan. Neither Lucy nor her brother were getting hurt on his watch, so he'd follow this path wherever it led.

He moved to the front door, glanced around the quiet lawn. Nothing and no one, as far as he could tell.

Carefully, he tried the knob. Locked. He looked around again, hoping for police backup, but still no sign of cops or sounds of sirens.

He'd have to move around the house, looking in what windows he could. Then if there was still nothing—and no cops—he'd simply have to break in and hope for the best.

He moved stealthily around the house, peeking in windows and seeing nothing—no people, no signs of struggle, just a perfectly neat but lived-in-looking house.

Until he got to the back porch. There were two big French doors that led into a dining room and kitchen area.

The bolt of shock at what he saw stopped him in his tracks. Stacy was sitting in the middle of the kitchen—tied to a chair. She had duct tape around her mouth. He could see her profile, and her eyes were wide and terrified.

There didn't appear to be anyone around her—though he could only see part of the kitchen and dining room from his vantage point. He looked around the expansive backyard. No one.

It could be a trap—the way his heart beat hard against his chest warned him that this could all end very, very badly for him.

But a woman was tied up in a kitchen and he was armed. The least he could do was try to help her.

He could tell the doors weren't fully latched—likely where whoever was in there had gotten in—so he began to slowly move forward, watching every inch of the backyard for a flash of movement.

Every last hunch inside him screamed *trap*, but he couldn't ignore the trickle of blood that started at Stacy's temple and slid down the side of her face and neck.

It was possible she'd done it to herself, possible she was *this* good of an actor, but he couldn't be sure.

Carefully, making as little noise as possible, Zach inched forward. He kept his gaze alert and his movements careful, gun at the ready. He moved up to the door and waited for some kind of movement.

When he reached forward and gave the door a slight nudge, Stacy's head whipped around. Her eyes went wide. Zach could only hope she recognized him as he stepped forward.

She didn't fidget or try to speak past the tape. She just watched him as she breathed heavily through her nose. Slowly, she moved her hand. Though her arms were tied to her sides and the chair, she lifted one finger and pointed upstairs.

At least, that was what he hoped she was pointing at. He moved closer and closer, studying the way she was tied. It would be best to free her arms and legs first, so she could run if need be, but he needed more information first. So the tape had to go.

"Brace yourself, okay?" he whispered, tapping the edge of the tape. "And try not to make a sound."

She nodded, tears trickling down her cheeks. Feeling awful, Zach pulled the tape from her mouth.

She gasped in pain, but she didn't make any extra noise.

"How many are there?" he asked, immediately crouching to untie the rope bonds.

"Just one. Just one. I don't know who he is. I don't know what's going on." She started crying in earnest, and Zach winced at the noise. "He's upstairs. He's looking for something, but I don't know what."

"That's fine. It's all going to be okay." He got the ropes off her and helped her to her feet. "Run outside.

The police will be here soon. I'm going to stay right here and make sure he doesn't leave, so you just make sure to tell the police there are two of us in here—and one of us means them no harm." Hopefully, between Stacy's recount and Lucy's call giving his description, he'd avoid accidentally entangling with police.

"What are you going to do?" Stacy whispered, rubbing her arms where the rope had been.

"I'm going to find out what's going on once and for all. You run. Now."

She nodded tremulously, but then she eased out of the back door and left in a dead run.

Zach took a breath and then began to move. He wished he knew the layout of Stacy's house, but he could at least hear someone upstairs. As long as he did, he knew the perpetrator was up there and not on the same level as him.

Zach just needed to find him, get him to talk and then let the police do whatever they had to do.

Easy, right?

He eased closer to the staircase, weapon drawn and ready. Here he couldn't hear the footsteps as well as he'd been able to in the dining area.

Still, he moved slowly and as silently as possible. As he went up the stairs, some of his old FBI training took over—the way his body would cool, tense and let go of the wild fear. Focused on the job—on the end result, and the rest of the chips would fall where they fell.

Doing what he came to do was the most important thing.

When he crested the top, he leaned forward and looked around. There weren't any hallways, just a circle of an area—with four rooms around him.

All four doors were open, but only slightly ajar. If he started to move forward, he'd be able to get a glimpse into them, but he wouldn't be able to do anything else without drawing attention to himself.

Not ideal, but it could be worse, so he started forward. The first room didn't have anyone in it that he could see. Neither did the second room. As he approached the third, his foot landed on a floorboard that made a creak as loud as a bomb.

Immediately, the third door burst open and a gun went off. Zach felt the searing burn of metal hitting flesh, stumbled to his hands and knees and swore, then rolled forward to knock the shooter off his feet.

His arm throbbed, but not enough to be anything more than a flesh wound. The gunman let out a howl of pain as he crashed into the dresser. Violent cursing and threats spewed from the man, but it was drowned out by the thundering of feet and shouted orders to drop their weapons and stay down.

Zach winced at the searing ache in his arm, but praised the timing of the police. The man he'd knocked into wasn't taller than Zach, but he was built like a Mack truck. Zach could take on a bigger man, but in this tiny room he would have been beat to hell in the process, no doubt.

Once the cops verified who he was and cleared him to get up, he moved toward the man he didn't recognize being handcuffed.

"Who do you work for?" Zach demanded.

"We'll handle the questioning, Mr. Simmons."

Zach leveled the officer pushing him back with a scathing look. Zach kept trying to push forward, but the one cop kept pushing him back while two others arrested the thrashing man on the ground.

Zach cursed. Demanded answers. Got nothing but a brick wall of blank-faced cops as they hauled the assailant down the stairs.

The last cop eyed him, nodded toward his arm. "There's an ambulance outside."

Zach looked down. Blood was trickling down his arm and onto the white carpet. He blinked at the tiny pool of blood. For a second he felt a little light-headed, but then he shook it off.

"I'm fine." He had to find some answers before this escalated any further. "I need answers. I need—"

"Nasty gash on his head. He'll be transported to the hospital, and then we'll take him in for questioning. I'd suggest calling one of our detectives tomorrow to get an update on the situation."

Tomorrow. An *update*? He didn't have time to wait until tomorrow. "Where's the woman?" Zach asked.

"What woman?"

Zach's entire body went cold, his gut sinking with dread. "The one who ran out of here a good ten minutes ago."

The cop's eyebrows drew together, and he pulled his shoulder radio to his mouth and muttered a few things into it. After a few seconds of static and responses, the cop shrugged. "No one saw a woman."

Hell. "There was a woman here, tied up and mouth taped." He went through the whole event, gave Stacy's name and description, and then rushed back to the farmhouse, trying to determine what on earth Stacy had been trying to pull. She'd been hurt, but now she was missing.

What was going on? He couldn't figure it out for the life of him, but one thing he knew for sure.

He had to get back to Lucy and make sure she was okay.

Lucy paced irritably. "It's taking too long. Why hasn't he called? Or come back? What if he's hurt and we're just sitting here—"

"If the police are questioning him, it'll take a while," Vaughn replied calmly. "These things take time, and unfortunately going half-cocked is likely what Stacy wanted. We have to stay put and wait and trust the police to do their jobs."

"Why would they question Zach?"

"Because they have to piece together what happened. If Zach sees anything over there, he'll need to explain. Maybe he's giving them more details on the case. You just don't know, and you can't read into the time that passes. Sit. Relax."

She snorted. "How can I relax when…when…" She plopped down on the couch next to Vaughn. She'd never told her brother anything about her personal life, and vice versa, but she didn't have anywhere else to put all this *stuff* roiling around inside her.

"I'm in love with him."

Vaughn leveled her with a bland gaze. "Gee. You don't say."

She frowned at him. She thought she'd get a lecture…one that would give her a reason to be mad and rage instead of be sad or worried.

Vaughn offered no such lecture and, in fact, seemed wholly unsurprised and unconcerned.

"You're okay with that?"

"Not *okay* exactly, but I know a thing or two about… falling in love under uncomfortable circumstances."

"He might not be in love with me," Lucy replied petulantly, because she wanted to be petulant about something if she couldn't be mad.

"Lucy, please. He's so head over heels even I can't be big-brother outraged over it. I might not be particularly comfortable with emotion, but I certainly recognize head-over-heels stupid love when I see it."

"It's just the pressure. He feels guilty. He had this

thing go wrong when he was in the FBI, and… You don't fall in love over the course of a few days. It's adrenaline and stuff."

Vaughn didn't even have the decency to look away from the computer screen he was still doing research on. "I'll be sure to let Nat know the only reason I fell in love with her was *adrenaline and stuff*."

"That's not the same."

This time he did look at her, but only to give her his patented condescending older-brother look. "How exactly?"

She didn't have a good answer, so she was more than happy that her phone trilling interrupted the question. She stood and answered without even looking at the caller ID. "Zach?"

"Lucy. No. No, it's me."

"Stacy?" She grabbed Vaughn's arm as he shot to his feet next to her. She was scared to death Stacy was calling to tell her Zach had been hurt or worse.

"What's happening? What is *happening*? I'm so scared. God."

"Stacy. Where are you? Where's Zach?" Lucy demanded through a tight throat.

Vaughn ripped the phone out of her hands. She thought he was going to talk to Stacy himself, demand answers, but he only put the call on speaker.

"He saved me," Stacy was saying over and over again. "He saved me, but… Lucy." Stacy was breathing hard, and the connection was spotty. "Listen to me."

The line cut in and out. "Stacy. Stacy. Stop… running? Or whatever you're doing. Stay in one place. I'm losing you."

"I'm so scared. Zach told me to run, so I ran and now… I don't know where I am. I ran into the trees and now… God, I'm so lost. I know I should have waited for the police, but I was so scared."

She started crying and Lucy's heart twisted, some awful mix of compassion and suspicion. What if this was another fake thing? "Stacy, tell me what's going on."

"I don't know. I don't understand it, but I think… Lucy, Jordan is Don Levinson's grand-nephew."

"What?" Daisy asked incredulously. The only reason she didn't lose her balance was because Vaughn held her up.

"Yes. God. He told me at some party eons ago. I didn't think much of it. You and I had already had a fight about Jordan and I didn't want to make you madder at me over Jordan. But then I mostly forgot about all that. He never brought it up again, and I never saw the old bastard. But I think Cory is involved, Lucy. I really do. I didn't tell anyone you'd been to Wyoming. Not a *soul*. But Cory could have been listening. It's the only possibility."

Lucy shared a look with Vaughn. He didn't look convinced, but Jordan was related to *Don*? Why would Don want to hurt her after all this time? How did it all connect?

"Okay. Okay. You just stay put," Lucy instructed. They needed her safe and coherent to figure out if her story made any sense. "I'm going to come find you."

Before Vaughn could mount his argument, Stacy gave one. "No, Lucy. You can't. Whoever was in my house… I didn't recognize him or know him. Whoever wants to hurt you is still out there, pulling strings."

Which was when they heard a car squeal to a stop in front of the farmhouse.

Chapter 17

Zach screeched to a stop in front of the farmhouse. He all but leaped out of the car and ran for the door. Stacy missing, the cops not having seen her at all, made every terrible scenario run through his head.

Stacy had already beaten him here. The whole thing had been a ruse to find out the location of the farmhouse. It was too late and Lucy was—

He stopped on the porch on a dime. What if he'd fallen for it, and led Stacy—or whoever—here right *now*? Stacy was a plant, but not the kind he'd expected. Not trying to lead Lucy to an ambush at her place, but a way to find Lucy at hers.

He turned, looked around the yard, but there was no sign of anyone that he could see. If someone had followed him, they were still far enough away that he could get to Lucy and keep her safe.

Unless they were already here. He jumped forward and shoved his key into the lock. He'd get to Lucy first.

Move them out fast. Then they could figure it out, but first they had to be away from any place that could be dangerous and breeched.

The sound of an explosion shuddered through the air in perfect timing with a blast of pain in his thigh. He staggered forward, the door opening as he did so. He crashed to the ground of the entryway, just barely recognizing the scream as Lucy's.

Lucy. Who he had to keep safe, no matter how his vision dimmed or the pain screamed through him. This wound was worse than his arm, but it wasn't fatal. Probably.

Even if it was, he'd do whatever it took to make sure nothing fatal touched Lucy.

Zach managed to scoot back and kick the door closed, but it wasn't fast enough. Before Vaughn could jump on the lock, it was being flung back open and Vaughn got knocked into the coffee table, which broke and splintered under his weight.

Two men stepped inside, one holding a gun, and one looking very, very smug. They shut the door behind them.

Zach didn't know why he was surprised. He'd known, hadn't he?

Emotion got people hurt and killed. He'd let his worry over Lucy cloud his thoughts, and now they'd all pay for it.

"Well, look at you, Daisy girl. All grown."

Lucy's stomach pitched. The years had not been kind to Don Levinson, and yet that smarmy smile of his was exactly the same and still reminded her of things she'd tried long and hard to forget.

That smile made her remember all too clearly a

young girl who'd thought her father would protect her and been wholly, utterly disillusioned.

But Dad was dead, and Don very much wasn't. Old, yes, but not dead, and certainly no less evil than he'd been all those years ago trying to take advantage of young women.

Vaughn sat in the wreckage of the coffee table. Zach lay on the ground, a concerning amount of blood pooling around his leg. Both were armed, but neither reached for their weapon. She supposed they wouldn't as long as Don's little buddy there had a very big and scary-looking gun pointed in her direction.

"I'm very disappointed in you, sweetheart. Your father always told me how smart you were, and yet you never once suspected your old pal Don. You didn't suspect that moron you married until it was too late."

Lucy didn't say anything. She barely let the words register, because she had to think. She had to survive this and get Zach and Vaughn out of this horrible mess.

"Don't worry. You're not half as disappointing as *him*," Don continued. "The time and effort I poured into that boy, and he's still dumb as a post. A bit of a coward, too. If I'd had my way, he would have killed you slowly and quietly when you were married, but *no*."

Killed her. Don and Jordan had plotted to kill her.

"He thought he'd use your fame instead of my know-how. Thought you being a wreck would sell him better than you being dead. Well, look where he is now. Like I said, dumb as a post."

"Yeah, I suppose we both were," Lucy replied, trying not to let the wave of nauseous regret fell her. Zach was bleeding. Vaughn would die to protect her and leave his family without a husband and father.

She couldn't—wouldn't—let that happen.

"What on earth do you have against me, Don?" Lucy asked, trying to sound bored and unaffected.

Don laughed. "Against *you*. Against *you*? As if you don't know. Your father told me what you did."

"Told him you were a dangerous pervert who couldn't keep his hands off teenage girls?"

"If you hadn't gone crying to him, pretending like you hadn't wanted my hands on you, do you know what I would have? He cut me out of his estate, and out of all I'd invested in *you*. So I had to bow and scrape and pay off my debts. The things I had to endure because I didn't get that money, all because you were a lying whore. Well, my hands'll be on you now."

Zach and Vaughn made almost identical sounds of outrage, and Don smiled down at them. "Don't worry," he said cheerfully. "It won't bother you any. You'll both be dead." His gaze went back to Daisy. "And boy, will the press eat this up. I'll have to figure out how I'm going to play it first. You'd think I'd know, with all the planning that's gone into it, but sometimes I do like to wing it. Murder-suicide? Or do I just frame you? So many options. But at least I finally realized I'd have to do it myself. The younger generation just doesn't have the chutzpa to get things done."

He turned to the other man. "Leave the one on the floor." He nudged Zach with his boot. Zach didn't so much as move or groan. Lucy tried not to panic that he'd lost consciousness. "He'll bleed out if he hasn't already." Don then studied Vaughn.

Lucy had to do something. Save her brother. Save Zach. But how? If someone was willing to kill like this, what kind of reasoning would work?

"You want money?" she demanded.

"I want *revenge*, little girl. I was supposed to have a

piece of your pie, but your father held your lying story over me for years. Made me jump through all those hoops and then not even a *cent* of his estate? Which should have been rightfully left to me for all I'd done to make him a star, if you hadn't come along."

"I never lied. You grabbed me."

"You begged for it."

"You're delusional. And insane, I think, to have spent your life so obsessed with me—"

"Shoot her," Don ordered of the man with the gun. Then he held up a hand, before Vaughn could lunge to her rescue, and sighed dramatically. "No. That's rash. I want my fun with her first. And yours, as well," he said, nodding toward the man with the gun, who smiled.

Lucy hoped she didn't go gray, because it felt as though the very blood leaked out of her. But she needed to keep Don talking, not acting. She had to make him feel…superior. Anger would make him act, but condescension would keep his diatribes going.

"You were never supposed to have a piece of my career. My career was always separate from Dad's."

Don tipped his head back and laughed, all too heartily. Lucy noted Zach's lifeless body. Vaughn's hesitant, slow and deliberate move for his hand to get closer and closer to his weapon without drawing attention.

She needed a scene. Not just from Don, but from everyone to get the man with the gun's attention.

"You were always meant to be your daddy's pawn. Problem was you got too many ideas, and that uppity assistant of mine fed them. And if your father had listened to me, you both would have been taken down a peg. But he let you go instead. Costing me millions. *Millions.*"

The rage was starting to seep back in and Lucy racked her brain for a way to fix this. Save them. But

Don just kept going, eyes gleaming with vicious rage, spittle forming at the corners of his mouth.

And all the while the man with the gun had the barrel pointed right at Lucy's heart.

"Then he didn't even have the intelligence to be sorry. Every time, every single time I had a better idea for your father's career, one he didn't agree with, what did he say to me? *I guess Daisy going to the police wouldn't be such a good thing for* your *career, would it, Don?*"

"That sounds like a problem between you and my father," Lucy managed, though her throat was tight with fear and pain.

"A problem I solved." He grinned and Lucy's knees nearly gave out.

"You killed him?" she rasped.

Don shrugged, but his smile was sharp. "Not so much. Supply him enough drugs and he killed himself." But his smile turned into a sneer. "Then I started getting your notes."

"I never sent you any notes, Don. I'd forgotten you even existed. That's why I didn't suspect you were behind this, because you're so far beneath me and behind me I didn't give you a second thought." Notes. Notes. As if this wasn't complicated enough, someone had been sending him notes in her name?

"Sure, little girl. Sure."

"Maybe Jordan isn't as stupid as you thought," Lucy shot out. "He knew, you know. About what you did to me." It was a flat-out lie. The only person she'd ever told aside from Stacy was Zach.

Oh, God, it all circled back to Stacy, didn't it?

But she couldn't get caught up on that. She couldn't let the tears that threatened, fall. She couldn't give in to panic or fear, because Zach was a lifeless, bleeding form on the floor and she had to save him.

Jordan was safe in jail. If she implicated him, if she got Don to believe it…well, he'd kill them all anyway, but maybe it would make him unbalanced for a few minutes.

Don narrowed his eyes at her. "I don't believe it."

"I didn't send you notes, Don. You would have been one of the top suspects if I had. It had to be Jordan. Unless you told someone else about it."

"Or your father did." He shook his head. "It doesn't matter. Result is still the same. This guy is dead." He pointed at Zach. Then he pointed at Vaughn. "That guy is going to be. And we're going to have our fun before you are, too."

No. That was not how this was going to go down, and the best way to get out of a sticky situation with a man who thought he was in charge was always, *always* act the overwrought female.

"Dead?" she moaned. "He's dead?" She made a choking, sobbing noise and flung herself on Zach's body.

She'd hoped it would be enough of an opening Vaughn would shoot, but Don just grumbled something about women. So Lucy sobbed as loudly as she could, moving her hand, discreetly trying to get to Zach's gun without anyone noticing.

It wasn't hard to keep crying when he didn't move. But he was breathing. Unless it was just the movement of her own body making his chest seem as though it was moving up and down. She was almost to his gun when she felt him twitch under her just a little.

She gave herself one second to just press her cheek to his chest and breathe in some relief. He was alive but he desperately needed help. She'd give it. Get his gun and—

"Scream," Zach whispered through bloodless lips, but he was breathing and talking, so she didn't wait around for anything else. She did exactly what he said.

Lucy's scream shattered through the air and though it hurt like hell, Zach whipped his gun out of his holster and shot the man with the gun—who'd been so intent on Vaughn's lunge he hadn't seen Zach move, and with Lucy sheltering his arm from Don, the old man hadn't been able to warn him.

Vaughn tackled Don to the floor amidst shouts and threats.

Zach tried to get to his feet, but leveling the gun had taken all his energy and focus. His vision wavered, and he wasn't all that certain he could feel his legs. There was only pain and a fog that he kept trying to fight.

It was starting to win.

"Get some pressure on the wound," he thought he heard Vaughn shout. Was Lucy hurt? No, she hadn't been—had she?

Zach had shot the right guy, and Vaughn had taken care of the rest. Lucy was safe. He relaxed a little into the fog, except there were still so many unanswered questions.

"Loose ends," Zach muttered.

Gentle hands were on his face. "Only a few. You just stay with me so we can figure them out, all right?"

"Lucy."

"That's right. That's right." There was a catch in her throat and even though he could only see black, he knew she was crying. But she was here and safe and that was what mattered.

He hissed out a breath, eyes opening as pain shot through his leg. Pressure, he supposed, but it hurt too much to hold on to consciousness. He tried not to slide away while Lucy whispered things in his ears.

"You're okay, baby. I promise."

Something floated around in his head, a feeling he had to tell her. But the words didn't form. Yet, it was imperative. He had to tell her so she knew, but every time he tried to speak it all floated away.

"Zach, stay with me. We need you here."

"I'm here." But he wasn't. He kept losing hold on himself, on her.

There was noise, and he was being jostled. Lucy faded away, and so did he, but words floated with him.

"I love you, Zach. I love you. So you just hold on to that or I'm going to be really pissed."

Those were the words he'd meant to find—*I love you, I love you*—if only he could manage to say them back.

Chapter 18

Everyone insisted she go to the police station. Vaughn was with her, but no one was with Zach. No matter what Vaughn said about him being in surgery and her not being able to be with him anyway, she could only think about him being alone.

The detective who sat at the desk across from them looked frazzled, which wasn't exactly comforting. "It doesn't add up. Let's go over it again."

"She's gone over it enough," Vaughn said firmly. "You have to find Stacy Vine. She'll fill in some of these missing pieces."

"Yes, I know. We're searching for her. We've got a team combing the woods as Ms. Delaney described to us from their phone call, and we've got someone watching her office as well as her car." The detective sighed, and then tapped a few things on his computer. "We've got someone searching Don Levinson's place of residence for evidence of these letters allegedly from you.

Also, obviously, any evidence pertaining to the murder of Tom Perelli, the break-in at Stacy Vine's house or any connection to the three hired men that have been involved in attacks on Ms. Delaney."

"That's all well and good, but it isn't answers."

"Answers take time, Ranger Cooper," the detective returned, losing some of his control as irritation snaked into his tone.

Lucy couldn't blame him. It seemed no matter how they dug, no one could find all the answers. And her being here wasn't changing that, so she had to go to the hospital.

Before she could thank him for his time, make her excuses to go to the hospital, a knock sounded at the door to the detective's office.

Lucy didn't know how long they'd been sitting here, but it felt interminable.

And then Cory, Stacy's assistant, was being walked in. Handcuffed.

"Cory?"

"I didn't do anything! I didn't do a *thing*." But Lucy's stomach sank as she noticed anger more than fear in the depths of Cory's eyes. The same kind of anger that had been in Don's.

"She was found in Ms. Vine's house. An officer found her placing these in Ms. Vine's belongings." The officer held out a ziplock bag and the detective studied them. Then he turned them to Lucy.

"Is this your handwriting, Ms. Delaney?"

Lucy studied the words. *You spineless lowlife, you owe me for what you did. I'm going to make you pay worse than my father did.*

"No. Not my handwriting and I didn't write those."

Cory started screaming, blaming Don and Lucy and

Stacy at equal turns, not making much sense in the process. The officer who'd led her in led her back out.

Lucy closed her eyes against the roil of nausea. She felt…sorry for the girl, almost. It was too easy to be manipulated by powerful men who'd always trusted their own influence, when you always questioned your own.

Vaughn's arm came around her and she leaned into it.

Hours passed as she sat in the awful police station. They finally found Stacy, and Lucy didn't know how to repair the damage of the past few days. But the police seemed to believe Stacy was innocent—that Cory's connection to Don had led her to ferret out information and supply Don with it.

Cory, a woman Don had groomed from the time she'd moved to Nashville with a dream of becoming a country music star. He'd pushed her into getting a job for Stacy, pumped her for information about Daisy over the years. Don had used that information to supply bits and pieces to Jordan. Who had, in the end, not used it quite the way Don had wanted.

But Don also hadn't helped Cory the way she'd expected, so Cory had begun using the information *she* knew about Don against him—writing threatening letters supposedly from Daisy.

Which had finally forced Don to act, instead of just stew. Especially when Daisy had filed for divorce from Jordan.

Jordan, who hadn't been released from jail yet, but it was looking like he would be.

Vaughn was insisting the detectives look into the legality of him getting off scot-free when he'd known Don had wanted her dead, but Lucy didn't care about that.

"I just want to see Zach. And then I want…" She wanted to go home. Only she didn't have one.

"We'll take it one step at a time, and I'll be here for

every step. Whether you want me to be or not. That's a promise for the rest of your life."

Lucy smiled, but she also cried. And Vaughn held her through the tears, no matter how uncomfortable he was. He always would have, but now she was promising herself to always let him.

Zach woke up, groggy and gray. Pain snaked through a void of numbness. He didn't know where he was or why he was here, except he was clearly hurt.

When he managed to open his eyes, blue ones stared right back at him. Something inside him eased. She was all right.

"Your mother will be so upset with me. I just convinced her to go back to her hotel and get some sleep and here you are waking up."

"Aw, hell. My mother?" Zach grumbled, his voice raw.

Lucy took his hand in hers. "She likes me, don't worry. Cam and Hilly wanted to come, too, but I think your mother told them to stay put so they could take shifts."

"Cam's probably pretty pissed I went dark."

"Cam will probably forgive the man who's been shot twice."

He looked at her, really looked, as he came back to himself. He didn't remember much of what had happened, and based on the itchy and uncomfortable scruff on his face, he'd been out for a while.

But he remembered her saying she loved him, like one bright, shining beacon in the middle of foggy dark.

"Supposed to be a Delaney that gets shot," he managed to say, earning one of her patented raised eyebrow looks that made the love sweep through him so hard, so fast, he'd never question anyone's view on meant-to-be again.

"You see, back in Bent, there's a feud," he said over the wave of pain.

"You've been holding another good story from me?"

A story she'd love. A story that didn't scare him anymore. Because when it came to love, there were lots of things to worry about, but none to be scared of. "Carsons and Delaneys. They don't like each other. My mother was a Carson. Your grandmother was a Delaney."

"Are we Romeo and Juliet, Zach?"

"No, because I'm willing to die for you, Lucy, but I'm not willing to kill myself over you. Besides, the past year or so it's been something of a…hate to love deal. Carsons and Delaneys kept pairing off. Until I was the only one left."

"So we're meant to be."

"I've never believed in meant-to-be," Zach replied, holding her hand in his. She was looking worse for the wear herself, worrying over him. So many loose ends, but she was here and okay, and he was here and okay, so the most important loose end was love. "But I believe we got thrown into each other's life for a chance at something I never really thought I'd have."

"A country duo?"

"You're on quite the comedic roll, aren't you?"

"If I don't laugh I might break down and cry, and I've cried myself dry. So, I'd rather laugh, if you don't mind."

"I don't mind. I don't mind anything, if you're here. I love you, Lucy."

She swallowed, eyes shining. "I want it to go down on the record I was brave enough to say it first."

"Or at least smart enough to realize it first. I needed to get shot. Twice."

"You're just more stubborn than me."

"Ha!" The scoffing laugh hurt and he winced.

"I need to call the nurse in."

"No, not just yet. Come here."

She scooted closer and brushed a gentle kiss across his cheekbone.

"Going to come visit me? A lot?"

"Nah."

The pain of getting shot had nothing on the simple slice of horror that cut through him, until he noted she was smiling and leaning forward.

"I'd rather come home with you instead. I've got some ideas for your little ghost town."

Relief coursed through him like a river. "Do you now?"

"I'll still make music, and tour, and you'll work with Cam and keep people safe even if it puts you in danger. Because my songs and your protection is who we are."

"Yes, it is."

"But I want to build a life with you where I can come home and be Lucy Cooper when Daisy Delaney wears me out."

"I want that, too." God. More than he could express.

"So you'll have to heal up quick. Nashville's got too many prying eyes, and one too many men named Jordan Jones."

"All right. I'm ready. Tell me the whole thing."

He fell asleep halfway through her explanation of Don's plans, Cory's role, Jordan's half guilt and Stacy's innocence. It took him another few days to make it through the whole story, and more time after that to get out of the hospital, and then back onto a plane to Wyoming.

With Lucy Cooper at his side. Just where she belonged.

Epilogue

Zach Simmons was not a sentimental man, or so he'd thought. The sight of his mother carefully assisting Hilly with her wedding dress outside the church that had been restored in Hope Town—the name Lucy had come up with for their little ghost town—shifted something inside him.

Hilly made a beautiful bride, and their mother's elegant form standing next to her, openly crying, made his heart swell—a mix of sweet and bitter. He knew Mom was missing Dad, but also happy for Hilly, who'd been through so much and deserved this pretty wedding.

"Mom, you're supposed to go take your seat."

She nodded, dabbing at her eyes. She gave him a quick hug, beaming at him.

"You're looking good," she offered before slipping out of the room.

Good was probably a tiny exaggeration. He still had

a ways to go on his recovery for his leg, but even Lucy had gotten to a place where she didn't get irritated about his jokes over it. After all, only Delaneys got shot in their pursuit of happily-ever-after. He'd bucked tradition—being the best of the Carsons and all that.

"You look beautiful," he said to Hilly once Mom had gone.

Hilly shook her head. "Don't say nice things to me. I'm trying not to cry until I see Cam. Is he nervous?"

"Cool as a cucumber." Which had been true on the surface, but his obsessive attention to detail at the church had been a sure giveaway Cam wasn't as calm as he pretended.

Lucy had called it cute. Zach had scoffed at her.

Zach offered an arm and then walked out of the small room Hilly had gotten ready in. They moved into the lobby of the church. Hilly and Cam had foregone bridesmaids and groomsmen since they had so many family members they would want to stand up with them. They'd said a church full of people they loved was enough—and that was exactly what they were getting.

So Zach waited for the signal—a text from Jen—and when it came, he opened the door. He led Hilly down the aisle.

There were people missing from the wedding. Their father and brother. The man Hilly had considered a father growing up. But Hilly and Cam were surrounded by family—Carsons and Delaneys, and the offspring of such calamitous pairings—and Zach was going to walk his baby sister down the aisle.

So he did, bringing her to a man he loved like a brother anyway. And he watched two people pledge their love to each other with the woman he loved seated next to him.

When the wedding ended, and the interminable pictures that tested his leg's endurance were done, they all drove back over to Bent to have the reception at Rightful Claim—filled to the brim with couples. Laurel and Vanessa made rounds with their girls in their arms before handing them off to Grady and Dylan respectively. Noah's adopted son ran around squealing as Addie looked tired with a little baby bump popping more each day. Jen had looked suspiciously nauseated for the past week—at least that was what Lucy had told him that Laurel had told her.

Lucy had jumped into Carson and Delaney life like she'd been born into it, and no one here called her Daisy Delaney, because she was Lucy Cooper here.

Except to Cam, on occasion.

Speaking of which, Grady and Lucy took the small makeshift stage shoved into the corner of the saloon's main room.

"All right, folks, we're going to have the first dance for Cam and Hilly, with our very, *very* special guest to serenade our couple. You all know her as Lucy Cooper, but let's give a warm round of applause for Daisy Delaney."

Everyone clapped, Zach cheered and whistled and Lucy took to the stage with her guitar. She grinned at the crowd and spoke into the microphone.

"When Hilly asked me if I'd sing Cam's favorite song at their wedding, I promised I would. But I also thought something as momentous as a first dance should be about two people, two families, coming together. A song about love and promises. So with Hilly's permission, I wrote a song not just for this moment, but for all of you, too. For love and family and hope. We'll save Cam's favorite song for later, and here's a tip. Get me drunk enough, I'll sing anything. But for now, this one's for all of you."

The crowd laughed, but it didn't take long for them to settle. For Daisy's amazing voice to fill the saloon. What's more, the words of the song Lucy had written, about love and forever and even a few lines about breaking curses, settled over a group made up of people who'd been brave enough to buck tradition and expectation and fall in love with the person they were never even supposed to tolerate.

Silence, tears, happy and hopeful smiles. Even the babies were quiet until Lucy finished her song.

She slid off the stage as Cam and Hilly still swayed to their own music while Grady hooked up the speakers to Hilly's curated playlist for the evening.

Though Lucy stopped and talked to anyone who called out her name, her eyes were on Zach's as she slowly made her way over.

When she finally reached him, she sized him up. "How's the leg, champ?"

"Good enough for a dance."

"So long as it's one and only one," she returned, letting him pull her into his arms. They swayed to the slow song, and Lucy rested her temple on his cheek.

"I wrote the song for Hilly and Cam, for all of them really, but I never would have had the words if I hadn't found you," she murmured into his ear.

He pulled her closer, overwhelmed by his love for her and the love in the air. "I never believed in curses. I still don't, but you convinced me to believe in meant-to-be."

And from that day forward in Bent, Wyoming, people didn't mention curses anymore. But they did talk about a love strong enough to stand the test of murder, loss, greed, terror and evil.

And a little bit about how some things are just meant to be.

* * * * *

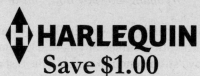

HARLEQUIN

Save $1.00

on the purchase of ANY Harlequin book
from the imprints below.

*Heartfelt or thrilling, passionate or
uplifting—our romances have it all.*

PRESENTS   INTRIGUE

DESIRE   ROMANTIC SUSPENSE   SPECIAL EDITION

LOVE INSPIRED

Save $1.00

on the purchase of ANY Harlequin Presents, Intrigue, Desire,
Romantic Suspense, Special Edition or Love Inspired book.

Valid from June 1, 2023 to May 31, 2024.

52617414

5 65373 00076 2   (8100)0 12532

HSERIESCOUP0623